THE BIRD IN THE TREE

BOOKS BY ELIZABETH GOUDGE

THE BIRD
IN
THE
TREE

ELIZABETH
GOUDGE

COWARD-McCANN, INC.
NEW YORK

MANUFACTURED IN THE UNITED STATES OF AMERICA
Van Rees Press, New York

TO

MARY AMBER

THE BIRD

I have grown tired of sorrow and human tears;
Life is a dream in the night, a fear among fears,
A naked runner lost in a storm of spears.

I have grown tired of rapture and love's desire;
Love is a flaming heart, and its flames aspire
Till they cloud the soul in the smoke of a windy fire.

I would wash the dust of the world in a soft green flood;
Here between sea and sea in the fairy wood,
I have found a delicate wave-green solitude.

Here, in the fairy wood, between sea and sea,
I have heard the song of a fairy bird in a tree,
And the peace that is not in the world has flown to me.

ARTHUR SYMONS.

THE TREE

My life is a tree,
Yoke-fellow of the earth;
Pledged,
By roots too deep for remembrance,
To stand hard against the storm,
To fill my place.
(But high in the branches of my green tree there is a
*   wild bird singing:*
Wind-free are the wings of my bird: she hath built no
*   mortal nest.)*

KARLE WILSON BAKER.

THE BIRD IN THE TREE

~~~~~~

CHAPTER ONE

I.

VISITORS TO DAMEROSEHAY, had they but known it, could have told just how much the children liked them by the particular spot at which they were met upon arrival. If the visitor was definitely disliked the children paid no attention to him until Ellen had forcibly thrust them into their best clothes and pushed them through the drawing-room door about the hour of five, when they extended limp paws in salutation, replied in polite monosyllables to enquiries as to their well-being, and then stood in a depressed row staring at the carpet, beautiful to behold but no more alive than three Della Robbia cherubs modeled out of plaster. If, on the other hand, they tolerated the visitor, they would go so far as to meet him at the front door and ask if if he had brought them anything. If they liked him they would go to the gate at the end of the wood and wave encouragingly as he came towards them. But if they loved him, if he was one of the inner circle, they would go right through the village, taking the dogs with them, and along the coast road to the corner by the cornfield, and when they saw the beloved approaching they would yell like all the fiends of hell let loose for the afternoon.

Their cousin David belonged to this inner circle, and

3

David would be here at five o'clock. It was half past four now. If they hurried they would reach the corner by the cornfield just as his car came jolting down the rutted lane from the main road. Madly they dashed down the back stairs from the nursery, raced into the kitchen to fetch the dogs, Pooh-Bah and the Bastard, and dashed out again into the hall and through the porch into the long drive that led down through the oak wood to the road. Every family has its particular bright stars, and David and Grandmother were the particular stars of the Eliot family, people in whose presence life was more worth living, people who warmed you, like the sun, and lit the whole world to a richer glory. Grandmother was always with them, the center of their life, but David only came on visits. He was like a meteor in the sky, or a rainbow, something that shone for a brief exciting moment and then was gone. They had to make the most of him, and for this reason it was important that they should not be a moment late at the cornfield.

"No time!" they yelled to Ellen, who called out something about thick shoes from the front door. "No time! No time!"

Yet even as he went leaping down the drive, going first because he was the eldest, with Tommy and Caroline coming after and the dogs flying on ahead, Ben was conscious as always of the beauty of the oak wood, and of the garden that he could see through the iron gateway in the old high red brick wall that was skirted by the drive as it wound from the east side of the house, where the porch

4

and the front door faced across the marshes to the silver line of the Estuary, down through the wood to the gate. But that one glimpse was enough for Ben. In his mind's eye, as he ran on, he could see the green grass paths between the lavender hedges, the purple masses of the michaelmas daisies with the butterflies sunning their wings upon them, the glowing spires of the goldenrod and the flames of the dahlias and peonies and petunias, the frail late autumn roses and the ilex tree by the house, where the blackbird sang. He could see the color of it, and smell the damp sweet scent of it, and feel how it lived and breathed within its old brick walls just to give sanctuary to those who needed it.

2.

And Ben was one of these. Though he was only nine years old he had come already to feel the need for sanctuary. He had been born in Egypt, and then gone on to India; and foreign countries had most violently disagreed with him. The first seven years of his life were now just a confused and painful memory of heat and flies, bands playing, riots when people got shot, a burning fever in his body, a pain in his head, a choking feeling in his chest that they told him was asthma, and his father and mother quarreling. The asthma, the grown-ups had told him, was an illness, but Ben had known quite well that he choked because his father and mother quarreled. He admired them so; his father so tall and splendid and his mother so lovely; and when they had quarreled his love and sorrow had swelled inside his chest like a balloon, and so of course he had choked. He had understood it all quite well in his own mind, but he hadn't been able to explain it; so he had had to go on choking.

And then they had come home to England, and the children had come to Damerosehay, where Grandmother and Aunt Margaret lived. That had been two years ago, but Ben could remember the day they arrived as though it were yesterday. Aunt Margaret had met the children in London and brought them to Grandmother, because their mother was going up north to stay with a friend and their father was staying in London to arrange something mysterious called a divorce. The children and Aunt Margaret had driven out from the station in the village taxi one spring evening just as the sun was setting, and the moment they had turned in through the broken gate into the drive that led through the oak wood he had felt better. And when ten minutes later he had sat on Grandmother's lap in the drawing room, rubbing his bare legs contentedly against her silk skirts, eating a sugared almond and looking out into that lovely cloistered garden, he had suddenly felt well. After tea he had gone out into the garden quite by himself and had seen how the old red walls were built all round him to keep him safe. It had been cool in the garden and the daffodils had made pools of gold beside the grass paths. There had been no sound except the far-off murmur of the sea and the blackbird singing in the ilex tree. He had known for certain that no one would ever quarrel here; there would be no bands or shooting to hurt his head and he would never feel too hot. . . . Nor would he choke here. . . . He had run up and down the grass paths and he had been happy.

But the difficulty was that now he could never g
from Damerosehay. He had to live here always :
lessons with Uncle Hilary at the Vicarage instead
ing to school. When his father had gone back to
and his mother had made a home for herself in London,
was working so hard that she couldn't have her child.
with her except sometimes on visits, he had been sent to
preparatory school. But he had choked there so badly tha
they had had to write and tell Grandmother. She had come
down at once, driven by David in his beautiful silver-gray
car, dressed in her black silk and with a little silver box
of sugared almonds in her black velvet bag; and while she
had sat on his bed and hugged him he had whispered to
her that it was because it was all so noisy, and the other
boys quarreled, and he wanted to go back to Damerosehay.
She had listened, nodding her head, and paying not the
slightest attention to the headmaster's remarks about the
wholesome discipline of school life, and the matron's asser-
tion that nervous disorders must not be treated with too
much leniency; she had wrapped him up in a rug and carried him straight off downstairs to David in his waiting
car. . . . That had been the first time he had seen David.
Sitting on Grandmother's lap, leaning back against her
shoulder and eating a sugared almond, he had looked at his
cousin's clear-cut features against the background of sky
and trees and hedgerows that streamed by as the car raced
them to Damerosehay, and thought him a god among men.
. . . Even so did the gods behave, dropping from the sky
in silver chariots and carrying one away from pain and
desolation to the place where one would be.

"This child is very like what you were at his age, David," Grandmother had announced over his head. "He has the Eliot coloring, of course, while you have mine, but I notice the same sensitivity."

"The same dramatic ability, you mean," had said David. "Nothing like turning on a bit of pathos to get what you want." But he had spoken quite nicely and had winked his eye at Ben, so that Ben's feelings had not been in any way hurt. . . . Indeed Ben had chuckled, remembering how he had coughed a lot harder when he had overheard the headmaster saying to the matron in the passage that they had better write to Grandmother. . . . "I used," David had continued, "to make myself sick at school by hammering on my front and then heaving. It was a useful accomplishment. I'll teach you, Ben, if you like."

"My dear!" Grandmother had exclaimed, shocked, and David had said no more but had tilted his head back and looked up at the flying clouds over his head, with upon his face that expression of ethereal beauty that was his to command at will. And Ben had chuckled again, and swelled a little with pride, because he as well as David had dramatic ability. . . . And David's dramatic ability was such that sometimes he had his name up in electric lights in Shaftesbury Avenue, the first Eliot to achieve this particular brand of fame.

And Ben, as well as David, had grace. As he went leaping down the drive his flying figure seemed less that of a boy than of the spirit of a boy. His lithe brown beauty was more of the essence of things than of their form. It was the loveliest of all types of beauty, his Grandmother thought;

more enduring than perfection of shape or color; more attractive because more elusive. In repose Ben was not a beautiful child; he was bony, with a sallow skin and straight lusterless dark hair, his only good points his shy brown fawn's eyes and exquisitely cut lips that lifted at the corners when he smiled with a swift movement that was the very epitome of delight. But any sort of movement, whether mental or physical, transformed him. When something touched his mind or spirit into awareness or delight, waves of light seemed to pass over his face, like the reflection of sun upon water; and when he moved, the suppleness of the body that in stillness could be so angular had in it almost the grace of wind-blown rushes, or weeds that sway with the current beneath the water. So unselfconsciously could he abandon himself to some thought or emotion greater than his body, as the rushes to the wind and the weeds to the water, that he himself became a part of the beauty of it. So, while his mind remained unsullied and his body capable of movement, would he always be beautiful, thought his Grandmother, for the loveliness that can be mirrored in mind and body is inexhaustible as long as the world endures.

Tommy was quite different. He was eight years old, and fat. He had fat dark curls, fat red cheeks and round bright dark eyes. He looked like one of Raphael's cherubs but unfortunately his character was most distressingly at variance with his outward appearance. "What have I done," his Grandmother would cry, "that I should have such a child thrust upon me in my old age?" At which cry of despair he would chuckle his fat chuckle, bump his incredibly hard head against her shoulder in what was meant to be a contact of affection but was in effect as that of the onslaught of a young goat, and go off to think out further devilry in the bathroom. He had twice been sent to school and twice been returned with thanks; so now he stayed at Damerosehay and in company with Ben did lessons with Uncle Hilary. He was, it seemed, better behaved at Damerosehay than anywhere else. He said it was the blackbird who sang in the ilex tree who helped him to be good.

Caroline was five and three quarters, and sucked her thumb. Nothing cured her of it; not spanking, nor bitter aloes put on the nail, nor coaxing nor expostulation. She just sucked, removing her thumb only when she wished to eat or smile. She seldom spoke, and it was impossible to say at her age whether her silence was due to the presence of great thoughts in her mind or to the absence of any thoughts at all. Time alone would show, and meanwhile she sucked, to the great distress of Ellen. "She must be cured of it, milady," Ellen would say to Grandmother. "It's her left thumb and it's swollen something terrible already. What'll her bridegroom say when she holds out her hand for the ring and he sees the thumb she has on her?"

"We can only do our best, Ellen," Grandmother would say soothingly. "Put on the aloes and trust in Providence."

Caroline had neither the dark good looks of most of the Eliots nor the golden beauty that had once been her Grandmother's and was now David's. She was thin and freckled, with straight fair hair cut in a fringe across her forehead. Yet she had an elfin attraction of her own. Her eyes were the green eyes of a fairy's child, she had the delicacy and precision of an exquisite old lady, and lovely little teeth that showed like pearls between her lips on the rare occasions when she condescended to remove her thumb from her mouth. She learned to read and write with her Grandmother, and Ellen had taught her to make cross-stitch kettle holders for her mother and aunts every Christmas. Ben was a child who could have lived in any age, tuned like a violin to respond with clear beauty to whatever moods and events might strike upon him, and Tommy was modern to the depths of his restless truthful little soul, but Caroline had stepped straight out of the age of Victoria the Good. She could not be dressed in shorts and jerseys, like the boys, she looked simply silly in them; she had to wear frocks of pastel shades, beautifully smocked by Ellen, worn in summer with sunbonnets that tied beneath the chin and in winter with bonnet-shaped hats and little pelissed coats trimmed with fur. Muffs became her, and coral necklaces, and little red shoes with pom-poms on them. She was inclined to be finicky over her food and already showed an old-maid tendency to like a place for everything and everything in its place. She kept a cat, and always said her prayers without being reminded, and, strangest of all traits in an Eliot, she was frightened of strange dogs. . . . Ellen was very much afraid that, the thumb-sucking apart, she would never get a husband.

Caroline was not frightened of their own dogs, of course, not even of Pooh-Bah, a chow possessed of the most mighty ancestry and a peculiarly crushing arrogance. Pooh-Bah's nose was permanently wrinkled, as though every smell that he smelt was beneath his notice, and he wore upon his fore-

11

head a frown that had been known to cause the most lo-
quacious visitors to fall uneasily silent when he turned the
light of his countenance disdainfully upon them. He was
superbly beautiful. His ears, stiffly erect upon his noble
cranium, were as delicately pointed as flower petals, his
eyes were like dark amber and his tongue was a royal
purple. His coat was the color of a ripe cornfield with the
sun upon it, and his tail, of a slightly paler shade of tawny
gold, was erected over his back in a strong curve that was
never untwisted and never lowered. Agitated back and
forth it might be in moments of pleasure and excitement,
but lowered, never. While life was in Pooh-Bah that tail
would stay erect above the proud curve of his furred, pro-
tuberant stern.

But with the tail of the Bastard it was not so. The Bastard's tail was tremblingly responsive to his every mood, and
his moods were many. Pooh-Bah was so proud that he
never permitted himself even to feel a weakness, let alone
to show it, but the Bastard, un-upheld by the arrogance of
race and beauty, felt many weaknesses and showed them
all. He was frightened, he was unhappy, he was penitent,
he was anxious, he was passionately loving, he was shy,
he was coy; and his tail, like a dirty uncurled ostrich
feather that had seen better days, trembled, drooped, rose,
fell, waved, rotated, or disappeared between his hind legs
altogether, according as these emotions ravaged his faithful breast. For faithful the Bastard undoubtedly was. In
spite of the extreme nervousness of his highly-strung tem-
perament he would have died in defense of the Eliots because he loved them, while Pooh-Bah would have died for

them only because they were his sacred property. The Bastard's loving faithfulness was very visible in his appearance, shining in the liquid depths of the dark eyes that gazed so appealingly out of the curious mat of whitish-gray hair that was his face, and dripping in streams of saliva from the end of the long pink tongue that he lowered out of the side of his mouth in moments of emotion. He always dribbled when he loved people; he couldn't help it, but it made him a little unpopular in the drawing room. For the rest, he was a large dog with flapping uncontrolled ears, sprawling legs that didn't seem to belong to him and a lanky body enveloped in tangled whitish-gray fur that had a slightly moth-eaten appearance. He had come to Damerosehay ten years ago as a puppy, having been deposited upon the back doorstep by persons unknown but thought to be of gypsy origin. Some thought he was of sheepdog ancestry. Others suggested elkhound crossed with pomeranian. Some few detected a flavor of collie with a dash of skye terrier. The vet made no suggestions; the problem, he said, was beyond him; but the dog was a sweet-tempered dog, and faithful, and let them thank God for that.

Which they did. The Bastard was a part of Damerosehay as no dog had ever been, or ever would be. Exiled Eliots could never think of the marshes that stretched between the oak wood and the sea without picturing the Bastard's busy body rabbiting through the rushes and the gorse. They could never dream of the ilex tree in the garden where the blackbird sang without seeing him sitting beneath it, pursuing insects upon his person, the sunlight striking down through the ilex leaves and patterning his white fur with a delicate diaper of light and shade. When they thought of Grandmother sitting in her black silk beside the drawing-room fire, the Bastard was always lying at her feet, his chin propped upon her shoe and his lustrous eyes rolled upwards in expectation of a sugared almond. And when they thought of the rutted lane that led down from the main road to the marshes, and the cornfield at the corner that was as the first sight of home, it was the Bastard whom they saw flying to meet them, his uncontrolled ears flapping with ecstasy and his feathery tail streaming on the wind.

3.

It was streaming now as he led the van of the party that was racing to welcome David. They were through the oak wood in a flash, and out of the broken gate that divided the demesne of Damerosehay from the village. That gate had not been mended for years. It stood open always, propped back with a stone, and would stay like that till it fell to pieces altogether. For why should Damerosehay shut itself off from the village and the marshes, the harbor and the sea? It didn't want to. It loved them. It lay encircled by them as a jewel in its setting. And it was a strange fact that only those who went to Damerosehay upon their lawful occasions ever passed through the open gate into the oak wood. Trespassers and sightseers had never been found within it. They stood at the gate and looked in, often, but their feet did not carry them from the hard surface of the village road on to the thick green moss of the drive. There was something about those oak trees that gave them a queer feeling. They felt warned off.

Perhaps it was because the oaks looked like people, and not normal people either, but gnarled, misshapen gnomes. Their trunks were covered with gray lichen, which made them look as old as time, and their branches were so twisted by winter storms that they looked like deformed arms with long clutching fingers stretched out in incantation. And the trees were blown all one way, as though they bowed towards the house of Damerosehay. Beneath them the grass grew thick and rough and tawny, jeweled in the spring with gold and purple crocuses that were the brightest that any one had ever seen, and the moss on the drive was so thick that it hushed every footfall to silence. There was seldom any sound in the oak wood except the talking of the trees themselves, for the birds preferred the sheltered garden to build and sing in, and passers-by in the wood never talked. But the trees said a good deal. In the spring, when their old branches were jeweled with flamelike coral-tipped leaves, they whispered together of the secrets that they knew, secrets that if communicated to the passers-by in the wood would have taken all sorrow from their hearts for ever. And in summer, when the warm rain pattered on the polished dark green surface of their full-grown leaves and their branches swayed rhythmically in the soft wind from the sea, they would sing beneath their breath a song about a far country that they knew of. The raindrops on their leaves were the words and the wind in the branches was the tune, and it ought to have been easy to overhear; yet not even Grandmother had succeeded in catching more than the echo of it. In winter they prayed and they meditated, or they cried out in anguish for the sorrow of the world. On windless days their gray heads were bowed and their knotted fingers, held up to the sky in supplication, were utterly still; but when the storms rushed in from the sea they wrung their hands in anguish and when night fell they screamed and moaned so loudly that sleepers in the house of Damerosehay woke up in sudden terror, conscious of the powers of evil abroad in the world and of great wings that passed in the night. . . . And then in the morning there would be a great quiet and the trees would stand exhausted, sodden with the rain, maimed and torn, with gashes showing white upon their branches and broken twigs strewn about their feet, yet at peace and triumphant because they had been for their people a bulwark against evil, and those wings that had passed in the night had done no harm. . . . Undoubtedly they had two faces, these trees. No Eliot, and no friend of an Eliot, could pass beneath them and not feel arms protectingly about them, and friendly hands leading them on to the inner sanctuary of the house and garden. But strangers were warned off and came no further than the broken open gate; for the trees could not feel certain about them, they could not know if they would bring to Damerosehay good or evil.

Outside the gate was Little Village, containing the Shop and Coastguard Station, the Eel and Lobster, a few cottages and some houses belonging to rich folk who came in summer for the yachting. Big Village, where abode Uncle Hilary and the Church, was some little way inland and was reached by a narrow winding lane where sloes grew and hips and haws were scarlet in the autumn sunshine. Both villages were really the same place, Fairhaven, but they were as different as chalk from cheese, and very jealous of their own particular attractions. Big Village, lying in a small valley and sheltered from the wind, had whitewashed thatched cottages ringed about with pasture lands, haystacks and prosperous farms. It had several shops, a petrol pump and a graveyard, and thought a lot of itself in consequence. It had a parish room, too, and a hoarding with advertisements on it, and its gardens were packed full of all the flowers that grow.

Little Village was quite different. Its houses, like the house of Damerosehay, were built of solid gray stone that knew how to withstand the onslaught of the winter gales, and were roofed with gray slate patched with yellow lichen. Its gardens, unprotected by high walls like the garden of Damerosehay, had little in them except the feathered tamarisk trees with their foam of pale pink blossom, and fuchsia bushes strung over with swaying lanterns of red and purple. But what did Little Village want with gardens? It looked out upon the harbor, and to right and left of it, stretching away to the far silver curve of the sea, were the rainbow-colored marshes.

Little Village considered that if you saw the harbor you saw Life. There were no less than two seats upon the harbor wall, and here the old salts would congregate in their off moments, smoking their pipes and blinking their old eyes at the sun: John Clutterbuck and Charles Beere, the coastguardsmen, William Urry from the Eel and Lobster and Obadiah Watson, who lived right out in the marsh and who helped Aunt Margaret and his grandson Alf, the Damerosehay gardener, with the weeding and the pruning. Any one who liked could sit with them discussing the bloody government, spitting accurately and with vigor into the bright waters of the harbor, and doing nothing else at all (beyond occasional adjournments to the Eel and Lobster for refreshment) from the time the sun got up till the time it went to bed again.... Nothing at all but listen to the sound of the incoming tide slapping against the harbor wall, and watch the broken fragments of light caught and cradled within each curve of the wind-rippled water. "Κυμάτων ἀνήριθμον γέλασμα," the Greeks had called those fragments of light, so David had told the children. "The many-twinkling smile of ocean." Precious they were, and beloved of seafaring folk since the dawn of the world.

In summer the harbor was always gay with color. The tamarisk trees grew right up to the wall and clumps of sea asters grew between the seats. The harbor itself and the creek that wound away through the marshes to the sea were dotted with fishing boats and yachts rocking at anchor, their hulls painted blue and green and their sails, tightly folded to the slender masts, looking like white lily buds folded about a flower stem. Yet it was only in repose that the sails reminded one of flowers; when they blossomed from the masts and the yachts sped down the creek to the sea they were no longer flowers but wings, their every movement a gesture of utter joy. Busy they were, and important, as thy sped about their business. Man had made them and they shared a little in the self-consciousness of their creator.

It was because it was so full of white wings that Fairhaven was such a happy place: wings of the yachts, of the seagulls, and of the swans who divided their time between the Abbey River, several miles to the eastward, and the blue lake in the marsh where the sea lavender grew. White wings are for ever happy, symbols of escape and ascent, of peace and of joy, and a spot of earth about which they beat is secure of its happiness.

The passing and repassing of the swans was one of the events of Fairhaven, something so lovely that no one ever got used to it and no one ever failed to look up when they heard the rhythmical powerful beat of those great wings approaching from the eastward. The swans would fly one behind the other in perfect formation, their long necks stretched out as though they yearned for the place where they would be, their flight, so different from that of the yachts, as unselfconscious and as unhurried as the wheeling of the sun and moon upon their courses. When they saw their blue lake the head of the foremost swan would point downwards like the head of an arrow that turns again earthwards, and, with a slow sinuous movement that was difficult to follow even though it enchanted the watcher, the whole long line of them would sink towards the water with tense necks relaxed into grace and white wings folded. Then, immobile, they would become, like the furled sails, no longer wings, but flowers.

And the gulls were quite different again. They, too, were unhurried, but when they were in flight their movement was unceasing and seemed without the direct purpose of that of the swans. All day long, sometimes, they wheeled and cried above the marshes, their wings seeming to trace some mystic pattern over the earth and sea and sky, their crying like the crying of prophecy or incantation. And then suddenly they would fall silent and unstirring, sitting hour after hour beside the lake, or perching in a solemn line upon a rooftree, heads all pointing one way and one foot tucked up. They seemed to be dreaming then, or brooding upon the mystery of the pattern that they traced over the earth and sea and sky. Sometimes they flew inland, but they returned always at night to sleep within sound of the sea. That place where the mystery of the earth met the mystery of the sea was in their charge, perhaps. Their crying and the beating of their wings had some purpose in it. They protected the marshes as the oak trees in the wood protected the demesne of Damerosehay.

With Little Village upon their right and the harbor upon their left the children ran on until the coast road brought them out again into the open. Now they had the earth world upon their right, plowed fields and wind-blown hawthorn hedges, and pasture lands where fat black and white cows placidly chewed the cud; and upon their left the mystical half-world of the marshes that linked the earth and sea.

These marshes were streaked with color like a painter's palette. There was the gold of the rice grass and the mauve of the sea asters and sea lavender, and the pools and channels that at high tide gave back the blue or flame or primrose of the sky above them, and at low tide flung back the light from the smooth mud like polished surfaces of steel and silver. Gorse grew upon dry patches of the marsh, and red sorrel and golden saxifrage, and the glasswort, a spongy sea-weedy plant that could take every shade of color from crimson to deep purple. Patches of bright green grass appeared now and again, with plovers sitting on them, and rushes bent in the wind with a soft cool sound that was indescribably peaceful.

With the sea to the south and the Estuary to the east, the marshes, Little Village and Damerosehay had water upon two sides of them. They lay between sea and sea, doubly protected, while at the junction of sea and Estuary reached by a long causeway of shingle, was the ominous gray mass of the old Castle, lying crouched upon the water like an animal on guard. And beyond the Castle was the Island, white cliffs leaping superbly from the sea and green fields sloping to the quieter waters of the Estuary. To the west of the marshes a high shingle beach piled itself up between Fairhaven and the world beyond, adding to its height with every storm, determined that what was outside should not get in.

At the corner by the cornfield, where the coast road swerved sharply to the right and became the rutted lane that led to the main road, you could know what you were protected from, for looking beyond the protecting shingle you could see the very distressing bungalows that formed the suburbs of the sea-coast town of Radford beyond, and if you listened very hard you could just hear the sound of the traffic passing on the main road at the end of the lane.

Tommy, whose tastes were of a material type, was always

fascinated by these rumors of the great world. Today, there being as yet no sign of David, he left Ben by the cornfield and ran up the lane to the place where he could sit on a gate and see the cars passing, and established himself there to enter their numbers in a little notebook. He always entered the numbers of cars in his notebook. It was very important, he said, that he should do so. He was going to be a policeman. Pooh-Bah went with him to watch the cars, for Pooh-Bah also was of the earth, earthy. Caroline went too, not because she liked the cars but because camomile daisies grew in the lane and she always picked a bunch of them for Ellen to make into camomile tea for Grandmother's weak inside.... But Ben and the Bastard stayed behind with the cornfield.

4.

Strictly speaking there were two cornfields, one in the marsh and the other just across the road in the angle of the lane, but it was the cornfield in the marsh that was the exciting one. For no one had ever planted it. It just grew by itself. Years ago, so said Obadiah Watson, a grain ship had been wrecked in one of the terrible winter gales that now and then, perhaps once or twice in a generation, sent the sea raging in over the marshes with the incoming tide, submerging the rushes and the sea lavender, galloping like mad horses over the blue pools and the patches of bright grass, leaping sometimes right across the road and attacking the very houses themselves, so that the inhabitants had to fly helter-skelter to their bedrooms and take refuge there until the tide turned. This particular wreck had taken place within the lifetime of Obadiah's grandfather, and Obadiah, by the exercise of a very constructive imagination, was able to tell the story as though he had seen it happen with his own eyes only yesterday. It had been at sunset, after a day of storm worse than any they could remember in those parts. It had been a wild sunset with a mad flaming light welling upwards as though the world rocked on the edge of a burning abyss that would presently engulf it. Outlined starkly against that terrible light the terrified inhabitants of Little Village had seen the great ship driving towards the marshes. She had been a merchantman, a splendid ship of graceful and lovely line and carven prow, such a ship as Little Village had seen launched time and again at the ship-building yards on the Abbey River where the greatest ships of the century were conceived in the minds of Hampshire men and wrought out of the labor of their blood and bones. Yet she was utterly lost, driven before the storm, two of her masts down and her spars and tackle, that had once lifted themselves in such beauty against tranquil skies, a tangled mass of wreckage upon her decks. They could see how the waves broke over her and how she was heeling over, her cargo perhaps shifted by the buffeting of the storm, and they could see the figure of her captain apparently lashed to the mainmast. A great groan and cry went up from Little Village, echoed by the wind and the screaming gulls; and then they all started running, for they could see where she was heading for; she was being driven straight across the marshes to the hideous bank of shingle on the west.

They could not go by the road for the sea was right

across it, but they fought their way through the drenched fields on the other side and reached the corner by the lane just in time to see the tortured ship shiver into stricken stillness, her prow wedged in the shingle and her keel held fast in the mud of the marshes. The inhabitants of Little Village had the same courage then as now. They hurled themselves into the swirling water and swam out to the ship. They saved the few passengers and the crew, including the unconscious captain, who was found to have a leg broken and his head injured by a falling spar; and they rescued from his cabin a young girl big with child, who was lying in his bunk large-eyed with terror but not crying out, and a blue bird in a brass cage who was singing away as though all that had happened was quite in order and nothing but what it had expected. It was Obadiah's grandfather who had saved the blue bird, concerning himself with its welfare rather than that of the girl because it was the prettiest bird he had ever seen, with a very bright eye to it; and the song it sang to him as he waded ashore with it, holding it high up over his head lest it should wet itself, was the prettiest he had ever heard. But the cargo they did not save. It was dark by the time they had got the last man ashore and they thought more of getting the poor creatures to warmth and shelter than of what might be in the ship's hold. In the morning it was too late. The ship was breaking up and the seas had raked her from prow to stern. They saved only some of the fine carving about her prow.

And there Obadiah's constructive memory gave out and the story abruptly closed down. No one knew what had happened to the unconscious captain, whether he had lived

24

or died, or what had happened to the girl and her unborn child, or the blue bird either. Obadiah's grandfather, apparently, had never got any further in his narrative than the song the blue bird had sung to him when he carried it ashore. At that point he appeared to have lost interest, or Obadiah had lost interest, or else, as Ellen declared was the case, Obadiah had made the whole thing up and was the most shocking old liar she had ever come across in all her born days. The other villagers, when closely questioned by the children, protested their total ignorance of the whole affair. They could not remember over a hundred years back, they said, and their grandfathers had not been as communicative as Obadiah's. . . . Nor such liars neither.

Yet there was the cornfield, mysteriously sprung up all by itself in the marsh. Every year the queer stunted blades pushed their way up, first the blade, then the ear, then the full corn in the ear. It was never reaped, for it was useless stuff, a mere travesty of what corn should be; so it fell and died and from its death fresh life sprang again, year after year, curiously persistent.

The villagers, of course, had their explanation all ready. In the angle of the rutted lane was the real cornfield, that had been there ever since they could remember. One spring some young sower must have taken it into his head to throw a few handfuls of his precious seed to the marsh. Daft young idiot! He must have known that marsh ground was no soil for good corn. Wasting the seed that way! The sun must have got to his silly head.

But Ben did not believe that theory for a moment; nor did David, with whom he had frequently discussed it.

For both of them had often watched, with souls caught up in delight, the lovely unwearied ceremony of the spring sowing in that field. They had watched the old-fashioned plow that was still used at Fairhaven pass up and down, John Barton guiding it, to drill a straight clean furrow for the precious seed, and the two horses Daisy and Florence, working with him in a steady patient rhythm that nothing seemed able to disturb or break. Back and forth they would go, turning at each furrow's end with a jingling of harness and a wheeling and rustling of the white wings of the gulls who followed after, but they never stopped until dinner time, and they never permitted any unusual act to mar the perfect order of events. Their work was as unbroken a thing as the rainbow that in those March days so often curved over the field in benediction.

And it was the same with Jack Hobson who sowed the seed on fine mornings when the sky was wide and pale after shed rain. He too went faithfully back and forth, his arm moving ceaselessly in that constant divine gesture of generosity, the seed sweeping fanwise from his hand to glint like gold in the sunlight before it fell. It was impossible to imagine that such men as these should break the rhythm of their work by such a disorderly act as throwing seed in the marsh. It was impossible to think it of them. Their work was part of the swing of the seasons and it diverted not a hairsbreadth from its appointed course. Why, there was even a local saying which declared that, "If when corn is sown a cast is missed, the farmer is doomed, or else his man."

No. The story of the wrecked grain ship was true. And

so was the unconscious captain lashed to the mast, and the blue bird in the brass cage who sang as it was carried over the water to safety. For the hundredth time, as he lingered now with the Bastard to look at the cornfield again, Ben reiterated his faith in these things. He believed them. They were a part of him.

It was autumn now and the corn was ripe. In the field in the angle of the lane it was cut and standing proudly in golden stooks, waiting to be carried away to make the bread that fed the world; but across the road in the marsh the stunted stalks stood uncut and the pale grains waited only to drop to the earth unwanted. As the wind passed over them they rustled a little desolately, and Ben's heart suddenly ached intolerably for that unwanted, ungarnered gold, and for the great ship that had gone to its death in this place. The field was its grave and the uncut whispering corn its epitaph. He wondered what it was saying. "Except a grain of wheat fall into the ground and die . . ." He had heard that somewhere, but he couldn't remember the end, and suddenly he forgot that he had been unhappy and began throwing stones for the Bastard. He could throw much further now than he had done a few months ago; he could send a stone clean over the field into a patch of sea lavender beyond. David would be pleased.

5.

"B.F.193," said Tommy, sucking his pencil loudly and winding his legs tightly round the gatepost in an agony of composition. "E.H.25. T.A.340. Caroline, what was that bus?"

But Caroline, squatting among the camomile daisies, with her pink skirts billowing round her, was paying no attention. She was talking to the camomile daisies, telling them how pretty they were with their golden faces and white bonnets, and how they mustn't mind being turned into tea because in this world we are all of us for ever being turned into something else and we've just got to put up with it. "I was a baby once," said Caroline, "and now I'm a big girl. Soon I shall be a grandmother and after that I shall be an angel."

"How do you know?" asked Tommy the materialist. "I don't believe there are any angels. A.B.59. They're just a make-up of Grandmother's. C.W.10. We're just eaten up by the worms when we die and that's all there is to it. U.V.590."

But Caroline was not disturbed, because she was not attending. Just as she seldom conversed with her fellow humans, talking only to flowers and herself because flowers and herself never contradicted her, so she never now paid the slightest attention to what they said to her. In her earlier days she had done so, but at the age of four she had realized that to those as desirous of peace and quiet as herself it was better not. The remarks of others, she had found, were invariably disturbing. Either they told you to do what you didn't want to do, or they told you not to do what you did want to do, or, like Tommy at this moment, they endeavored to undermine your nice ideas about angels with unpleasant ones about worms. So it was much better not to listen.

She tied a piece of grass round her bunch of daisies and

28

sat down beside Pooh-Bah, with her arm round his neck and his woolly cheek held tightly against hers, while she tried to recollect something that she had thought she wanted to say to him. She did occasionally talk to Pooh-Bah, as well as to flowers and herself, because he and she were of exactly the same age, five and three-quarter years old, and this gave them a certain sympathy with each other. No one year is ever quite the same as any other year, and the souls whom it cradles through their first months on earth are of a particular vintage and know each other when they meet. Caroline and Pooh-Bah, being so young, could both of them still just remember a place where they had lived before they were born upon this earth, and sometimes they talked about it together in whispers, generally towards evening when the blackbird was singing in the ilex tree.

For Pooh-Bah and Caroline knew quite well that it is at times and in places of transition, at that moment of the sunset or the dawn when it is neither night nor day but both, or out in the marshes where there is neither sea nor land but a mingling of the two, that the veil slips a little between one world and another and for one brief moment one belongs nowhere, neither to day nor night, to land or sea, in this world or the other. At these moments it made little difference to Pooh-Bah or Caroline that the soul of the one was encased in golden brown fur and the soul of the other in pink freckled skin. They forgot these slight physical differences and cheek to cheek they communed together of the things about which the blackbird was singing.

The gulls told about these things too, as they wheeled over the marshes, and the plover in the reeds by the front door when he cried out like a shrill trumpet in the dawn, but they were not as explicit as the blackbird. In the gulls' cry there was a note of warning and in the shrillness of the plover there was something of a challenge; but the blackbird at evening seemed to have no further need of courage or of struggle; he forgot about them for the moment and sang only of that which they win.

It was of something the blackbird had said yesterday, something about a blue bird, that Caroline wanted to talk to Pooh-Bah. Suddenly she remembered what it was, lifted her cheek from his and put her lips to his ear. He pricked it and rolled a sympathetic amber eye in her direction.

"M.V.590," shouted Tommy above their heads. "Gosh! Look! There's David!"

The bonnet of a silver-gray car had nosed its way round the corner of the lane, like an animal smelling its way home, and a humming contented throbbing sound rose in the quiet of the lane. The engine of the car was purring as though it was happy, and the silver racing greyhound on the bonnet, flashing in the sun, seemed to take a leap forward as though it saw the end of the journey. Forgotten was the blue bird, forgotten were those passing cars upon the high road with the important numbers plastered on their tails, forgotten was the well-bred dignity of a long and royal line of Chinese ancestors. With one wild bark Pooh-Bah was on his feet and rocketing down the lane like any vulgar mongrel. With a surprising shrill sound like a train whistle, instantly stoppered by the insertion of her thumb, Caroline was after him, easily outdistanced by Tommy who leaped from the top of the gatepost clean over her head and reached the bonnet of the car neck and neck with Ben, whose long strides had brought him flying up from the cornfield at the first shout. But it was the Bastard who was the first to leap through the opened door of the car and land heavily upon David's chest, the Bastard mad with excitement, ears flapping, legs flying and tail half out of its socket with its agitation. David dropped his arms to his sides, closed his eyes and lay back in the driving seat, suffering with passivity the Bastard's muddy paws upon his chest and the Bastard's long pink tongue swirling over his face with a circular motion which though of an extreme rapidity left no particle of the countenance of the beloved unmoistened. It was always better to suffer the Bastard thus, so the Eliots had discovered. If one endeavored to dodge the expression of his affection, or stem the torrent of his love, it but prolonged the agony. Expressed the Bastard's feelings must be, lest he burst, and it was best to get it all over as soon as possible.

Meanwhile the other four surged over David and the Bastard and fell heavily into the back seat. "What have you brought us?" shouted the children, picking themselves up.

"Sausages," said David weakly, and felt for his handkerchief.

He always brought them something amusing. Once it had been a large tin moneybox to encourage thrift in them; but when the lid was lifted there were two white mice inside. And the next time, just in case they were tired of the mice and were at a loss as to how to get rid of them, it was an old boot with a kitten inside, a kitten called Tucker with a white patch under its chin that was subsequently given to Caroline. And the next time it was an exceedingly shrill cuckoo clock. And the next time it was a chameleon and a box full of live spiders to feed it on. And after that Grandmother turned a little difficult and said no living gift could be received in future unless it was a vegetarian, and no mechanical gift unless it could refrain from calling attention to the passing of time by shrill noises in the night. Life fed on life, one knew, and time passed, but Grandmother did not wish her attention called to either distressing fact.... So now David had brought a string of five sausages with a large pink bow tied in each joint. "Pork," he said. "Quite silent and very nourishing. One for each of you and one each for the dogs. Now, for the love of Mike, sit down, and let's get a move on."

Gradually the turmoil inside the car subsided, and David, holding the Bastard down with his left elbow, was able to get at the self-starter. There were times when he wished his arrival at Damerosehay could be less like a minor earthquake and more like what it was, the return of a tired man to the place that he cared for the best on earth.... Yet he would have missed that riotous welcome in the lane and by the time they reached the turn by the cornfield the children were generally sufficiently engrossed in their gifts to let him watch in comparative peace for the landmarks that he loved.... The car took the corner and he greeted the first, the old cornfield itself, with a leap of recognition. The window beside him was down and he could hear the wind sighing in the shivering, uncut stalks and feel it cold and clean on his skin. Beyond stretched the marsh, crimson and amethyst and gold and blue under the level rays of the sun. White high clouds were passing, sweeping upwards from the far line of the sea, and their shadows swept the marsh like the wind made visible. The old Castle was visible now, and the Island beyond. The car slid on, past the remembered creeks and gullies and the fields where the cows were browsing, past Little Village and the harbor, with the blue swans' lake beyond. The swans were lying at rest upon their own reflections, and the gulls contemplative upon the roofs of Little Village, but a yacht was speeding out from the harbor to the sea and Clutterbuck and Charles Beere, Urry and Obadiah Watson, turned slowly round upon the harbor seats and removed their pipes from their mouths. More they would not have put themselves out to do had the new arrival been the king himself. David shouted a greeting to them and their mahogany faces creaked into grins of welcome, which was more than they would have done for his majesty.... But then David was David and the most popular of the Eliots of Damerosehay.

"Everything all right?" he asked as the oak wood came into sight. He asked the question casually, as he always did just at this bend of the road, but Ben sensed the undercurrent of anxiety in his tone. David could never come back to Damerosehay, Ben knew, without that shadow of a fear that something might have been changed and the old rapture of homecoming not be quite the same. Ben understood. That was the worst of going away, like David had to. If you stayed at home, as he did, you knew that everything you loved was safe; day by day you watched over it, and if something had to change a little it changed so gradually that it did not hurt.

"Everything's all right," he hastened to assure David. "Tucker's had a kitten; at least I think she had six but something seemed to happen to the other five; and Tommy has smashed his mug with the robin on it, but that's all that's different."

"I didn't smash it," said Tommy indignantly. "I just threw it at Ben and he ducked so that it hit the wall. It was his fault. If he hadn't ducked it wouldn't have hit the wall."

"I can bear it," said David. "I wasn't keen on that robin; too like Lloyd George. I suppose I'm too late for the butterflies on the michaelmas daisies?"

And again there was anxiety in his tone and again Ben grieved for him. For David had been away all the spring and summer. He had missed the gorse on the marsh and the fruit blossom in the kitchen garden. He had missed the shut-eyed stage of Tucker's kitten and all the Victoria plums. He had missed Grandmother's birthday and cook's new hat with the cherries on it that the Bastard ate, and the fête at the Vicarage when the donkey had knocked down the crockery stall. He had, in fact, missed all the beauty and excitement of five glorious months. "But you've not missed the butterflies," cried Ben triumphantly. "The purple michaelmas daisy by the gate had a painted lady on it this morning, and three red admirals and a cabbage. . . . And Tucker's kitten is called Bib because it has a white patch on its chest like Tucker."

And then they spoke no more for they were in the oak wood. The moss was as velvet beneath the wheels of the car and the trees, bending a little, gathered them in.

CHAPTER TWO

I.

MEANWHILE LUCILLA, THE children's grandmother, sat at tea with her maid Ellen in her firelit drawing room. Her daughter Margaret was at a missionary meeting at the Vicarage and the children had gone to meet David, so only Ellen was with her. She liked this, for a strange peace came over her when she and Ellen were alone. They had been together for sixty years now, ever since Lucilla had come back from her honeymoon, and what they didn't know about each other wasn't worth knowing. It was their utter knowledge that gave them their happiness together; that and the fact that they saw eye to eye in the matter of always having the window open a little bit, but not too much, and always having a wood fire burning in the grate unless there was actually a heat wave on. More happy homes have been wrecked, Lucilla was apt to say, by not seeing eye to eye about how much window to have open than by any other controversy known to man. It is quite possible to live happily with a person who does not think as you do about the eternal verities; but it is not possible to live happily with some one who wants the window open when you want it shut, or shut when you want it open, or with some one who likes a fire when you don't, or doesn't like it when you do. Lucilla and Ellen were utterly at one about the fire. The Damerosehay drawing room was beautiful, but it was damp, and it was no good saying it wasn't. Lucilla and Ellen didn't say it wasn't. . . . They lit the fire.

It was, however, only Lucilla who drank the delicate China tea out of a white and gold fluted tea cup of Worcester china, and ate two pieces of wafer bread and butter and one sponge finger; Ellen merely stood looking on at the rite, her bony hands crossed on her black silk apron and her face folded into stern lines of determination. She was very firm with Lucilla over her tea. Lucilla might drink two cups of tea, but no more, and she might not eat less than two pieces of bread and butter and one sponge finger, and she might not feed the cat Tucker, who had her tea in the kitchen before she came to the drawing room. Lucilla was a very strong-minded old lady, but in the hands of Ellen she was as wax.

It was because she loved Ellen more than any one else, except perhaps David, that she permitted herself to be domineered over in this way; for even the strongest succumb sometimes to this luxury of yielding love; it is good to have one person upon earth to whom one gives oneself in submission as a child to its mother. There were other people to whom Lucilla appeared outwardly to yield; to her daughter Margaret, for instance, who was unmarried and poured out upon her mother all the devoted fuss which she would have given to her children had she had them. To this devotion Lucilla yielded. It was, she thought, her duty as a mother. . . . It was also her cross. . . . But her yielding was only skin-deep, given for Margaret's sake and not

36

for her own, while her yielding to Ellen went right down to the depths of her spirit and was one of the sources of her strength. Without Ellen she would have made a poor thing of her life. Unseen, mysteriously, Ellen's spirit had always supported hers. The different quality of this yielding was seen in the fact that if Ellen put a shawl over her knees it remained there until Ellen took it off again, but if Margaret put it there she whisked it off the moment her daughter's back was turned.

Lucilla was a truthful woman and so she did not mind admitting to herself that she loved Ellen more than any of her children, more than the memory of her dead husband, more than any of her grandchildren, with the possible exception of her grandson David. Ellen knew all her secrets. She knew things about her that Lucilla's children and grandchildren had never even guessed at, would hardly have believed had they been told of them, things that were a shame to Lucilla, and things that were a glory. Ellen knew all the heights and all the depths. In such knowledge there was peace.

But that did not prevent her getting very irritated with Ellen at times, especially when, as now, Ellen insisted obstinately upon keeping between them that barrier of mistress and maid.

"Sit down, Ellen, for goodness sake!" she exclaimed. "Why stand on those varicose veins of yours when the room is full of chairs?"

Ellen chose an extremely uncomfortable chair against the wall and sat gingerly upon the extreme edge. Her eyes were mutely reproachful.

Perhaps she was right, thought Lucilla, pouring out her second cup of tea. Perhaps Ellen's insistence upon the outward forms of respect added to the richness of their relationship. On second thought she was sure that it did. On Ellen's side that outward respect had as the years went by become a habit of mind, so that even though she knew all her weaknesses she did indeed respect Lucilla. And on Lucilla's side that dignity which as a young mistress she had always tried to practice before her young maid, encouraged and trained in it by that same respect of Ellen's, had become automatic. Not even when they clung together in grief or pain need they fear now to lose those two attributes of their mutual relationship. And that, Lucilla saw, was good. "You're quite right, Ellen," she said with seeming irrelevance. "One should build, as we have done, from the outside inwards."

Ellen sniffed with a slight suggestion of sarcasm. All their life together she had been astonished by Lucilla's perpetual questioning of facts that seemed to her to be obvious. But then Lucilla had been so beautiful always. Facts had come to her softened by the loving determination of others that they should hurt her as little as possible. This had perhaps a little blunted her understanding of them. But upon Ellen they had descended with that uncompromising hardness of impact that the plain woman learns to expect in all her dealings with life. She never questioned them, as did Lucilla, she merely accepted them. It was that acceptance that had made her the rock against which Lucilla leaned.

And now Lucilla found herself, as often before, thinking about this fact of service.... Mistress and maid.... She

38

shut her eyes for a moment against the westering sun and pictures of their life together flashed quickly through her mind, little cameos that were bright and living among dark tracts of forgotten time. Very vividly, for a few moments, she lived in them.

2.

She was once again dressing for dinner for the first time in her married home. She was tired after the long journey back from Italy where she and James, her husband, had spent their honeymoon, tired and very frightened of her new, austere maid. She had not had a lady's maid before her marriage; she had shared her mother's, but now they said that as the wife of such a brilliant young barrister she must certainly have one. She owed it to her husband's position, they said. There were a good many things, she was beginning to see, that she would owe to her husband's position that she would not like at all. This London house, for instance, so dark and gloomy after the home in the country where she had been brought up, and the many servants she would have to manage, and the strenuous social life that James was expecting her to lead. Married life was not going to be altogether the earthly paradise that her mother had led her to expect, she thought. She had not liked her honeymoon very much. She had been horribly scared. Her mother had not explained what was going to happen to her, and James had been married before and was so much older than she was that though he meant to be kind he made her feel more like his captive than his mate. She had had to keep telling herself all the time, as her mother had kept telling her during her engagement, how wonderful it was that a man like James, thirty-five years old, a widower, and with a great future before him, should have fallen in love with a little chit of eighteen like herself. She had been very fortunate, for what, her mother had frequently demanded of her during that terrifying engagement, would have happened to her if he had not? One of four daughters, the offspring of an impecunious country squire undistinguished by anything except a gallant death in the hunting field, she would have had to become a governess, she, Lucilla Marshall, the daughter of a long line of aristocratic forebears who had never stooped to do a hand's turn at anything except losing their money. . . . That would have been her fate but for James. . . . And so, bewildered by her father's death, by her mother's arguments and James's impassioned pleadings, she had got married, and sat in front of her mirror on this first evening in her home with her head held high, her cold hands locked in her lap and her voice very carefully controlled so that her new maid should not see how frightened she was. "It is a cold evening, I think," she said, and wished that Ellen did not look so like a horse.

"Yes, milady," Ellen answered, though as a matter of fact it was rather warm and sultry. "Will your ladyship wear your white satin tonight, and the diamonds?" And her bony hands, that had been busy arranging Lucilla's golden curls in the elaborate puffs and coils of the late eighteen-seventies, pressed the girl's head with a light, tender pressure, so light and so instantly withdrawn that Lucilla would not have known it had happened had it not been for the quick sense of warmth that suddenly ran through her cold body.

"Yes, Ellen," she said. "Whatever you think right."

And Ellen, looking at her in the glass, had smiled a comical smile that showed all her yellow teeth, and made her look more like a horse than ever; but that yet was full of reassurance. "White satin for a bride," she said, "and diamonds for joy."

And then Lucilla realized that to Ellen this was a great occasion. Vicariously and unselfishly she too was decking herself in honor of a bridegroom. Behind that grim and horselike exterior were beating all the emotions that should have been Lucilla's, and Lucilla felt suddenly shamed and humbled, shamed that Ellen should have been quicker than she to see the inherent beauty of a given moment, humbled by the selflessness of this older, plainer girl who could live the drama of womanhood only through another. She was quick to respond, quick to give Ellen what she wanted. She stood joyously to be decked in her white satin, lingered over the choice of earrings and bracelets, and gave Ellen a shy eager kiss before she went tapping across the polished floor in her high-heeled shoes and laughing down the long stairs to the great drawing room where her husband waited for her. . . . Ellen, she knew, was leaning over the bannisters watching her, listening to hear the greeting that she gave to James, listening for the triumphant rolling of the gong and watching for the processional entry into the dining room. All through that evening she was aware of Ellen, and all through that evening she made her husband happier than she had done since the day she married him.

That picture faded and others slipped through the mind of the old Lucilla. Once again she was lying in the big gloomy bed in her big gloomy bedroom in Eaton Square, waiting through hours of undrugged agony for the birth of her first child. She made no sound, for she had been trained to courage, but her mind was a fevered whirl of anguished questioning. Why? Why? Why? Why must she bear this child to a man she did not love, why must she bear it in this pain? And then she became aware of Ellen standing beside her, questioning nothing. With her lips tightly compressed and her forehead beaded with sweat, because when Lucilla suffered she suffered too, she was knotting a towel to the bedpost for Lucilla to cling to. But her face was quite serene. There was no "why" about this for her. It just happened to a woman. One accepted it. She gave Lucilla a glance that was almost stern before she was whisked out of the way by the midwife, the proper mistress of these terrible ceremonies. But her glance remained with Lucilla, steadying her through the nightmare that came after.

It was Ellen, Lucilla thought, as she opened her eyes and the little pictures slipped away from her, who had taught her how to love her children. Upon each babe as it arrived, and there were six of them before Lucilla's childbearing was over, Ellen poured out such a passion of maternal love that Lucilla herself had at last caught the infection. At first the children had been to her little nuisances who periodically robbed her of her youth, her health and her beauty; but later her mind changed towards them; they became to her what they were to Ellen, the crown and glory of her life. To the last child of all, Maurice, the father of her grandson David, Lucilla had given a love that was considered even by Ellen to be out of all proportion to what a mother should feel for her child; a love that had been, and still was, though Maurice had been dead for twenty years, the great emotion of her life, the emotion through which she had reached out to some measure of comprehension of the glory and the agony that are human existence. . . . And it had been Ellen who at long last had taught her to admire her husband. It had been Ellen's respectful devotion to him, her appreciation of "the master's" justice and generosity that had opened Lucilla's eyes to them. The knowledge came almost too late, of course; James died very soon after she had learned to appreciate him; but when she came to mourn for him she needed no teaching from Ellen. She had worn her widow's weeds with an outward correctitude which was for the first time in her life matched by her inward emotions. Ellen had, at last, made of her a woman cut to the proper pattern.

But was it fair, she wondered now, that she should have had all the substance while Ellen had had only the shadow? And Ellen had been so ready for the substance, so well equipped with the right reactions to all the circumstances of a woman's life, while she, Lucilla, had been always questioning, always straining away from the things that she must meet and face. No, it was not fair, but yet, in this contradictory world, it seemed the normal thing. More often than not a human creature seemed cast for the role that suited him least. There was a purpose here, perhaps.

To swim with the stream was too easy; it was swimming against it that increased one's strength. But it had surely been hard on Ellen. Sighing, Lucilla reached for the teapot to pour herself out a third cup of tea.

3.

"You've had two cups," said Ellen.

"So I have, Ellen," said Lucilla, and set back the teapot on the tray.

"If you've finished I'll clear," said Ellen, and raising herself stiffly from her uncomfortable chair she lumbered on her flat feet to Lucilla's side, adjusted her spectacles and bent over to take a firm grip of the tray with her bony hands. Ellen was eighty, two years older than Lucilla, and lifting trays was now for her something of an achievement. It required her whole attention and concentration, and Lucilla hated to see her do it.

"Why can't you let Rose clear?" she asked with that irritation which was always hers when in anxiety for those she loved.

"Rose!" snorted Ellen. "That girl shall not touch our Worcester china while I'm above ground; and when I'm in the churchyard I'll not lie easy, thinking of her way with a teacup. Believe it or not, milady, but her notion of washing up is to fill the sink with water and then shoot the whole tray-load into it like rubbish into a dump. I've told her and told her, but every word I say to these girls goes in at one ear and out at the other."

"It's very trying, Ellen," agreed Lucilla. "But we must remember that we are very lucky to have kept Rose so

44

long. The servant problem is so very acute in the country, and so very trying for Miss Margaret."

It was indeed; the more so that Ellen did not get on with modern servants. Her standard was too high. They could not, like Lucilla, learn to adjust themselves to it.... And so they usually left at the month, and Margaret did their work until others were found.

Ellen snorted again, then carefully raised the tray of Worcester china and bore it, as a priestess a holy relic, towards the door.

"How I love you, Ellen," cried Lucilla impulsively. "Was I irritable just now?"

"I'm used to it," said Ellen.

"Better than any one else, I think, Ellen," said Lucilla.

Ellen paused at the door and her face creased itself into its rare, slow smile. "Master David will be here in half-an-hour," she said.

"What? So soon?" cried Lucilla, and was instantly in a flutter. Her face flushed a delicate shell-pink and her hands went instinctively to her white hair to see that it was tidy. Ellen sniffed. The extravagance of Lucilla's love for her grandson David, as for his father before him, always slightly irritated her. It was out of proportion. It was not quite the correct reaction of maternity. It was almost more the love of a girl for her lover.... And Lucilla was seventy-eight.

"Tell Rose to make fresh tea as soon as Master David comes," said Lucilla.

"He don't take tea," Ellen reminded her. "Only cocktails."

"Not in my house," said Lucilla with sudden heat. "The grandsons know perfectly well, Ellen, that I will not have those horrible drinks, those Sidecars and highballs and what-not, shaken all over the place between meals. A glass of wine with their dinner, yes, and a whisky and soda if they've got wet out shooting, but no more. They know that, Ellen."

"Ah," said Ellen, and departed, closing the door with a little more noise than was actually necessary.

"She's jealous," thought Lucilla.

But here she misjudged Ellen, who was never jealous of David. She slammed the door because she was in a bit of a hurry, having forgotten to see if the necessary ingredients for the kind of cocktail beloved of David were put ready in the cupboard in the dining room where Lucilla never went. She knew all the tastes of the grandsons in regard to drinks, and never confused them. Sometimes her conscience reproached her a little at this deception of Lucilla, but these qualms were rare, and she did not let them worry her. She had been an excellent disciplinarian in her youth, and was so still with the children who lived in the house, but the others she just wanted to have what they liked. Lucilla wanted them to have what they liked too, of course, but only if it was good for them. Ellen did not care a rap if it was good for them so long as they enjoyed it.

Left alone, Lucilla laughed again, a clear girlish laugh that was echoed by the little gold clock on the mantelpiece jubilantly chiming half-past four. Another half-hour to wait; or more probably three-quarters, for he was always later than he said he would be. Lateness was a matter of principle with him, she thought, for he knew quite well, the rascal, that he was one of those who are always waited for with a beating heart. There was no need for him, as for less fortunate ones, to woo popularity with punctuality and consideration. He could, and did, trade upon affection. That was wrong of him, of course, but she could not scold him because she had done the same when she was young. She remembered how, in London, when she was at the height of her beauty and popularity, she had always been careful to be the last arrival at a party. It had been such fun to hear the sudden thrilled little silence that fell at the announcement of her name, to walk slowly down the long drawing room with every eye upon her, to feel the envy of the women and the admiration of the men. . . . And how it had annoyed poor James. . . . But she had grown out of that, as David would, for the acceptance of homage, she had found, gave no permanent satisfaction; it was better to give it; what is given to you you are always afraid will one day cease to be given, but what you give you can give for ever. Life had taught her that at long last.

And now that she was old she found so much to call forth her homage. Now that she had to count her springs they burned for her with a glory to which she could not give less than worship. She felt that she could almost pray to the sun as it warmed her, and to human kindness when she met it she had hard work not to bend the knee. Above all did she worship youth, especially the youth that had flowed from her own life. This, she was aware, might be called a perverted form of egoism; but she did not think it was, for though they were life of her life, she regarded her adored grandchildren with a certain detachment. The gulf of time was so wide between them that she could not fully share their thoughts or their outlook, their torments or their battles, which were of their generation and not of hers; she could only love them and tend them and make for them a refuge to which they could fly when those same thoughts and struggles had wearied them beyond endurance.

For that, she thought, was the mission of a grandmother. It was for that purpose that twenty years ago she had bought Dameroseshay. She belonged to the past and she had bought for her setting an old house in a strip of country rich in history. The past, she knew, is inviolable, one of the few things in life that cannot be marred by present foolishness, and in it the present may find its peace.

4.

And so she had made Damerosehay for her grandchildren, and especially for David. The day when she had found Damerosehay, and the days leading up to that day, bound up as they were with the greatest anguish of her life, were almost the most vivid of all her memories. Swiftly, her eyes closing again, she relived them.

Only a few weeks before she found Damerosehay she had sat by the bedside of her son Maurice, watching him die after weeks of pain so hideous that even now she dared not let herself think of it, lest she should be once more the mad woman she had been at that time. It had been April, 1918. Maurice had been wounded in France, and his wife, as worn by his pain as he was, had died from the spring scourge of influenza only a few days before. Lucilla's son Roger had died at Jutland and of her remaining three sons, Hilary, George and Stephen, only Hilary the parson, badly wounded as a chaplain in the early days of the war and now relegated with his wooden leg and his injured lungs to a country parish in Hampshire, was in a place of safety. "Spring," she said to herself that day. "Spring." And she gazed stupidly at a patch of sunlight on the wall. Maurice was already unconscious and beyond her reach, Maurice who had been the most gay and gallant and vividly alive of all her children. He would have loved life to the full, enjoying it as none of the others would; yet she had borne him only for agony and death. If only she and James had known, in those far-off days when they had had their children, for what purpose it was that the delicate bodies of their sons were shaped in the womb, that their minds unfolded and their spirits grew, if they had only known, then they would have seen to it that their union was unfruitful and rejoiced that their line died with them. She was glad that James was dead. She was glad that he did not know.

She supposed that there were other people with her in the room, but she did not notice them, she only watched the patch of sunlight on the wall. She hated it. "Spring," she repeated stupidly. How dared the spring break through again upon an earth drenched in the obscenity of war? How dared the sun shine upon men and women mad with pain...? Surely God mocked.... The shadow of a bird's wing flashed across the patch of sunlight on the wall and they told her that Maurice was dead.

Such little things can loom so large in life, and it was that shadow of a bird in flight that saved her reason in the days that followed. She saw it constantly, blue against the patch of golden sunlight, so brief and so fragile an appearance, yet instinct with such joy. The picture of it in her mind was almost more vivid than the picture of her dying son; when that second memory swept over her, threatening to destroy her, the first came quickly upon it, drawn over it as a fair sheet is drawn over the face of the dead. "Look not upon that but upon this," it had seemed to say, and she had looked and been comforted.

And when she had to tell the five-year-old David that now his father as well as his mother had left him, groping a little desperately among the symbols of angels and heavens above the stars with which grown-ups try to comfort stricken children, it was the symbol of the bird's wings that helped her most. "They fly away," she told David. "They fly away and are at rest."

"Birds," said David, savoring the word. "Birds. I like birds. There are lots of birds in the country. Grandmother, shall we go to the country?"

And then Lucilla knew what she was going to do with the rest of her life. She was going to build some sort of a refuge, somewhere, to which her children and her grandchildren could escape. Not a permanent escape; even in her grief she still knew that a selfish isolation is the sure road to hell; but that temporary one which is the right of every man. They were talking a lot just now about the war to end war, and a country fit for heroes to live in. She thought they deceived themselves. She had seen now what life could be, and what man could do when the devil was in him. She had not much hope of any wholesale change; only of the creation of isolated homes of beauty from which, please God, the loveliness should spread. Such a home would she make for her children and her grandchildren. They should come to it weary and sickened and go away made new. They should find peace there, and beauty, and the cleansing of their sins.

"It sounds very far-fetched and absurd," she said to her eldest son. "But what it boils down to, Hilary, is just that I want a house in the country."

"Come and stay with me," Hilary said, "and we'll look for it."

So she and her daughter Margaret, and Ellen, and little David who was to live with her now, went down to the ugly red brick Vicarage of Fairhaven, in Hampshire, where Hilary lived contentedly in a state of discomfort and confusion which seemed to him, after the mud of Flanders and the rigors of the slum clergyhouse that had preceded it, the height of luxury. Plenty of women would have been happy to undeceive him, but Hilary was, and had always been, one of those born solitaries who can live to the full only in loneliness. He was very like his father. It was partly because James had been like that, only without Hilary's good sense in realizing it, that Lucilla, naturally gregarious, had not been very happy with him.

But Hilary, like his father before him, was very practical and very kind. He had provided for Lucilla photographs and descriptions of all the desirable residences in the neighborhood, taking great care that they should be well within her means and of a type that Margaret, who was to be her mother's housekeeper, would find easy to run. . . . But Lucilla, when taken to see them, hated the lot. . . . None of them had either that loveliness or that unearthliness for which she was looking.

"They're no good," she said one evening wearily to Hilary. "They are all far too ordinary."

"You know, Mother dear," Hilary said gently, smiling at her, "I am afraid your ideas are a bit too large. You can't afford the sort of house you want, darling. You'll just have to put up with the best that we can do."

"I will do no such thing, Hilary," Lucilla said, aggrieved. "I will have what I want for my children and my grand-children or I will have nothing." And she cast all her "orders to view" despairingly upon the floor.

Hilary and Margaret looked at each other and smiled and sighed a little. It was almost impossible to make Lucilla understand that though before this horrible war she had been a comparatively rich woman she was now not so well-to-do as she had been. Investments had gone down. She couldn't expect to get the price for the town house that she would have done in days of peace. "Why not?" she had asked. They had tried to explain why not, but she hadn't bothered to listen. She was too tired. And all her life long those about her had exerted themselves to spare her the tiresome details of practical affairs. . . . She was too lovely to be bothered with such things, they had thought, and she had quite agreed with them. . . . So now she couldn't take those things in. She had lost the habit of it.

"Wouldn't you consider this one, Mother?" Margaret

asked a little wistfully, pushing forward the photo of a particularly hideous modern house. "It was so convenient inside. I could run it quite easily with two maids."

"That!" cried Lucilla in horror. "You expect me to buy that thing as a home for little David? Are you mad, Margaret?"

Margaret propped her aching head on fingers that trembled a little, and her eyes, again seeking Hilary's, filled with tears. She was absurdly sensitive, and Lucilla, who seldom cried, come what might, always had great difficulty in keeping her patience with her. At this moment, worn out as she was and not quite normal in her grief, she almost hated these two children of hers. They were worthy and good, but oh, so distressingly plain. Hilary at thirty-nine was already bald and stout, and Margaret, with the only man who had ever loved her dead at Gallipoli and what small good looks she had ever had destroyed by years of strenuous war nursing, was now at thirty-five quite the dowdiest frump Lucilla had ever seen. She could not conceive how she could have produced these two. Only Maurice of all her children had had beauty...Maurice ...Maurice.... Suddenly she got up and left them, fumbling blindly for the door. They heard her stumbling on the stairs.

"Let her alone," Hilary said sternly to Margaret, who with her usual tactlessness would have flown after Lucilla. "Let her alone. It's all we can do."

Margaret, her thin elbows set upon the litter of Hilary's study table, hid her face in her hands and cried. "It is so dreadful," she sobbed, "not to be able to give her what she wants. I would die to do it, Hilary, if I could. You know I would."

Hilary, taking his pipe from his mouth, limped round to her and held her head clumsily against the tobacco ash that strewed his waistcoat. "I know you would," he said, and suddenly wondered if Margaret was not a much finer woman than any one ever suspected. Everyone loved Lucilla so much that they seldom noticed Margaret. . . . And Margaret did not mind. . . . Surely it was rather fine of her not to mind. He would have liked to tell her so, but he couldn't find the words. He rubbed his hand over his rough, thinning hair, stuck his pipe back in his mouth and bent patiently to pick up the papers that Lucilla had thrown upon the floor.

"What a mess," he said tolerantly.

"Darling Mother," said Margaret, and laughed a little through her tears. The childlikeness of Lucilla was a perpetual delight to her children. Even in their grief they could rejoice in it. It kept them young.

And in the end it was David who gave Lucilla what she wanted. "Grandmother!" he cried, leaping up and down in his cot in her room at five o'clock the next morning. "Grandmother! I want to go to the seaside!"

This was a grievance with him. They had been in the place four days, only a mile from the sea, and they had not been near it. Instead they had gone rattling about the inland country in the village Ford, looking at hideous houses that interested him not at all. At least the grown-ups had looked at them. He hadn't looked at them. He had

had more sense. He had stayed in the car playing bears under the back seat and wanting to go to the seaside.

"The seaside!" he yelled now, smacking an imperious fist upon his pillow.

"Certainly," said Lucilla, and got out of bed.

She had also not been to the sea yet. There was nothing at Little Village, Hilary had told her, except a handful of cottages and a harbor. It was rather pretty, and he would take her there one fine day when the house question was settled. And she had acquiesced. But now, of course, she saw the iniquity of keeping a small boy of five and the seaside separated for longer than was absolutely necessary.

"I'm so sorry, darling," she said, pulling on her stockings. "We'll go to the seaside."

"Now," commanded David.

"Of course," said Lucilla. "As soon as we're dressed."

"Right," said David. "I can take off my own 'jamas."

They performed extremely sketchy toilets, crept downstairs very softly so as not to wake Margaret and Hilary and let themselves out into the garden, all wet and glimmering and deliciously scented with the rain and the sun and the flowers of April. David giggled his peculiarly entrancing giggle. Grandmother was great fun. She never used those hateful words "presently" or "perhaps." She understood that if you wanted to do a thing you wanted to do it now, while you remembered about it, and not tomorrow or next week when you would probably be wanting to do something entirely different. Daddy had been the same. Daddy also had always wanted to do things "now." He could remember that once he and Daddy had played cricket out in the street at four in the morning because they felt like that, and had subsequently gone to bed at three in the afternoon because they felt like that too. Mummy, he remembered, had had difficulty in understanding their point of view.

"Grandmother," he said suddenly, the thought of Daddy bringing another thought to his mind, "will there be birds at the seaside?"

"Lots," said Lucilla. "Sea birds. White ones."

"A blue one?" he asked.

"They're not generally blue at the seaside," said Lucilla, "but as it's so early in the morning we might see a blue one."

"Is it easier to see blue birds early in the morning?" asked David.

"At dawn and sunset," said Lucilla, "one sometimes sees beautiful things that one does not see at other times."

"Why?" asked David.

"One just does," said Lucilla.

"Right," said David, and accepted her statement. He was not as yet old enough to be one of those tiresome children who have to go on asking why until they have plumbed the utter depths of adult ignorance. He was still an explorer, finding the world so full of wonders that it was all his small mind could do to accept these wonders without fatiguing itself to ask questions about them.

"Come on," he continued, pulling at Lucilla's hand. "It's nice."

It was indeed. The lane that led from Big Village to Little Village was an enchanting place at half-past five on an April morning. The thick high hedges of sloe and briar and hawthorn, blown all one way by the wind from the sea, so that the seaward hedges tossed long sprays of emerald green leaves like foam across the lane, were bright and sparkling with sun-shot raindrops, and nestling in the shelter of them were celandines and speedwells that were still asleep. Through gaps in the hedge they could see the east still barred with gold, and the sky curving up through lovely gradations of color that ended over their heads in a clear deep blue that was reflected on the earth below, by the pools in the lane and the polished surfaces of the wet green leaves, as though the depth of the firmament was something the earth must at all costs reach up and catch hold of. The light was the strange light of dawn, cool and bright yet deep and warm, the light of the sun and the moon and the stars mingling together for a moment as the dominion of the one yielded to the rule of the other.

There were quantities of birds already, little ones that sang praises madly in the hedges and big ones that moved in long lines against the golden east, flying from north to south in slow rhythmical ecstasy. Some of them were black and some were white. "Crows and gulls," said Lucilla, "and they fly like that because they are so happy that the sun has risen. They can't sing like the little birds and so they have to praise God with the movement of their wings."

"What an awful thing it would be," said David, "if suddenly one morning God forgot to tell the sun to get up."

"I think that's what the birds feel," said Lucilla. "They

do get so excited, don't they, when they find it's all right and He hasn't forgotten."

"Could He ever forget?" asked David anxiously.

"Of course not," said Lucilla. "He always remembers everything."

"How clever He is," said David. "See me jump this puddle."

And then the lane topped the crest of a little hill and suddenly, breathlessly, they saw the marshes and the sea. They stood still for a moment, clutching each other, and then quite silently they took hands and ran. They did not stop until they reached the harbor wall, where they sat down very suddenly and looked about them. The gorse was out, flaming under the sun, and all the colors of the dawn were caught in the waters of the harbor and in the pools and channels in the marsh. The gulls were everywhere, and, as they watched, the swans arrived from the Abbey River, flying one behind the other, their great wings touched with gold. From the old gray cottages behind them a few spirals of blue smoke crept up from the chimneys, and over to their left the sun touched the coral buds of a twisted oak wood to points of beckoning flame.

"And Hilary said this was rather pretty," gasped Lucilla. "Rather pretty! Oh, my poor Hilary!"

She said no more, for David was pulling at her hand again, and she was running with him towards the oak wood. They were through the broken gate and their feet were running silently on the moss-grown drive. The gnarled boughs stooped about them, gathering them in and closing the ranks behind so that they should not turn back. To their left was an old red brick wall and to their right, through the delicate patterning of twigs and buds, they could see the sea. Then the wall turned at right angles, they with it, and they stood before a gray house where a porch with a battered front door within it faced across the marshes to the silver line of the Estuary. Lucilla, who when all was said and done was fifty-eight years old, sank down upon the stone horse block that stood there, utterly out of breath, but David flung himself against the door like a wild thing.

"It's locked!" he shouted. "It's all shut up! Open it, Grandmother! Open it!"

Instantly Lucilla, an utterly unscrupulous woman when in pursuit of what she wanted, was up and smashing the hall window with the heel of her shoe. Then she put her hand through, unlatched and opened it, and climbed in, David after her.

They were in the hall of an eighteenth-century house, empty, mildewed and desolate, but with a fine shadowy molded ceiling and a broken fireplace that Adam might have designed. A wide, shallow, curving staircase led away into the darkness above, the carved banisters festooned with cobwebs that drifted like gray ghosts in the soft breath of dawn. But Lucilla and David were not dismayed. They took hands and went forward.

Almost without speaking they went everywhere. They opened doors into queer rooms lit only by the long fingers of bright sunlight that smote through the chinks in the shutters, setting all the dust motes dancing and the shadows piling themselves one upon the other in the darkened corners. They pursued long twisting passages to their strange conclusions in unexpected flights of steps and small closets through whose broken windows creepers had grown, trailing their tendrils on the floor. They disturbed families of mice and regiments of spiders, and found a starling's nest that had fallen down a chimney. They explored attics under the roof where the plaster had fallen and the slates had slipped, so that patches of blue sky smiled in upon them, and exciting cellars where toadstools like orange flowers were growing in the must and damp. And at long last, worn out with excitement, they came back to what they knew was the heart of the house, the long low drawing room with the wide hearth and the high mantelpiece and overmantel of dark carved wood that stretched from floor to ceiling.

Hand in hand they stood before it, peering at it through the dimness of the shuttered room. It seemed to tower above them, the carving of it lit here and there by the dusty beams of light that came through the shutters. Looking at it Lucilla suddenly felt that a great ship was sailing towards her, driven fast on a rising sea. She fancied she could hear the roar of the water as it surged away from the proud curve of the prow, and see a shadowy figure moving high up upon the deck. With a sudden gesture of panic, she pushed David back, lest that sharp prow should run him down.

"What is it, Grandmother?" he asked. "Are you frightened?"

Lucilla laughed. "I was so silly, David," she said. "Just

for a moment I thought the mantelpiece was a ship. Let's open the shutters, and then I shan't be silly any more."

There were two windows, both facing southwest, long windows with windowseats below them set in the thickness of the wall. Lucilla and David, standing together on the first windowseat, had hard work to push up the heavy iron bar that closed the shutters. Yet when they had at last done it they were well rewarded, for the shutters creaked back to show them what lay within the old red walls that they had passed as they came through the oak wood—the garden.

Lucilla and David gasped and clutched each other, for it was such a garden as neither of them had seen before. It was a wild, crazy garden, the kind of garden in which the sleeping beauty and her court lay sleeping for a hundred years. Once it had been planted with orderly care and neatness, but now all the flowers and trees and bushes had gone mad together with a sort of jubilant madness that was one of the loveliest things Lucilla had ever seen. The rose trees, bright with their new green leaves, were running riot everywhere, climbing up over the old wall, festooning themselves over the cherry trees and oak trees, cherry trees to the east and oaks to the west, that grew in the tangle of wild grass that had once been lawns and flower beds, and flinging out greedy suckers over the bushes of silvery lavender and rosemary that were struggling gallantly to keep their heads above the tide of green that threatened to wash over them completely. The cherry trees were out already, a foam of white against the blue, and below them daffodils flowed through the grass in drifts of gold. Somewhere, it seemed, violets were growing, for the scent of them drifted in through the open window; but they couldn't be seen, they had been submerged long ago; and just outside the window, standing up sturdy and strong above the general riot, its stiff little leaves like blobs of dark green paint against the bright sky, was an ilex tree.

"Grandmother," said David, "could I go out into the garden?" And then he added in a whisper, "Could I go alone?"

"Of course, darling," said Lucilla, and she lifted him over the sill, setting his feet down among the daffodils below the window. In a minute he was gone, running quickly, hidden from sight by the green sea of grass and the swelling waves of the rosemary and lavender. Lucilla did not fear for him. No harm could come to him in a walled garden. House and garden, oak wood, marshes and sea, it was all of it a children's paradise, and a paradise that would not lose its glory as the children grew older. . . . She had found what she wanted. . . . She leaned her head back against the folded shutters and her hands fell idly in her lap. She was worn out by sleepless nights, by traveling and arguing and desolation. Her eyelids, deeply shadowed by the grief that had found no relief in tears, quivered a little, as though resisting the fingers of the sun laid gently upon them, then they yielded and she was asleep.

As she slept she dreamed one of those astonishingly vivid dreams that make the dreamer feel that his soul has actually left his body and gone voyaging. She was walking through a forest in a strange country. About her the great trees soared upwards, stretching their branches against the sky like arms held up in adoration. They were like living creatures, those trees, and so were the myriad flowers that grew about her feet. In their color and scent they were as an army that praised God; the ground was singing-bright with them. There were caroling birds in the trees who did not fly away when she came near them, and little brown furry beasts in the undergrowth who had never known the meaning of fear. There was water not far away. She could hear the murmur of it and see the calm blue of it shining through the trees. And yet behind this music there was a deep quiet. Though she moved onwards, yet she was resting. The music and the silence, the movement and the rest, seemed co-existent together. She felt happy with a quite indescribable happiness that was yet best described by the word cleanliness. In body, mind and spirit she felt clean, with her thoughts unmuddied and her body a perfect instrument of the spirit within her that she could feel was as a polished mirror to reflect and transmit the light about her.

That light, too, was indescribable. It was something like the light of earthly dawn that she had seen before she slept, holding the same depth of color, the same coolness and warmth as the light of the sun and moon shining together; yet it transcended that as greatly as the light of the sun transcends the flicker of a candle. The music that was all about her, lovely yet diffuse as light, seemed to gather itself into one single phrase, as when the voice of a solo singer soars out above the harmony of orchestra and voices, and she heard the words of it. "They have no need of the sun, neither of the moon, to shine in it, for the Lord God giveth them light."

Then she laughed out of her joy, for she knew where she was. And she knew, too, why she was here, and why she had been born into that life that she had left, and why those whom she loved had been born into it, had suffered in it and had left it: to reflect and transmit this light from the mirror of a pain-cleansed spirit.

"Who sang to me?" she asked, and there was a flutter of wings above her. A small blue bird was with her, not flinging her snatches of song as she passed like the birds in the trees, but accompanying her all the way that she went with his music and the flutter of his wings. She could not hear the words of his song now, but she had heard them. He had been with her all the time, she was sure, but just at first she had not seen him. As she became more familiar with this country, she knew that as she went on the boundaries of it would widen. It was the glorified beauty of the familiar and habitable earth that she saw now, the trees and flowers and creatures that made up the sweetness of it, but soon she would see more. She would see the spirits of those she loved going about the purposes of God, bathed in the light of His perpetual compassion; and at the last she would see even further; but of that she dared not think. . . . Yet, thinking of it, she began to run, effortlessly, almost as though she were winged, and the bird, tossing like a blue flame in the air about her, sang and sang and sang.

And then she saw nothing but the darkness of her closed

eyes, and with a sickening sense of frustration she knew she was awake. But the bird was still singing; the liquid cascades of his song fell in showers all about her. For a long time she listened, then she opened her eyes and saw him sitting in the ilex tree. . . . But he was only a blackbird after all. . . . For just a moment the blueness of the morning had been reflected in his shining feathers as it had been reflected in the pools and the polished leaves in the lane.

Yet how happy she was. One part of her mind was telling her that her dream was just a mix-up of the dawn and the flowers in the garden and the singing blackbird, but another part of it was saying that one world interpenetrates another; we live in them both, but of the greater we know now only that which the lesser tells us of it; and the language of the lesser is the language of dreams and birdsong, sunshine and the kindliness of man.

David suddenly appeared beneath the window. "Grandmother!" he cried excitedly, "I saw a blue bird!"

"Did you, darling?" said Lucilla. "So did I." And she helped him to scramble back through the window and curl himself up on her lap.

"Shall we live here?" he suggested in commanding tones.

"Yes," said Lucilla.

"Right," said David, and wriggled himself comfortable, his smooth golden head laid against her shoulder and his eyes following the sunbeams as they caressed the room that was opened to life again after so many years.

And here they were found by a rightly incensed Hilary, Margaret and Ellen.

"Mother!" exclaimed Hilary. "Do you know the time?"

"Nine o'clock, darling," said Margaret. "Breakfast was to have been at eight."

Ellen merely sniffed.

"Hilary," asked Lucilla, "why did you not tell me about this house?"

"We're going to live here," announced David.

Ignoring his nephew's remark as unworthy of attention, Hilary concentrated upon Lucilla's question.

"I didn't think you would be interested, Mother. It's an awful old barn of a place that's been empty for years. It would cost a fortune to get it into order now. What ever made you come here? We'd not have known where to find you if someone in Little Village hadn't seen you go in." He smiled indulgently at his unaccountable mother. "What a jaunt to take before breakfast! You're as much of a child as David."

"And the surroundings," continued Lucilla, gently preparing her children for the coming blow, "the marshes and the oak wood and the garden. It's all a paradise."

"In the spring and summer," said Hilary darkly.

"We're going to live here," continued David, who felt that this point was not being sufficiently stressed.

"Don't be silly, darling," said Margaret, brushing cobwebs off her skirt. "No one could possibly live here."

"Margaret, my dear," said Lucilla kindly but firmly, "I am very sorry, but I am afraid that we *are* going to live here."

5.

And so it was that the Eliots came to Damerosehay, for Lucilla wanted Damerosehay and Lucilla had to have what she wanted. Her children, worshiping the very ground she trod on, saw this as clearly as she did herself; but what they did not at first see as clearly as Lucilla was how the purchase and restoration of Damerosehay was to be reconciled with the condition in which the family finances unfortunately found themselves. "I'll sell my diamonds," said Lucilla happily, and thought she had found the solution of their difficulties. They did not undeceive her. They let her think, since she wanted to think it, that the sale of the diamonds, which just about mended the roof and modernized the drains, but no more, had purchased the whole estate, but secretly they all of them, Hilary, George, Stephen and Margaret, dived into their pockets and laid the last available halfpenny upon the altar of Damerosehay. The sons suspected that they would be helping to pay for the upkeep of the place until their dying day; and Margaret, facing year after year of struggle with an understaffed house and garden and ends that could be persuaded to meet only with the greatest difficulty, had felt sometimes that her strength and her courage must surely break. Yet, twenty years later, in this autumn of 1938, they were all agreed that it had been worth it. Lucilla had been quite right. Damerosehay was their inevitable home. From the very beginning, almost as though it were alive, it had taken them all to its heart and held them there.

And things were easier now; though still they couldn't afford to install the electric light plant that Margaret longed for, but Lucilla didn't because the softness of oil lamps was, she felt, more suited to the age of Damerosehay; it was Margaret, of course, and not Lucilla, who did the lamps. George, the father of Ben, Tommy and Caroline, was now a major, and Stephen had become as successful a barrister as his father before him. In spite of George's polo, wife and children, and Stephen's wife and children and collection of first editions, they could contribute more to Damerosehay than they had done, though not as much as Margaret thought they should do; and Hilary's careful juggling with Lucilla's investments, and Margaret's unselfish economy, had further pulled them through rough waters into a comparatively smooth harbor. As Lucilla sat waiting for David that September evening, she looked what she was—a leisured and lovely old lady securely enthroned in a home where there was enough money for the creation of dignity and beauty, but not enough for luxury or ostentation.

For it was one of the special mercies of Providence, Lucilla was apt to say, that beauty and shabbiness are quite compatible. The great thing, she would tell her grandchildren, is to start well. A thing of beauty is a joy forever, but it must be a costly and strong beauty, purchased at a high price of service or sacrifice, not skin-deep but bone-deep, if it is to be as desirable at the shabby end as it was at the sumptuous beginning. Pointing a moral to the grandchildren she would wave a hand towards her Sheraton chairs with the petit-point seats worked by her grandmother in a pattern of purple pansies and crimson gilliflowers. She would tell them how the exquisite curves of the wood had been created by the hands of a craftsman, each tool in its aptness and simplicity itself a thing of beauty in his hands as patiently, line by line, he fashioned the vision that was in his mind. And the same with the great-grandmother's needlework. She had spun the wool herself and dyed it to its lovely colors with the juices of plants picked upon her walks, she had seen with the eyes of her mind a vision of her garden, formalized and touched with perpetual stillness, and painted the picture with her needle upon canvas. And now though their legs were scratched and their colors were faded the chairs were as lovely as ever. Lovelier, Lucilla declared, because a work of art is like a human being, the more it is loved the more beautiful it grows, reflecting the gift of love like light back again to the giver.... The odes of Keats, she had heard it said, are lovelier now than when they were written.... And the same with her Sheraton chairs, which had been loved now for so many years. And everything in the house, she had told Margaret twenty years ago, must be as love-worthy as they were if Damerosehay was to be a perfect refuge for the grandchildren. Margaret had sighed and asked if this dictum applied to the saucepans. "Certainly," Lucilla had replied. "I'll have none but the very best saucepans."

The furnishing of Damerosehay with works of art from attic to cellar had been a crushing expense at the time, for very little of the furniture from her London house, bought originally by James, was considered by Lucilla to be worthy of Damerosehay; but it had been worth it. Looking round at her drawing room Lucilla could note with satisfaction that though Margaret had had to darn the Persian rugs in places, those places concealed by the tactful disposition of the armchairs and sofa, yet the colors of them, the rose and amethyst and midnight blue, were as bright as ever. And it was the same with the stiff eighteenth-century chintz; it was cracked here and there but the posies on it were as fresh as those in the garden. The Dresden china, that no one but Ellen might touch upon pain of death, was still in its first Arcadian perfection: not a shepherdess had lost her pretty head, not a lamb its garland; and the crowning glory of the drawing room, the great carved mantelpiece and overmantel that reached from floor to ceiling, swirling upwards in a bewildering polished luxuriance of sweeping curves and spirals that looked like the breaking waves of an ebony sea, was surely as perfect today as when it had been placed there by no-one-knew-who.

For what Lucilla could not discover was the history of her house. The last owner, before the arrival of the Eliots, had been a Mr. Jeremy Martyn, a bachelor of peculiar habits, who had sat tight within its walls for a lifetime, studying the habits of birds and letting the roof fall quietly in over his eccentric head while he gave away the whole of his substance to the deserving poor. He had died of heart failure at the age of ninety-five, only six years before the arrival of the Eliots, but oddly enough no one seemed to know where he was buried—probably in the churchyard at Big Village, but there was no headstone to say so. His dilapidated property had descended to his nearest relative, a distant cousin already in his dotage, from whom the Eliots had bought it.

And before Jeremy a French woman with the lovely name of Amarante Emilie du Plessis-Pascau, had lived there, probably a descendant of one of the many refugees from the French Revolution who had formed a colony not far from Damerosehay, at the little town of Seacombe on the Estuary. No one knew how she had come there, or anything about her, not even Obadiah who had been a little boy of four at the time of her death. He only knew that she had died, and that she had been very beautiful but no better than she should be, and that was all. She had not been as mysterious in her choice of a burying place as Jeremy, for her grave was to be found in the churchyard at Big Village; but the texts she had chosen for her tombstone were not exactly what one would have expected. They were from the Apocrypha. "He was overtaken, and endured that necessity which cannot be avoided. For gold is tried in the fire, and acceptable men in the furnace of adversity." And then, lower down, "A melodious noise of birds among the spreading branches, a running that could not be seen of skipping beasts. The whole world shined with clear light, and none were hindered in their labour." Such odd texts to choose, and not, apparently, referring to herself. It was very peculiar.

Lucilla would so have liked to know the whole story of her home, but she had no hopes of ever doing that now. Only Obadiah of the village folk was left from those old days, and the gaps in his memory were abysmal; nothing at all could be fished up out of them. Not to be wondered at, said Ellen, seeing that in her opinion Obadiah's memories were not memories at all but the most outrageous romancing she had heard in all her born days. "We can know only one thing," David would say teasingly to Lucilla, "that the inhabitants of Damerosehay appear, one and all, to go completely barmy. A cheering thought for us, isn't it, darling?"

The memory of his laughing voice was with her in the room. Soon he would be here. She got up and moved to the gilded French mirror that hung between the windows, to see what she looked like. David often told her that she was beautiful; he often told her that he loved her. The second statement she knew was true, but the first might not be, for David was undoubtedly a flatterer. And if it was not true would she be able to hold his love? She looked at herself critically, but what she saw did not tell her very much. She was tall and still slender. Her white hair was lovely, springing away from her face in soft waves that had never lost their vitality, and, though her blue eyes had sunk a little and looked a trifle bewildered because she ought to have worn her spectacles all the time, but didn't because they were not becoming to her, they were still wide awake, aware and interested, the purple shadows about them intensifying their deep color. She had kept the shape of her face, wide across the cheekbones, then tapering to a narrow heart, and though her lips had lost their fullness, they had kept the delicate wavy line that seemed always ready to break into a smile. Her skin was wrinkled, and slack about her throat, but it was clear and pale, like ivory, and when she was happy her whole face, as well as her eyes, seemed to shine. She could be very happy, happier than most people, and unhappier too. All that she felt and did she felt and did with the whole of her being. Nothing of her ever lay unused and every little happening of her day was tremendously important to her, and she lived in it as a child would do. It was this vitality that gave her her undying charm, for it gave everyone who was with her a strange sense of assurance. The value of little things was heightened by her enjoyment of them; the value of life itself was heightened because she had bought her knowledge of it with bitter sorrow and yet in her old age could wear it with such grace. Life was worth while when Lucilla was there, but when she was not there the light went out.

But Lucilla, looking at herself in the glass, could see no reflection of the charm that was so apparent in her when she lived and moved. She noted only with dissatisfaction that the skin of her neck was slack and her hair not so thick as it used to be. But she could see for herself how well her clothes suited her, and she smiled a little. She had always been able to make herself look nice for she had the kind of body—long and slender and graceful—that makes any material fall into attractive lines, and the kind of hair that any hat becomes. Not that she was careless about either her materials or her hats. She bought the best and softest materials and the finest straw, gave all her attention to line and none to ornament, employed the most expensive dressmaker she could find and wore the result for years, looking splendid and spending less on her clothes than most women did. The few jewels that she had left she always wore; her diamond ring that almost extinguished the thin worn hoop of her wedding ring, her big emerald upon the other hand, her pearls, the lorgnette on a long thin gold chain that she used if she wanted to look at something in a hurry and hadn't time to get hold of her spectacles, and the little gold wrist watch that David had given her with his very first earnings. They seemed a part of her, and her family could not imagine her without them. Equally a part of her was the faint fresh scent of verbena that clung to all her clothes, and the large black velvet bag that contained her spectacles, her handkerchief, her purse of small change, the letters she had had during the past week from absent children and grandchildren, her bottle of eau de cologne and the silver box of sugared almonds that she kept for the delectation of her younger grandchildren and the dogs. Without this bag she stirred nowhere. She dared not leave it behind her as she moved about the house lest the maids or children should purloin a sugared almond or a sixpence and so have sin upon their souls. Nor dared she let anyone else carry it, heavy though it was, for they might drop it and smash the spectacles that, becoming or not, were essential to her reading and writing and needlework. It lived always in her hands, showing up to perfection her long white fragile fingers and her two superb rings.

"But I don't really know what you look like," she said to the old lady in the glass. "I don't really know what you are. I don't think we any of us know much about ourselves. I don't even know if I like you. But it doesn't matter if I like you. What matters is that David should like you."

She went back to her chair and she felt a little breathless, for it was an exhausting thing for an old lady to love anyone as she loved David. She clasped her hands tightly upon the bag in her lap and watched the iron gate in the garden wall through which, in a few minutes, she would see the silver-gray car sliding by over the moss in the oak wood. Ten minutes passed and she saw it. Another five and a great clamor broke out as the children and dogs erupted into the hall. Another two minutes and David was in the room, struggling to shut the door against the onslaught on the other side, for he would not have them in the room when he greeted Lucilla. She stood up, tall and slender, and waited while he grappled with them. "Get out, you little demons," he commanded them, "wait a minute," and he leaned against the door as though a gale of wind were blowing upon the other side. Then it closed and latched itself inexorably upon the tumult without and he came across to her in a sudden peace.

"Are you all right, Grandmother?" he asked her, and took her face in his hands and smiled at her. He could not kiss her yet because he had not had time to wash his face. No arriving Eliot ever could kiss Lucilla until after a wash because of the Bastard.

"Yes, David," she said. "Are you all right?"

For years they had always given each other the same greeting when David had come home. He had chosen it himself of his schooldays, considering this form of words adequate and informative without being sloppy, and always the answer had been satisfactorily in the affirmative. But now, with sudden panic, Lucilla knew that David for the first time was not all right. Something had happened.

CHAPTER THREE

I.

MARGARET WENT STRAIGHT from her missionary meeting
to her bedroom, cast her hat and gloves from her, buttoned
on her cooking overall and hurried to the kitchen. Cook
had given notice after the Bastard had eaten her fruit hat
and not for love nor money could Margaret find another.
It was strange how few domestics were attracted by the
thought of living in a marsh; or by the prospect of cooking for children and dogs. Lucilla thought it very sad that
the hearts of the proletariat should be so singularly un-
susceptible to the beauties of the country, to the loveliness
of child nature and the charms of canine character. She
mourned a good deal over this unsusceptibility, which she
felt to be a not altogether reassuring characteristic of modern national life. Margaret had no time to mourn. It was all
she could do to get the work done.

Standing in the old kitchen, with its window looking
out on to the kitchen garden, its raftered ceiling where
the hooks were still fixed in the beams for the home-cured
flitches of bacon that were never hung there now, the
great built-in range and the rose-red tiled floor scrubbed
to a velvet softness, Margaret rolled up her sleeves and
wondered a little desperately what there was still left to

do. Having to help Hilary with his missionary meeting had put her dreadfully behindhand. She hadn't yet even cooked Pooh-Bah's meat and cabbage.... Pooh-Bah had to have special dishes all to himself because his well-bred inside rebelled against the bones and oddments and fruit hats that agreed so excellently with the Bastard's less aristocratic interior.... And then Lucilla liked fish but not pheasant and David liked pheasant but not fish, so she must do both. The soup and the cold soufflé, thank heaven, were prepared already.

For just a moment, as she rolled up her sleeves, Margaret moved to the window and looked out. After Lucilla, the garden was the passion of her life. The marshes and the sea, though like Hilary she thought them rather pretty, never touched her so deeply as they did Lucilla and David, and the house was such a heavy burden that she did not enjoy it so much as she should have done, but the garden was her inspiration and her strength. Unmarried though she was Margaret was no frustrated woman. Her love for Lucilla and the grandchildren satisfied her heart and in the garden her creative instinct had full play. She had "green fingers" and knew them to be one of the happiest gifts that the gods can give.

The day, twenty years ago, when she had found she had them, had been one of the fortunate days of her life. She had been desperately unhappy when they came to Damerosehay that first spring. She had lost so much in the war—her lover, and with him her hope of marriage and motherhood, two of her brothers, her youth, her looks and much of her strength. There had seemed nothing left;

77

nothing except the back-breaking task of getting Dame-rosehay fit for Lucilla to live in. And Lucilla had not been as appreciative as she would have been in more normal times; she had been absorbed in her grief for Maurice, in little David, and in spending far too much money on the furnishing of his home; she had hardly seemed aware that Margaret existed. Margaret had understood, of course. She knew Lucilla and her utter absorption in the person or occupation of the moment. She had only to wait patiently for her mother's love to flow back to her again; but, loving Lucilla as she did, she never found this waiting easy.

She had been so desolate one evening that she had wandered out to the far end of the flower garden to try and get out of earshot of the song of that wretched black-bird in the ilex tree. His song had been so self-confident, so utterly abandoned to joy, that by contrast it had only intensified her misery. Screened by the cherry trees and the lavender bushes she had sat down on the rough wild grass, her fingers twisting in it and her eyes shut against the tangle of weeds that she would have to cope with sooner or later. Her head and her back were aching and her eyes behind their shut lids were smarting and burning with fatigue. And then she had been suddenly aware, as Lucilla had been, of the scent of violets. "I didn't know there were any," she had thought, and pulling herself up on to her knees she had begun eagerly pushing aside the weeds and grasses. Presently she had found them; a few strangled plants under the wall that must once have been a violet bed, gallantly struggling up to the light, holding up their purple flower heads on stalks almost too weak to bear them. "Oh, my poor dears!" Margaret had cried and in a moment, tired as she was, had been hard at work pulling the weeds and grasses out of their way. She had worked on and on, with no tools but her fingers and a sharp stone, taking no notice of the supper bell or of Ellen's voice calling her, and by dark she had quite a large patch cleared. By the end of the week she had the whole bed cleared, and the freed violets, living creatures sun-warmed once again, had been flinging out their scent to her in a passion of rejoicing. . . . And even though she had as yet done no planting or pruning she had known by the feel of the magic running through them that she had "green fingers."

Now, twenty years later, she could see the faces of those freed violets more clearly in her memory than she could see the face of her dead lover. "How awful of me!" she thought, scandalized at herself, and then forgot to be scandalized in noticing that there were three more ripe figs on the tree by the kitchen window. The kitchen garden, like the flower garden, was walled. Espaliered fruit trees covered the walls and in the space between were orderly rows of currant bushes, raspberry canes and vegetables. Margaret and Alf Watson, Obadiah's grandson who helped her in the garden, and old Obadiah, who ambled up from the harbor to lend a hand when he felt inclined, and to criticize their efforts when he didn't, were very proud of the kitchen garden. Nothing ever went to waste in it, and the Damerosehay vegetable marrows were always the largest and shiniest at Hilary's harvest festival. . . . Margaret could see them now lying out there under the sun, self-consciously fattening themselves for it. . . . The runner beans, too, growing always the way of the sun and never widdershins, were invariably the finest in the neighborhood, though less suitable for harvest festival decoration, and her carrots and her turnips were miracles of the gardener's art.

But it was the flower garden that Margaret loved best. It was to her as a canvas is to an artist, only to her mind more splendid. "They shall splash at a ten-league canvas with brushes of comets' hair." Kipling's description of the artists in heaven applied equally well to gardeners upon earth, she thought. She had such a splendid space to splash about in, and the pictures she painted there were forever changing. No sooner had she finished planning pools of purple crocus and rivulets of daffodils than she was lying awake at night intoxicated by the thought of mauve Canterbury bells and pink phlox in the herbaceous border, bright against the curtain of honeysuckle over the wall, with purple pansies to edge the border and tall white lilies to give it dignity and strength.

But in September Margaret threw all careful color planning completely to the winds and went berserk. Restraint would come later when she had to nurse her iris stylosa in sheltered corners, put glass over her Christmas roses, and thank God if the frost spared the chrysanthemums a little longer than usual, and meanwhile she just went mad. Year by year she had been adding to the ranks of her Michaelmas daisies, heaping up her blazing dahlias, her globed peonies, her goldenrod and her red-hot-pokers, and now whenever she had a bit of space to spare she poured out floods of pink and purple petunias with an abandon that reduced

Lucilla to a shocked and blinking silence. . . . For Lucilla never interfered in the garden. She knew it to be essential to Margaret's salvation and she endured the September display of savage color with the same patience which she showed when Margaret draped an unwanted shawl over her knees on the hottest evening of the year. . . . Margaret was not very sensible always, but she meant so very well.

As she did when, her thoughts wandering to the garden, she held the tin with the basted pheasant in one hand while she tried to open the oven door with the other, and the wretched bird slipped sideways and stepped neatly out on to the floor just as Ellen, arriving at just the wrong moment as was her invariable habit, entered with an empty decanter in one hand and the key of the cellar door in the other.

"There!" said Ellen. "How many more times am I to tell you, Miss Margaret, that you need to take two hands to a baking tin? A basted bird is bound to slip. I've told you and I've told you, Miss Margaret, but never a word I say is attended to by any of you children."

Margaret, as much under Ellen's thumb at fifty-five as she had been at five, said meekly: "I'm sorry, Ellen," and stepped aside, pushing her short gray hair nervously back from her flushed face. Ellen, she knew, would not allow her to pick up the pheasant for herself. It was Ellen's prerogative always to be the one who put things right. Others might make mistakes, but never Ellen. This was a fixed principle in the Eliot family, fixed there by Ellen.

"There!" she said, resetting the pheasant and warming to Margaret since the child had accepted her rebuke with becoming meekness. "What the eye does not see, the heart does not grieve for. I'll give him a bit of dust up and your mother'll be none the wiser." She prodded the pheasant with a knowing forefinger. "Nice bird. Good firm breast. You've seen he was properly cleaned, of course?"

"Yes, Ellen," said Margaret.

"No shot left in him so far as you know?"

"No, Ellen."

"You've got the string tied right?"

"Yes, Ellen."

"You've not forgotten the breadcrumbs, dear, have you?"

"No, Ellen."

"And you've got the onion in the milk ready for the bread sauce?"

"Yes, Ellen."

"There's a good girl," said Ellen, and suffered herself to be helped to her feet. The two women smiled at each other, and Margaret had a twinkle in her eye. She did not mind being treated like a child by Ellen. She liked it. One would know the first cold breath of old age, she thought, when one found oneself in a world where there was no one left to whom one was a child.

"Now I must get me down to the cellar for Master David's burgundy," said Ellen, and lumbered on her flat feet towards the cellar door.

"For heaven's sake, Ellen," cried Margaret, "let me go!" She hated to see Ellen on the dark cellar stairs as much as Lucilla hated to see her lifting the tea tray.

But Ellen gave her a sour look. "I trust nobody on these

stairs but meself," she said with the air of a martyr. "If legs are to be broken, it'll not be the children's."

"But why keep the wine down there, Ellen?" complained Margaret. "We have so little of it that it might just as well be kept in the dining room."

But Ellen, unlocking the cellar door and hitching her skirts well up above her elastic-sided boots, only sniffed. ...She liked being a martyr.

Half an hour before dinnertime Margaret left the heavy-handed Rose in charge and hurried up the back stairs to change. Lucilla would never permit the Eliots to sit down to dinner without changing into evening dress first. Even if she and Margaret were quite alone, and their dinner consisted of a boiled egg and a baked apple, they still had to change. Lucilla said it kept up their self-respect. Margaret didn't know if it did or not, because she had never been allowed to see what happened to her self-respect if she didn't change. Even if Lucilla was ill in bed and she ate her favorite supper of Heinz baked beans on toast quite alone (she couldn't possibly have eaten it when Lucilla was there because Lucilla thought it a vulgar dish) she still had to change because she would not have dared to go and say good night to Lucilla attired in anything except her perennial black silk and her pearls. But they didn't suit her. Looking in her glass, she acknowledged this fact with a sigh. Out in the garden, wearing her boots and her weather-pulled tweeds, Margaret could look quite nice, for the roughness of them suited her short rough gray hair, sunburnt, weather-beaten face, tall angular figure and roughened gardener's hands. But her silk didn't suit her at all.

"I look simply silly," she said to herself, and snapped the pearls that her father had given her on her twenty-first birthday angrily round her thin throat. Generally she did not mind in the least that she was a plain woman; she only minded when David was here. Like Lucilla, she had always been extravagant in her love for David, and also like Lucilla she had wanted to keep the love he had given her when he was a little boy. But she hadn't kept it. She wasn't attractive like Lucilla.

She took a clean handkerchief out of her drawer and moved restlessly to the window, suddenly tormented again by the old pain that she always thought she had conquered, yet always found was not yet quite conquered; why must it be only the women of charm who can know the fullness of life? Then suddenly she saw her garden and the pain was gone. She leaned out of the window, smelling the fresh scent of it, seeing how the colors glowed in the sunset. "I live to the full," she told herself. "All gardeners do."

She heard David's bedroom door open and shut and heard him running lightly down the stairs to the dining room where Ellen would be waiting for him with a beaming smile and the cocktail shaker, and she turned back to the room with a smile. Poor David! He loathed deceiving Lucilla about those cocktails, but if he didn't Ellen's heart would be broken; so what on earth, he had once demanded of Margaret, was he to do? "Drink them," she had advised. "It is better to deceive one old lady than to have to disappoint another." Thinking of Lucilla and Ellen, she smiled again. What beloved old ladies, but, oh, what autocrats!

She waited in her room until the gong went, fearful of bursting in upon Lucilla and David when they did not want her. She spent her whole life in terror of disturbing people when they did not want her and so catching was her frame of mind that they too, when she entered anxiously upon them, were inclined to agree with her that, no, they did not want her. Lucilla had spent a large part of her life in unsuccessful endeavors to teach Margaret that [people will generally take up towards you the attitude that you take up towards them; shrinking will be met with shrinking and friendliness with friendliness;] but Margaret, painfully conscious of her own lack of charm, was too scared to put that theory to the test. So she held aloof always, afraid to give herself lest her gift should be scorned, and possessions that she most deeply prized, like David's love, slid away from her.

Yet as she opened the drawing-room door she utterly forgot herself in the picture that she saw. The drawing room was always lovely in the evening light; even Margaret whose whole heart was in the garden could never see it at this time without loving it. The glow of the sunset lit it with an unearthly light that both deepened and softened the colors of rugs and chintz, and the flowers in the vases burned like flame. Even that great grim overmantel of polished wood was transformed, taking on the softness of velvet rather than the midnight murk of ice-cold water.

And Lucilla, enthroned in her armchair, the Bastard at her feet with his chin resting on her shoe and Pooh-Bah beside her, the flames of the wood fire painting roses on the wide skirt of her purple silk dress, was as lovely as her room. Her cheeks were a little flushed because David had come, and her eyes were shining in welcome to Margaret.

"Margaret, darling, we've been wondering where you were," she said, and stretched out her left hand in that desperate yearning of hers that Margaret should be able to enter with her into the gracious ease of family love. But Margaret could never do anything easily; she was as rigid as a scarecrow by the door and Lucilla's hand, its hoop of diamonds shining in the firelight, fell to her side in a little gesture of discouragement.

But David, standing where all the Eliot men always stood, in front of the fire so that none of the warmth could reach their female relatives (though to do them justice they did not think of this, Lucilla not having the heart to point it out) threw the evening paper quickly aside and went instantly to meet Margaret. He never forgot for how many years she had done for him all the things that it would have bored Lucilla to do: darned his socks, packed his box for school, ministered to him when as a small boy he was sick in the night; he did not forget, and he never failed to show her a punctilious affection that hurt her intolerably.

"How are you, Aunt Margaret?" he asked, and bent to give her one very gentle but very dutiful kiss.

How well he had done it, she thought. The flinging aside of his paper, as though he would not allow it to keep him from her for an instant, the swift movement towards her and the bend of his head to kiss her; it had all been done apparently in one graceful movement. . . . No wonder that as an actor he could earn more in a month than many men did in a year.

86

But Margaret's moments of bitterness were rare and soon gone. As she moved to the fire with David's arm through hers she was exclaiming delightedly, as she always did, at his likeness to Lucilla. She had made the same remark for fifteen years, and David would have felt his homecoming to be incomplete without it.

And this time, she saw, it was truer than usual. Since he had grown up David had always had Lucilla's height and slenderness, her eyes and the vitally growing yet smooth gold hair that Lucilla had handed on to him and to his father alone of all her children and grandchildren. But today for the first time Margaret noticed that the actual structure of David's face was just like Lucilla's; she noticed because his face had lost its youthful roundness and had changed in a few months from a boy's face to a man's.

"You've got very thin, David," she said, as they crossed the hall to the dining room. "Have you been ill?"

"Of course not, Aunt Margaret," said David evenly. "No Eliot is ever ill. . . . Not unless he wants to get his own way with it like old Ben with his asthma."

"You're tired?" pursued Margaret.

"This last show did seem to run for a century," admitted David.

"Margaret, how beautifully you have arranged these flowers," said Lucilla, and put a long slender finger under one of the purple petunia trumpets that Margaret had placed upon the dining-room table in a bowl that contained also yellow goldenrod, pink petunias and small scarlet dahlias.

Margaret flushed suddenly, for she was well aware,

though Lucilla never said anything, that her lavish autumn color schemes were anathema to Lucilla. Then, looking up, she saw by the warning glint in her mother's eye that she had been tactless again. She was forever being tactless. She ought to have remembered, for Lucilla had told her often enough, that when something had obviously gone wrong with one of the elder grandchildren they must not ask questions, or they would be told nothing. To Caroline or Tommy or Ben they could say, "Have you a pain? Did you have a nightmare? Are you missing Mother?" but when the grandchildren had grown up, as had now Stephen's four children as well as David, one could not force their confidence. If one tried to they closed up like clams. One had to wait patiently to be told what was the matter with them. . . . Or perhaps alternatively not to be told, in which case one must pretend very hard to have noticed nothing at all. . . . Margaret sighed and upset the salt.

David took instant and skillful charge of the conversation, directing it to the Chelsea flower show, to politics, to things that had nothing to do with Damerosehay. He talked easily and amusingly, setting himself to make Lucilla smile her lovely smile and win from Margaret her low rare laugh. Not tonight, said a voice that was beating like a little hammer in his brain, not tonight. Let it be the same as always tonight. Keep it the same as always. Tomorrow is time enough to tell them. Make them happy tonight. Old ladies are easy to deceive. They don't guess anything. Make them happy tonight. . . . And Lucilla, with Margaret rather heavily following her lead, was so gay that he never guessed that of the two dramatic performances hers was even more accomplished than his own.

The dining room as well as the drawing room faced the garden, but its windows were not so wide. It was dim and a little musty, paneled in dark wood and curtained and carpeted in a somber crimson. The late Sir James Eliot, painted in oils, legally bewigged and gowned and framed in a gilt frame six inches wide, hung over the fireplace and looked down upon his descendants with the rather frigid kindness which had been so characteristic of him. The large sideboard was weighted with all the heavy Eliot silver and the mahogany table was polished until it gleamed like the shining ominous surface of some black bottomless tarn. The dining room was Ellen's especial pride, as the garden was Margaret's and the drawing room Lucilla's. It was she who had chosen the carpet and curtains, hung Sir James and chosen his frame; it was she who polished the silver and the gleaming table. The dining room was the only room at Damerosehay that David disliked. At all times he hated its darkness and heaviness, and tonight it seemed to him like some sort of stuffy shrine of Victorian family respectability. He felt as though there were no air in the room and as though the stolidity of it were pressing upon him like an actual physical weight.... That awful heavy silver and that ominous table.... He looked away from them and encountered the painted eyes of his grandfather looking at him from the wall. They were kind gray eyes in a heavy kindly face; they were exactly the eyes of his son George, the father of Ben, Tommy and Caroline and the divorced husband of Nadine. David abruptly drained the one glass of wine which the grandsons were allowed at dinner, and which they usually made last as long as possible, but he kept his eyes courageously upon his grandfather's. He imagined that his grandfather had been just like George; professionally clever but insensitive in his personal relationships, just, kind, conservative, and a gentleman to the marrow of his bones. He, too, like George, would have always done what the code of his generation considered the decent thing, at whatever cost to himself and without it occurring to him that the code itself might need examination. Had he lived in the twentieth century and been faced with George's problem, that of a middle-aged man with a young wife who had tired of him and was unhappy with him, he would have done what George had done, yielded to her pleading and arranged matters so that she was set free and called innocent while he, also innocent, must lose his children and carry about with him always the stigma of a divorced man. . . . Only in Grandfather's day, of course, that wasn't the code. . . . In Grandfather's day the decent thing had been to whiten the sepulcher and carry on within it at whatever cost of truth and happiness. How stifling it must have been inside. A stifling hell. As stifling as this loathsome room.

"Open the window wider, dear," said Lucilla's quiet voice.

David flung it wide with a quick grateful glance at her. The room wasn't really hot, he supposed, but the movement had eased his choking misery.

"Is Nadine quite well?" asked Margaret conversationally.

How like Aunt Margaret to ask that particular question

at that moment! But he had control of himself again and answered easily. "Quite well, Aunt Margaret."

"And you see her often?"

"Fairly often. But she's busy, you know, with that shop of hers."

"That I should live," said Lucilla tartly, "to have a daughter-in-law in trade!"

Lucilla definitely disliked her daughter-in-law Nadine. She knew it was wrong of her but she couldn't help it. She had disliked her on sight, when George had first brought her to Damerosehay, a charming dark-eyed creature of nineteen, as sophisticated as Lucilla at not much younger had been unsophisticated, marrying a man twenty years her senior with an awareness of what she was doing that had been denied to Lucilla. Just why Nadine had married George, Lucilla had never known. George, in spite of the Eliot heaviness, had been attractive at thirty-nine, straight-backed, tall and a V.C., but Nadine had not been the kind of girl to be swept off her feet by a soldierly figure and a bit of bronze metal won in a moment of heat that was not likely to occur again, and she had responded to George's doglike devotion with a laughing acquiescence that had not looked like love. Then why had she married him? He had no money worth mentioning. And why had she, who openly avowed she hated babies, given him three in quick succession? There might even have been others had not Nadine's illness at Caroline's birth put an end to all hope of further childbearing. Lucilla had never found any satisfactory answers to these questions, but when after nine years of stormy married life the break at last came, she vowed she had always said there would be trouble (though as a matter of fact she hadn't, and was for some reason she could not explain to herself surprised at it) and was quick to lay possessive hands upon her grandchildren, Ben, Tommy and Caroline, lest worse befall them. . . . A merely temporary measure, she said, to tide over the time until Nadine and George came together again. . . . For she insisted that, for the children's sake, the break should not and must not be permanent. She did not believe that it would be. The divorce she swept away as being a lying thing of no consequence; though she considered it both wrong and silly of George to have acquiesced in it. She had fought him with all her strength, but he had not listened. When what he considered to be Nadine's happiness was at stake he could be as obstinate as he was brave.

Nadine had submitted to this grabbing of her children by Lucilla with surprising meekness in one so spirited; for after all they were her children, and she loved them. She had listened quietly, her sleek head bent, her quick tongue curbed, when Lucilla had held forth to her about the excellence of sea air for asthmatic subjects, the unsuitability of a London flat as a dwelling place for little children, and the impossibility of Nadine's looking after her children properly if she were living her own life and running an antique shop, and when Lucilla had at long last finished, Nadine had whispered meekly, "Yes, Grandmother," and lifted her head and looked at Lucilla with dark tormented eyes that had haunted her mother-in-law for a week or more.

No. Lucilla had never been able to understand Nadine,

and blamed her lack of understanding upon Nadine's Russian grandmother. There was no understanding the Russians, a tiresome people, all quite mad.

But she had succeeded in capturing her grandchildren, and this had been some satisfaction to her in her sorrow for her son George, going back alone to India with bewilderment in his kind doglike eyes and an undeserved stain on the name that James had handed down untarnished to his upright sons. . . . Yet still hoping against hope, they all knew, for reunion with his wife; still loving her intensely, longing for her, perhaps even believing that in giving her the freedom she wanted lay his best hope of winning her again.

How she disliked Nadine! She brooded on the depth of her dislike while David talked cheerfully on about the Chippendale chairs that Nadine had picked up for a mere song. Nadine was clever, there was no doubt about that, and Lucilla hoped she was enjoying herself selling chairs and living her own life. It was that declaration of Nadine's, that she wanted "to live her own life," that had exasperated Lucilla beyond anything else in the whole wretched business. It was a remark frequently on the lips of the modern generation, she knew, and it annoyed her. For whose lives, in the name of heaven, could they live except their own? Everyone must look after something in this world and why were they living their own lives if they looked after antique furniture, petrol pumps or parrots, and not when they looked after husbands, children or aged parents? Lucilla didn't know; and Margaret didn't either when

Lucilla asked her; nor Ellen. Nadine was beyond the combined comprehension of the three of them.

"Unaccountable," said Lucilla to herself, and cracked a water biscuit between her delicate fingers with the sound of a pistol shot.

Then she thought that perhaps she was being uncharitable.

"There is good in all," she announced rhetorically to the room in general. "Another fig, David? Margaret? Then we've finished, haven't we?"

David came round to her and she was glad of his arm as she got up out of her chair, for though she was a wonderfully healthy old lady she found a little difficulty in getting up once she was sitting down, or sitting down once she was standing up.... It was because she was so tall.

"But I'm not as tall as you, David," she said, and she kept her hand on his arm as they went back to the drawing room because his nearness made her so happy. But she wished he would tell her what was the matter. Had he, perhaps, told Nadine? At the thought that he might have told Nadine, such a storm of jealousy shook her that she had to pray to be forgiven, her lips moving soundlessly as David brought her her footstool and Margaret plumped up a cushion that she didn't want at all and pushed it down against her backbone in a position that was positively painful. "Thank you, darling," she said, and hoped it wouldn't be long before Margaret made the excuse of letters to write to go and help with the washing up.

It wasn't long, for it was the nursery maid's evening out

and as well as the washing up Margaret had to see that the mess the children had made in the bathroom over their baths was mopped up before Lucilla had hers. "The Indian mail must go tomorrow," she explained to David, and shut the door quietly behind her. Thankfully Lucilla withdrew her cushion.

"Chess, Grandmother?" said David, and before she had time to answer he had lifted forward the little table with the old scarlet and white carved chessmen, that stood for the most part unused in the corner of the drawing room between David's visits, because he was the only member of Lucilla's family whom she considered had sufficient intelligence to play with her without doing himself an injury. Hilary tried sometimes, but the stertorous breathing and the agonized writhings that were the outward sign of severe mental effort in Hilary terrified Lucilla. If people could not look nice when they thought, said Lucilla, then let them cease from thought, for evidently they were thinking more than was good for them. The great thing, in her opinion, was to look nice; especially during that hour after dinner when all sensible people assist the processes of digestion by aesthetic enjoyment, which while taking the mind off what is going on inside is not sufficiently intellectual to draw away the blood from the part where it is most needed at the moment.

But she didn't want to play chess with David tonight. She wanted him to tell her what was wrong with him, now at once, so that she need not endure the misery of uncertainty all through the long hours of the night, when, in any case, she never slept very well because old people never do; especially when they have brought six children and eight grandchildren into a world that is not as good to them as they thought it was going to be.

But he wasn't going to tell her tonight; perhaps he was never going to tell her. He was determined to do everything just as usual and she, too, must do everything just as usual because he wished it.... Increasingly, as one got older, she found that one did things because the young wished it.... She pushed her lace ruffles back from her wrists, bade David light the lamp that stood beside her and turned her attention to the delicate kings and queens, prelates and nobility and humble horsemen whom David's quick fingers were arranging in battle formation.

A sudden panic possessed her. Was there going to be a battle between her and David? Was the great love that had always been between them going to be strained by bitter disagreement? Was the peace of Damerosehay, that had been utterly unsullied all these years, to be soiled and torn at last? The far murmur of the sea, coming very faintly through the utter stillness, sounded to her like a mutter of warning. David generally beat her at chess, for he was cleverer than she was, and generally she rejoiced in his greater power, rejoiced to feel his mind grappling with hers, bearing it down, subduing it. But tonight, in the grip of this fantastic panic, she wanted to beat him.... She wanted most desperately to beat him.... Her hand was trembling as she stretched it out to move the first pawn.

Presently she found herself studying her grandson almost furtively. The daylight had faded now but as he leaned forward over the table the one lamp threw his face into vivid relief above the black of his dinner jacket and against the shadows of the darkening room. He was much thinner than he had been, as Margaret had already noticed, and that made the character of his face more apparent. There was something of fanaticism, she thought, in the hollows at the temples and the deep shadows round the eyes, and the line of the jaw was harder than she had realized. He was thinking and his lips were folded so tightly in concentration that the smiling curves of them were lost in a straight line that was a little ruthless. She suddenly did not recognize his face. This was not the boy she had known but a man capable of passion and of action that was strongly willed. She looked at him intently, almost weighing her chances against that face. Then he made his move and leaned back, lost in the shadows, and she tried to get a grip upon herself. It was nonsense. It had been just a trick of the light that had made him look so changed and so hardened. She would think no more about it. She would attend to her game. . . . Yet when she made her next move it was a false one.

"Grandmother!" exclaimed David half-an-hour later. She was losing all along the line. He had never known her put up so poor a fight. He looked across at her, startled, and saw that her blue eyes were piteous in her delicate, heart-shaped face.

"No, David, no!" she cried, and caught his hand as he was about to lift a crowned queen upon the road to victory. "No! Don't let's play it out! I don't want you to win. I think I'm tired tonight. Don't let's play it out."

"Of course we won't," said David, and kissed the hand

that clung to his. "But you still had a chance to win, you know."

"No," said Lucilla. "No chance."

"Yes, you had," said David. "Listen." And lifting the table away he stretched himself beside the sleeping dogs on the rug before the fire, his arm across her knees, and lectured to her softly but inexorably upon the royal game of chess. Instantly the years rolled back and she was reassured. So had all her sons and her grandsons, stretched upon that same hearthrug, lectured to her through so many years, instructing her ignorance about tadpoles, cricket, submarines, howitzers, communism and the habits of ants; and always she had listened so patiently, expressing astonishment, ignorance and agreement just at the points where these emotions were expected by the lecturer. So familiar was this situation that her ridiculous panic left her. David was still only a boy after all. There could be no real quarrel between them; nothing that mattered. "Yes, dear," she said as she had said a hundred times before, relaxing comfortably in her chair. "Yes, I see what you mean. Yes, indeed, I quite see."

Then the Dresden china clock struck shrilly, the dogs awoke and blinked at the firelight, and bringing his lecture to a graceful conclusion David rose to his feet. "Ten o'clock," he said. "Time for us to visit the children and then you must go to bed, Grandmother."

And again Lucilla was uneasy. Not by a hairsbreadth was he deviating from the accustomed routine. Nothing was he leaving out. It was almost as though it was for the last time. "For the last time," whispered the flames in the wide hearth, and a shower of bright sparks fled up the chimney as a log crashed and fell apart. The sudden glow sent a ripple of light up over the dark carved overmantel and it seemed to Lucilla to move and sway.

"It is so funny," she said to David as she lowered the lamp by her chair, "but I always feel as though that overmantel were the prow of a ship. You won't remember but I felt it the very first time we ever saw it."

"A ship?" said David, looking up in the half-dark at that massive brooding presence of dark wood.

"Yes," said Lucilla, "and sometimes there seems to me to be a man up there too."

David only laughed as he slipped his arm through hers and drew her away towards the door. He did not tell her that as a little boy he had always been frightened of that overmantel, nor that tonight, for the first time, he had been conscious of some presence in the room that was just at the moment inimicable to him. His profession was one that took toll of the imagination and the emotions and he had learned to discount "queer feelings." They came when one's emotional experience had strained the mechanism of the nerves too severely.... That was all.... He shut the drawing-room door behind them and picked up from the hall table the little shaded lamp that Lucilla carried when she said good night to the children.

Every night before she went to bed Lucilla visited each sleeping grandchild in its bed to see that all was well with the child and to pray for its safety through the coming night and through the life that stretched before it. So had Lucilla's own mother brooded nightly over her children, and her mother before her. Lucilla understood that the custom was dying out now, but she still kept to it. And David on his first night at home always went with her because it amused him. Lucilla did not mind his amusement, for it was not mocking; it was merely the laughing delight that all her actions and remarks seemed to arouse in her family. She did not know why they found her so deliciously funny, but she was glad that they did, for she knew that the people who can be loved and laughed at together are the most adored.

They went slowly up the shadowy dark stairs, Lucilla going first with David's arm through hers and the dogs following after, her silk skirts falling from stair to stair with a whispering murmur and the dogs' paws padding very softly, with little clicking sounds as their nails touched the polished boards on each side of the narrow strip of carpet. How familiar it was, thought David; their shadows leaping on ahead of them as the lamp he carried illumined the well of the staircase, the faint scent of wood smoke, oil lamps, damp and dried rose leaves that always pervaded the house, the feel of Lucilla's silken sleeve under his hand and the soft cool breath of air that came from some window open to the marshes and the sea; these things stabbed him with their sweetness. Odd that such trivial things could have such a hold upon one.

Caroline slept in a dressing room that opened out of Lucilla's bedroom, the same little room that David had had when he was a child. She slept tidily in her white cot, the sheet turned down neatly over the pale blue blanket and her right cheek turned confidingly to the pillow. Her favorite doll Gladys lay beside her and her other dolls lay in a precise row at the foot of the bed. She was flushed by the depth of her sleep and looked prettier than she did when she was awake. Her eyelashes, lying on her cheek, were like curled golden fans. David, standing at the foot of the cot with the shaded lamp, looked at her somberly as Lucilla bent over and skillfully withdrew Caroline's left thumb from her mouth. For a moment the small hand lay where Lucilla had placed it, tidily upon the sheet, then it moved upwards and the thumb popped back again where it had come from, without the incident having in any way disturbed the depth of Caroline's slumbers. "Hopeless," murmured Lucilla, and folded her hands upon the top rail of the cot to pray for Caroline. Then she glanced up, expecting to see the usual gleam of amusement in David's eyes. It was not there. His eyes looked like cold blue stones in his set white face.

Ben and Tommy slept together in a little room looking out on to the flower garden and called "the chapel room" because on each side of the main window were two others filled with stained glass. One showed a man carrying a little child upon his shoulder across a waste of turbulent water towards a quiet shore where a cornfield grew, and it was a rather striking picture. The waves, sweeping in stylized swirls that were queerly reminiscent of the carving in the drawing room, were full of dark menace, and behind them the sky was heavy with storm; only one ray of sun pierced the dark clouds to touch the cornfield to gold. The man who struggled through the waves seemed scarcely able to keep his feet, big burly fellow though he was; he gripped a great staff with both hands and the veins on his bare arms stood out like cords, his face was gray and strained with exhaustion and his back was bowed as though all the pain of the world weighed upon it. But the child was not afraid. Enthroned upon the man's shoulders he rode secure above the waves. He seemed to know that he was safe in that man's care and his smiling face was like a white flower against the storm clouds behind his head.... It was, the Eliots supposed, a picture of Saint Christopher and the Christ Child.... The other window showed a strange jumble of beasts of all sorts running through a forest; very happy beasts, full of jubilation; the garden of Eden, Lucilla thought, but Ben said it was the animals let out of the ark, and pleased about it.

Tommy's bed, after slumber had claimed him, looked like a jumble sale. Everything that was dear to him he took to bed with him: his engine, his boxes of tin soldiers, his water pistol, his notebook with the numbers of cars in it, various pebbles and bits of wood which he liked for some reason or other, and the remains of a perfectly revolting fur hearthrug with which he played at Robinson Crusoe when he woke up in the mornings. Could these possessions have remained in neat rows, as Caroline's did, his bed would have been a more pleasing sight, but he was a restless child and within ten minutes of falling asleep he had kicked everything, including his bedclothes, into such confusion that it was difficult to tell what was what. "It's no good my trying to do anything," said Lucilla, sadly regarding her grandson's tousled head, which had slipped from its resting place and was pillowed on the engine, his outflung uncovered arms and the curly toes protruding from beneath the covers. "If I try to straighten him out he only bites me...in his sleep, of course, the darling."

She touched Tommy's riotous curls tenderly but with caution, lest he bite, and turned to Ben, who slept with the head of his bed pushed under the stained glass window of the man carrying the child across the water, because he was so fond of it.... The man's face reminded him of his father, whom he missed quite dreadfully, though no one knew it.... But slept tidily, like Caroline, lying high on his pillows in case he should cough, one hand under his cheek and the other lying palm up upon the covers, the fingers a little curved. His physical delicacy revealed itself very clearly when he was asleep. The shadows under his eyes looked enormous, intensified by the thick dark lashes lying upon them; the mouth, relaxed in sleep, dropped poignantly at the corners, and in the curved fingers there was something that beseeched.

"It's not fair, Grandmother," whispered David suddenly and a little fiercely. "It's not fair on the old boy. He's too old now to be looked at when he's asleep. Sleep shows too much. It's not fair."

Lucilla looked at David in surprise. She had always known there was a special link between David and Ben.... They were a little alike and understood each other.... But she had not known that David felt quite so deeply.

"He has always been delicate," she said gently. "Nervy, frightened about things. The eldest so often is. I want him to have only happiness and peace all through his childhood, to settle his nerves."

But David, holding the lamp high, was no longer looking at Ben but at the window above his head. "Like him, don't you think?" he muttered.

"The child? Like Ben?" said Lucilla. "Yes. A little. He has that look of peace that Ben has when he knows he is safe."

David sighed twice, with difficulty, almost as though he were Ben oppressed by the asthma, and led the way rather abruptly back to the passage.

Lucilla's room was next to the boys' room and over the drawing room. It too looked out over the garden, and beyond to the marshes and the sea. It was a noisy room when the storms were sweeping in, but Lucilla did not mind that. She was never afraid of natural things, winds or lightnings or the flooding of great waters; they might deal out death now and again but they had not got it in their power to poison life; it was the things that poisoned that she dreaded, war and disease and the canker of creeping sin.

But there was no wind tonight. When David lit the candles on her dressing table, the flames burned steady and straight, illumining her beautiful room with its four-poster hung with blue-flowered chintz curtains, the dim blue shabby carpet, the old kidney-shaped dressing table with its chintz petticoat, the miniatures of children and grand-children over the mantelpiece, and the old Spanish crucifix of ebony and ivory that hung above the *prie-dieu* in the corner.

"What a lovely shape candle flames have," said David,

looking at them. "Living so long with electric light I had forgotten. Like a perfect laurel leaf, or hands set palm to palm in prayer. 'And palm to palm is holy palmer's kiss.' "

"You're getting absurdly fanciful, David," said Lucilla.

"No, only quoting Shakespeare. Do you remember when you came all the way up to town to see me play Romeo for the first time? Do you remember the party we had afterwards? You liked that. You behaved as though you were eighteen. I don't know what Aunt Margaret would have said if she'd seen you."

"I've liked all the good times I've had with you, David," said Lucilla. "Now I come to think of it I don't believe you've ever done a single thing that made me really unhappy."

David was still looking at the candle flames and had his back to her.

"We like the same things," went on Lucilla. "Beautiful things, and funny things.... And Damerosehay.... That reminds me, David; I made my will for the last time the other day and I left Damerosehay to you."

David swung round as though she had struck him, the color blazing up into his white face, and as though he had struck her she put out one hand and clung to the bedpost so tightly that her fingers were white and bloodless, though she kept herself erect with head held proudly.

"You can't," he said hoarsely. "You can't."

"Why not?" she asked, and her voice was very cold.

"Hilary—George—Stephen. Your sons must come first."

"I have consulted them," said Lucilla, and she was still very cold and rather distant. "They are willing and glad that it should be yours. You were brought up here. It is your home as it never was theirs, and you love it more than they do." David was silent and she forced herself on again. "You are successful in your profession. They tell me that as you get older you are likely to be increasingly so. You are the only one of the family who is likely in the future to have enough money to keep it up. And I know that you will always keep it as a refuge for the children whom perhaps I'll never see—your children—Ben's—it was for the children that I bought it." Again she stopped and forced herself on. "And you love it so, David, you love it so. . . . David, what in heaven's name is the matter with you?"

David laughed and came to her. "Nothing," he said, his cheek against hers. "Nothing except that I'm tired. It's absurdly early, but I'll go to bed I think."

"You've your usual room?" asked Lucilla dully. "That funny little room you're so fond of?"

"Of course I have. It's the best room in the house for making one feel sleepy. The sound of the wind in the rushes is so peaceful; and then you don't know any more until you hear that plover in the dawn."

He still stood with his cheek against hers. Lucilla felt that if he didn't stop talking and go away, or alternatively sit down and tell her what on earth was the matter with him, she would scream. She was at the end of her tether. "Go to bed, darling," she said, and gave him a little push.

"Good night," he said. "Sleep well." Then he kissed her and went away.

Lucilla crossed the room with trembling knees, sank into

her fireside chair and pulled the old-fashioned bell long and passionately for Ellen. She was distracted, quite incapable of undressing herself. Why could children never tell one anything? "Sleep well." How could she possibly be expected to sleep well when no one told her anything?

CHAPTER FOUR

I.

DAVID'S ROOM LOOKED east across a level stretch of feathery rushes to the Estuary and the Island. He loved the view, and the room too, and now, without lighting the candles, he sat in the chair by the window for a little while looking at it as it lay quietly waiting for him, patterned by the moonlight. He had used this room ever since he had been too old for Lucilla's dressing room. It was very small, built out over the porch in the eighteenth-century style, and in cold weather it could be very cold indeed. But David did not mind that. There was a streak of austerity in him that welcomed hardship, and even, he imagined, was ready to welcome pain. It bred courage, it sifted the true from the false, and courage and truth were companions who could outpace all the others; when dreams had withered and happiness was forgotten they were still there. For their sakes he was prepared to suffer much himself and to see others suffer. Lucilla had been right to recognize in his face that night a hint of ruthlessness.

Yet perhaps ruthlessness was the wrong word, for there was no cruelty in David, perhaps resolution was a better one. He would inflict pain, if he had to, as a good surgeon does, outwardly unmoved by the patient's outcry, steadily pursuing the ideal of health that is greater than individual distress.

He remembered suddenly, at this moment, as he looked at the squares of moonlight lying on the floor, the time when he had first realized that pain is a thing that we must face and come to terms with if life is to be lived with dignity and not merely muddled through like an evil dream.

It had been when his father was dying. His mother had not troubled overmuch to keep him out of sight and sound of his father's pain; she had thought he was too little to understand. But he had understood. He had been old for his age and already sensitivized by more than his normal share of those terrors of childhood of which no child will ever speak: the horror of a creeping shadow on a wall, the sudden awakening at night to the terrifying dark, the conviction that a nightmare beast is stabled beneath the bed and the strange panting fear awakened by lightning and big bangs; these he had known to the full, and they had seemed to him all summed up in this terrible thing that he had seen, this pain that had gripped his father. Terrified by it he had fled one evening to the dark attic, slammed the door and flung himself down sobbing upon the floor. He had sobbed for an hour, sobbed himself sick and exhausted until at last, childlike, he had forgotten what it was he was crying about and had become instead absorbed in the moonlight on the floor. It had been like a pool of silver, enclosed and divided up into neat squares by the bars of the window. He had counted the squares and the lines, dark and light, and had been delighted with them. He had touched each with his finger, this way and that, and had been utterly comforted.

"Whatever are you doing?" his Nanny had demanded, coming in to fetch him to his bath, irritable and anxious because he had been lost.

"Making a pattern, Nanny," he had said joyously.

"Strange little boy," had said Nanny, who though not a bad Nanny had not been very understanding. "All this trouble in the house and you make patterns!" And then, overwrought as she had been, she had shaken him for lying on the floor and making his jersey dusty. Then he had cried again, of course; but later, in bed, he had been comforted once more by the thought of that pattern. In some vague way he had understood that dark things are necessary; without them the silver moonlight would just stream away into nothingness, but with them it can be held and arranged into beautiful squares.

And here was that same moonlight pattern lying on the floor of this beloved little room at Damerosehay. He would not see this room very often in the future; perhaps not at all. He was going to cut himself adrift from Damerosehay. He loved Nadine Eliot and was going to marry her. That, in the eyes of Damerosehay and Lucilla, would be treachery to the place and to the family and they would not again receive him with intimate gladness. The thought of that separation was misery to him; yet he had no doubt at all as to what he must do. His love for Nadine was the most shatteringly real thing that had ever happened to him. It was the truth, and it must be served. Damerosehay must be cut out of his life, Lucilla must be dealt a blow that would hurt her intolerably, and yet he must do it. He had not shirked the pain of what he had to do. He had come himself to tell Lucilla; he had not taken refuge in the easy way of a letter. Courage and truth must be served.

Truth. He would have to try and make Lucilla understand how he felt about it, how it was to him the lamp that lit all life. It would be difficult, for her generation and his felt so differently about this truth. Her generation had built from without inwards, had put the reality of law and tradition above the reality of personal feeling; but his built from within outwards, the truth of personal feeling must come first; when there was no longer reality in a union, smash the union; never mind what laws were broken or what lives were crippled; live the truth. He tried to, in art as in life. Life, to him, was the fearless facing of reality, and art was its illumination. It is the business of an artist, he thought, to show how the truth, even an apparently ugly truth, can be transformed by fearless acceptance into a thing of beauty. Living this acceptance it is hard to realize the beauty; watching it objectively we see and understand.

But he doubted if Lucilla would look at the situation like that. His marriage to Nadine would not seem to her a blow struck for the truth but a blow struck at her son George, a death blow to all his hopes of reunion with Nadine. It would not seem to Lucilla loyalty to reality but treachery to the Eliot family. She would be unable to take a broad view. For a moment, knowing that she wouldn't, he felt exasperation with her. Then he pulled

SALEM COLLEGE LIBRARY
Winston-Salem, North Carolina

himself up. In the awful arguments that were bound to come he must try and understand her point of view as well as try to make her see his. That was only fair.

Then his man's problems fell from him and he just thought, childishly, that he didn't want to lose this room. He was so fond of all the things in it. That was womanish of him, and he was ashamed, but he couldn't help it. There was a lot of the woman in him, he knew; a lot of Lucilla. His room was not cluttered up with school groups and fishing rods and all the paraphernalia of a departed boyhood; he loved beauty too much for that. There was just the bare minimum of furniture, old and cherished, and a bookcase full of the books that he loved best: most of them the poetry that he read always when he was at Damerosehay and that seemed to him a part of it. There were several reminders of Lucilla in the room: the sunshine-yellow quilt that she had worked for him, the yellow curtains that she had chosen and the exquisite Chinese model of a galloping horse that she had given him when he first learned to ride. It was of great value, and Lucilla had had no right to spend the money on it that she had done. . . . Only Ellen was allowed to dust it. It was made of china, blue with green lights in it, the deep blue and translucent green of a windy summer sea. It was a sea horse, perhaps, for there was a swirl of green water about its plunging hoofs and a hint of spray in the flying mane. It stood upon the chest of drawers, and would always stand there. Looking at it now, mysteriously drowned in the moonlight, David knew that he would never be able to take it away when Damerosehay was no longer his home. It was part of the sea and belonged to it.

And he didn't think he would be able to take away his picture, either, even though that was his own gift to himself, bought with almost the first money that he had earned. It was a reproduction of Van Gogh's painting of a lark tossing joyously over a wind-blown cornfield. He had seen it some years ago in a shop window and had stood at once utterly spellbound, feeling the hot sun that beat down out of that clear blue sky, hearing the swish of the corn as it bent before the wind that was surely racing in from the sea, caught up in the ecstasy of the fluttering bird. The whole feeling of Damerosehay was in that picture. He had gone straight into the shop and bought it, and hadn't had quite enough to eat for the rest of the week in consequence. It hung now over the bed, the yellow of the corn matched by the yellow of Lucilla's quilt. It must always hang there. He could not take it away.

He flung the window wide and looked out. Even though it was so still a night, the rushes, lost in shadow, were yet rustling softly. Beyond them he could see the lights of a ship sailing down the Estuary to the open sea, and beyond that again was the dark mass of the Island blocked against the stars. In the morning the plover would wake him and he would get up and watch the dawn. Perhaps it would be one of those quiet dawns of early autumn; the Estuary would be a silver ribbon and the Island would be folded in veils of amethyst mist, very withdrawn and far away, almost a part of the gray dreaming sky. Or it might be one of those bright clear dawns when the Island was a patchwork of colored fields, so near that one could almost touch them, with the Estuary a sparkling gold and the sky like flame. He knew all the dawns. His window had framed them for many years.

He undressed and got into bed. These first nights at home were always a joy; he fell asleep so blessedly soon, lulled by that cool murmuring that sometimes seemed to come from the rushes outside the window and sometimes from the bending corn in the picture over his bed. But tonight he could not sleep. He lay quite still, tormented, listening hour after hour to the strident voice of that wretched cuckoo clock that he had given the children. Where had they hung the confounded thing? In the nursery? As time went on it seemed so near that he felt it must be in the room with him, and then it seemed in his own brain, cuckooing there with an insistence that made him feel distracted. . . . He would smash the thing in the morning.

The striking of three o'clock was, as always, the cue for the entrance of self-pity. It submerged him. He rolled over on to his face and groaned. Why must it happen like this? It was just his luck that it had to happen like this. Love had come to him for the first time, glorious, over-whelming, passionate, the love for the one woman in the world, far greater and far more lovely than he had ever dreamed it could be, returned in full measure and with equal passion, but she had been his uncle's wife. He could not take her without pain—pain for himself, for her, for the whole family. Why had it had to be like this? God in heaven, why had he had to fall in love with Nadine?

But David was not given to self-pity and it did not submerge him for long. The thing had happened. It was true. His love for Nadine would be all the more precious because he had to sacrifice a good deal for it. He turned over again and lay quietly watching for the first lightening of the dawn, and listening for the trumpet call of the plover that would be followed soon after by the ecstasy of the lark. It was not the season of larks now, but at Damerosehay there were always a few who sang in snatches all the summer through.

I shall wake presently, he thought, at daylight.
It is the season of larks. They will be flinging
the bright seed of song in the furrows of grey light,
till the East is gold with the smooth sheaves of singing.

Who had said that? Humbert Wolfe? Had he been thinking of Van Gogh's picture when he wrote it? *The Uncelestial City* was in the bookcase. He would read it again to help himself through the bad days that were coming.

2.

Yet, as it happened, sleep unexpectedly overtook David and he missed the dawn completely. He awoke in broad daylight to find Tommy sitting on his chest.

"David," said Tommy, "will you teach me how to be sick, please?"

It took David a little while to adjust his ideas.

"Why?" he asked at last.

"You see," said Tommy, "I'm so bored by lessons with

115

Uncle Hilary. You can't think how bored I am. I want to stay home today and if I could be very sick Grandmother would let me. Ben says you taught yourself how to be sick when you were at school."

"It's a difficult technique," said David seriously. "And you have to have breakfast first."

"Why?"

"Every artist must have material upon which to work. There must be something in your tummy."

"Oh," said Tommy, and pondered. "But it's those sausages you gave us for breakfast. It would be a pity to waste them, wouldn't it?"

"It would," said David. "And an insult to my gift."

"Yes," said Tommy. "I think I'll try on a haddock day."

"Horrid little brat," said David. "You're as horrid a little boy as I used to be. Go and turn on my bath." And he heaved the horrid child off onto the floor.

Tommy in his red and white striped pajamas, chuckling in a round fat heap on the floor, was an engaging sight. He had a way of looking always completely circular which was very reassuring. His bones and nerves were so well covered by fat that his body would bounce through life, one felt, with consummate ease. His mind, too, was very compact. It had no sensitive tendrils to get broken, it gave forth no impossible delicate dreams to be shattered. Tommy's tendrils were of the octopus type, strongly acquisitive, and his dreams of that practical sort that can come true with effort.

"I'm going to be a policeman," he said suddenly, and with one leap was back again on David's chest.

"Quite," said David weakly. "Only I should have thought a gangster was more in your line."

"It's much the same thing," said Tommy. "I mean, whichever you are you can knock people down. I'm training myself. I practice jumping onto people, like I have onto you, and I take all the numbers of cars."

The door opened and Ben, clad in a sky-blue dressing gown, stood in the patch of sunshine on the threshold like an apparition from another world.

"Tommy," said David, "get off my chest and go and turn on my bath."

"Ben," said Tommy, "go and turn on David's bath."

"Shan't," said Ben, who though delicate was not without spirit. "You're the youngest."

Tommy arose, trampling on David, and poised himself on the bed as though for flight. "Watch me," he commanded, and in two gigantic leaps was over the foot of the bed and out of the door. It was amazing that anyone so solid could be so swift in movement. He reminded David of an American robin, six times the normal size and rotundity yet capable of airy leaps which astonish the watcher.

"You saw that?" asked Tommy, returning for a moment. "Good, wasn't it? If I'd had more take-off I'd have done it in one. Good-by." And he disappeared, leaving the door open.

Ben carefully closed it and sat down on David's feet. "David," he said earnestly, "I want to tell you something. It's very important."

David, tired after a bad night, could not but feel that

the early morning is hardly the best time for contact with the very young. It is desirable to have breakfast first.

"What about my bath, old boy?" he hedged. "The water will be running over the top."

"Oh, no it won't," said Ben. "Tommy won't have turned it on. He never runs errands for people. He says it's better not."

David, listening, recognized the truth of Ben's statement. There was no sound of running water, only a succession of heavy thuds that suggested that Tommy was leap-frogging along the passage. He resigned himself to the inevitable.

"All right, old boy. But get off my feet, will you? You're not so heavy as Tommy but you're quite heavy enough."

Ben settled himself at the foot of the bed, cross-legged and very upright. With his thin brown hands folded and his wide dark eyes absorbed in something very far away he looked like a young Indian mystic. David wondered where his mind had gone to, but not for the world would he have interrupted Ben's train of thought to ask. There was something about Ben that made his silences respected.

Instead he found himself thinking about the children in relation to their mother. He had scarcely done that before. Until now they had just been his cousins, jolly little beggars whom he was fond of. But now they were something more, they were the children of the woman he loved. He could see Nadine in them. Tommy had her driving force, her power of doing and getting what she wanted. And all the qualities that he loved best in Nadine were in Ben also: the grace, the elusive beauty that defied definition, yet led one on to try and define it, like a will-o'-the-wisp dancing on the marsh, the intensity and the almost painful capacity for feeling. About Caroline he seemed to know very little as yet. She was a small girl-child, a creature as mysterious to him as a mer-baby from the ocean. But he would have to try and understand her. He would be her stepfather as well as Ben's and Tommy's stepfather.

That had really come home to him for the first time last night, when he went with Lucilla to say good night to the children. It had struck him like a blow, almost terrifying him. It had seemed especially alarming that he should be Ben's stepfather. Why? He and Ben were fond of each other. They ought to be happy in their new relationship. Yet last night he had known they wouldn't be, and this morning, looking at Ben's upright figure and dreaming face, he thought he knew why. For there was a look of discipline in Ben's straight back and quietly folded hands, in his thin legs folded neatly under him, not sprawling as Tommy's would have been; a look of discipline and of pattern. They were the same thing, of course; just an orderly arrangement of the things that make up life; an arrangement that delivered one from the bewilderment of confusion so that the spirit could go free . . . as Ben's was doing at this moment. . . . His was a nature that needed orderliness. Maladjustment would always injure him, as his parents' quarrels had already done. The family distresses that were bound to come when David married Nadine, the final tearing apart of the threefold pattern of father and mother and child, would injure him even more.

Delicately-balanced creature that he was, it might upset his equilibrium altogether.

David thrust the thought away. As usual, he was letting his imagination run away with him. It would be quite all right if everything was very carefully explained to Ben. And, anyhow, risks must be taken for truth. Such a blazing love as his and Nadine's could not be denied, and it would be a finer thing for a child to see and live with than the perpetual quarrels that had disfigured the marriage of Nadine and George.

"I can't help thinking about it at night," said Ben, "and it makes me feel awful."

David felt suddenly cold. Did Ben know already? Had some gossip reached him through the servants? That would be fatal.

"And I can't tell Grandmother or Aunt Margaret," said Ben, "because Obadiah said I wasn't to. But it's horrid to know about it all by myself. Tommy knows, of course, only Tommy doesn't understand how bad I feel about it. Tommy never feels bad about anything."

"What do you feel bad about?" asked David.

Ben did not move but his dark eyes were full of fear and horror. "David," he said, "Jeremy is buried under the ilex tree, and buried very shallow."

The relief was so great that David was utterly at sea. "Jeremy?" he repeated stupidly. "Jeremy?"

"Yes," said Ben. "Jeremy Martyn who used to live in this house. He's buried under the ilex tree and buried very shallow."

In his relief David laughed. "Good old Jeremy!" he said.

"So that's where he's buried? What a first-rate place to choose. I think I'll be buried there when my time comes."

"It's horrible!" said Ben. "It's horrible!"

"Not at all," said David. "While he's lying waiting for the last trump he can listen to the blackbird singing. . . . Not that one would hear the last trump through that blackbird."

"He's buried very shallow," repeated Ben in a monotonous voice.

David perceived that Ben was really in the grip of horror, and stopped laughing. "Tell us about it, old man," he urged. "Start at the beginning."

"Grandmother and Aunt Margaret went away for the week end," said Ben, "and Alf and Obadiah were working in the kitchen garden, and there was no one to see what we were doing in the flower garden, and so Tommy thought it would be fun to make a dugout under the ilex tree."

"A dugout?"

"Yes. To put Grandmother in if there was an air raid."

"Even if war should come, which God forbid, there'll never be an air raid in this back of beyond, old boy."

"Tommy hopes there will be. We've made one dugout already, behind the rubbish heap in the kitchen garden. It's a bit smelly but then it's only for the servants."

"Well, go on about Grandmother's dugout."

"We worked frightfully hard, and we got the grocer's boy to come and help a bit on the Saturday. His brother is the gravedigger, you know, and so it's in the family. We dug the whole week end. It had rained a lot and the ground was very soft. The dogs dug too, and the deeper we got the more excited they were. The Bastard was dreadfully excited all Sunday. He got down in the hole and he just scratched and scratched." Ben stopped, shivering.

"But you didn't uncover anything, did you?" asked David, catching a little of the horror.

"No," said Ben, "but we would have if Obadiah hadn't found out what we were doing on Monday morning. He was dreadfully angry. He said we were just exactly over where Jeremy was, and Jeremy wasn't in a coffin and was buried very shallow."

"Obadiah," said David, "is an old liar."

"Oh, no he isn't," said Ben. "He buried Jeremy there himself, and the old parson, the one who was here before Uncle Hilary and was very eccentric, read the burial service over him. Jeremy had wanted to be buried under the ilex tree. He was eccentric, too, you know. He wanted to be buried there so that he could listen to the blackbird, like you said, and he wanted to be buried shallow, and not to have a coffin, so that it would be easy to get out on the judgment day."

"The more I hear of this tall story," said David, "the more unlikely it sounds. If ever there was an expert liar in this world it's Obadiah. Hasn't the old scoundrel told us time and again that no one in Little Village knows where Jeremy is buried?"

"But Obadiah says they do," said Ben. "The whole of Little Village knows about Jeremy. But they decided not to tell Grandmother and Aunt Margaret because they know Grandmother likes to sit under the ilex tree, and it's very near to the drawing-room window, and they thought she might feel upset if she knew that—that— David, what do people look like when they've been buried for twenty-six years?"

David got out of bed, put on his dressing gown and pulled Ben out of his strained Indian-yogi position to sit beside him on the edge of the bed. The little boy was trembling all over.

"So that's the trouble, is it?" he said gently. "After twenty-six years, Ben, and no coffin, there'll be nothing left of Jeremy but a nice clean respectable skeleton. You're not frightened of skeletons, are you?"

"Yes," whispered Ben. "I saw pictures of them once. They're horrible. They grin. Obadiah has horrible pictures of dead bodies and skeletons in a book at his cottage. I saw them. I think about it in the night."

"What do you think about in the night?"

"About what the people I love will look like when they're dead. Father and Mother and Grandmother, and you and Aunt Margaret, and Ellen, and Tommy and Caroline. You'll look like the people in Obadiah's book."

"Now look here, Ben," said David strong-mindedly, "it doesn't matter a damn what people look like when they're dead because they're not people any more. A body is like a suit of clothes. When it's finished with, it's thrown away and the soul that lived in it goes off somewhere else. You don't worry about what's happening to your old clothes, do you?"

"It's not a bit the same," said poor Ben. "Not a bit. You and Grandmother and Mother, you're beautiful. I like to look at you. I can't bear it that—that—" He stopped. "I think about it in the night," he finished lamely.

"And you the eldest son of a V.C.," said David, applying bracing treatment. "If your father had let himself get scared of death in the night he wouldn't be a V.C. now."

"No," whispered Ben. "No. And I shouldn't be afraid if Father was here."

David felt stabbed. "Why not?" he asked.

"Because I never felt afraid of things when I was with Father. When he went out I used to feel afraid, and I used to hide on the veranda and watch for him to come home. Then when I saw him coming I used to run and meet him, and when I was very small he used to put me on his shoulder. One felt very safe with Father."

David came to a decision. "Now look here, Ben," he said, "I'll tell you what to do when something you have seen has frightened you. You don't run away from it, you look at it again. Any fear, when you face it instead of running away from it, turns out not to be so bad after all. Those pictures of Obadiah's terrified you, didn't they? You wouldn't have been so upset by Jeremy if you hadn't seen them?"

"No," whispered Ben.

"Well, we'll go out to Obadiah's cottage and look at those pictures together. I'll explain them to you, and then, you'll see, they won't frighten you any more."

"No!" cried Ben, and he began to sob. "I can't look at those pictures again! I can't! Not ever!"

"Shirker," said David. "Coward."

Ben began to tremble again. He trembled for five min-

124

utes, as a thoroughbred dog trembles, but his voice was quite steady, though muffled, when he spoke. "I'll come," he said. "We could go this afternoon. It's Saturday and Obadiah is always out at his cottage on Saturdays. He does his own garden then."

"Then we'll go this afternoon. You're a fine fellow, Ben. Proud of you. There's that confounded cuckoo shouting again. What's the time?"

Ben counted. "Eight."

"Eight? Go and turn on my bath."

Ben slipped off the bed and vanished like a blue shadow. David searched wearily for sponge and shaving things. He seemed to have been talking for hours, and it was going to be a brute of a day. In the morning there would be Grandmother and her reactions to the Nadine affair to be coped with, and in the afternoon there would be Ben and his skeletons. Yet in spite of his weariness and apprehension there was a tiny gleam of interest flickering in his mind. What *was* this terrifying book of Obadiah's? And how much more, that he had never told, did Obadiah know about the former owners of Damerosehay? Like Lucilla, David had always wanted to know more about Jeremy and Aramante. He would pump Obadiah. He would pump him hard. . . . The cheerful sound of running water told him that the obliging Ben had turned on his bath, and with almost a feeling of impending doom he sallied forth to confront the new day . . . the first time in his life that he had confronted a day at Damerosehay with foreboding.

It was an understood thing that on his way down to the dining room he should visit the children at nursery breakfast. On his way there, in the passage, he encountered Margaret on her hands and knees.

"Have you dropped anything, Aunt Margaret?" he asked.

"No, but I thought I saw a spider," said Margaret.

"Did you want a spider?" asked David politely.

"For Queenie," said Margaret.

"Queenie?"

"That chameleon you gave the children. She'll eat nothing but live spiders. It's very difficult to keep her supplied."

"For heaven's sake!" ejaculated David. "Can't the children catch the spiders?"

"Children are very difficult with their pets, dear," explained Margaret. "They'll feed them with great enthusiasm for a fortnight, but after that they lose interest. They like the pets, of course, but they won't be bothered with the commissariat."

David fell silently to his hands and knees. He was too penitent to speak; he could only spider hunt. He had presented the children with two white mice, a chameleon, and a cat that had taken to heart rather too literally the divine command to replenish the earth. . . . And Margaret had the bother of them.

"I *am* sorry, Aunt Margaret," he said at last, lying flat to take a particularly juicy spider by the back leg from beneath the wainscot. "What a lot of trouble I've given you."

"It's quite all right, dear," said Margaret patiently. "This is an old house, you see, and spidery. I don't know what we should have done if we'd lived in one of those modern chromium-plated things. Poor Queenie would have died, I think."

"And a good riddance," said David savagely. "I wish that cuckoo clock would die. It kept me awake all night. Was it always so noisy?"

"Yes, dear," said Margaret. "It was always very noisy. I think that will be enough. I've more in this tin."

David inserted his spider into the toffee tin with a perforated lid that was Queenie's larder, got to his feet and sighed. It struck him that though he might be, after Lucilla, the most beloved member of the Eliot family, yet he was, what with one thing and another, an inveterate troubler of its peace. And he didn't want to be that. He wanted to be the preserver of it. With a face of gloom he followed Margaret into the nursery.

It was a cheerful place, looking west over the kitchen garden. It had a blue oilcloth on the floor, and a blue wallpaper decorated with white ducks hurrying to some invisible enchanted pond. The windows were curtained with blue curtains patterned with white butterflies and across them were very ancient iron bars that had been there before the Eliots came, showing that this room had been a nursery before. Another child had leaned out of these windows, holding the old iron bars with fat hands, watching the unfolding of the apple blossom in the garden below and laughing to see the gold of the sunset spread behind the tall pear tree. David could dimly remember how in his own rather lonely nursery days he had created for himself a little dream boy who played here with him; he had felt along the window bars for that other boy's hands and listened for his voice shouting in the garden.

The Eliot nursery was in some ways more like a zoo than a nursery. In one corner of it was stabled Job, the rocking-horse who had in turn carried all Lucilla's children, then David and his dream-child, and now Ben, Tommy and Caroline. Job was worn with his patience. His tail and mane had disappeared completely, his eyes were filmed with age and his once glossy dappled body was faded and dented. Yet, round about sunset, he could go as fast as ever. He creaked abominably, it is true, but he could fling back his head as gallantly as ever he did, paw the golden air with his feet, and arrive at the gate of the city of dreams in a mere twinkling of an eye. He could not go so fast at other times; it was sunset that inspired him.

Next to Job dwelt Snowflake and Lily, the two white mice, in a little house with a knocker on the door. They were very beautiful and much beloved and they had not been given as food to Tucker, according to David's original outrageous suggestion; though Tucker, dozing with the kitten of the moment before the fire, always kept one green eye half open and glinting at them in a way which made them a little nervous.

Queenie lived in a sort of miniature sheep pen on a table. She was incredibly ugly, though she seemed not to know it. In the table drawer was her wardrobe, a selection of colored handkerchiefs upon which she was displayed when visitors came to the nursery. Smiling fatly she was placed upon each in turn and would turn red, blue, green or pink as the case might be. She had on the whole an amiable character and never failed to oblige.

"Auntie!" cried Ben, as Margaret and David entered. "Hurry with the spiders! Queenie's dreadfully hungry!"

Queenie certainly seemed much enraged. She was racing round her pen lashing her tail and looking exactly like a crocodile. When she was in a bad mood she looked like the worst kind of crocodile and when she was in a good mood she looked like the nicest kind of lizard. Like all of us she had a higher and a lower nature. The children thought that when she got to heaven she would always look like a lizard.

Margaret took the lid from the tin and spilt the unfortunate spiders into Queenie's pen. Out shot her long serpentine tongue and they were licked up. It was like a conjuring trick. One did not see them go. They just went. Bulging with repletion Queenie sank to rest in the corner of her pen.

"It's a revolting sight," said David. "Simply disgusting."

But the children, their porridge spoons suspended in mid-air, were chuckling with delight. Queenie's meal was a sight of which they never tired. It seemed to give them just the right start to their breakfast.

Ellen always presided over nursery breakfast. She was behind the teapot now, standing no nonsense, for though she could be wickedly indulgent with the older grandchildren, who came to Damerosehay on visits, she was not so with the younger ones who lived there. She knew her duty. Bits of porridge couldn't be hidden beneath the spoon when Ellen was there, and on haddock mornings the loathly creature had to be finished up to the last flake. The feeding of young Eliots had always been Ellen's duty, for somehow Lucilla had never been lucky with Nannies. They never seemed to stay. They didn't seem to like being taught their duty by Ellen. They went, and Ellen once more reigned supreme in the nursery, assisted by one of those battered nursery maids, meek, loving and devoted, who never give notice no matter how bullied they may be because they belong to the rare company of those who love little children; really love them; love them when they are dirty, greedy, noisy and rude; love them through bilious attacks, colds, measles and the whooping cough. Of these the world is not worthy and of their blessed company was Jill, the present holder of the office.

She was seated by the window, darning Tommy's tattered socks. She had lately staggered up from the kitchen with the loaded breakfast tray, and would presently stagger down with it again. She was thin, round-shouldered and pasty-faced, but very tough and wiry. She had far too much to do, Ellen used her as an outlet for any bad temper she might happen to be feeling, and Tommy teased her unmercifully and tried out upon her all his newest inventions in practical jokes. But her life was not without its compensations. Alf walked out with her on Sundays, and was one day going to marry her, and between her and Caroline there was a quiet understanding companionship that was one of the best things that either of them had in their lives. She did not look up when Margaret and David came into the nursery; she did not even glance under her eyelashes at David's good looks, as Rose the parlormaid would have done; she was absorbed in her work for the ungrateful Tommy...who had his back to her and, unseen by Ellen, was ladling his porridge into the marmalade pot. Jill, he knew, would not give him away.

The boys greeted David with torrents of conversation, quite as though they had not met this morning, but Caroline only gave him a shy smile and went on eating her porridge very slowly and daintily. She wore a white bib with a pussy on it, but she never spilt anything, out of consideration for the feelings of the pussy. Tommy, on the other hand, breast-plated with Humpty Dumpty sitting on the wall, was always a horrible sight down the front. Ben wore no bib. He was too old for such things.

"Don't stay, dear," said Ellen to Margaret. "I'm having trouble to get these children through their porridge.... Sausages excite 'em.... And I'll trouble *you*, Master David, not to bring home sausages again. Too heavy on the stomach, as I've told you time and again."

Tommy leaped to his feet. "I've finished my porridge," he yelled. "Bags I the burst sausage—the big one."

"Now! Now!" said Ellen. "Ask properly or you'll get nothing.... There's the gong, Miss Margaret, love."

Margaret and David went downstairs. Lucilla, who thought it a weakness of the flesh to have breakfast in bed, was already behind the silver coffee pot in the dining room, worn and heavy-eyed. She had slept badly. With each striking of the cuckoo clock through the night David's trouble had taken on more and more alarming proportions. She was convinced, by the time her early tea came, that he was suffering from some incurable disease. The only question which now remained to be decided was, which one. A great-uncle upon her husband's side of the family had died of diabetes, and her own great-grandmother had fallen a victim to an interesting decline, but otherwise both families had enjoyed an almost vulgar healthiness. What *could* David have? Something he had picked up on the stage, no doubt. She had always considered the stage a most unhealthy place; no fresh air, too many drinks, late hours; it had been entirely against her wishes and advice that David had had anything to do with the thing. And now look at the appalling result of disregarding her wishes. There was always disaster in the family when her wishes were disregarded. She was grieved that it should be so, but such were the facts.

"Good morning, darlings," she said evenly, lifting her face to be kissed, "did you both sleep well?"

Margaret said that she had. David talked hurriedly about the weather. "Perfect," he said. "Shall we have a 'heart-to-heart' in the garden this morning, Grandmother?"

"Heart-to-heart" was a phrase used in the Eliot family to describe that type of conversation which was only possible with Lucilla; only to Lucilla dared one show those hurts of the mind and spirit that any other touch than hers would have only lacerated further.

Only today, for the first time, David was not looking

for healing from Lucilla, only a deepening of his pain. Their eyes met and their mutual apprehension lay between them like the first shadow of an opening rift.

"After Caroline has had her lessons," said Lucilla with a touch of severity. She allowed herself to show no favoritism. Little Caroline should not be deprived of her daily hour of instruction even though David was threatened with tuberculosis. . . . Lucilla had made up her mind while she drank her coffee and ate a piece of toast (somehow she had not felt able to tackle her boiled egg) that David had tuberculosis. The great-grandmother's decline was probably that, and it was a disease that was rather liable to attack actors, she had heard, because they had to breathe so deeply in such vitiated air. He should go to Egypt, she decided, and she would go with him for a few months. It only took her two minutes to decide what clothes they would both need. Lucilla was like that. An acquaintance had only to sneeze, or to smile at a member of the opposite sex, and she would have the funeral or the wedding planned down to the last detail. Her prevision was good mental exercise but rather exhausting.

Yet after breakfast she was able to switch her mind completely off David and fix it upon Caroline. That was Caroline's right, and her duty as a grandmother. They sat side by side upon the drawing-room sofa, Lucilla dressed in one of her severe but beautifully cut black frocks that showed off to perfection her white hair and her shapely hands, and Caroline in a buttercup yellow smock with knickers to match. Her short bare legs were not long enough to dangle over the edge of the sofa seat, they stuck straight out in front of her as though she were a doll with no knee joints. Her straight bobbed hair, which had been well brushed by Ellen and polished with a silk handkerchief, looked like a smooth red-gold bell about her thin earnest little face. She sat very upright, her hands clenched firmly upon the covers of a battered blue book which she held very close to her button nose, and read aloud to her grandmother about a Cat who ate a Rat and afterwards, feeling replete, no doubt, Sat upon a Mat. She was working very hard. Her toes, visible through the latticework of her sandals, were curling and uncurling with the violence of her mental effort and her hands clutched the book so hard that the knuckles showed white through the sunburn. Yet her voice was a very small murmuring voice, almost religious in its tone, as though she were saying her prayers. Caroline was a true scholar. She stood before the mystery of wisdom with a single and a reverent mind.

Lucilla also was working hard. With her hands folded in her lap she listened intently to every word spoken by the murmuring little voice, carefully correcting the intonation and explaining the full and glorious meaning of such words as Brave, Save and Wave, Light, Sight and Bright. She tried very hard to teach her grandchildren how to extract the last drop of beauty out of all the small things of life, words and scents and sounds. Many little joys, weighed against the few heavy griefs of existence, could give some sort of balance to the scales and preserve the sanity of life.

"It is the Light of the sun," she explained to Caroline, "that gives us Sight to see the Bright world. When the sun sets it is as though we had gone blind. We see nothing any more."

David, sitting just outside the drawing-room window under the ilex tree with *The Times,* lowered it and listened. "The bright world." It was unusually bright this morning; one of those cloudless autumn days that seem to burn like a flame, not hot but brilliant, the last leap of the fire before the ashes and the dying sparks of winter. The garden lay like a mosaic of color all about him and upon every bush lay the silver filagree of spiders' webs hung with dewdrops. In spite of the deep blue of the sky and the bright gold of the mounting sun the whole garden was still jeweled with dew. But it did not dim the color, it gave to it a clear still purity that was strangely healing. David felt a sudden overwhelming affinity with this bright world of Damerosehay. It was his own place. He knew a quick surge of joy, as though his spirit leaped to meet it, and then a stab of pain and a darkening before his eyes, as though it receded from him and the lights went out.... Only a cloud over the sun, but it had given him a jar. ... It had shown him what he would feel like when this was no longer his place.

The lesson in the drawing room was apparently over. Levering herself forward Caroline slid off the sofa, showing a lot of knicker in the process, pulled down her abbreviated skirt with a maidenly gesture taught her by Ellen, kissed her grandmother and put her book away in the bookcase. Then she took her doll Gladys from the corner of the sofa, trotted out into the hall and through the garden door into the garden, smiled at David but refused to speak, and disappeared into the recesses of the garden. She would not be seen again until nursery dinner. This was her hour, her own secret hour, and what she did with it no one knew.

Lucilla, taking her sunshade from the hall stand, followed Caroline out into the sweet sunshine. She put up her sunshade and walked slowly towards the ilex tree. David got up to meet her.

"I'm ready," she said.

4.

They walked up and down the lawn together, moving with the unconscious grace that was habitual to them both, their long lean shadows dark upon the dew, and David told her, simply and straightforwardly as he knew she would wish to be told. She didn't say anything for a few minutes, and then she said, "I think I shall have to sit down, David."

They went back to the chairs under the ilex tree that Obadiah had already set for them, a deck chair for David and an upright wicker one for Lucilla, who hated lounging, and sat down; and in spite of his unhappiness David remembered with a jerk of grim amusement that Jeremy's skeleton, if Obadiah's story was true, was just about exactly underneath them. Then he looked at Lucilla and suddenly went white, for her face was like the face of a dead woman, some stranger, hollow-cheeked and hollow-eyed. He passed his hand quickly before his eyes, as though to shut it out, and when he looked at her again she was Lucilla once more; but a much older Lucilla. It must have been some trick of the light that had made her look like that; the light or his thought of Jeremy. He found that his hand was shaking and stuck it savagely into his pocket.

"I see," said Lucilla in a hoarse exhausted voice. "So that's what it is."

She did not say anything else and she seemed unaware that in spite of the shade of the ilex tree she was still holding up her sunshade. She looked at him and he forced himself to meet her eyes. They were blazing with anger.

It was far worse than he had thought it would be. He had thought he knew all the arguments that she would use, the arguments of a Christian and of a Victorian woman to whom family unity was very dear, and he had steeled himself to hear them, and now she said nothing at all. There was nothing but her silence and her anger and the aging of her beloved face. The tension between them was almost unbearable.

"Grandmother," he said desperately, "you look as though I had committed a crime, when all I have done is to get engaged to a woman I love who by the law of the land is free to marry me."

"The law of the land," repeated Lucilla dully. He waited for her to speak to him of the law of the Church, but she didn't, and he had to go on, talking for the sake of talking, uncertain if she heard a word he said.

"Listen, Grandmother," he said, "I want to tell you how I feel about this. I want to make you understand."

He told her of the nature of the love that had grown between himself and Nadine, of its power and depth and beauty, and of his other love that was as strong, his love of truth. He tried to make her understand what he felt about this truth, that it was a thing that should live in one's inner life, compelling outward things to its own likeness and not suffering their shape to impinge upon its beauty. Now and then she bowed her head as though she had understood, but he could not be certain. When he had finished he waited again, ready to hear her point of view; but she seemed not to have one.

"And so you see, Grandmother," he said at last, "that I cannot inherit Damerosehay."

"Why not?" demanded Lucilla harshly.

He stared at her in astonishment. Surely she could not, her opinions being what he knew they were, still consider him a fit heir for Damerosehay.

"I am waiting," said Lucilla, "to hear why you think you cannot inherit Damerosehay."

"Because I did not think that after this you would want me to."

"Why not?" asked Lucilla.

Then he saw her meaning. She knew why not but she wanted to see if he did.

"Because, Grandmother, you will not want to leave your most precious possession, that you made to preserve the family unity, to a man who is dealing such a blow at that unity. It would be an insult both to the family and the place if I lived here. At least that is what I expect you to feel, Grandmother. You will feel, too, that I am smashing forever any chance that Nadine and George might come together again, that I am injuring the children and breaking the law of the Church of which I am a member.

And it isn't only you who will feel this, all the others will too, Margaret, Hilary, Stephen and his children. And, of course, George. And George will feel much more. Whoever Nadine married he would feel it, but her marriage to his own nephew will hurt him unspeakably. Damerosehay is the family home; it is where we belong, our own place; in a way it *is* the family. If I cut myself off from one I must cut myself off from the other."

"There is no need for me to say anything," said Lucilla, still in that harsh dry voice. "You have expressed my point of view perfectly, quite as well as a minute ago you expressed your own. I heard what you said about your own. I heard and understood."

"I could say a little more on my own side," urged David. "I could tell you that even had I never existed Nadine would not go back to George. A divorce is a far more final thing than you realize. And I could tell you, too, that she would never stay single; she's not that sort; if it were not me it would be some other man. And as for religion, Grandmother, you know that I don't feel bound by that. You brought me up to be a churchman but I'm not one now. I keep the law of the land but not the law of the Church."

Lucilla sighed and moved a little restlessly. David's loss of the faith she had taught him was a trouble to her, though she had not given up hope that he would find it again.

"As for the other thing," went on David, "the distress that I shall cause you all, well, I'm sorry, Grandmother. I'm bitterly sorry. I don't mind so much about the others, but to hurt you is damnable. Yet I must do it. If I'm to be honest I must do it. I must serve the truth as I see it. You understand that, don't you, Grandmother?"

"What I understand, David," said Lucilla, "is that your infatuation for Nadine has blinded you to every consideration of honor and duty, and even sense. I see what you mean about truth, and I know that you mean to be honest, but I think that unconsciously you are using your ideals to justify action that you would take in any case. What is possessing you, David, is not a passion for truth but a man's utterly selfish longing to possess the beauty of a very lovely woman."

David flushed angrily. "Selfish?" he demanded. "My love for Nadine? Grandmother, I don't believe you know what love is. How should you? You were just a girl when you married Grandfather. I expect you were always just the affectionate Victorian wife. I expect—"

"That will do, David," interrupted Lucilla. "I believe that I know far more about love than you do. And more about truth. One day I'll tell you; not now, I'm too angry. Yes, angry. With you and with Nadine, but especially with Nadine. She should have stopped it before it came to this. She is years older than you, a woman of the world while you are a mere romantic boy."

David's simmering anger blazed out. "No man is a boy at twenty-five," he flashed. "And there's only five years between Nadine and me. What's five years?"

"In middle life, nothing," said Lucilla, "at your age, everything; all the difference between inexperience and maturity. You would never be happy with Nadine, David." Suddenly she stretched out her hand and put it on his.

"Now we are both angry," she said. "That must not be. We have always loved each other so much. Nothing must spoil it, David. Not even this."

"No," said David wretchedly, his anger evaporating, and he held her hand in both his, twisting her rings round and round as he had done when he was a child. "No. But what can we do, Grandmother?"

He spoke in bewilderment, like a small boy, and Lucilla was quick to take advantage of his weakness. "Do you feel that after all these years you owe me anything?" she asked. "That I have the right to ask some little sacrifice of you?"

"Yes, Grandmother," he said. "Yes, of course."

"Then you will do nothing for a few weeks," said Lucilla. "You will not write to George or say anything to anyone of your intentions. You will stay here quietly with me for a little while, you and Nadine."

"Nadine?" he asked sharply. "Grandmother, that would be impossible. Nadine and I here together—it would be unbearable. I hadn't even meant to stay myself. I had meant to go tomorrow."

"We will both write to Nadine," said Lucilla inexorably, "and ask her to come down. I shan't bother the two of you. Just once I will tell you both what I feel, but only once. You shall go about together as much as you like. Just for two weeks. Not longer. I don't merely ask this, David, I demand it. I have the right."

"Very well," said David, but his mouth set in a hard line and he no longer caressed Lucilla's fingers. She withdrew her hand.

"I'll go in," she said, and got up. But she was not so

141

steady on her legs as she had expected to be and David went with her to the garden door.

"Grandmother," he implored, "these next weeks are only going to be bearable for the three of us if we keep the thing to ourselves. Don't tell Aunt Margaret. But above all don't tell Ellen."

Lucilla hadn't been going to tell Margaret, whose distressing efforts to be tactful, did she know, would obliterate the lot of them, but she *had* been going to tell Ellen. She had always told Ellen everything. It cost her a hard struggle to say, "Very well, David, not Margaret or Ellen or, of course, the children. But I must tell Hilary. He is my eldest son and I lean upon him."

"I don't mind old Hilary knowing," said David, and suddenly thought of his steady, sensible uncle with a sense of relief, as though struggling in a dangerous sea he had felt firm ground beneath his feet. "I don't mind Hilary knowing anything."

"I am all right now, David," said Lucilla. "Don't come in."

He stood at the door and remorsefully watched her slight figure go slowly up the stairs; then he turned back towards the ilex tree. He thought he saw a dark figure moving in the drawing room, yet when he looked through the window there was no one there. Later, once more under the ilex tree with *The Times*, he saw Ellen in the dining room, polishing the table with a display of energy such as he had never witnessed before.

But he could not stay under the ilex tree. Every murmur of birdsong in the old garden, every movement of the little wind that had come in from the sea now that the tide was turning, seemed a reproach. He strode down the garden, through the oak wood, and down to the harbor where the sun was bright on the water and the white wings of the yachts were unfolding in the rising wind. He took his own little boat, that Obadiah had got ready for him, and sped down the creek to the sea. Out there, if anywhere, alone with the sea and the wind, there was freedom from tormenting thoughts.

Lucilla, seated at her bedroom window, saw him go. She sat very still, her hands folded tightly in her lap. The shock of what David had told her was wearing off now and she was moving through anger to pain. She had not been so desperately unhappy since David's father had died. It was so unexpected. As always with one's personal disasters the thing that had happened was the one thing that she had not thought of. She tried to tell herself that perhaps this marriage would not be the appalling disaster that she thought it. It was perhaps true, as David had said, that the breach between George and Nadine was too deep now to be healed. David and Nadine seemed really to love each other and by the law of the land David had every right to marry her. And David would be a kind stepfather to the children, though she could not but feel that it would upset Ben terribly to see David in his father's place. She said this over and over again to herself but yet she could not be comforted. What had happened was a tragedy to her because it meant the total overthrow of all for which she had worked for twenty years. It meant the disunion of the family and, to her, the death of Damerosehay that was the symbol of it. No, more than twenty years, for most of her married life she had been working for her children's unity, making for it sacrifices of which they had never dreamed; and Damerosehay, before it had come into existence as an actual physical fact, had always existed in her mind as a sort of spiritual country in which she held them all secure. She felt she was confronted now with the ruin of her life's work, and no greater tragedy can confront a human being.

"What nonsense!" she said to herself. "What nonsense! Though David leaves me, David and Nadine and her children, I still have the others."

But the others would not make up to her for the loss of David. He meant more to her than they did. And, too, he was the one whom all the others loved best. She had expected that when she died he would take her place as the focal point of the family. He had all the gifts that would have fitted him to do that, the sympathy, the love of hospitality, the strong sense of family and of place. "But never now," she thought, "never now. Even though he comes back to see me sometimes he will never be the same David. This will be between us always. And the others, too, Stephen's children, George's, they will never take him now into the place that was mine. He is right. I cannot leave Damerosehay to him now."

Dully she wondered to whom she could leave it. All the others loved it but not, she thought, sufficiently to want the expense and bother of keeping it up. Only David really understood how she felt about it, only he who had grown up here loved it with that strong personal love of a man for his own bit of earth that was, she thought, one of the best things in life, yet was under modern conditions so fast being lost.

As David must lose it when he married Nadine. Suddenly she forgot everything in her anger against Nadine. She would not make David happy. Lucilla considered her a selfish woman, who would love only in a selfish way. She would be the worst wife possible for an artist, unaware that creative work demands a singleness of mind that must at times put everything else aside. Nadine would never be content to be put aside even for a moment. She would always be insistent with her claims; the clamor of them would exhaust David and spoil his work.

Her anger brought Lucilla to the realization that she was taking up the attitude of defeat, she was taking for granted that in the struggle before them David would win, even as she had taken it for granted during their game of chess last night. She drew her breath sharply and sat up straighter. She would fight. She would not be defeated. Though she was old and he was young, she would fight him and win. Looking back over the past conversation in the garden she thought she had taken no false step. Her wish that David and Nadine should stay quietly with her at Damerosehay for a while had been simply intuition, but she thought it had been right. Damerosehay would, she thought, in some mysterious way fight its own battle, bring its own pressure to bear upon David; the place was alive in every stick and stone, rich with some unknown history that was molding both the present and the future. She was in sympathetic touch with that history; she felt its touch very often; it would be on her side.

Yet she would have her part to play too, and quietly she began to make her plans: what she would say to David, what to Nadine, in that one discussion that she had claimed, what she would make Hilary say. For a moment or two something of the old exhilaration of battle that she had known when she was younger came back to her and the color rose in her cheeks. But it soon passed and she found that she was crying, a thing she never did, the tears making her head ache abominably. She was so dreadfully sorry for her son George. Until now she had selfishly hardly considered him, but it was the thought of his grief that finally broke her down. She cried and cried. She was dreadfully lonely in this trouble, she found, horribly lonely. . . . If only she could have told Ellen about it.

And just at that moment Ellen entered, almost as though she had been listening outside the door for the first sound of weeping. In a grim silence she pulled the curtains, took Lucilla out of her dress and put her into her dressing-gown, laid her upon the bed and handed her the bottle of eau de cologne from her black velvet bag. "You'll stay there, milady," she commanded, "till lunch, and if you're not a lot better by lunch I'll have something sent up."

"I must come down to lunch, Ellen," sobbed Lucilla into her pillow, "because—because—oh, I can't tell you, Ellen. And I can't think why I'm crying. It's a thing I never do."

"Ah," said Ellen, and sniffed savagely. She was very angry, it appeared, though not apparently with Lucilla, for she put out a horny forefinger and very gently touched her cheek. Then she set upon the table beside her the smelling salts, the sal volatile, two clean handkerchiefs, and a mirror and a powder puff for when she should be sufficiently recovered to take interest in her appearance again. Then she went out. "The idea!" she said indignantly at the door. "Did you ever hear? Well, I never!"

CHAPTER FIVE

1.

THERE WAS ANOTHER garden at Damerosehay besides the flower garden and the kitchen garden, and that was the wild garden, which lay to the west of the flower garden, the kitchen garden being on the north and the oak wood on the south. It had originally been the part of the flower garden where the oak trees grew and Lucilla had made it by erecting another brick wall to divide them, and moving one of the beautiful wrought-iron gateways with which Damerosehay abounded from the kitchen garden to give access from one to the other. The wall was almost hidden now by the mind-your-own-business which tossed its sprays like white foam over it, and the gate was hidden by a great bush of guelder-roses, so that the wild garden was very secret indeed. Lucilla had wanted to keep some reminder of the Damerosehay that she had seen on that first spring morning, that overgrown place where she had dreamed of the blue bird and David had seen it, and so she had simply left the wild garden more or less alone to go mad as it liked. The grown-ups thought Lucilla was as crazy as the garden, but the children blessed her foresight every day of their lives.

Especially Caroline. When she was here, with the boys

at their lessons and the grown-ups busy over their mysterious employments, she knew that she would be quite alone, undisturbed by anyone except Jill bringing her eleven o'clock milk and biscuits, and she liked Jill so much that she hardly counted as a separate person.

Clasping Gladys, and smiling at David where he sat beneath the ilex tree, she ran through the tame garden, slipped behind the guelder-rose bed, and lifted the latch of the gate that led to the wild garden. It latched behind her and she gave a deep sigh of content and stood still for a minute to survey her kingdom.

The oak trees in the wild garden, sheltered by the wall and by their brothers in the wood, were less wind-blown and stunted than those outside. Their branches were less twisted and more graciously spread, their foliage thicker and their hoary lichened trunks stouter and straighter. They were less like battle-scarred warriors and more like wise and mellowed councilors, set there not for defense but for encouragement and support.

And certainly the other growing things in the wild garden took every advantage of the encouragement offered. The honeysuckle raced up the oak trees and in summer blew its trumpets victoriously at the very top; the mermaid rose, that hardy rambler that will go anywhere and catch hold of anything, clambered along the branches and sent festoons of creamy golden-hearted blossoms to sway in the wind beneath them like fairy swings. As for the mind-your-own-business, sadly restrained by Margaret as it was on the flower-garden side of the wall, it let itself go completely on the wild side. It leaped exultantly off the wall and hung in thick curtains of ivory blossom that swept the moss-grown path and even encroached upon the rough grass beyond.

All the loveliest wild flowers grew in this grass in their seasons, primroses about the tree trunks in April, bluebells in May, ragged robins in June and daisies at all times. There were still garden flowers running riot here, Michaelmas daisies, hollyhocks and Japanese anemones, lavender and rosemary, for Obadiah was allowed in now and then to scythe the grass and keep the brambles down so that they should not be choked completely out of existence. But there was never any suggestion of real cultivation in the wild garden, it was just a glorious natural wilderness of color and scent.

And how the birds loved it! They seemed scared of the strange twisted oak trees beyond the wall, but these beneficent creatures inside were their friends, and the whole garden was their sanctuary. The children put food here for them in winter and Tucker was severely chastised if she dared to come in over the wall. Even the dogs were discouraged, in case they should bark at the birds and frighten them. The blackbird, at such times as he was not singing in the ilex tree, was singing in the wild garden, and on the very top of the tallest tree a big missel thrush was forever crying out to the world that God is good. A robin lived here too, a bullfinch and a chaffinch, and the wives of these creatures, every kind of tit and wagtail, called by Jill "Polly dishwashers," willow wrens, hedge sparrows and tree creepers. On rare occasions a goldfinch was seen flashing his splendor through the trees, and a couple of exquisite rose-breasted redstarts fluttered over the bushes, so fragile that they seemed each of them more like a gasp of wonder than a bird. Only the sea birds never came here. They knew better. It was not their province. Once a Sabine's gull had tried to take refuge in the wild garden from a violent storm, but all the other birds had risen up in a cloud of fury and attacked him with savage beaks and raucous cries, and he had fled back to the comparative kindness of the wind on the marshes.

Spring, when the birds were nesting and the bluebells were budding, was the best time in the wild garden, but autumn could be lovely too. As Caroline stood gazing, the Japanese anemones were like fallen moons beyond the gray trunks of the oak trees and there was a soft mist of mauve where the autumn crocuses were growing in the rough grass. The fires of autumn had already touched the leaves over her head, and spun from twig to twig and from bush to bush was that exquisite silver filigree of dewy spiders' webs. Caroline went slowly forward along the path that led in and out through the tree trunks to the secret center of the garden where Methuselah was.

He was the oldest of the oak trees, taller and larger and hoarier than any. It was on his topmost branch that the missel thrush sang, and among his leaves that the willow wrens nested. In spring the loveliest primroses grew about his gnarled old roots, and in autumn the crocuses grew here thicker than anywhere else.

When Lucilla had first come to Damerosehay she had found the remains of a battered swing hanging from the stoutest of Methuselah's branches, showing that once a child had played here. She had taken it away and put a new one for David, and as the years went by an even stouter one to sustain the weight of Stephen's children, and then a very strong one indeed to carry the sometimes combined weight of Ben, Tommy and Caroline. It was a perfect place to have a swing, for here you were as secret and safe as though shut up in the heart of a flower. No one could see you and you saw nothing except leaves and birds' wings, flowers and grasses. No one visited you except the sunbeams or a silver shower of rain, and, sometimes, the lady and the little boy.

Caroline, like David in his boyhood, was a lonely child. Except for Lucilla and her adored Jill she thought but little of the human race, and Grandmother and Jill were so often busy about other things that she did not see a great deal of them. Not that she minded. She liked solitude, especially in the wild garden. Yet like many solitaries she felt the need for some sort of companionship, even if it was only a companionship of her own creation. Talking to oneself palled, but Caroline found that if one shut one's eyes and just talked, not to oneself but to someone unknown outside oneself, when one opened one's eyes that someone was there. . . . And she thought the person really was there. She forgot, if she had ever realized, that her own wish had had creative power. . . . That was how she had come to know the lady and the little boy.

It had happened first last year, when Mother had been staying with them, on an autumn day like this one, when she had been feeling particularly forlorn. She had eaten all the sugar out of the nursery cupboard, and there had been a good deal of unpleasantness with Ellen, from which she had fled to the shelter of Methuselah's kind arms. Sitting in the swing with the slow tears oozing out from under her shut lids she had felt the urgent need to tell somebody about it, and so she had just begun to tell.

"I was *not* greedy," she had said. "It was because Mother said I was a skinny little shrimp, and I thought that if I got fatter she might love me as much as she loves the boys, and so I ate the sugar. Then Ellen scolded and Mother said I was a greedy little pig, and I couldn't tell her why I had eaten the sugar because if I had I would have cried, and Mother doesn't like cry-babies."

At the end of this recitation she had opened her eyes and at first she had thought that all the autumn crocuses that were growing about her feet had flown up into the air like a cloud of butterflies, because there was a sort of mauve mist before her eyes, but when she looked again she saw that it was a lady in a mauve dress, with a lovely full skirt that swept over the grass like a wave of the sea.

At first Caroline thought this lady was Mother, because she was tall and dark and slender like Mother, but when she looked again she saw that she wasn't really a bit like Nadine. Her face was rounder and softer and her eyes shone in a way that told Caroline without any words that she, unlike Nadine, liked little girls every bit as much as little boys, and that she quite understood about the sugar. And then a funny little boy dressed in green, with red curls and a head far too large for his body, had popped out from behind the lady's skirts and grinned at Caroline; and Caroline had wriggled out of the swing and had run to him, and they had played in the garden together all the morning, and the lady had sat on the grass and laughed.

Thinking it over afterwards, Caroline could not remember what they had said to each other, if indeed they had said anything. But they had been blissfully happy. This mother had not been so much a mother, as the mother, the mother of everything in the garden, of herself and the little boy and the flowers and birds and everything. Though she was dressed in mauve instead of in blue, and wasn't really a bit like her, yet she had somehow reminded Caroline of the picture of the Madonna that hung in the nursery. But her name wasn't Mary. Caroline knew quite well it wasn't Mary, though she didn't know what it was.

And as for the funny little boy, well, he was the perfect companion, that companion of whom we all of us dream under so many disguises, the outward form altering as the years go on, but yet seem somehow never to find.

So often since that day Caroline had seen them, though only in the wild garden; indeed it sometimes seemed as though she could make them come at will simply by shutting her eyes and talking to them. She knew, as she trotted along to the swing with Gladys, that she was going to see them today. . . . And she did.

When Jill brought out her milk and biscuits at eleven she was sitting in the swing, very demure and bright-eyed and rather more rosy than usual.

"Funny little thing that you are!" exclaimed Jill. "Happy all alone?"

Caroline took her mug of milk and buried her nose in it. She vouchsafed no remarks but her eyes twinkled at

Jill over the top. She could not tell even dear Jill about the lady and the little boy, but she could let her share her joy.

Jill sat down on the grass beside Caroline with a sigh of relief. It was a joy to escape from Ellen's perpetual harrying and be alone with Caroline for a little while in this lovely secret place. And mercifully Caroline was always a very long time absorbing her milk and biscuits, for she liked food and always made it last as long as possible. Jill sat very still, with Gladys in the crook of her arm, and lifted her face, her eyes closed, to the warm sunbeams that struck down through the branches of the oak tree. She could hear the flutter of wings near her, and birdsong and the murmur of the sea; and her free hand, pressed down hard upon the earth, lifted itself unconsciously to caress the cool grass and the crocuses and the rough sun-warmed bark of the tree. "Well," she ejaculated suddenly, "it would not be so bad to be blind, after all. The sound and feel of things is that nice."

Caroline gulped down the last of her milk, removed her countenance from her mug and looked at Jill a little anxiously. Jill was talking to herself and she was rather afraid that when she opened her eyes she might see the lady and the little boy.

Yet all she said when she opened her eyes was, "Wipe your mouth, lovey. You've milk all round it."

Caroline took a microscopic handkerchief from up her knickers and wiped her mouth with relief. Somehow she did not want even Jill to know the secrets of this secret garden.

Jill got up with reluctance. This old tree, with the patch of flower-jeweled turf around it and the trees and bushes closing it in on every side, always made her feel so safe. Had she been able to express what she felt she would have said that it was the inner sanctuary of the Damerosehay garden, as the drawing room with the carved overmantel was the heart of the house. It seemed that in both of them the best of all that had ever been at Damerosehay was very safely kept. From them its life's blood flowed out. She picked up Caroline's mug and went away very slowly. It was always hard to leave the wild garden.

When Jill had gone the little boy came out from behind the tree trunk and Caroline played with him for a long time, while the lady sat in the swing, her mauve skirt billowing out over the crocuses, and laughed. And then suddenly they were not there, and Caroline wondered why until she heard a clear whistling in the garden, like the blackbird but yet not the blackbird. It was David's whistle that he always used to tell the children that he was coming.

That was one of the things that the children liked about David. He understood quite well that grown-ups were invaders from another country, and that one did not want to be caught unexpectedly by them doing something which they would probably neither understand nor approve of. He always gave warning of his coming.

So he found Caroline seated once more upon the swing, as composed as a queen waiting to give audience.

"Dinnertime, Caroline," he said. "Tommy has been ringing the nursery dinner bell out of the window for some minutes. He's very hungry, he says. Aren't you hungry?"

156

Caroline shook her head, slithered out of the swing and slipped her hand into David's. But David seemed reluctant to leave the old oak tree. As Jill had done, he laid his hand against the bark.

"I used to have a swing here, too," he told Caroline. "It's a jolly place. Do you play here every morning?"

Caroline, her thumb in her mouth, nodded her head.

"All alone?"

Caroline, a truthful child, shook her head.

"I invented a dream boy to play with," said David. "Do you invent playmates, Caroline?"

Caroline took her thumb out of her mouth and lifted puzzled eyes to his face. "Invent" was a word Lucilla had not taught her yet. She did not know what he meant. Then she hung her head and whispered something that David had to bend low to catch. "A lady and a little boy," she said. And then a tear rolled down her button nose because she had told her secret, and to a grown-up. She couldn't think what had made her do it. And she was terrified of that word "invent." She was afraid that David was going to explain it to her, and that its meaning would be one that she would not be able to bear. She burst into floods of tears and clutched David with both hands. "No! No!" she said. "Don't tell! Don't tell!"

David, much embarrassed and totally at sea, sat down in the swing and took Caroline on his knees. "Of course I won't tell," he assured her, though he had no idea what it was he wasn't to tell. "Is the little boy you play with a nice little boy, Caroline?"

Caroline nodded, once more withdrew her microscopic

handkerchief from her knickers and applied it pathetically to her minute face.

"And the lady? Is she a nice lady? What's her name?"

Caroline shook her head, but David seemed to feel that the lady ought to have a name. "Aramante," he suggested.

Caroline looked up at him and smiled through her tears, for that was a name that exactly suited her lady. She had known it wasn't Mary, she had known it ought to be something longer, though she hadn't known what. Vigorously and joyously she nodded her head, blew her small nose triumphantly and put away the now quite unnecessary handkerchief. David was delighted with his success. The mysterious grief was now apparently assuaged, and he thought they might safely go in to dinner. Amicably, hand in hand, having become in some queer way very close to each other, they threaded their way through the tangled sweetness of the wild garden to the place where the curtain of mind-your-own-business swept the path and the iron gate was hidden behind the guelder-rose bush.

Here Tommy met them, feverishly ringing the nursery dinner bell. "Come *on!*" he urged them. "Come *on!* It's liver and bacon and I've a hungry raging wolf in my tummy!"

2.

But Ben, when David made polite inquiries after lunch, said he hadn't been able to fancy liver and bacon. "Liver seems more like a dead animal than other sorts of meat, don't you think?" he said.

David said he didn't really think he'd thought much about it.

"I have," said Ben with a shudder. "I've thought a lot about it, and I wish I was a vegetarian."

They were walking through the oak wood, the dogs at their heels, on their way to the marshes and Obadiah's cottage. David perceived that Ben's haunting had gone deep, and his anger rose against Obadiah. He had had no business to show the sensitive little boy whatever it was that he had shown him. But then Obadiah was a poor man, familiar with all the worst facts of life and death from his babyhood up. He could not be expected to understand that disastrous sheltering of the rich man's child which, carried on from generation to generation, makes his spirit increasingly vulnerable in a world where year by year the horrors that lie in wait for him proportionately increase.

For a moment, as they turned out of the oak wood and the loveliness of the marshes and the sea lay before them, David felt himself gripped by his own particular nightmare beast.... War.... He had glibly lectured to Ben on courage that morning, but he was no more successful than anyone else at applying his advice to himself. He was no more afraid of death and wounds than most men, but the fear of having his life's work taken from him and destroyed by war was like an insidious poison in his system, perpetually weakening his effectiveness. It was so difficult to concentrate upon creative work, so difficult to carry on one's particular battle for truth and beauty, when all the time those great forces of man's hate and greed were lying like a dark sea on the horizon, ready to sweep over the world—

as in great storms the sea submerged the marshes—and carry away all individual creations of joy and loveliness as though they had never been. There was only one way to go on without weakening, and that was to hold on to the conviction that what has been, has been and in some mysterious way is immortal; to believe that every work of art has its spiritual as well as its physical life and is indestructible by material fate. But he found it increasingly hard to do that. The faith that Lucilla had taught him he had largely lost; nothing was left of it but an exceedingly vague hope that the soul lives on beyond death; when he had spoken of immortality to Ben with such certainty he had only been saying what he knew Lucilla would wish him to say; so how believe in the immortality of the little he had created? No, it was no use. He felt that without length of days in which to bring his life's work to fulfillment a man is of no more value than a leaf that flutters by on the wind and is lost. And length of days was a thing of which, in this generation, one could have no reasonable expectation.... It behooved a man to seize every chance of joy, of work and of love as it came, even as he and Nadine were doing, for the time was not long.

"Are you unhappy, David?" asked Ben, tugging at his coat.

Confound the little beggar! He was far too perspicacious. Without a word spoken one's moods were clear to him. David pulled himself together and began to be very heartily cheerful. It was very important, he knew, to make children think that life was a splendid thing. How persistently grown-ups struggled to do it, what lies they told, what fears they battened down that the very shadow of them should not be seen. They worked so hard to create this illusion, obeying an overwhelming instinct, that one was tempted to wonder if it *was* an illusion, if it was not, after all, a dimly perceived truth. Well, anyway, while with Ben he would pretend it was. For Ben, this afternoon, life must be splendid.

And he was not an actor for nothing. Never had Ben been so gloriously entertained. He forgot his fears. His laughter rang out and his eyes were bright with delight in his thin brown face.

The effort that he made reacted upon David, and he too began to cheer up. There was, at any rate, this afternoon with the sun bright in the sky and the beauty of the marshes all around them. They were walking east along a rough road that led to Obadiah's cottage. This was a drier part of the marshes, where the sea never came now, for big dykes had been built to keep it out. Cattle were put to graze here, and one day the mayor and corporation of Radford hoped to put up bungalows for holiday makers. ... Though only over their dead bodies, said the Eliots.... In spring it was a sheet of flaming gorse here, but now it was mostly rough grass, fragrant with wild thyme and bright with pink swift and golden lady's-slipper, with occasional patches of sea lavender and golden rice grass.

"Isn't there a break in one of those dykes?" asked David, and he pointed it out to Ben.

"Yes," said Ben. "They'll have to mend it before the winter. They don't think the dykes are going to be the use they thought they'd be. They tell Obadiah he'll have to turn out of his cottage one of these days, or he'll be drowned dead."

David laughed. "Not much fear yet," he said. "But Obadiah is rather an ancient old party to live in so lonely a place."

"Not at all," said Ben defensively. "He's only just over eighty, and his great-grandfather lived till a hundred and three."

David hastily agreed that it was more than probable that Obadiah would outlive them all.

His cottage was ideally placed to promote long life. At the back of it a half-moon of woodland protected it from the north and east winds, while from the south, across the marsh, the life-giving wind from the sea and the full flood of the sunshine swept unchecked. And all around it was such beauty of sight and sound: birdsong and windsong in the wood, with the flowers in their seasons and the changing tapestry of budding, unfolding and then falling leaves, and then the gorse on the marsh, the white wings of the gulls and the far line of the gleaming sea. And to crown everything else a stream ran through the wood. It came from the high Forest land to the north and flowed through the wood fast and strong, passed by Obadiah's cottage and then sang its way across the marsh to the sea in an ever-widening, deepening channel. Its waters were sweet to drink, said Obadiah, pure and untainted; he never bothered to boil it.

But when they came to it David noticed that the stream was unusually full and rapid for the time of year. He hardly ever remembered, even in winter, seeing it so full.

"It's been such a wet summer," explained Ben. "Lots of the Forest is under water just as though it were January."

They crossed the rough wide plank bridge that spanned the stream and found themselves in Obadiah's strip of flower garden, bright with the hydrangeas, nasturtiums, tamarisks, marigolds and fuchsias that did not mind the wind from the sea. Behind the cottage was the vegetable garden, where the vegetable marrows were a sight to behold.

But Obadiah himself was in the flower garden, tending the giant blue hydrangea that grew beside the two snowy steps leading to the front door. The cottage was built of weather-stained gray stone, like the cottages at Little Village, but it was only one story high and contained only three rooms: the kitchen, Obadiah's bedroom and the little slip of a room occupied by Alf. The village woman who "did" for them came only in the mornings and did not live there. Should there at any time come another great storm and flood, such as had wrecked the grain ship, there would, for Obadiah, be no escaping upstairs for safety.... But then his part of the marsh was so safe with all those dykes.

"You all right, Obadiah?" asked David as he shook hands with the old man.

"Pretty tar'blish," said Obadiah. "Pretty tar'blish. Oi 'opes ee be well, Master David."

He was hospitable and garrulous, was Obadiah, and was delighted to see David and Ben, much deploring the absence of Alf at Big Village for the first football match of the season. "Though 'ow they can play football in this 'eat," said Obadiah, "beats me. But there, these things keep to date, look see, an' if the English climate ain't keepin' to date along wi' the football us can't 'elp it. If us was to start relyin' on the climate us'd get nowhere, look see."

"Tides are more reliable, eh, Obadiah?" said David. "You know where you are with a tide."

"Ah!" said Obadiah, and shaded his eyes to look at the distant line of the sea. "Yet Oi've knowed tides what be-'aved pretty contrary at times. The autumn an' spring tides, now, Oi've knowed 'em be up to their tricks. Like 'orses, they be. They'll run in 'arness quiet as you please fur many a year an' then one day sudden loike, one on 'em will kick free an' savage ee."

David had a sudden vision of chaste Diana, charioteer of the moon, driving a great team of blue-green plunging horses, like the sea horse in his room at Damerosehay. He could see her, tall and serene, driving them backwards and forwards, controlling them at will; until one day one of the reins broke and one solitary horse dashed in too far, swift and terrible, galloping in over the marshes with a welter of mad white foam flying up from the spurn of his feet. Obadiah was like that; with just a few growled words he had the power to create strange, satisfying pictures in the mind.... Or, judging by poor Ben's state of mind, rather horrible ones.... David controlled his imaginings and remembered what he was here for. The book would be indoors. He must maneuver the party there.

"Got that clock still, Obadiah?" he asked.

Obadiah, who had been doing the honors of his garden, smiled broadly and promptly led the way indoors. His

164

grandfather clock was his most cherished possession and a joy not only to him but to every child who ever entered his cottage. It was a perpetual delight to Ben, Tommy and Caroline, and it had been an even greater one to David in his childhood. . . . He and his dream boy, he could remember, had visited it constantly.

And even now he went to it with eagerness, sparing hardly a glance for Obadiah's charming neat little kitchen with its snowy scrubbed stone floor, gay rag rugs and gilt-framed oleographs of ships in storms, gallant ships climbing "hills of seas Olympus high," with behind them inky-black clouds rent by lightning.

But the grandfather clock was truly remarkable and the crown of Obadiah's possessions. He never said how he had come to possess it, and his reticence upon the subject had led to the current belief that the old scoundrel had stolen it.

David was immediately, as ever, so enthralled by it as it stood opposite the window, bathed in light, that he failed to notice that Ben, after entering hesitantly behind him, had slipped back into the garden as though afraid, taking the dogs with him. And Ben was usually such a passionate worshiper of Obadiah's clock.

It was very old, quite small as grandfather clocks go, and must have been made, its admirers thought, at the Hard, the ship-building yard on the Abbey River where more than a hundred years ago the greatest of England's ships had been built and launched. The slender length of it was built of forest oak, beautifully fashioned and carved, but its chief glory was the clock face where at each hour, instead of the usual numeral, there was the picture of a sailing ship. The ship at one o'clock had bare masts, with just one little sail hoisted to indicate the hour, and then as the day went on the sails blossomed out upon the masts one by one until at twelve o'clock a great ship like a blossoming rose was seen sailing triumphantly into the sunset. The little pictures were faintly colored, with blue and green for the sea, scarlet and gold for the setting sun and green dolphins and rainbow-tinted sea horses disporting themselves around the ships. The clock did not go any more, and the hands stood perpetually at one o'clock, that hour when something that has ended begins all over again; yet if it was no longer of practical use it was still a glorious work of art, and rejoicing in it afresh David looked round for Ben to share his delight.

"Why, he's gone!" he exclaimed.

Obadiah, coughing sepulchrally behind his horny hand, looked exceedingly self-conscious.

"Look here, Obadiah," said David suddenly, sitting on the table edge. "That boy's scared stiff at something you showed him here. What was it?"

A look of relief spread over Obadiah's mahogany features. "Oi'm right glad to tell ee of it, Master David," he said. "It's worritted me considerable as the boy should 'ave seen. It weren't Oi showed un. 'E found un 'isself, look see. Real put about Oi was. 'E opened the clock when me back was turned. Out in the garden, Oi were, an' 'im alone inside."

"The clock?" exclaimed David, and immediately was on his feet, opening it. Wedged behind the pendulum that now swung no longer was a battered old book with worn brown leather covers. With an exclamation David took it out.

"Bring un outside," suggested Obadiah. "There's sun outside. More 'olesome, look see."

They carried out Obadiah's two Windsor chairs and sat beside the glorious blue hydrangea. Then, at Obadiah's suggestion, they lit their pipes. When these were well started, and they were settled as cozily as cats in the sun, Obadiah signified that David might open the book. He was being very careful of David's nerves. To him David was still a little boy, and his experience of Ben had taught him that the nerves of educated little boys were what he called "roight gaggly ..." Ben and the dogs had completely disappeared.

David lifted the cover and immediately gave an exclamation of delight. He was looking at a spirited picture of dancing dolphins executed in pen and ink, with faint washes of color. It was lovely, the work of a fine artist. He ruffled the pages of the book and saw that it was full of drawings. Then he turned back to exult in the dolphins again. The edges of the page were stained and spotted with damp and age, but the picture itself was hardly hurt at all. It was almost as fresh as when it had been drawn. He turned the page and saw a ship in full sail; he turned another page and saw some exquisite studies of sea horses. Something familiar about these challenged his attention.

"Obadiah!" he exclaimed, "these are studies for the clock face! Did you realize that?"

"Aye," said Obadiah, puffing unmoved at his clay pipe.

"But they're beautiful," cried David. "They're exquisite. There's nothing here to frighten a child."

"Ee'd need to turn on a bit further, look see," said Obadiah ominously.

David turned on further, but he still saw only great beauty; more sailing ships and strange, richly imagined sea creatures, the graceful shapes of sea birds in flight, minutely observed and evidently most passionately loved; a splendid little sketch of a launching at the Hard, with the ship lying ready in the slips, the cheering crowd and a group of seamen, the ships' officers no doubt, standing tense and expectant on a raised platform. David recognized this scene quite easily; he knew the lovely curve of the Abbey River and the woods beyond, and the row of workmen's cottages that was still to be seen at the Hard. After this picture came another of a sailing ship, the best of all. She was a grand creature with a fine carved poop and forecastle, wind-filled sails crowding up aloft and the foam curling back in delicate curves and arabesques from her splendid prow. Something was written very faintly beneath this picture, and David bent low to make it out. First came some illegible name, and then these words, "The first ship I have had the honor to command. Launched at the Hard on April 6th in the year of Our Lord 1816. May God bless her, and find me worthy of my trust."

David leaned back in the hard Windsor chair and gazed through the sun-warmed spaces of limpid air to the far-off sea. Those quiet yet proud words had somehow touched him very deeply. The artist in him leaped out to meet the artist in this unknown sea captain. It was as though at that moment they were made friends. There is always, he thought, this communion between the men who follow the great professions—doctors, priests, artists and sailors. Those are the selfless professions that demand all that a man can give, even sometimes to his very life, the professions that make him or break him according as he has it in him to give what they demand. David sagged a little in his chair, feeling suddenly overwhelmingly conscious of his own many failures, of the times when as an artist he had aimed rather for personal power than for the power of interpretation, of the times when he had shrunk from giving the last ounce of his strength to his work, holding always a little back through fear of fatigue, of those other times when the applause of a great audience had been too sweet to him. He did not think that other man would ever have shrunk from personal danger, however great the tempest, or that anything whatever would have deflected him from the course he must pursue. David had no real reason for his conviction; yet he had it. For he knew this man, knew him to be courageous, indomitable, yet sensitive and highly strung too; his drawings showed that; a man who would feel weakness and fear but who yet would never yield to them. In the quiet and silence of the marshes one spirit mutely reverenced the other.

"Ee'd best turn on," said Obadiah's voice, suddenly shattering the silence with an almost brutal note.

Startled by it, David pulled himself upright in his chair and turned on. There were a few blank pages and then, turning another, he had a hideous, a sickening shock. His mind seemed to reel under it, he felt physical nausea and a sense of terrible desolation. It seemed that he fell quite suddenly from the sunshine to the slime of the pit. Yet he turned on and on, page after page. In spite of his horror he could not stop himself.

What had happened? It was the same artist, possessed of the same genius, but some fearful change had taken place in him. He was seeing the world differently, seeing it with a mind distorted. His pictures now were of death, of agony and despair. They were pictures of war, of famine and pestilence, of cruelty and hatred. David had never seen anything so horrible.

Yet, as his mind grew steadier and he turned back the pages to look at them all again, he found that they were not evil. They were drawn not with a love of evil but a hatred of it. There was a strange mystical feeling in them all that reminded him a little of the drawings of William Blake. In one of them what at first sight seemed a plowed field waiting for the corn was really a bare ridged plain where each ridge was a long line of dead bodies, slaughtered soldiers laid head to feet unendingly; yet the whole of the sky, that formed the background, was composed of clouds shaped like outspread wings. Another, that showed the corruption going on beneath the surface of a graveyard, showed also a little copse above it filled with singing birds. Undoubtedly these were the pictures of a man whose full sanity had left him but who still retained at the core of his being something changeless that his friends could know him by. David felt that he still knew him, still reverenced him, and in spite of the horror wanted to know him better.

"Obadiah," he said, "may I take the book? It's appalling, but I want it."

Obadiah removed his clay pipe from his mouth and spat significantly. "That's more'n Oi do. *Oi* don't want un," he said. "Never knew 'twas in that dratted clock till after Oi'd brought un 'ere."

"Obadiah," said David, "how in the world did you get hold of that clock?"

"Ah," said Obadiah, and, reinserting his pipe in his mouth, closed his old lips on it very firmly.

"Come on, Obadiah," urged David. "Tell me. It's between friends."

"Oi took un, look see," said Obadiah. "Always partial to that thur cloak, Oi wur, an' the old Master, old Jeremy Martyn, did say Oi should 'ave un after 'e died. But 'e died sudden loike, an' thur warn't no will found. So Oi just up wi' un one evenin', afore the lawyer chap 'ad time to get 'ere, lays un on me barrer an' wheels un out 'ere."

"Very sensible of you," said David with a grin. He always *had* vowed that clock had come originally from Damerosehay. It had a sort of Damerosehay flavor about it. "I'll not mention it, of course."

"Ah," said Obadiah.

"That yarn you told the boys," said David, "that yarn about Jeremy being buried under the ilex tree, was it just a yarn?"

"True as gospel," said Obadiah. "Shoveled earth in on un meself, Oi did. Don't ee go fur to tell 'er Ladyship or Miss Margaret, an' don't ee let those young varmints, what nearly dug un up, tell 'em neither. Mid a bin all over trimble, them two ladies, look see."

David was not at all sure that Lucilla and Margaret would be scared. With women, you never knew what would scare them and what wouldn't. But he promised. There was a lot more he wanted to find out from Obadiah and he wanted him in a good temper.

"Obadiah," he said, "was Jeremy Martyn any relation to Aramante du Plessis-Pascau?"

"'E told Oi," said Obadiah, "as 'e wur 'er son. But ee couldn't pay no attention to what 'e said. Childish, 'e wur, at the last. Put flowers on 'er grave, 'e did, summer an' winter; grew un special."

"You never told us that, Obadiah," said David.

"Ah," said Obadiah. "No better than 'er should be, from all Oi've 'eard, look see."

"There was no husband that you ever heard of?" queried David tactfully.

"Not that Oi ever 'eard on," said Obadiah, and suddenly spat again, reinserted his pipe and shut his mouth upon it like a trap. His old face had a very closed look now, and David saw that he was going to get nothing more out of him. He did not know whether Obadiah's sudden reticence came from loyalty to the past or a desire not to contaminate the present, or whether it was simply the wish of an old man not to be bothered with questions when he didn't feel like it. Anyway he realized that as far as Obadiah was concerned the session was now closed, and he got up and held out his hand.

Obadiah got up too, removed his pipe and gripped

172

David's slim hand in his huge horny one. He was devoted to David. The loyalty he had once given to Jeremy Martyn, and then to Lucilla, he now gave to David, who from many little signs that he had seen he did not doubt would be the heir of Damerosehay. He was of the old school. This bit of earth, comprising the marshes, his cottage, Little Village and the house of Damerosehay, with the owner of Damerosehay as the symbol of it, was his whole world and had his whole devotion. " 'Tis good," he told David, "to 'ave 'ad proper sensible folk in the old 'ouse this last twenty year. Not but what Oi weren't rarely fond o' the old Master, Oi was that, proper good to the poor 'e wur, but 'tis good to 'ave sensible folk. Master David, Oi 'ope ee'll be at Damerosehay many a long year. All on us 'opes that i' these parts."

He wrung David's hand hard, then jerked his pipe stem over his shoulder. "The lad's in wood," he said. "Goo' arternoon, Master David. See ee termorrer-day," and he turned immediately back to his labor in his garden. He could express himself well, with all a countryman's fine simplicity of feeling, but it was not his way to prolong a sentimental moment.

David, the book under his arm, went into the wood in search of Ben with feelings suddenly grown cold and desolate. He too, like Obadiah, was old-fashioned in his feelings about place and service. It was good to have a bit of the earth that was really your own, and good to be served by men whose hearts were as bound to it as yours. It was this mutual bond that justified the fact of service, even glorified it. It was bitter that he must lose all this.

Bitter but inevitable. And it would have been harder still, impossibly harder, to lose Nadine.

But in the wood he recovered himself; it was so long since he had been in a wood, and he found the magic of the trees as healing as ever. The pungent autumn smell of the wood, the crackle of the twigs under his feet and the soft squelch of the wet moss, the pattern of the intertwined branches over his head and the sighing of them as the wind passed over them, these were good things and not to be exchanged for all the riches of the world.

He found Ben and the dogs where he expected to find them, in a place that all four of them knew of, a clearing in the wood where a fallen tree trunk lay like a bridge across the stream and where the swiftly flowing water, tinted golden-brown by the iron in it that came down from the forest land above, was so clear that you could count all the pebbles on the bottom. Bramble bushes grew all round, colored by the autumn to the brilliance of fire, and the moss here was deeper and greener than anywhere else. Ben sat on the tree trunk, dangling his legs over the water, and the dogs splashed happily in the sun-flecked shallows of the stream.

"You ran away, Ben," said David.

"Yes," said the little boy and hung his head.

David swung himself out along the tree trunk to sit by Ben. It was a rather perilous position in which to examine a precious volume, but a perfect one in which to face a terrible fact of life. The book might fall into the water at any moment, but all around them was such loveliness and peace, and in front of them, through a break in the trees, they could see a perfect view of the marshes, the sea and the sky.

"The pictures are perfectly horrible, old man," said David. "I don't blame you for panicking. I was scared stiff myself, and even Obadiah doesn't think them pretty."

Ben let out a shuddering sigh of relief. It was extraordinarily comforting that other people should be frightened too. Ben had all the horror of being abnormal of a supersensitive person. So often he had found that other people didn't feel about things as he did, and it made him feel very lonely. It was consoling to have David's companionship in fear.

"But you see, Ben," David went on, "they're not quite true. They're exaggerated. I grant you that death can be dreadful, but it's not as bad as this. You see it was a sick man who drew these last pictures, and a healthy man who drew the first ones, and the truth about things is somewhere between the two. When we feel well and jolly we see the happy side of life, and are inclined to think that's all there is to it, and when we're sick we see the seamy side and are inclined to think that's all there is to it too. You've got to get both sides, and not exaggerate either of them, before you get the truth.... And even then you only get the shadow of it."

Ben did not quite understand, but he took the book from David and began bravely to look at the pictures again, first the happy ones and then the awful ones.

But he found, this time, that the awful ones were not quite so awful as he had thought they were. He had not noticed, for instance, until David pointed it out, that in that picture where the dead soldiers lay line upon line like the furrows of a plowed field the clouds above were formed of spread wings. And there were other comforting things, in the other pictures, that he had not noticed either until David showed them to him.

"How odd that I shouldn't have noticed," he said.

"The nice things aren't drawn in a noticeable way," said David. "Besides, you weren't looking properly before. The horror of the pictures stunned you and you didn't look them steadily in the eye, so to speak."

"Well, I have now," said Ben, "and it's not as bad as I thought." He gave a great sigh of relief. "I shan't think about it in the night any more; or if I do I'll remember the wings. . . . Surely it's tea time?"

Examination of David's watch proved that it was long after. David was heartily thankful, for he found the guidance and instruction of the young most exhausting. In fact he had found the whole day most exhausting. There had already begun in him a mental conflict of which he was not fully aware, and of all things in this life an unrecognized conflict is most wearing to nerves and body.

Because they were so late they had a tray of tea brought to them in the drawing room and Lucilla sat with them while they ate it. At least David, thirsty after the walk in the sun, merely drank, but Ben ate everything there was to eat with an appetite astonishing in one who had so recently been in the grip of distress. He seemed very happy now. David hoped the load of horror had been left behind in the wood forever.

Lucilla, except for dark circles round her eyes, seemed

176

herself again. While her grandsons ate and drank she sat by the fire, a piece of needlework in her hands, and told them tales of when their fathers had been boys. She excelled at these tales; the long past that stretched behind her, upon which she looked back as though she saw it framed in a window at sunset, was more precious to her now than it had ever been; she could take from it one incident after the other, seeing them now with their inevitable past and future as perfect rounded things, and show them to her hearers as jewels of great price. "You cannot judge anything without its context," she said now, suddenly, after several tales. "And you cannot judge the value of what happens to you until many years afterwards. Then you see how one thing led to another and how it was all, even the little trivial things as well as the big ones, somehow necessary."

David thought that she was trying to comfort herself in this grief that he had brought upon her, trying to feel that this tangle of family life would somehow get unraveled and the perfect pattern that she was trying to weave for them all be seen again. He got up abruptly and went to her, standing before the fire looking down at her, his hand resting on the old carved mantel. But when she looked up and smiled at him he could not bear it; he loved her so much. "I'll go upstairs," he said.

"You've letters to write?" said Lucilla evenly. "The post goes at seven, dear. When you've finished put yours with mine on the hall table and Rose will take them to post as usual."

As David went through the hall he noticed that she had

written only one letter, and that it was addressed in her clear beautiful handwriting to Mrs. George Eliot. She did not usually, he thought, use her son's Christian name when addressing her daughter-in-law; it was generally just Mrs. Eliot. But now it was different; now the battle was joined; and even on an envelope Lucilla was insisting that Nadine belonged to George, divorce or no divorce, and should to the end.

Upstairs in his room David put away the book in the drawer of his writing table and sat down to write to Nadine. He wrote persuasively. She must leave her partner in charge of the shop, take her holiday now, and come. It would be hateful, but they must go through with it. It was only fair to Lucilla. How could they expect her to try to understand their point of view if they made no effort to understand hers? And she must understand their point of view. He couldn't bear it if she didn't. He wanted her to realize the greatness of their love, and to understand too that what they were doing they were doing for the sake of truth.

Yet when he had written the letter he wondered a little uneasily if Nadine would obey the summons. He never felt quite sure of what she would do under given circumstances; he did not know her well enough yet; he was never sure to what extent their outlook coincided. So often, when he talked, she just smiled and said nothing. But she loved him, he believed, as deeply as he loved her. His letter finished, he dropped his head in his hands and thought of her love, and instantly his body was burning and his pulses throbbing as though she were with him in the room. Against the darkness of his closed eyes he could see her adorable beauty, and his longing for her was almost unbearable. Everything else was forgotten. There was only Nadine. The fact of her filled the whole of life. She was the only reality.

Half an hour later he went downstairs to put his letter on the hall table beside Lucilla's. He had addressed it to Nadine by her professional name—Miss Nadine Marsh.

CHAPTER SIX

I.

NADINE ANSWERED BY return that she would be at Damerosehay in a couple of days. She wrote charmingly to Lucilla in a letter that Lucilla handed David to read, even though she knew that the sweetness of it would increase his infatuation tenfold. But she was determined that in this struggle she would have no secrets from David. Come what might they should respect each other throughout, for if they lost their mutual respect they would to a certainty lose their love.

David could not be so open in return, for Nadine's letter to him could not possibly be shown to Lucilla. "Very well, David," she wrote, "since you want it I will come. But I think you are making a mistake in giving way to Lucilla over this. It is never pleasant for a man to have two women fighting over him, especially when he loves them both. You will be horribly mangled, darling. For that is what it comes to, David; are you to belong to Lucilla or to me? It is a measure of my trust in you that I dare to come, for Lucilla will be a powerful adversary. But I do dare to come. I love you utterly, as you love me. I shall win. But one thing I do refuse to do, David, and that is to see you first in the bosom of the family and dogs. I have told Lucilla

I will arrive at four o'clock. I won't. I will be at the corner by the cornfield at half-past two."

David wished she had not said that. It jarred upon him. Now he would have to slip away furtively, or else to prevaricate. It was odd how the finest of women seemed to love intrigue. It would be good to have that hour and a half with her alone, but not worth it at the price of honesty. They would have many other times of being alone, times when they could walk off together openly. Then he resolutely crushed his momentary disappointment in her. Nadine was perfect in thought and word and deed.

The children were wild with excitement. Mother coming to stay! Mother coming to stay for perhaps two whole weeks! They rooted up armfuls of flowers out of the garden, Margaret enduring their onslaughts with stoical, smiling fortitude, and garlanded the staircase and the hall, the nursery and Nadine's bedroom. With amazing unselfishness they denuded themselves of their white mice and Queenie the chameleon, and ranged these upon Nadine's mantelpiece. Suggestions that Mother might not appreciate livestock in her bedroom were not attended to. Of course she would! They had not yet arrived at the age when they could conceive it possible that tastes differ. If they gave people what they liked themselves they were then quite sure that they had given pleasure.

The children's attitude to the mother whom they did not now see very often was very individual. They all adored her, greeted her comings with ecstasy and her goings with grief; she was to all three of them the sun and moon and stars, all the more adorable because she seemed nowadays to be always a little out of their reach.

But apart from their adoration their attitude towards her varied with their characters. Ben had for her a feeling of chivalrous protection. He was old enough to recognize her beauty and to worship it, and her quite misleading look of frailty made him long to fight dragons on her behalf, protect her from gangsters and their like, even die for her if occasion should arise. Only occasion never did seem to arise, and his protectiveness was accepted by Nadine with a tolerant amusement that hurt him quite horribly.

Tommy was never hurt by his mother; he was perhaps the only person whom she did not, at times, hurt rather badly. It is possible that he unconsciously understood her better than anyone else did, and certain that he was her favorite child. She made no secret of the fact that he was her best beloved and he traded upon her love with the utmost wickedness. Everything that he wanted to possess he got out of her when she came to stay, anything forbidden that he wanted to do he did while she was there, so that she might take his part when Ellen's wrath fell upon him. He knew that she always would. He knew that she, like himself, could not, simply could not, live without what she wanted. To both of them what they wanted was like a shining lamp hanging in the darkness. If they could not have it then they were in darkness indeed, a terrible outer darkness that only they could understand. And to both of them, restless as they were, this lamp was rather like a will-o'-the-wisp. It was continually on the move. No sooner had they grasped one joy than they wanted another. Such restlessness should have made them miserable; yet in Tommy's case it troubled him not at all, and Nadine only sometimes, for their will-o'-the-wisps led them on to such glorious adventures, and they loved adventures. And then again each fresh joy as they captured it was so full of satisfaction that they were apt to forget all that was past and all that was to come in the joy of the present. Denied adventures they both had it in them to be desperately, terribly unhappy.

Caroline's love was infinitely pathetic in its hopelessness. She still looked to Nadine for that love of a mother who loves her child more than any other being in the world, but she knew in the depths of her that she would never get it. Her unconscious knowledge was at the root of her shrinking from human contact, her low opinion of the human race; personified in Nadine, it so cruelly failed her. Yet Nadine couldn't altogether help her failure; she did try very hard to be all that she should be to her funny little daughter; but the fact was that she did not appreciate women at all, not at any age. Her mother had died in her babyhood and she had been brought up in a family of brothers, the only girl, and could not understand her own sex. She was a man's woman through and through. . . . But she would have wept could she have known what was Caroline's most precious memory, a memory of her father sitting by her on the nursery hearthrug, just before he left her apparently forever, stroking her shining bell of hair with his forefinger and telling her that he liked little girls better than little boys, yes, much better. Only Caroline's remembering mind, because her father had gone away and now she could hardly visualize him at all, tried hard to substitute her mother's figure for that of her father, tried hard but did not quite succeed.

When David left the house at a quarter past two, ostensibly for a walk, they were all three on the stairs tying tall sunflowers to the banisters so that it seemed that the stairs, all the way up, were lit by flaming torches. "Don't be back late," they called to him. "Mother will be here at four."

"Shall just Tommy and Caroline and me meet her at the cornfield at four?" Ben asked David. "Or will you come too?"

His tone was sweetly courteous but his eyes were pleading and his meaning was quite plain, and David's heart smote him.

"At four I'll be out somewhere," he said. "Not at the cornfield. Your mother will want you to meet her quite by yourselves. Call the dogs, will you? I'm not taking them."

"Not taking the dogs? Why ever not?" gasped Ben. It was unheard of that anyone should go for a walk and not take the dogs. They were already expectantly present, barking joyously, Pooh-Bah dancing on his hind legs and the Bastard alternately crouching on the ground, tail violently in motion, eyes shining through his mat of hair, and making sudden rushing onslaughts upon David as though to push the dilatory man out of doors into the wind and sunshine and the glorious smells that live there for all God's four-legged creatures.

"No," said David. "I don't want them today. No. Not today."

A sudden terrible blight fell upon both dogs. A cold proud grief froze Pooh-Bah's leaping body to an awful stillness, and the Bastard's tail, though still waving, waved ever more faintly, and his eyes, fixed upon David with a pleading that hoped on to the very last, dimmed as though with tears.

"Oh, David!" mourned Ben, sharing to the full in this awful desolation.

David had to clear his throat guiltily before he could speak again. "Not today," he said at last. "No. Some other day. Tomorrow. Not today."

"You might at least say you're sorry," said Tommy, outraged.

"I *am* sorry," said David. "I'm awfully sorry. I can't say how sorry I am. Tomorrow we'll go. Tomorrow."

Pooh-Bah turned his back with great dignity and stalked away into the furthest recesses of the hall, where the door of a particularly dark cupboard had been left open. He entered the cupboard and lay down in the darkness upon a heap of croquet mallets. He was suffering, but he came of a great and royal race and no one should see him suffer. The Bastard did not care who saw him suffer. His tail sank to the ground and he crouched yet lower, laying his chin dejectedly upon his paws. His eyes became dark pools of sorrow and tears trickled out of the corners of them.

The children, grouped upon the stairs in utter silence, gazed at David in reproach too deep for words. He opened the front door and fled. It had been even worse than he had expected.

2.

But once through the oak wood his sense of guilt gave way before a winged, exultant joy. Winged, he thought, is the only word for that joy that is like a live creature within one striving to lift one off one's feet. It is hard to walk; one wants to run, to fly. The body seems bound about that joy like bands of iron; there is physical pain in the restriction of it, throbbing temples and panting breath, a mortal body with immortal longings in it. For joy is born of longing, thought David: longing that is running to its satisfaction.

Once past Little Village, David began to run along the coast road as excitedly as a few days before the children had run to meet him. It was absurd of him, he knew, and extremely childish, but he didn't care. In a first onslaught of joy or grief we are all of us children; it is only as we deal with the havoc that they have created that we show what the years have taught us. He was vaguely aware, as he ran, of the beauty of the day, clear-shining after a spell of rain, of the misted sea, the golden sun and the shimmer of white wings. It looked as though a spell of fine weather was on the way, for the country people had a saying:

> *When the mist comes from the hill*
> *Then bad weather it doth spill;*
> *When the mist comes from the sea*
> *Then good weather it will be.*

That was as it should be, and as it always was. Nadine had that kind of beauty which seemed to impel natural things to give her always the perfect setting.

He was too early, of course. He had time to sit on the gate opposite the cornfield in the marsh and laugh at himself; to think how silly it was that his pulse should be racing and his head swimming. To steady himself he tried to fix his attention on the silver mist that drove in from the sea and listen to the wind in the corn and a lark dipping and soaring above it like the lark in Van Gogh's picture. But it was no good. Nadine was in the mist, the wind, the birdsong, everywhere. The thought of her seemed the pulse that kept the world alive.

Yet when she actually did come she took him by surprise. Her battered old car had crept round the corner and was beside him before he knew it.

"David," she said, stretching her hand out through the window.

He did not respond very much; not here; not in this public place.

"Get out," he commanded her hoarsely. "Back the car up here into the gate and get out."

Nadine laughed. She enjoyed the love of young men. The depth of feeling that was almost rude in its savage eagerness was delightfully stimulating to a woman whose first youth was lost. She felt deliciously young again, as young as David.

He had opened the door and pulled her out before she had time to clutch bag or scarf. Then he took her wrist and ran with her over the hard brittle stalks of the cornfield, up over the ridge of shingle that had once wrecked the grain ship, across another stretch of marsh, over another shingle bank and so down to a strip of silver sand. The sea washed right in here. Stretches of blue water flung themselves in lovely half-moons of wind-rippled color almost to their feet, and at their backs the piled shingle hid them from sight.

David let go of Nadine's wrist and put his arms round her, gently at first, then straining so tightly that she was breathless. She could feel the pulse throbbing in his cheek as she put up her hand and held it against hers and the beating of his heart pressed so tightly against her body. Tears pricked her eyelids. It was sweet, this love that had come to her just when she had been so saddened and so weary, it was lovelier than anything she had ever known. She yielded to David's passion for a moment or two, returning it to the full, then withdrew herself a little. She never gave a man quite all that he wanted. That was no way to foster love.

"David," she said. Her voice was very gentle, but a little maternal. "David, let go at once."

"I'm sorry," he said, and flushed a little. His love for Nadine was so overwhelming that it always made him go a little too far. He was ashamed then. Nadine was too fine a woman to be treated like that.

"It's all right, darling," she said, and touched his hot cheek with her finger. "I love your bear hugs, only I didn't want my ribs cracked. I still have Tommy's affection to face."

David felt absurdly stabbed. So often, by classing him

with her children, she made him feel a child, and it hurt him. This love of his, that was driving him to sacrifice and outrage so much, was surely no childish thing. But then Nadine did not quite understand the depth of his love for Lucilla and Damerosehay. She did not, could not, know how much she was costing him.

But she sensed the hurt in him and was quick to heal it. Her momentary passion, her assurance, left her, and one of her enchanting little-girl moods was upon her like dew on a flower. This was the one of her many moods that David loved best, and she knew it. It made him feel mature, older than she was, more certain of her, when she stood still and straight like that, waiting for him to take the initiative, her mouth sweet and shy and her eyes wide with expectation like a little girl at a party. He was smiling as he took her arm protectively and led her over to the old rowing boat, half buried in the sand, where they could sit and watch the ripples creaming up to their feet and the stately passing and repassing of the gulls across the sky.

"Isn't it quiet, Nadine?" he said. "Isn't it quiet?"

Nadine nodded. Though she did not love Damerosehay as the rest of the family did, yet she loved it. She sat still, folded in its peace, her hands linked lightly round her knees.

David watched her, worshiping her. "With my body I thee worship." He had always liked the sentences in the marriage service. Lover of words as he was, he was sorry that a marriage in a registry office gave one nothing lovely to say to the woman one loved. Never mind, he would say them now. "For better for worse, for richer for poorer,

189

in sickness and in health, to love and to cherish, till death us do part. With my body I thee worship, and with all my worldly goods I thee endow.... And thereto I give thee my troth."

"David!" laughed Nadine. "You're absurd!"

Her laughter might have hurt him again, only Nadine when she laughed was so enchanting. Her dark eyes, then, were so full of light, and her low laugh had a soft caressing quality that warmed and comforted and was a lovely contrast to the white austerity of her beauty. It was her contrasts that gave Nadine so unique a loveliness. Her great dark eyes and softly curling dark hair were almost startling against the ivory pallor of her face, and her gallant, almost boyish figure, combined with her very feminine and rather sensuous grace, made people look and look again, touched and even troubled by her beauty. "Troubling" was an adjective that very accurately described Nadine. Her joyousness, together with that hint of intensity that suggested that she might be able to suffer very deeply, were very troubling; so was her rather reckless courage, that took delight sometimes in flying in the face of all safety, law and order.... Even her clothes were troubling to those conservative minds who take a fancy to a particular fashion only when it is going out.

Nadine, somehow or other, always managed to be almost ahead of fashion. If they wanted to know the latest, the female Eliots only had to look at Nadine; and when they did look at her they experienced shock and incredulity not unmixed with envy. For Nadine was so clever over her outrageous clothes. She had never had much money to spend on them, but she could knot a vivid scarf round her shoulders with just the right air of devilry, pin a bunch of camellias on the shoulder of an evening dress in exactly the most enchanting position, and wear wicked hats at an angle that however outrageous did not detract one whit from her austere and lovely dignity.... Though how it was that she gave this impression of austerity no one had the slightest idea.

Except David, who knew it was because she always possessed herself. Whatever mad thing she was doing he knew she had planned to do it, willed it, and was in perfect command of the situation. Even this love that had come between them never swept her off her feet as it did him. In the beginning he had fought against it and been beaten. Nadine had not done that. When she had found that she loved David she had taken her love, looked at it, known it was what she longed for and resolutely taken it to her.

"David, dear," she said, "have things been very detestable?"

"It was detestable telling Grandmother," said David slowly.

"I told you it would be," said Nadine. "You should have written. There's something so decisive about a letter. What is written is written, down in black and white, not to be altered."

David did not answer. This question of the best way to tell Lucilla had led to the one and only quarrel that he and Nadine had ever had. He was still astonished and marveling that he had been the victor in that quarrel. He did not know that, just at the end, Nadine had let him win.

She had known instinctively that he needed, just then, to feel his power over her, and in the vital question of this marriage she was sure enough of her power over him to let him have his own way in smaller things. She was so certain that she could even afford to be sorry for Lucilla.

"Poor old Grandmother!" she said, and there was real compunction in her tone. She was much fonder of Lucilla than Lucilla was of her. She was genuinely sorry that she had to hurt her.

David felt a little shock of surprise. Somehow he never thought of Lucilla as old. Her unaging spirit in her aging body burned so strongly that he forgot the one in the other.

"I know it seems cruel to hurt so old a woman," went on Nadine; "yet when it is a question of sacrificing the happiness of two young people to the happiness of one old one I don't think there's any question of what the choice should be. Grandmother's life is nearly over. We have ours before us."

David did not answer because he was doubtful of her argument. If life went on beyond death this question of how much longer one had to live just did not apply; if one had all eternity there was neither youth nor age to be considered. Besides, the young of this generation had always hanging over them the nightmare of impending war. It was quite probable that Lucilla would live longer in this world than he would. No, the whole question was one of truth. But Nadine, he knew, did not quite see it like that. Where he sought truth she sought happiness. It was to her a divine and shining thing and she thought it her right to grasp it when she could.

"So let's be happy, Nadine," he begged. "We know we are doing right, so let's not question it for just this hour."

The appeal to happiness was one that never failed with Nadine. She jumped up and held out her hands to him, her eyes bright again with her party mood. Turning their faces eastward they walked quickly on the firm sand. To their left, though hidden from them by the ridge of shingle, were the marshes; the sea was on their right. The wind and the sun-shot mist blew over them and they laughed like children, swinging their clasped hands. The air and sunshine seemed to enclose them in a translucent crystal globe. Through it they could see dimly the sorrow of the world, but just for a little while they were safe inside it with their happiness.

It was David who remembered first that they ought to turn back. "The children want to meet you by themselves," he told Nadine. "I'll leave you by the car to wait for them and walk on towards the Forest."

They turned quickly, crossed the patch of marsh and the banks of shingle and were back in the old cornfield again. But they were too late. The children and the dogs were standing there by the car in a bewildered, puzzled little group, and Nadine's heart smote her intolerably.

She cried out to them, an inarticulate cry filled with her love and her remorse, and dropped on her knees among the stiff corn stalks with her arms held out. But they did not come to her with their usual headlong rush, and it was, most unexpectedly, Caroline who was first in her mother's arms. Never before had she been the first to get there; usually she hung back because she knew Mother liked little boys better than little girls. But today the boys were so slow that she couldn't help getting there first.

Nadine, her little girl clasped in her arms, looked questioningly over her head at her two sons. They were regarding her with a most unusual concentration: sorrowful upon the part of Ben, tinged with scorn in Tommy. For the first time in their lives they were highly critical of her, and she found it quite difficult to meet their eyes with smiling steadiness. It must come sooner or later, she knew, this moment when the children know for the first time that their mother is only a frail human creature after all, and can at moments fail them. But it is a bad moment. Very bad.

David fled from it. He went on up the rutted lane, and then across the main road and on through the lanes towards the Forest. He walked for miles, walked himself into the quietude of weariness, and was guilty of that unforgivable sin in the Damerosehay household: being late for dinner.

3.

Lucilla sat in the drawing room waiting for Nadine, as a few days ago she had waited for David. But her feelings now were very different. Then, relaxed by her happiness, her mind had wandered back into the past, and she had seen the way that she had traveled bathed in the rosy light of her present joy. In spite of its sorrow it had seemed an inevitable way, leading to the haven where now she was. Now, that haven threatened, she dared not look back; she feared to see too clearly the mistakes and failures of her own that had perhaps helped to bring about her present trouble. Somewhere, in her training of David, she must have gone wrong, or else his adherence to the Church she loved would not have been lost; she had, she remembered, pushed her own beliefs far too vigorously down his throat. Somewhere, in her handling of George's and Nadine's quarrel, she must have erred disastrously. She had been too interfering perhaps; probably it had been unwise to take her children from Nadine and leave her so lonely.

But it was too late now. She took a grip on herself. She had meant to do right and it did not do to dwell morbidly on mistakes that were past. She must continue to believe, as she had said to David and Ben a few days ago, that everything, even perhaps our mistakes, are necessary to the pattern. "But I must not make more now," she said to herself. "I must force nothing. Just once I will tell them the truth as I see it, that's my right, then I will be quiet. Surely the place will teach them: the house and its history, the garden, the birds and the children."

Then she laughed at herself a little, for she realized she was taking it for granted that she and Damerosehay thought alike, whereas it might be that Damerosehay would think with David.

"We all of us try to make God in our image," she said. "It is one of the worst of our temptations."

Then she did not think any more because through the gate in the garden wall she saw Nadine's car slide by. She had a quick feminine impulse to look at herself in the glass, to see if the beauty that still remained to her was at its best as a weapon in her hands, but she resisted the impulse; she was old and Nadine was young; that sort of warfare would be ludicrous now.

And then the door opened, Nadine and the children were with her, and every other feeling was drowned in intense curiosity as to what in the world Nadine had done to her hair. She erected her lorgnette and stared and stared again. Lucilla was a woman to her fingertips; even on her deathbed she would have postponed departure to investigate a new style of hairdressing upon the head of her nurse.

For she saw the new fashions so seldom at Damerosehay, and she delighted in fashion; though slightly scandalized by this new one of a married woman going about out of doors with no hat on and her hair brushed up on top of her head and held there in a bunch of curls like a baby in the bath. But how well Nadine dressed! Her plain tweed coat and skirt, though ridiculously short, were superbly cut and of the loveliest shade of green imaginable, and the bright silk scarf knotted round her throat perfectly and exactly matched her lipstick. Nadine's shoes were green too, Lucilla noted, and her pearl earrings lustrous and very large. Lucilla would have liked to have been able to describe these extras as vulgar, but in honesty she couldn't; there was that about Nadine which made whatever costume she wore appear dignified and seemly.

Lucilla's examination, though thorough, was swift. It was not polite to use her lorgnette in this way, she knew, and she was ashamed that the astonishment at Nadine's hair should have betrayed her into this momentary discourtesy. She came very sweetly to meet Nadine, took her face in her hands and kissed her; being very careful not to get anywhere near the lipstick, for though repeatedly assured by her family that the thing was kiss-proof she nevertheless had her doubts. "Welcome, my dear," she said gently.

A tiny flush stained the pallor of Nadine's face. Few things in this world embarrassed her, but her mother-in-law's lorgnette did. Somehow it always made her feel perfectly certain that she had a smut on her nose. She glanced for a moment into the glass to see, but her lovely face was unblemished as ever.

And lovelier than ever, thought Lucilla. She always forgot, between visits, how very arresting her daughter-in-law's beauty was, and today the sight of it made her feel almost weak with fright. What chance had she against it? It was a beauty to drive men mad. She understood David, and a little of her anger against him ebbed away. And some of her anger against Nadine too; such a woman could not help but be blinded, now and again, by the smoke from the fires that she kindled.

> *Love is a smoke raised with the fume of sighs;*
> *Being purged, a fire sparkling in lovers' eyes;*
> *Being vexed, a sea nourished with lovers' tears.*

The words came to her in David's clear voice, and she remembered that he had spoken them when he played Romeo.

> *Love is a flaming heart, and its flames aspire*
> *Till they cloud the soul in the smoke of a windy fire.*

197

She had read that somewhere, too. They were blinded, always, these poor lovers. They could not help themselves.

"You look very well, Nadine," she said gently. "Sit down, dear. Tea will be here in a moment."

Nadine sat down very meekly in a low chair by Lucilla and untied her scarf. How slender her hands were, thought Lucilla, and how exquisite the column of her throat. Now she came to look at it again, that absurd new style of hair-dressing suited her. It was like a coronet set upon her beauty.

"The children are going to have tea with us since you are here," said Lucilla. "And Margaret will be here in a moment. I don't know where David is. You met Mother, did you, darlings?"

"Yes," said Tommy, loudly and a little rudely, and bit deep into a bun, though the teapot had not yet arrived and no one had invited him to help himself. Ben said nothing. He just gazed at the sugar basin very, very sadly. Caroline, not fully understanding her mother's delinquency and much elated by having somehow or other been the first to be hugged by Mother, stood very close to her, her hand on her knee.

"Nice little midget," murmured Nadine, and kissed her daughter's smooth shining head. Caroline, overwhelmed with speechless joy, sucked her thumb ecstatically and gazed at her grandmother with shining eyes. It really almost seemed as though Mother had changed her mind and liked little girls best after all.

Lucilla could not understand it. Ben and Tommy were exuding from every pore that icy disapproval which a man, disappointed in his female relatives, can express so well in utter silence. Nadine and Caroline, on the other hand, feeling no doubt the bond of their sex, seemed drawing together. Yet while she talked to Lucilla and fondled Caroline, Nadine's eyes were continually wandering appealingly to her sons. But they would not meet her eyes. They were very, very displeased with her. Surely, thought Lucilla, Nadine had not already told the children about David? Lucilla could not believe it. Yet, if she had, it was obvious upon whose side the children were. With a lifting of the heart Lucilla realized that consciously or unconsciously, the children would be most potent advocates.

And then Ellen came in with the second-best teapot. Lucilla stared in astonishment. Why the second-best? They always had the best when there were guests.

"Good afternoon, madam," said Ellen coldly to Nadine, and set down the teapot with a resounding bang that all but cracked it.

"Good afternoon, Ellen," said Nadine. "It's a lovely day, isn't it?"

Ellen deigned no reply. She drew herself to her full height, sniffed, folded her bony hands at her waist and with one keen swift glance through her steel-rimmed spectacles told Nadine exactly what she thought of her. Then she left the room, closing the door with quite unnecessary firmness.

The incident was somehow completely shattering. At Ellen's glance Nadine had braced her shoulders as though she feared a blow and now, so unnerved that she quite forgot the children's presence, she turned startled eyes upon Lucilla. "Grandmother," she whispered, "did you tell her?"

"No, dear," whispered Lucilla, equally unnerved. "I didn't. David told me not to."

"Told you not to what?" demanded Tommy suddenly and very loudly.

Lucilla, who had also been momentarily oblivious of the children's presence, jumped, and turned anxious eyes on Nadine. Now she would know if Nadine had told the children.

"Nothing," said Nadine. "Hand me my tea, darling."

So Nadine hadn't told them. Lucilla was trembling so much that she had to use both hands to lift the teapot. It almost seemed as though children, like dogs, could sense things without being told.

It was a profound relief when Margaret, in her gardening clothes and bringing the freshness of the garden with her, came in to greet Nadine with that awkward admiration which was always hers when confronted with her beautiful sister-in-law. Her unawareness of strain in the atmosphere, her complete lack of envy as she sat there delighting shyly in Nadine's loveliness, were utterly refreshing. Dear Margaret! thought Lucilla, and her strained figure relaxed thankfully.

But in a moment Margaret had her taut again. "Why in the world," demanded Margaret, "are we welcoming Nadine with only the second-best teapot?"

CHAPTER SEVEN

I.

By TEN O'CLOCK in the morning Hilary had already done
what many people would have considered quite a good day's
work. He got up always at six, had his tepid bath, shaved
and dressed, donned the threadbare cassock he always wore
in the house as protection against the Vicarage draughts,
went downstairs to his study and prayed and meditated for
an hour. At seven forty-five he crossed the garden and the
lane to the small gray church half hidden among the great
churchyard yews, and struggled into his surplice and stole
in the vestry while Thomas Trickup, the verger, who was
also the village butcher, and a very excellent churchman
besides, tolled the bell. At eight Hilary said mass, his weekday congregation consisting, winter and summer alike, of
Trickup, Miss Marble from Lavender Cottage, Margaret
when she could get away, and a robin. On Sundays he had
quite a large congregation, for he had been Vicar of Fairhaven for over twenty years and had brought it up very
firmly in the way it should go, but it would take him another twenty years, if he lived as long, to persuade any but
the faithful four to come to church on a weekday. Yet
Fairhaven liked to hear the bell tolling out every morning,
sounding through the winter darkness as though to tell them

that the night was over or ringing through the spring and summer birdsong like another bird calling in the sky. The ungodly, rousing from sleep, set their watches by this bell, and the godly, whilst also setting their watches, remembered that at this hour Hilary was praying for them. They were glad of that, for they liked Hilary.

The least intuitive among his colleagues sometimes wondered why it was that Hilary was so popular a parish priest. He was not very clever, and certainly nothing to look at with his limp, his bald head and his tendency to stoutness; and evidently the powers that be thought little of him, for, having more than twenty years ago rewarded his patriotism with the gift of a parish and a stipend almost too microscopic to be seen, they had now apparently forgotten all about him: vicar of Fairhaven he still was and would be, presumably, forever. But there were others who did understand why Hilary was so well liked, and they envied him. For Hilary was an utterly unselfconscious and therefore a completely happy man, and none are so well-loved as the utterly happy.

Not all the credit was his; Lucilla had handed on to her eldest child her own delightful enjoyment of little things; but a good deal of it was. He had found out early in life that people did not find him very interesting, and his humility had decided that they were probably quite right. If they didn't bother about him neither would he bother about himself. To the best of his ability he would do the work he loved in the world he loved and think no more about it; if it turned out at the last that the one had helped the other he would be glad, but it would be arrogant to feel any certainty about that in this present life, and weakening to worry over it. A wise countryman, not gifted with great and compelling gifts, should pass steadily and quietly on his way, not questioning too much or expecting too much, unhurried as the seasons that regulate his life, disciplined by their rhythm, facing ever outwards to the wide horizons that are his special treasure. So Hilary argued, and so he lived, and as the years went on was, unknown to himself, regarded with ever-increasing affection.

Yet even had he realized the world's changing attitude towards him it is doubtful if he could have been much happier. He had adjusted himself so well to the shortcomings of his personality and the hardships of his life that they fitted him as comfortably as the lumps in his hard bed. He was quite at home now with his inability to write a good sermon and the draughts and ugliness of his red brick vicarage, and the physical pain that had been with him since the wounds of the war was now an old friend. Against the background of these things the riches of his life shone as gaily as the little red berries on the somber churchyard yews. He was very rich, he considered, above all in the possession of that old gray church, the way that led to it and the prayers that he said in it. These things seemed to him peculiarly his own, and beyond price.

Nearly a week after Nadine's arrival he crossed his garden as usual at seven forty-five. It was a glorious morning. The summer had been drenchingly wet, but since Nadine came they had been enjoying one of those glorious mellow spells of autumn sunshine that last on and on until they are finally shattered by the equinoctial gales. It had been splendid harvest weather, thought Hilary with satisfaction, and stopped still in the lane outside his garden to rejoice in the warmth and the clear light, and the thought of all those golden stooks of corn that had ringed in his parish like the tented encampments of fairy sultans. Country life was good, he thought. Among all the terrible complexities of modern life it was blessedly unchanging.

> *Here in the country's heart*
> *Where the grass is green,*
> *Life is the same sweet life*
> *As it e'er hath been.*

> *Trust in a God still lives,*
> *And the bell at morn*
> *Floats with a thought of God*
> *O'er the rising corn.*

> *God comes down in the rain,*
> *And the crop grows tall—*
> *This is the country faith,*
> *And the best of all.*

Hilary's memory was stored with the hymns that he taught his squeaking little choir boys and he murmured this one to himself as he turned in under the lich gate to the sounding of the bell.

The yews of Fairhaven churchyard were far-famed. Once they had made the great bows that the yeomen of England carried on foreign battlefields, but now they towered in undisturbed majesty over the weather-worn headstones beneath them. Even when the sunshine touched it their green was deep and opaque, but in the shadows over the graves it was black as pitch; yet everywhere the little red berries were strung in the darkness like lanterns in the night. "The jewels of the just," murmured Hilary.

> *Dear beauteous death! the jewel of the just,*
> *Shining nowhere but in the dark;*
> *What mysteries do lie beyond thy dust;*
> *Could man outlook that mark!*

He paused in his leisurely journey up the moss-grown path to the vestry door to look for the hundredth time at the inscription on the headstone under the largest yew tree of all. "Aramante Emilie du Plessis-Pascau. . . . A melodious noise of birds among the branches. A running that could not be seen of skipping beasts. The whole world shined with clear light and none were hindered in their labour." Never before had he seen that text upon a gravestone, yet surely there was none so instinct with glorious freedom. The singing birds, the skipping beasts, the men set free from pain and disease to be forever unhindered in their work, "the whole creation, that groaneth and travaileth in pain together until now, delivered from the bondage of corruption into the glorious liberty of the children of God." He was in the vestry by this time, struggling into his surplice, filled as always with a sense of leaping expectation as he prepared to celebrate that sacrament where he believed that the two worlds met.

The quiet of the old church seemed filled with the stately loveliness of the familiar prayers as he repeated them, yet this morning, beyond the slow fall of his words and the procession of his pleading thoughts, he was unusually conscious of the sights and sounds and scents that he knew so well. Though his back was to his church he could see in imagination the slanting beams of light falling through the windows, the dust motes dancing in them, the upward leap of the pillars to the lovely curve of the arches above and the dusky gloom of the roof over his head. He could hear the robin's chirp and the flutter of its wings, the soft swish of a woman's skirts as she knelt and a cock crowing somewhere in the village. The smell of must and damp was mingled pleasantly with the scent of the late roses in the altar vases and the very faint and lovely scent of verbena. Verbena? When he turned round he knew why all his senses were so unusually sharpened. Instead of Margaret, Lucilla was here. Such was his love for his mother that when she was near him he was always more wide-awake than usual to the beauty of familiar things.

Yet he felt a pang of sorrow at seeing her there. She always came in the village taxi on Sundays but on weekdays she did not usually feel justified in running to the expense. If today she had felt justified it must be because her mind was unusually troubled. He knew that she was taking this business of Nadine and David very much to heart.

When the service was over and he came out of the vestry he found her standing on the moss-grown path by Aramante's grave. "I am having breakfast with you, dear," she said.

She always had breakfast with him after she had been to mass. Sunday breakfast was one of the high lights of his week.

"That's fine, Mother," he said. "Only I don't know if

there's anything for breakfast that you'll like to eat. We didn't expect you, you know."

"Uninvited guests know what to expect upon your table, Hilary," said Lucilla sweetly. "Leather. . . . But I've not come for nourishment but to enjoy your company, darling."

Hilary laughed as he slipped his arm into hers and walked with her under the yews to the lich gate. He was a little suspicious of her sweetness. He rather thought she wanted to give him a scolding. He knew that he had exasperated her by the calm with which he had taken the news of David's delinquency, and that he had further outraged her by doing nothing at all about it. The fact was that he didn't know what to do about it, and when Hilary didn't know what to do about anything he waited in perfect placidity until he did. This he called "waiting upon God." Lucilla called it "Hilary's dreadful inertia."

Seated in the high bare dining room of the Vicarage, hideous with oilcloth and ecclesiastical pitch-pine woodwork, regarding the table spread with leathery toast, leathery cold ham, and tea that had not been made with boiling water, Lucilla sighed in a great depression of spirits. Hilary's Vicarage always depressed her. It was so cold, so bare, so ugly, and she could see no reason why godliness should go hand in hand with leathery food.

"If only you had married, Hilary," she sighed.

"Why, Mother?" asked Hilary, drinking a cup of tepid tea with every appearance of enjoyment.

"This ham," said Lucilla, regarding it with a revolted eye. "It has a very odd green tinge. Your old Mary is the worst housekeeper in the world. No wife would allow you to eat ham like this."

"Shall I ring for an egg for you?" asked Hilary, worried.

"No, dear, don't bother. It would probably be a curate's one and I don't like that sort. I'll just have toast. . . . You should have married, Hilary."

"If I had, Mother," said Hilary, "you would have taken a great dislike to her."

"I daresay, dear," Lucilla agreed. "I dislike the two daughters-in-law I have quite intensely. Laura is so dreadfully unworldly and Nadine so terribly worldly. It's so hard to strike the happy medium with a daughter-in-law."

"And then, Mother," said Hilary, smiling, "I've never met a woman who could hold a candle to you. A man should love his wife more than his mother, and that's a thing I could never do."

Lucilla was more annoyed than mollified. "Hilary," she announced, "you are one of those cowardly men who shelter behind the love of a mother from the bother of supporting a wife. Had you married, and possessed even the most elementary knowledge of women, you would have had the courage and intelligence to bring Nadine to a sense of her duty."

Hilary lay back in his chair and laughed delightedly. So she wanted him to tackle Nadine. He had thought there was more in her desire for his company than had met the eye.

"I don't know why you're laughing," said Lucilla miserably. "I am most dreadfully unhappy."

"Poor Mother," said Hilary, instantly sobered. "It would

do no good for me to talk to Nadine, darling. I shouldn't in the least know what to say. I'm always a tongue-tied idiot with women of her type. I don't understand them."

"You shirk women," said Lucilla severely. "You ought to be ashamed of yourself. What's a parson for but to cope with silly women?"

"I don't shirk all women," said Hilary with pardonable pride. "Have you ever known me to drop a female infant when baptizing her, scream she never so loudly, or fail to hale a young mother off to be churched, no matter how reluctant?"

"Don't be flippant, Hilary," said Lucilla. "It is your duty as a priest to help me in this miserable affair of David and Nadine."

"I know," said Hilary seriously. "And I mean to have a talk with David. But I don't want to force things. I'm just waiting until an opportunity arises easily and naturally, and until I am clearer in my mind as to what I should say."

"Your mind always takes such an age to clear, dear," mourned Lucilla.

"I know," agreed Hilary placidly, putting four lumps of sugar into his second cup of tea. "It's a slow mind. And guidance never comes to me other than gradually."

"So gradually, dear," sighed Lucilla, "that when at last it does come the thing that you wanted to be guided about has long ago passed into the realm of legend."

Hilary stirred his tea serenely and his mild brown eyes beamed affectionately upon his mother. Lucilla pushed her untouched plate impatiently away and sighed. Hilary was being hopeless as usual. In spite of his gentleness she found him quite the most difficult of her children to bend to her will. ... And yet she relied upon him more than upon the others; which was odd, because he did not always agree with her, and Lucilla, like everyone else, seldom sought advice unless she was sure it would bolster up the conclusion she had herself already come to.

"You are the person to talk to Nadine, Mother," said Hilary.

"I mean to, dear. I am going to talk to her and David today. But I doubt if I shall do much good with Nadine. A woman of her type only listens to men. That's why I wanted you to talk to her too."

"She is more likely to be touched by you than by me," said Hilary with conviction. "You will be able to speak to her out of your own experience of great love and great loss, the kind of love and loss of which I know nothing. Your experience, long ago when we were young, was so like hers. And also, though I don't think you know it, she is extremely fond of you."

Lucilla started and gazed in astonishment at her son, but he did not meet her eyes. "Great love and great loss long ago." But Hilary could not know anything about it. He had only been a little boy at the time. Perhaps, dear simple soul, he took it for granted that she had loved his father as David loved Nadine. Her strained figure relaxed.

"Of course, you mean your father," she said.

Hilary looked up and smiled at her. "No, not Father," he said. "Tolerant affection was the deepest emotion you ever felt for poor Father."

Lucilla got up and said in a trembling voice that she

thought she ought to be going. He was startling her so much that she felt incapable of sitting still where she was or of staying longer in his company. Soon, she thought, he would be telling her of her inmost thoughts, those half-formed things that were hardly clear even to herself. And this was her slow, her obtuse Hilary!

"But at least you're wrong about Nadine liking me," she gasped, feeling like a blind woman for her bag and sun-shade. "She can't bear me."

"She's very fond of you," insisted Hilary. "I'll come with you down to the gate, Mother."

In the shelter of a lilac bush he took her in his arms. "You see," he explained, "children always know more than their parents think they do. I so often saw you with him, and I happened to be in the garden that evening when you came home again. I did not understand then, of course, but later, putting two and two together, I did. I have always loved and reverenced you for the decision you made. If I were you, Mother, I should tell Nadine."

"I never meant to tell a living soul," whispered Lucilla, her face hidden against his shoulder. "I thought no one knew except, of course, Ellen."

"Tell Nadine," insisted Hilary.

"Not Nadine," exclaimed Lucilla. "David, perhaps, but of all people, not Nadine! I don't like Nadine. It's unbear-able to have to tell one's most private affairs to a woman one dislikes."

"Especially Nadine," insisted Hilary, "because she is so fond of you."

The purr of David's car, coming to bring the boys to

211

their lessons and drive Lucilla back to Damerosehay, was heard in the lane.

"Well, Hilary," said Lucilla, withdrawing herself tremblingly from her son's arms, "you've astonished me. All these years you've known more about me than any of my children. You're far cleverer than I thought you were. Far, far cleverer. The most astute of all my children. . . . But I still think you're wrong about Nadine liking me."

"You'll take my advice?" asked Hilary.

"Must I?" pleaded Lucilla. "I should so hate to tell Nadine."

"I think you must," said Hilary. "That old story of yours is the best weapon that you have."

"Very well," said Lucilla meekly.

And then David and the two little boys appeared upon the garden path. David looked a little troubled, Tommy was white under his sunburn and Ben looked not quite himself.

"What's the matter with Tommy?" demanded Lucilla in instant anxiety.

"It's nothing," David hastened to assure her. "It's just that he hasn't been very well this morning."

"It was a haddock morning," explained Ben.

"And you were out," said Tommy resentfully to his grandmother. "You ought to have told me you were going out, Grandmother. It's all been wasted because you were out."

"What's been wasted?" asked the puzzled Lucilla.

"The haddock and Tommy being sick," said Ben. "He thumped himself on his front and was sick, the way David

212

taught him, but you were out and couldn't give him permission to stay home from lessons, and we couldn't find Mother, and Ellen was cross and said he'd done it on purpose and must come. It's been hard on Tommy. You really *ought* to tell us when you're going out, Grandmother."

Lucilla, outraged, was no longer interested in Tommy's pallor. "You're a horrid little boy, Tommy," she said. "And you, David, you're not much better," and she swept indignantly to the garden gate.

"But, Ben?" asked Hilary, looking at his favorite nephew's strained face with considerable concern. "Did you part with the haddock, too, Ben?"

"No," said Ben sullenly, and kicked at a stone on the garden path.

David, still looking worried, made a half movement towards Ben, but Ben drew away from him towards Hilary. David followed Lucilla out to his car.

2.

Hilary conducted his two young nephews sternly indoors. He thought that they were considerably spoilt by all the women at Damerosehay and that but for his instruction and discipline their characters would have stood a poor chance. He was fond of them and he did not grudge the hours that he gave to them, even though it meant getting behindhand with parish business and staying up half the night to get it done. He was also extremely fond of his brother George, whom he considered the bravest and the stupidest man he had ever met, and he was anxious that George's sons should grow up to give him pride and joy and make up to him for the tragic disappointment of his marriage. With this end in view he thrust Latin verbs down the little boys' throats with a zeal that was almost ruthless, and kept in the drawer of his desk a very thin ruler that was not infrequently used for purposes of discipline. Hilary was rather an old-fashioned educationalist. He believed that to spare the rod was to spoil the child, and that it does not much matter what you teach a boy so long as he hates it enough.

Yet his nephews were exceedingly attached to him, and Ben liked his lessons. Tommy didn't, but then no matter who had taught him Tommy would have disliked instruction of an academic type. His mind was far from academic.

Hilary sat on one side of his dining-room table, from which the debris of breakfast had been cleared, and his nephews sat facing him upon the other, twisting their legs about their chairs and breathing heavily, and for half an hour instruction followed its normal course. Then Tommy spoke.

"May I go and lie down in the study, Uncle Hilary?"

"Certainly not," said Hilary.

"But I don't feel well inside," complained Tommy.

"That's your fault," said Hilary. "Your indisposition was self-induced and you are now bearing the consequences of your own action. Parse that sentence again."

Work continued for another half hour and then Ben said, "Uncle Hilary, please may I lie down?"

Hilary gave one keen look at his nephew's face, then without a word picked him up and carried him to the study. He laid him on the shabby old sofa, covered him with a rug and went to the kitchen to tell his housekeeper to take Master Ben some hot milk. Then he went back to Tommy who had, as was only to be expected, disappeared.

But Hilary knew Tommy's habits and ran him to earth in the little room where the apples were stored. "I didn't expect you back so soon," said Tommy with bulging cheeks. "You've been jolly quick tucking up Ben."

Hilary made no reply but haled him back to the dining room and made strenuous use of the ruler.

After that his heart warmed to his nephew, for Tommy neither cried nor made excuses. Nor did he say, as he very well might, that Ben had received favored treatment. He knew that Ben really felt bad, while his indisposition had vanished the moment he scurried down the passage and smelled the apples. Tommy, though wily, was honest.

"You took that well, Tommy," said Hilary, replacing the ruler and looking a little ruefully at Tommy's scarlet, smarting little palms. "Now you'll learn those verbs while I go and see what's the matter with Ben."

"Could I learn them in the linen cupboard with the cistern?" asked Tommy.

Hilary agreed. He was unable to understand Tommy's passion for the cistern but he felt that his honesty and courage merited reward. "But don't mess about with the linen," he cautioned.

Tommy vouchsafed no reply, but made a hasty exit.

Hilary found Ben lying exactly as he had left him, flat on his back staring at the ceiling. His milk was untouched beside him.

"Drink up your milk," said Hilary kindly.

"I don't want it," said Ben.

"Nonsense," said Hilary. "Do as I tell you."

Ben sat up and drank some of it obediently.

"Why did you turn queer like that?" asked Hilary. "Didn't you have any breakfast?"

"No," said Ben.

"Why not?"

"It wouldn't go down," said Ben. "I tried, but it wouldn't. Haddock doesn't if you feel upset. It's very thick and woolly in one's mouth, haddock is."

Hilary sat down on the sofa and put an arm round him. Sharp, quick tremors were passing through the little boy's body. Never had there been a child so exactly like a thoroughbred dog. Hilary was deeply distressed. "Ben," he commanded, "tell me what's worrying you."

Ben shook his head.

"Try, Ben."

"I can't," said Ben. "You see, I wasn't meant to see it and so I can't tell what I saw."

"I think you could tell me," said Hilary. "You see, I am a priest, and you can say things to priests that you would not say to other people because it is part of their duty never to repeat the things that are said to them."

"You mean it's as safe as saying things to God?" asked Ben.

"Quite as safe," said Hilary, and was immediately overtaken by the almost overwhelming sense of humility that was always his in the confessional. "As . . . God." Truly a priest carried the weight of an almost insupportable dignity. No wonder if staggering beneath it he appeared sometimes completely ridiculous in the eyes of the world. Atlas no doubt looked very silly, and Saint Christopher staggering through the whirling water bearing the Christ Child with him.

"It was in the wild garden," said Ben, with another of his thoroughbred shivers. "I went out there before breakfast, like I always do, and David and Mother were there under Methuselah, and David was kissing Mother. I ran away again and they didn't see me."

"There is no reason why David shouldn't kiss your mother," said Hilary evenly. "He is her nephew. Nephews always kiss their aunts. Don't you ever kiss Aunt Margaret?"

"But he wasn't kissing her that way," said Ben. "He was kissing her the other way."

"What other way?"

"Like Alf kisses Jill. I saw them at the back door once and when I asked Jill why they kissed like that, going on so long and with Jill sort of disappearing into Alf, she said it was because they were going to be married. . . . Uncle Hilary, could Mother marry David now that she doesn't live with Father any more?"

"Would you like her to?" asked Hilary.

"No!" shouted Ben, and burst into a storm of angry sobs.

"But you like David, don't you?" asked Hilary.

"I used to, but I'd hate him if he married Mother!" sobbed Ben furiously. "So would Father hate him. I want Father to come back again. I won't have David be Father!"

He sobbed stormily on while Hilary, patting him mechanically upon the back, gazed grimly over his head at the garden. Lucilla's previous anger against David and Nadine was as nothing to Hilary's at this moment. The wild garden was the children's own. What right had David and Nadine to indulge their selfish passion there, in the kingdom of the children they were injuring? Their behavior showed an insensitivity that sickened him. He was so angry that he had hard work to control himself. He felt that he knew now what to say to David. What was more, he was longing to say it.

"You're quite wrong, Ben," he said at last. "David is not going to marry your mother."

"How do you know?" demanded Ben.

"Because I know your mother and David wouldn't do such a thing," lied Hilary glibly. "Neither your mother nor David would ever do anything to hurt your father. I'm sure of that. What you saw was only an ordinary kiss, going on a bit longer than usual because it was such a lovely morning, and probably that missel thrush was singing in Methuselah. There's nothing like a bird singing to make people kiss longer than they meant to."

"You're quite sure?" asked Ben anxiously.

"Quite sure," asserted Hilary, but the grimness of his expression was by no means changed. He had, so to speak, burned his boats behind him. If he failed, now, to bring David to his senses his attempt to save for Ben his love for his mother and David would have done more harm than good, he would merely have deepened their guilt in Ben's eyes. He must bring David to his senses. Failure was inconceivable.

218

Yet Hilary was only slightly alarmed by this burning of boats. It was a method of establishing good that he frequently adopted, for he knew himself to be diffident and self-distrustful and he liked to put it out of his power to turn back from a job that he had at long last decided must be done. In this he was unconsciously true to his own and Lucilla's generation; he built from without inwards; his courage began as an outward show and only gradually, as the burned boats made it a necessity, penetrated to his feelings.

"So now that's all right," he reassured Ben. "Blow your nose and finish up your milk. You've upset yourself quite enough for one day. It doesn't do, you know, it weakens you. You wouldn't find Tommy losing his appetite because his relations kissed under an oak tree. Come to think of it, I don't believe I've ever seen Tommy cry."

As if in answer there was a sudden tremendous crash in the hall, followed by such a loud and sustained roaring that it seemed the very rafters shook. Hurrying to the scene of the commotion Hilary and Ben found Tommy and a black tin tray lying at the foot of the stairs, inextricably mixed up with Hilary's best pillow cases and his umbrella. Old Mary, Hilary's housekeeper, wailing and lamenting, was vainly endeavoring to separate the roaring confusion into its component parts. Tommy had apparently fallen from the top to the bottom of the stairs but the noise he was making satisfied them that his bodily vigor was in no way impaired by the accident.

"I was shooting the rapids!" he yelled when finally

219

scooped from the debris by Hilary. "In a boat with sails," he added, and hiccuped pathetically.

"And I said you never cried," ejaculated Hilary, regarding the streams of water that were pouring down Tommy's scarlet peony of a face and disappearing into his wide-open roaring mouth. Yet on second thoughts he decided that this explosion of noise and moisture could hardly be called crying. It was too elemental, too impressive. Hilary was almost stunned by the force of his nephew's powers of expression.

"Never mind," he said to old Mary. "Go back to your cooking. I'll see to this."

"Me best pillow cases!" wailed Mary.

"Never mind," said Hilary again, gathering them up. "Come on, boys." And he led the way back to the study. Arrived there he shut Tommy's roaring mouth with a peppermint bull's-eye from the tin that he kept for the delectation of his choir boys and suggested that they should continue the game of sailing ships with the pillow cases.

It was unheard of for Uncle Hilary suddenly to turn flippant like this in the middle of lesson time. Tommy's wet scarlet cheeks dried immediately, as though fanned by a breeze from the land of make-believe, and hastily crunching up his bull's-eye he began roaring with delight instead of sorrow. Ben said nothing, but a few airy leaps about the room found him in Hilary's big armchair, tying fishing rods to the four legs for masts and pillow cases to the fishing rods for sails. Hilary helped with a will and Tommy opened the French windows that the great ship might sail out.

"It's the grain ship," said Ben in low excited tones, his

thoughts as completely turned as his uncle had hoped they would be. "It's the grain ship that was wrecked on the marshes. I'm the captain and Tommy can be the crew if he likes. You're the storm, Uncle Hilary, pushing behind. We'll sail across the lawn and get wrecked in the sunflowers by the gate. See? They're gold, like the corn."

"What about my game leg?" asked Hilary mildly, hitching up his cassock.

"You must do the best you can," said Ben kindly. "Tommy will get down and help if you stick. Not me. I'm lashed to the mast. Where's the blue bird? Where's the blue bird in its cage? Tommy, fetch Mary's budgerigar!"

Tommy raced to fetch it from the kitchen, quite indifferent to Mary's wails as he carried it off from beneath her very nose, and soon the great ship was driving across the stormy green sea towards the sunflowers with the bird cage erected on the umbrella and all the pillow cases fluttering in the breeze. Old Mary, who was attached to her budgerigar, watched from the kitchen window in considerable anxiety. It was as she feared, when they reached the edge of the lawn the whole thing tipped over and the two little boys and the bird cage went flying into the bed of sunflowers.

"Me bird! Me bird!" wailed poor old Mary. "The cage'll come open!"

It had come open. The blue budgerigar, a silent creature who when confined within the kitchen never so much as opened its beak, flew up into the heights of the hawthorn tree above the sunflowers and sang and sang and sang.... At least so the little boys afterwards declared.

Meanwhile Nadine sat in the wild garden under Methuselah reliving the events of the early morning and most bitterly reproaching herself. She had got up before breakfast that morning and gone out into the garden. She was not usually an early riser but used as she was to the soothing sound of London traffic she found the birds in the country so dreadfully disturbing. They woke her up appallingly early, and very annoyed with them she always was. They were not now, of course, making the row that they made in the spring, when they all sang with such abandon that one would have said the very earth itself was singing, but this morning they had made quite noise enough. There had been the plover, for instance, crying out in the marshes almost before it was light, and the sea gulls mewing like kittens, and then laughing their strange deep ha! ha! as though someone had told them a joke in rather doubtful taste and they were a little uncertain as to how much mirth it would be seemly to show. Then there had been a robin, repeating his sharp metallic phrase of music over and over again under her window, and somewhere that everlasting blackbird had been, as always, singing his everlasting song. . . . It had got on Nadine's nerves to such an extent that she had had to get up.

In the garden she had found David gloomily smoking over the blight on one of Margaret's rose trees. Margaret herself did not smoke and always felt a little guilty about it, because all good gardeners should smoke over their blight, but she salved her conscience by driving every smoking guest out into the garden to do it for her. David no longer needed driving. The minute he struck a match he remembered his duty.

"David," had said Nadine, slipping her hand into his.

David had gripped her hand hard but had not looked at her. He had continued to breathe out over the blight in a way that had irritated her a little, suggesting as it did that he was more concerned over the welfare of Damerosehay than over her own.

"David," she had whispered, "I feel blighted too. Couldn't you smoke at me for a bit?"

Then he had looked straight at her and she had been shocked by the misery in his eyes. "What is it, darling?" she had whispered.

"Everything," David had said hopelessly. "Every damn thing. Why is life always such a mix-up?"

There being no answer to this question Nadine had made none. Besides, life never seemed a mix-up to her. She always knew what she wanted and made straight for it. She had known then. "Come into the wild garden," she had said. "We'll be alone there, with no windows looking at us."

"Not the wild garden," David had said. "That's the children's own."

"But they aren't up yet, darling. It's very early. We can't hurt anyone by being happy in the wild garden."

He had given in and they had gone. It had been almost absurdly beautiful there, like some childish fairy story with the wet bright leaves like veined silver and the air heavy and sweet with the scent of the flowers. There had been so many birds that the blue air had seemed flashing with wings like a Botticelli canvas.

"I'm not at all sure that I like birds," Nadine had said. "Uncanny things."

David hadn't agreed with her. "They're the jolliest creatures alive," he had said. "Birds and butterflies and all flying things. If there's a war I'll take to the air. If I must die I'd like to die in the sky, high up, near Apollo."

"But you wouldn't, my dear," Nadine had said grimly. "You'd die crashing out of it."

"Even that's better than being gassed in a corner like a rat in a hole," David had retorted.

> *"This is life: to keep*
> *Steadfast to the light.*
> *This is death: to leap*
> *From the topmost height*
> *Of ecstatic being straight into the night.*

Rudolph Besier wrote that about death in battle. It'll be the air for me, Nadine. There is still some sort of romance left about war in the air. Not much, but some."

He had spoken with the bitterness that was always his when he mentioned war, and Nadine had hastened to change the subject.

"I think I'm not fond of birds because they make me feel inferior," she had said. "How *do* they fly? It annoys me that such little silly things should fly so high when I'm so earthbound."

They had been under Methuselah by this time, with Nadine sitting in the swing and David leaning against the gnarled trunk. Looking up it had seemed to her that the tree was full of the green wings of the tits.

"It's because of their mystery that I love them," David had said. "Their wings seem a sort of prophecy. More than other beautiful things they might be an evidence of things not seen."

Nadine had smiled amusedly but when she spoke her voice had been tender. She was always gentle with the childish fantasies that were still not done to death in David. She enjoyed them. They were such a change. "Do you think all beauty is just the evidence of things not seen, David?" she had asked.

"If it's anything it's that," he had said. "I should say that faith is the belief in something that you don't understand yet, and beauty is the evidence that the thing is there."

"And birds' wings the bit of the evidence that vouches for eventual freedom," Nadine had suggested. Then she had sat up straight, listening. "What on earth is that?"

What she had heard had been a harsh exciting sound. David, hearing it too, had smiled. "Apollo's swans," he had said. "Look."

She had got up to look, strangely stirred, and had seen them flying one behind the other, slow and strong, their white plumage turned to gold by the sun god whose servants they were.

"And they," David had said smilingly, "are the evidence of immortality. They sing for joy when they die because they know they will live forever."

"Duffer!" had said Nadine. "They sing, if they do sing, and I don't believe it, for sorrow because their life is over."

David had laughed at her and softly begun to quote the *Phaedo*. With his trained actor's memory he was capable of quoting anything forever. There were times when Nadine found this most annoying, and this had been one of the times.

" 'But men,' " had quoted David, " 'through their own fear of death, belie the swans too, and say that they, lamenting their death, sing their last song through grief, and they do not consider that no bird sings when it is hungry or cold, or is afflicted with any other pain, not even the nightingale, or swallow. But neither do these birds appear to me to sing through sorrow, nor yet do swans; but in my opinion, belonging to Apollo, they are prophetic, and foreseeing the blessings of Hades, they sing and rejoice on that day more excellently than at any preceding time. But I too consider myself to be a fellow-servant of the swans, and sacred to the same god, and that I have received the power of divination from our common master no less than they, and that I not depart from this life with less spirits than they.' "

"Really, David," she had protested. "Before breakfast!"

Then he had taken her in his arms and given her the kisses she was longing for; very gentle kisses on her closed eyelids and the tip of her lifted chin. "What nonsense you talk!" she had whispered, leaning against him. "Or do you believe it?"

"I wish I did!" he had whispered back. "Oh God, I wish I did!"

She had pressed closer to him to comfort him. It was a bad moment in history, this, in which to live and love. The

Rider on the Red Horse seemed advancing ever more and more quickly, his shadow creeping before him over the light of the sun.

"At least we have this to believe in," she had said, "this love of ours. It is real, David. Not a dream or a hope or a prophecy but a fact. The loveliest fact in all my life."

After that she hadn't been able to blame David that he let go completely. And she had not checked him, this time. Breathless with her joy she had let herself go slack in his arms, abandoned to him. So great was her love for him that at that moment, had it been possible, she would have been willing to let her whole personality be lost in his. She would have foregone conscious knowledge of her own existence if by that sacrifice his could have been enriched . . . just for the moment.

It had passed quickly, for self-abnegation was not really Nadine's strong point, yet as she slipped back into herself again she had known that she had just passed through the best moment of her life. And David had given it to her. She could never part from David now. Never.

It had been a slight sound, the sharp snapping of a twig, that had brought her back to herself. And David too. They had both looked round and Nadine had seen a little figure slipping away through the trees, running quickly as though afraid.

"Ben!" she had cried, and there had been a sharp pain at her heart.

"I don't think so," David had said. "I heard a bird or something but I didn't see anyone."

"It was! It was!" Nadine had exclaimed.

They had followed quickly, but there was no one in the wild garden, and when they looked through the iron gate there was no one in the other garden either.

"You're seeing spooks, Nadine," David had laughed. "You're seeing Caroline's little boy." And then, as they wandered about the moss-grown paths, he had told her about Caroline's little boy and the lady in the lilac frock.

4.

And now it was after breakfast and she was alone in the wild garden. David was taking the boys to the Vicarage and fetching Lucilla, and Ellen had taken Caroline to the dentist, one of her little pearly teeth having most unaccountably decayed, so Damerosehay was denuded of its children and Nadine could not harm them by sitting alone in their kingdom.

We should not have come here this morning, she reproached herself. David was right, this is the children's own place. I believe it was Ben. Yet it couldn't have been, or David would have seen him too. But I believe it was. If only it had been Tommy. But *Ben*.

Nadine was in a most unusual state of maternal worry and fuss. Usually she carried her responsibilities as a mother lightly, but this visit to Damerosehay was making them nag at her mind with alarming insistence. She had not realized until now what complications there would be with the children when she married David. Or rather with Ben, for she did not think that Tommy or Caroline would be much disturbed by a change of father. But Ben would. He was old enough to remember his father and he was a very

228

faithful little boy. And if that *had* been Ben in the garden this morning the gentle preparation for change that she had planned for him would be completely upset by what he had seen. . . . But perhaps it hadn't been Ben. . . . She thrust the thought away from her and began to worry instead about Caroline's tooth.

The poor scrap was no beauty and if she was going to have bad teeth she would indeed be a plain Jane. Nadine had no wish for a plain daughter; it would increase the difficulty of marrying her off. Nadine was very anxious to marry off Caroline; otherwise she would be landed with her forever, as Lucilla was landed with Margaret, and she was very much afraid that she and Caroline would never get on together as Lucilla and Margaret did; and if a mother and daughter did not get on their relationship was the most difficult on earth.

"I love the children so, yet I believe I'm a bad mother," Nadine reproached herself. "I'm good with men but I'm bad with children. I oughtn't to have had them. I only had them because George wanted them so. In everything else I disappointed him. I tried to make up for the other things by giving him children."

Sitting in the quiet of the wild garden she found herself most unexpectedly grieving a little over the wreck of her marriage. She supposed it was because Damerosehay was George's family home that she found herself, even in the full flood of her love for David, thinking more about George than she had done for ages. At the time she had been so glad to marry him. Before she had met him she had been in love for the first time, that is very romantically and desperately in love, with a man who turned out upon intimate acquaintance to be all that most revolted her. Nadine had no religion, she submitted her life to no stern moral law, but she was fundamentally clean and fastidious and she had been shocked and sickened by her discoveries, so much so that for a little while her world had seemed to crash about her. Then she had met George and had fallen at once for his sheer goodness. He had satisfied her desperate craving for love with cleanliness, and for a while she had been very happy.

But if George was good he was also slow, and he had a rather sullen temper, and if there were two things in this world that Nadine could not stand they were slowness and sullenness. Nadine was, and had been from her cradle, an outrageous flirt. She could not help herself. She flirted as naturally and as charmingly as a bird sings. But she was fastidious and she was self-controlled and she never let her flirtations get beyond the bounds that she herself set for them. But George had been too stupid to understand this; he had continually reproached her, had been continually outraged; and, worst of all, though he loved her he had not trusted her. His sullen temper and her quick one, his slowness and her cleverness, had clashed and clashed again. It had all become impossible and they had been glad to part. . . . At least she had, but she believed that poor old George in the depths of his heart still longed for her. He was so tenaciously faithful, so conservative, that he hated anything that had been to end. He was bound always to the past with bands that could not be broken.

It had been grievous, heartbreaking, that crash, not only

for the grief that it had been to George but for the sorrow it had caused Lucilla; Nadine had tried to make up for that sorrow by letting Lucilla have the grandchildren. Yet she told herself that she must not grieve, because it had opened the way for David to come to her. At the thought of David her mouth curved into a lovely smile. He was everything that she had always longed for. He had beauty enough to satisfy her fastidious taste and though he was not clever he was intelligent and sensitive, and above all he combined tolerance with decency. Her flirtations would not upset him any more than his upset her; they had mutual trust in each other. And she had proof of his sense of honor that delighted her. She knew that he longed most desperately to be her lover; yet he had never once asked her if he might come to her before their marriage. That was not his code. It augured well, she thought, for her future happiness.

There were, of course, things about him that irritated her a little. His absorption in his work, for instance. She could not quite understand that passionate dedication to an art, and she was jealous of it. The value of his work in her eyes was that it would provide them with a home in which to love, but she was not at all sure that he did not unconsciously twist things the other way round; he had said once that his love would be the inspiration of his work. That, Nadine thought, was all wrong. With her, love came first. She did not like to think of it as being anything but an end in itself. No woman did.

She was sitting on the grass beneath Methuselah, her head leaning against his hoary trunk, and through her half-closed eyes she saw a swirl of mauve, as though a woman's skirt swayed over the grass. She opened her eyes wide and saw that the autumn crocuses were bending in the wind. She wondered if it was the crocuses that had made Caroline imagine for herself a woman playmate as well as a child. Poor little scrap, she must have been very lonely. Nadine felt reproached by the thought of that imagined woman. It was natural that Caroline should have created the child playmate, all lonely children did, but the woman— Had Caroline wanted the right kind of mother so very badly?

There was a rustle among the bushes, and a sigh, and Nadine sat up and looked intently in that direction. Then she laughed at herself, for it was only the wind. But she could understand Caroline. This wild garden was undoubtedly a very haunted place. She was glad to see David, his fetching and carrying over, coming back to her.

"We're for it," he said with a rueful grin.

She raised her eyebrows.

"Grandmother is enthroned in the drawing room," he said. "She has chosen this morning to give us our Talking To."

Nadine got up immediately. One of the things she liked about Lucilla was that she never nagged. For five days she had said no single word of what her daughter-in-law knew must be to her a great trouble. There had been no difference in her manner to Nadine; it had been the one of sweet but rather distant courtesy that was always hers when she did not like people very much. When the Talking To was over Nadine knew that the matter would not be referred to again. She admired Lucilla's self-control. She was controlled herself and she hated nothing so much as the lack of it. She put her hand in David's and went with him through the garden.

"Strange, sweet, wild place," she said. "I've felt quite haunted, David, by that woman of little Caroline's in the lavender skirts. Are you ever haunted by her?" And she laughed to show him that she was only joking.

"Never," said David. "But according to Grandmother there's some sort of a spook in the drawing room. A man this time."

"Ever felt him?" asked Nadine.

David did not answer, but allowed his answering laugh to show her that he didn't believe a word of it. They needed to joke a little, for they dreaded the ordeal that was coming. As they left the wild garden it seemed to Nadine that the air was a rush of wings. "Those birds!" she sighed.

CHAPTER EIGHT

LUCILLA ALSO DREADED the Talking To. She sat in her arm-chair, the Bastard at her feet with his chin on her shoe, and wished it was over. She was so dreadfully afraid of saying the wrong thing, of forgetting all her arguments if the children interrupted, or losing her temper from sheer fatigue. That was why she had chosen indoors instead of out of doors, for she found it much easier to concentrate indoors. Out of doors one's mind, if one was old, was continually being deflected by something else, a cold wind on the back of one's neck, or midges. When one was old one felt things like cold or midges very acutely. Indoors she was protected from both and her mind was more at rest. The door opened and gripping her hands together on top of her black velvet bag she looked up almost piteously at the two who came in.

How beautiful they were, and how strong. David had got very sunburnt these last days and his hair was more than ever like a cap of smooth gold. He might have been the young Apollo. And Nadine in her slim green dress looked like a dryad. She had a yellow autumn rose stuck in her belt and there was a little wriggly green caterpillar caught in her hair. Unconsciously Lucilla put up her lor-gnette. "You've a caterpillar in your hair, dear," she said.

Standing in front of the French mirror Nadine removed it. "Don't, Grandmother," she laughed.

"Don't what, dear?"

"Put up your lorgnette. It completely unnerves me."

An astonishing influx of confidence and strength came to Lucilla from this statement. She was surprised, and delighted, to find that she still had it in her to unnerve another woman, and a young one at that. She waved the two erring ones to low chairs with dignity and calm.

"I want to tell you something that happened to me when I was young," she began abruptly and bravely. "I had not meant ever to tell anyone but this morning I changed my mind. Or rather Hilary changed it for me. He made me see that if I told it, you would realize that I sympathized with you, and that I understand your feeling for one another. I do not think one has the right to give an opinion on any subject unless one has oneself experienced the emotion of it."

"May I smoke, Grandmother?" interrupted David politely but firmly. If Lucilla was going to tell them tales of her youth they would be here all the morning, for there was no holding her when once she embarked upon the past.

"Of course, dear," said Lucilla, but she felt a little put out. When men smoked they became so somnolent. You could never tell if they were listening to a word you were saying. The interruption, too, had upset her. "Where was I?" she asked a little plaintively.

"...oneself experienced the emotion of it," prompted Nadine gently, and gave Lucilla a little comic glance of commiseration that was very warming. Nadine, unlike every other woman of her type and generation, did not smoke. She was too fastidious. She didn't like the way her lipstick came off on her cigarette.

"I was very young when I married," said Lucilla. "I was younger than you were, Nadine, when you married George. And I was not in love with my husband; he was a widower and much older than I and, poor dear, so plain. And I did not know when I married what marriage meant, either. Young girls never had things explained to them in those days. It was all a great shock to me. And then, you know, having been married before, there was no romance about marriage to James, and though he meant to be kind he treated me in such a way that there was none for me either. I had five children much too quickly, and I am afraid I did not want them at all. Later, when I was older, I loved all my children very dearly, but when they were little I am afraid I did not think them worth the bother and pain. I was so very young. Though I am a naturally happy person I was very unhappy all through those early years. I was quite dreadfully unhappy and I am afraid I almost hated my good kind James."

She paused and her two listeners looked at her in astonishment. Somehow they had both always imagined Lucilla's married life as one of idyllic Victorian bliss. Now her short, difficult sentences gave quite another picture.

"I was very ill when Stephen, my fifth child, was born," said Lucilla, "and after that I rebelled. I told James that I would not have any more children. He was very upset, poor James. He was an ardent man, and he loved me. His mother had had thirteen children and had given him very decided ideas about the duties of a wife. He thought I was failing him very badly.... I think," sighed Lucilla, "that if he hadn't gone on about his mother so much my married life might have been happier."

Nadine was now definitely very interested. Her married life, too, would have been very much happier if George had not gone on so much about Lucilla. One of the odd things about men was that though they always swore that women were the very devil yet they always thought their mothers perfect.... Lucilla, so George had told her, had delighted in bearing six children to an adored husband, Lucilla had been utterly contented with the home circle, Lucilla had never flirted, Lucilla—

"Grandmother," asked Nadine wickedly, "did you ever flirt at all?"

"Just a little, dear," confessed Lucilla modestly, "but not enough for James to notice. You see, dear," she added with a touch of pride, "I was very pretty when I was young."

"Grandmother," said Nadine, smiling, "this is getting most exciting. I feel as though your life story was going to be a Victorian melodrama. Surely, Grandmother, you didn't behave like the heroine of *East Lynne?* I can't believe it of you."

"'Dead, and never called me mother,'" quoted David delightedly.

His amusement hurt Lucilla and put her out again, and she stopped dead in her story. He was instantly penitent. "I'm sorry, Grandmother," he cried, "I'm sorry," and threw his cigarette into the fire to please her.

Nadine was sorry, too. "Forgive us," she said. "It was

because we don't believe it of you that we teased you. Please go on, Grandmother."

"I am afraid, my dears," said Lucilla slowly, "that you must believe it of me. I think a woman's history is very often like one of those old romances that you laugh at. Mine was, and so, Nadine," she added a little sharply, "is yours. You may laugh at them but they were truer to life than many of those psychological novels you young people read nowadays. We women don't sit half the day and night analyzing our emotions but we do perpetually fall in love out of wedlock, and over and over again we have to fight out the same old battle between love and duty. Human emotions are very monotonous," sighed Lucilla. "Poor human nature doesn't get much change. . . . Now where was I when you interrupted me?"

"I believe we were just getting to a most exciting lover," said Nadine, and her eyes were still dancing though she kept her mouth serious and grave. "Was he a brilliant young artist, Grandmother?"

"I'm sorry to disappoint you, dear, but he wasn't. He was only a doctor, a perfectly ordinary country G.P., and I met him through the children's measles."

Nadine and David forbore to smile, for Lucilla spoke with such quiet intensity. She was back in the past now, recapturing deeply felt emotion, and even the room seemed gathering round to listen as she went on with her story.

"James and I took a house on the Island, our Island that we see from Damerosehay, for the whole summer, because the children had been so ill with measles in the spring. I was there all the time, of course, and James came down for

238

the week ends. Michael Forbes was the doctor there. The village where we had our house was a quiet little place and he came in to see us a great deal, as a friend as well as a doctor, because he was lonely. At the beginning I only liked him, but I liked him better than anyone else I had ever met. He was young, just my age, and he cared about all the country things just as I did, but as James did not. James, you know, was always a thorough Londoner, but I was brought up in the country and I've always hated towns. Michael could ride well and we often went out together. Riding had been the joy of my life before my marriage, but James never cared for it; his seat on a horse was a heartbreaking thing. Michael read a lot, too, and though he wasn't actually an artist, Nadine, he had an appreciation of beauty that enriched my life forever. He could be very amusing and he made me laugh a lot. It was so long since I had really laughed. But best of all he was so sensitive in all his contacts. It was wonderful to see him with a sick child or a frightened little animal. Had he been married I know he would have been very gentle with his wife, far more gentle than James had ever been with me. There was something about him that seemed to heal the wounds of the mind as well as the body."

"What did he look like?" asked Nadine with eager feminine curiosity. David was a little impatient with her. What on earth, at this immense distance of time, did it matter what the fellow had looked like? Yet in a minute he found that, to him, it most surprisingly did matter.

"He was good to look at," said Lucilla. "I shouldn't have loved him if he hadn't been, for I was hungry for every sort of beauty. He was tall and graceful and he looked his best on horseback; all good-looking men do. He was fair, with very smooth gold hair."

She raised her head suddenly and found her grandson looking at her with most painful intensity. He was almost, she thought, a little white. After a moment's puzzlement she understood. "No, no, my dear," she cried, a little amused in spite of herself. "Don't look like that, David. It never got to that. Your father was James's child, not Michael's. You've every right to the name of Eliot."

David relaxed, a little shamefacedly. Lucilla's eyes, he noticed, were still twinkling. She had caught him out. He, who was all for truth rather than law in human relationships, had, caught unexpectedly, not wanted to find himself with no legal right to his own name. . . . He grinned at Lucilla.

"After Grandfather," pronounced Nadine, "you must have fallen for a man like that very badly indeed, Grandmother."

"I did," said Lucilla, "but gradually. There was nothing violent about it. I just woke up one morning to find that in him all my desperate unsatisfied longings were satisfied completely, and that his companionship was the only thing in the world I wanted. This love was, I thought, the one and only really true thing that had ever happened to me. My marriage and motherhood had always seemed like a sort of play that I acted. This was real. It was the same with his love for me. It seemed to him, he told me, the only truth there was. It dwarfed everything else. Even his beloved work seemed an unreal thing beside it. I don't need to explain such a love to you. You know all about it, and how the power of it can numb thought and memory and drive the sanest and best of men and women to the maddest of acts. . . . Unless fate gives them a quiet breathing space in which to recollect themselves. . . . I had it, and it saved me from doing incalculable harm, and I am hoping that this time at Damerosehay will give it to you."

There was naturally no response to this, and Lucilla went on.

"We arranged to go away together. That was the way one did things in those days. There were none of these arranged divorces," and here her eyes fell upon her daughter-in-law and her voice grew a little hard, "none of this ridiculous business of making the man take the blame as though the fault were his only. In those days, if a woman wanted to leave her husband for another man, she did so openly, and the blame was hers; and very severe blame it was, too; she and the man she went to were socially ruined to an extent that can hardly be understood nowadays." She paused, then went on again. "Looking back after all these years I can understand myself, for I was a selfish creature when I was young, I had next to no religion, I was not happy with my husband and I did not love my children as much as I should have done. But I find it hard to understand Michael, for he was so fine a creature. It is strange to me that he should have been so completely overturned by a silly young woman."

"I can understand him," said David, and his smiling eyes told her how utterly adorable the young Lucilla must have been.

"Don't interrupt, dear, because I cannot remember where I am, if you interrupt. . . . Well, we made our plans. We were to go to France. Michael had a little money of his own and on that we planned to live, for we knew, of course, that his professional life would be smashed by what we were doing. James was in London, and I told the servants and the children that I was going to him. Michael had established a locum and was supposed to be taking his annual holiday. It seemed quite natural to everybody that we should go down together to catch the morning boat to the mainland. Even now I can recapture the happiness as though it were yesterday. We went down to the boat in Michael's dog cart, through lanes full of honeysuckle. In spite of days and nights of anxiety and torturing indecision I was half crazy with joy. And then, just as we were getting on the boat, a frantic man came running to say that a favorite patient of Michael's, a little boy of three, had burned himself most dangerously. They did not trust the locum, they wanted Michael." She paused and sighed, as though even now the memory of that moment oppressed her. "And Michael went. Before I came along he had been mad about his work; the best men always are. He just dumped down his bag and ran down the gangway, calling to me to take a cab home and we'd go by tomorrow's boat, and was off like a flash in his dog cart before I'd even got time to protest. I was furious, of course. I thought he ought to have left the child to the locum and considered me first. He had put me in a very difficult position. He had, I thought, been very cruel. I did not go home. I was too angry. I put our luggage in the little office on the quay and walked to the nearest lonely bit of seashore and tramped up and down and raged and stormed, and cried until I was utterly exhausted. Then, I think, I must have slept a little. I was worn out and it was quiet and warm in the sunny little bay. Then I sat up and ate my sandwiches and looked across the Estuary to the mainland on the other side. I saw the cloud shadows passing over the wide flat marshes and flocks of sea birds wheeling up into the sun. I did not know, of course, that I was looking across at the Damerosehay country, but the peacefulness of that wide landscape had a very powerful effect upon me. It seemed to clear my mind and lull my torment to sleep so that I was able to think, and to think hard and straight. I stayed there all day, thinking."

She stopped, and David, to give her time to rest a bit, went over to a window and pulled the curtain a little to keep the sun out of her eyes. He was touched by her story. Lucilla was such a serene old lady that he had never pictured her torn by any sorrows except those of inevitable bereavement. It astonished him that she too had known passion and conflict. Nadine, he saw, was also moved. He supposed that all human experience is very much the same. We think our own sufferings are unique and then we find that everyone else has been through much the same ... or worse.

"I want to try and tell you the conclusions I arrived at that day," said Lucilla. "This is what I really want to tell you. My silly little love story isn't really important, and at one time I had not meant to tell it, but the conclusions one comes to about living are important. They mold our lives, and sometimes other people's lives too.... My thinking all started from the fact, so bitter to me, that Michael had put his work before his love for me. And he had done that instinctively. He had had no time to reason things out; if he had I expect he would have come with me; he had simply acted upon instinct. Now in those days I had great faith in instinct. It was instinct, I thought, that guided the world aright, that sent the wild birds flying across seas and continents to find their home, that taught the animals to care for their young, even to die for them if need be. Instinct, I thought, was the voice of God. . . . I still think that very often it is, though I realize now that there is such a mixture of good and evil in all we think and are that everything, every instinct and every thought, needs to be tested by the teaching of Christ. . . . And if that were true it meant that Michael, in instinctively putting his work before his love, was doing right. Yet he had said that his love for me seemed a truer, a more real thing, than his work. So great was his love that he had been quite ready to have his work ruined by it.

"That made me think very hard, even as you have thought, David, about the nature of truth. What is it once one moves beyond the narrow conception of truth as the correctly spoken word? You must remember that I had never read very much and that I had to think it out very crudely for myself. I thought it out and I said to myself that true action is the creation of perfection while lying action is the creation of something that falls short of the ideal. 'That is a true line,' we say, when it is drawn as near to the straight as we can get it. 'That is a bad portrait,' we say of a picture that is not like the original. From there I went further and I said that truth at its greatest is something made in the likeness of God."

" 'Beauty is truth, truth beauty,' " quoted David softly, smiling at her.

"Yes, dear, but don't interrupt. I was very uneducated, as I said before. I don't believe I had even read Keats in those days. I had to struggle on by myself to the idea that if truth is the creation of perfection, then it is action and has nothing to do with feeling. And the nearest we can get to creating perfection in this world is to create good for the greatest number, for the community or the family, not just for ourselves; to create for ourselves only means misery and confusion for everybody. That made me see that acting a part is not always synonymous with lying, it is far more often the best way of serving the truth. It is more truthful to act what we should feel if the community is to be well served rather than behave as we actually do feel in our selfish private feelings."

"In other words, Grandmother," said David, smiling, "it is more truthful to pretend that you love your husband when you don't, rather than run away with another man because you do. That, you think, is the best way of creatively building up the idea of faithfulness in marriage, which to your mind is a better thing for the community, and therefore a truer thing, than adultery."

"You put it crudely, dear," complained Lucilla.

"Life is a bit crude," agreed David.

"Yes, that's what I thought," said Lucilla. "Only I thought no more about my work for the community as a wife and mother than Michael's as a doctor. I thought all day about his work. A doctor's work is splendidly creative, I thought; building strong bodies and healthy minds; it is more creative even than the work of painter and sculptor, for he deals in flesh and blood and thought, materials that are living. It seemed to me appalling, as I thought it over, that all this should be sacrificed to his passion for a pretty woman. It was every bit as bad as that my work for my husband and children should be sacrificed to my passion for a charming man. The love of a man and a woman, I saw, should never be allowed to be an end in itself; it should be the helpmate of their work."

"Do you know, Grandmother," said Nadine gently, "if you could reason this all out so clearly I don't think you could have been so desperately in love as you thought you were."

"Oh, but I was!" said Lucilla, and her tone was so piteous that they had to believe her. "I don't know why it was that I could think so clearly then, for I'm not usually a clear thinker. Perhaps it was the shock of Michael's action. A shock can have two effects, you know; sometimes it stuns you and sometimes it quickens you; I suppose it did the second to me. I had pencil and paper in my bag and sitting on the shore I wrote to Michael, telling him why I could not go with him after all. Then I tore up the letter I had written to James, and had meant to post on the mainland, and threw it in the sea, and I walked quietly home, posting Michael's letter on my way. As I went in at our garden gate Hilary came running to meet me, he was a little boy of eight years old then, and he hugged me. He was so glad I had not gone away after all. 'Don't ever go,' he said. 'No,'

I said, 'I won't,' and I cried and hugged him hard. Next day James came back and I told him I was tired of the Island. So we moved and went back to the mainland."

"Were you very unhappy, Grandmother?" asked Nadine.

"For the whole of the next year I was so unhappy that I did not know how to go on living. Every day when I woke up in the morning I used to hope that this day would be my last on earth—I was as unhappy as all that. The fact was that I loved Michael more than all my children put together. It's a dreadful thing to say, but it's true. I did not see how I could live without my best-beloved. But I did, of course; one so often has to. It was Ellen who saved me."

"Ellen?" asked David, astonished.

"Ellen knew all about it, of course; I don't know how because I didn't tell her; perhaps I left a letter about, for I'm very careless. Ellen doesn't think it wrong to read my letters. She thinks it her sacred duty to know all that's going on in the family, no matter by what means. She knew and told me that she knew. She was kind, but stern. 'What you need, milady,' she said, 'is to love your poor children a bit more.' 'But I do love them,' I protested. 'I have sacrificed my happiness for them.' 'You don't love 'em as much as I do,' said Ellen. 'What you need is to do a bit more for 'em. It's I who do all the work, not you. Never a hand's turn do you do for those children. . . . And if I was you, milady, I should have another.'

"What Ellen said made me think again. Love at its highest, I thought, like truth at its highest, is a creative thing. Perhaps it is action, not feeling. I was playing the part of a good wife and mother quite successfully in the outward ways but that, I saw now, was not enough. That was not love. Creative love meant building up by quantities of small actions a habit of service that might become at last a habit of mind and feeling as well as of body. I tried, and I found it did work out like that. Feeling can be compelled by action not quite as easily as action by feeling, but far more lastingly. You may not believe me, but it's true."

They smiled at her, but their faces looked as though blinds had been drawn over them. She had no idea what, if any, effect she was having upon them.

"And the last baby?" asked Nadine. "Maurice? David's father?"

Lucilla's face softened and shone, as it always did at the mention of Maurice. "I took Ellen's advice and I had him," she said. "James had been very upset, not to say outraged, by my refusal to have more children. I told him I was sorry and I asked to have another; and Maurice, as you know, was the glory of my life. After he came, living was not only possible but actually happy again. I suppose a psychologist would have said that in my love for Maurice I sublimated my love for Michael. And the odd thing was that though he was not his son Maurice was very like Michael. He had a sensitiveness and a beauty that none of my other children had. . . . And yet I suppose it was not so odd, for our children are the children of our minds and souls as well as our bodies, and my mind and soul belonged to Michael."

"What happened to Michael?" asked Nadine.

"Nothing dramatic, dear. He just went on with his work. But he never married, and I suppose he was unhappy on the Island after what had happened, for he left it and went to the north of England, and later he came to London and before he died he was considered to be one of the greatest child specialists of his day. He must have saved the lives of a multitude of little children. He would never have done that had he married me. When we were both middle-aged I met him once at a London dinner party, and I think I was rather expecting him to tell me that I had broken his heart and ruined his life; not that I thought I had but I thought it would be nice of him to say so. But Michael was never one to say the proper thing if it wasn't the truth. 'Sensible young woman that you were,' he said to me. 'You saved us both from a great disaster.' I asked him, a little wistfully, if he hadn't been upset at the time. 'Just for a twelvemonth,' he said. 'A year of hell, though it seems long at the time, isn't really long compared with the span of a man's working life.' I said no, I supposed it wasn't, and we said good-by very politely and I never saw him again."

"And Grandfather never knew a thing about it?" asked Nadine.

"Oh no, dear," said Lucilla, horrified at the bare idea.

"How odd of you not to tell him, Grandmother," said David. "Now I couldn't have gone on living with him if I hadn't made a clean breast of it."

"Your Grandfather would have been very upset if I had told him, dear," said Lucilla. "I wanted to tell him, of course, but I saw no reason why he should be upset just to give me peace of mind. Confession is often a rather selfish luxury, I think."

David marveled at her. Inward integrity meant so much

to him that her ruthless sacrifice of it to the common good knocked him speechless.

Lucilla sighed. She was dreadfully tired. "Well, I've finished," she said. "You've both been very patient. I've said my say and I've no doubt I've said it very badly, and I shan't bother you any more. Your ideals and mine are so different, but please just think about mine, for they have been tested and I think experience has proved them trustworthy." She looked round her beautiful room. "I have tried to make life a creative art. I saved Michael's work from disaster. I built up a happy and united family, that will be disunited if you two marry, and I made this lovely home that may pass away from us if David forsakes it. Happy homes are very important. I think, far more important than you realize, and God knows how many of them have been built up by the sacrifice of private longings. I am inclined to think that nothing so fosters creative action as the sacrifice of feeling. It's like rain coming down upon the corn. I think it is David's beloved Shakespeare who says somewhere, 'Upon such sacrifices the gods themselves throw incense.'"

Her voice trailed away and no one said anything for some minutes. "Do you know, Grandmother," said Nadine at last, "that through all this you have never even mentioned George and the children to me?"

Lucilla got up and slowly crossed the room. "I saw no need to, dear," she said at the door. "Since you have been here they have haunted you night and day. I've seen it." And she went out.

"Is that true, Nadine?" asked David. He was standing

by the mantelpiece, looking unutterably weary, for his love for Nadine and his love for Lucilla, so completely opposed, seemed dragging him in pieces. Nadine sat on in her chair, her hands moving restlessly upon its arms.

"Yes," she said. "Grandmother has built up such an atmosphere of family feeling here that it affects one. And then there's something else, something older and deeper than Grandmother's atmosphere. I can't describe it. A sort of climate. It's in the wild garden as well as the house."

"Just the atmosphere of age," said David. "All old places have it. Age and tradition."

Nadine got up and moved to the window. "That's it," she said. "Tradition. But a particular tradition. In this place there is a tradition of faithfulness."

"Faithfulness to what?" asked David sharply.

Nadine did not answer. She went slowly out of the room and up the stairs to her bedroom to wash her hands for lunch.

David turned round and held on to the mantelpiece with both hands. He had seen what Lucilla had not seen, that that old story had touched Nadine very deeply. The likeness of their experience had given her a strong link with Lucilla, and when we feel ourselves linked to someone whose experience, up to a certain point, has been our own, the tendency is not to break the link but to follow on along the full way that the other has taken. For a moment an agony of apprehension seized him. Then he shook it off. Nadine had a very strong character. Of all the women he had ever met she was the least easily influenced.

But he was still holding on to the old carved mantelpiece when the little boys came dashing in to tell whoever they could find about the game of the ship in Hilary's garden, and he kept one hand upon it as he swung round to listen to them.

"Nothing was saved," finished Ben dramatically. "Nothing but the blue bird and some of the carving about the prow."

Then they ran out again, for Margaret's voice was heard demanding that they should go and wash their hands for nursery dinner.

"The carving about the prow." Without realizing what he was doing David looked up at the old carved overmantel that had come from no one knew where, and in spite of his anxiety a thrill of excitement went through him. At the Hard, in the old Master-Builder's House, he had often seen prints of the great ships that had been built and launched there more than a hundred years ago, and many of them had had glorious carved poops and forecastles. Surely some of them had been decorated with arabesques like swirling water, rather like these that curled from floor to ceiling of the Damerosehay drawing room. Why had he not noticed that before? Had this carving been taken from the wreck of the grain ship? Was the story of the grain ship true, and its captain the same man who had drawn those appalling pictures that had been found in Obadiah's clock? Before Jeremy, before Aramante, had he lived at Damerosehay? David gladly seized upon something to turn his thoughts, and he felt as excited as his battered condition would allow. Had it not been for his preoccupation with Nadine he thought he would have connected the drawings with the captain of the grain ship long ago. He liked that man. He felt him to be his friend. How in the world could he find out about him? Could anything be discovered at the Hard?

The telephone rang and he answered it. It was Hilary. "You haven't taken me for a run in your car yet," complained Hilary. "You always do when you come down. How about tomorrow?"

"Nadine and I hope to ride in the Forest tomorrow," said David. "Sorry."

"The next day then," said Hilary with such determination that David smiled a little grimly. He had been in daily expectation of an expression of Hilary's views upon the Nadine affair. He did not dread them. Hilary in the expression of views was always blessedly terse.

"The day after tomorrow, then," said David. "Let's hope the weather lasts. If there's nowhere else that you particularly want to go to I'd like to go to the Hard."

"Right," said Hilary. "Pick me up at two-thirty. By the way, will you all keep your eyes open for old Mary's blue budgerigar? By mistake we let it out this morning."

"Mary upset?" asked David.

"Weeping," said Hilary.

"We'll keep a look out for it," promised David.

But, as it happened, he forgot about Mary's blue bird, for the rest of the day was one of extreme woe. At nursery dinner Tommy cut the top of his finger off with the bread knife, and, Ellen being absent and Jill one of those who faint at the sight of blood, David had to help Margaret bind it up, to the accompaniment of ear-splitting roars from Tommy, while Nadine revived Jill with Lucilla's sal volatile. After lunch Caroline returned from the dentist in a very tearful condition, not having enjoyed her first extraction, and much depressed by the thought of the many more she would have to have before she was old enough to be an angel in heaven, where, she was assured there were no dentists; or at least, if there were, for presumably dentists as well as other people went to heaven if they were good, only winged dentists in a state of bliss in which it was no longer necessary to extract teeth for a living. For, said Lucilla, in heaven our teeth will not decay. They will be made of chippings from the gates of pearl and no corruption shall touch them. But in spite of Lucilla's comforting remarks they all had to play animal grab with Caroline until her bedtime to bring her round, and so exhausting was the grab that before the grown-ups' late dinner Lucilla retired to bed with a headache, saying she thought she was getting a bit old to be a grandmother; but after dinner she had to get up again for Ben suddenly and unexpectedly had a violent attack of asthma, his first for a year, which was not subdued by the ministrations of the whole household until close on eleven o'clock, when it occurred to Ellen to give him a good hard slapping.

"What can have happened to upset him?" Lucilla kept demanding miserably. "Whatever can have happened?" And Nadine and David, haunted by the vision of a little boy running through the trees of the wild garden, were careful not to look at each other.

Altogether it was a depressing evening, and David, climbing wearily to bed, thought that though there is a lot to be said for being the father of a family it is by no means, what with one thing and another, all jam.

CHAPTER NINE

I.

"WE'RE ONLY JUST in time," said Hilary, climbing laboriously into David's car. "The weather is on the change."

"Splendid today," said David, as his silver-gray monster slid smoothly away from the Vicarage gate. "Southwest weather. The best there is."

The warm still blue days, and the quiet nights bright with the harvest moon, had left them. There was a fresh southwest wind today and brilliant masses of sun-lit cloud passed like a pageant before it, their shadows sweeping the earth beneath them. Far up, beyond and between their mighty shapes, stretches of sky shone like aquamarine and crystal, cold and tranquil. The distance was hard and clear, a brilliant royal blue, and the nearer landscape a flung quilt of color with the bright emerald of the well-watered pasturelands, the pale buff squares of the shorn cornfields, the dark swaying masses of the trees and the cottage gardens blazing with their dahlias and hydrangeas. A few larks were tossing over the fields, wind-blown and delirious, and the wings of the sea gulls, as they beat up into the wind, were like streaks of silver in the hurrying sky. Hilary did not speak. The hood of the car had been opened to the sun and the wind and he settled into the comfortably padded seat and prepared to enjoy one of the greatest pleasures of his life.

He loved speed. Tied as he was to a lame leg, his only form of locomotion a monotonous chug-chugging round the parish in the second-hand battered Trojan that was all he could afford in the way of a car, these expeditions with David often fell little short of ecstasy. Journeying in his Trojan was a painful business that he undertook for duty only, but David's glorious car went like a bird, so painlessly that he almost forgot he had a crippled body. For a moment his eyes went to the distant hills over which other men could tramp at will, and the woods in which they could lose themselves in the springtime, as he had once done, and his forehead contracted, for no one, no matter how resigned, ever quite gets used to the restrictions of an injured body. . . . Freedom. . . . He watched the strong beating wings of the gulls and the tossing of the larks, and rebellion surged bitterly through him. Why have wars and diseases to rack and weaken men's bodies and make their lives mere things of endurance instead of things of joy? So pointless and useless. He pulled himself up sharply. He knew himself to be a happy man. He had come to terms with life. He was certain he was enjoying this drive far more than David, who, if he wished, could have stopped the car and tramped to the horizon and back again without a twinge. He glanced at his nephew. He looked confident and carelessly happy, abandoned to the delight of the day, yet there was that in the rather hard set of his mouth and the challenging glance of his eyes that gave him away. The young, thought Hilary, are not happy in this generation. They are greedy for joy but their joy is too precariously held. . . . There was a good deal to be said, Hilary decided, for middle age and infirmity. The years in which one demanded much of life were left behind, together with the bitterness of not getting what one wanted. One's values, too, were altered. Gifts that once one took for granted, sunshine and birdsong, freedom from pain, sleep and one's daily bread, seemed now so extraordinarily precious.

The car, racing at full speed, had carried them from the low-lying coast country to the Forest land above. Then the trees dropped away behind them and they were up on the high bleak moor, still purple with the fading heather. The sky seemed immeasurably high and the wind here was keen and shrill. It was cold, for the sun was momentarily hidden by the clouds. It was like being on a ship at sea. Here space seemed a great and terrible power and one was tossed through it like a dying leaf or a shred of sea foam.

"It's always very grim up here when bad weather is on the way," said Hilary.

But David was enjoying it. He was on his way to enquire into the fate of a sea captain, and the cold wind and the racing clouds were in tune with his mood. At the limit of the moor was the lake where the monks from the Abbey below used to catch their fresh-water fish. Its waters were steel gray, whipped by the wind. Hilary turned his coat collar down with a sigh of relief as they turned away from the moor and slid downhill again towards green fields and human habitation.

At a cross-roads he asked hopefully, "Are we going to the Abbey first?" Hilary liked the Abbey ruins down below them in the valley as much as he liked any spot on earth. They held a mystical stillness deeper than any he knew. Magnolias and myrtles bloomed against the gray walls and when the sun was hot, rosemary scented the air. Great yew trees were black against the sky and among them, at the entrance to the Abbey, a carved calvary stood facing the river, where the Fairhaven swans rested when stormy weather drove them inland. Hilary, unemotional though he was, almost loved the place.

David was not quite so obliging as usual today. "The Hard first," he said, "we may not have time for the Abbey," and turned to his right along quiet lanes and through woods where in spring the primroses grew so thickly that the air was scented with them.

But at his first sight of the Hard, Hilary forgot his disappointment over the Abbey, for there were few places lovelier when, as today, the holiday season was over and the trippers mercifully absent. The Hard, too, had its stillness; not the living stillness of a place where many prayers have been said that cry on still in the silence, but the stillness of a place where once there has been great physical activity and now there is only the memory of it; the kind of stillness that comes at sunset after a storm has passed. For the Hard had once been one of the most important shipbuilding centers in England and now it was only a short little street of eighteenth-century cottages leading down to the quiet reaches of the river.

They parked the car at the top of the hill and walked slowly down, amiably accompanied by a kindly gray donkey. The sun was out again and the old brick of the cottages glowed rosily as it touched them. Their windows were latticed and grown around with creepers and above them the roofs were wavy as a ribbed sandy seashore. They were still quietly inhabited and smoke curled up lazily from some of the tall chimneys. Beyond the wide river the marshes were green and tawny, threaded with channels of blue water, and the horizon was shut in with thick somber woods. The gulls, as usual, were everywhere, and a few yachts rode at anchor on the river. The peace was indescribable.

Yet to David today it was alive with past activity. He could picture the prosperous town that once stood here, the shipyard, the slipways, the forges and the shops. He could hear the ring of hammer on anvil and the sound of the saws that fashioned the Forest oak trees into timber for the ships. He could hear the men singing as they worked and far away in the woods he almost imagined he could hear the sound of the ax that felled the trees. Merchant ships had been built here, men-of-war, brigs and frigates. Glorious ships had slipped down the slipways at their launching and passed down the tranquil river with flags flying and cheering crowds bidding them Godspeed on journeys to India or the China seas; and as they reached the sea and lifted to the swell the sails had blossomed like flowers upon their masts. They had passed by Damerosehay on their way to great adventure, and Aramante, perhaps, from David's own little room over the porch, had watched them go. Those had been great days, thought David, days that his friend the sea captain had known well. Simpler days than these, quieter and more spacious and with more beauty and laughter in daily living; cruder and more cruel in many ways but more hopeful and not cursed with such bitter weariness. In those days men had gone to work or war on sea or land possessed of a faith in the worth-whileness of what they did that made their sufferings light.

"All things are light to bear for those who love God." It was Hilary who had spoken, and David discovered that they were sitting on a bench in a sheltered hollow on the bank watching the sun-flecked river slipping past them on its journey to the sea. A yacht was moored close to them and the water slapped softly against its sides. There is no more soothing sound in the world. What with his dreams and the sun, and the bad nights that had been his since he came back to Damerosehay, David found that he was half asleep. For how long had old Hilary been talking? What was he saying?

"We churchmen have such an unfair advantage over you others," said Hilary, happily unconscious that though he had been speaking for five minutes he had not been attended to for any of them. "To have certain principles laid firmly down, certain things that are done and certain things that are not done, makes life comparatively simple for us. Faith, too, real faith, precludes anxiety. I am a very happy man in my possession of it. My grief is that I seem unable to hand it on. It seems to me a dreadful thing that I should sit here so rich and yet unable to give any of my riches to you."

"You can make yourself envied, Uncle Hilary," said David. "That's something, isn't it?"

"Is it?" queried Hilary doubtfully.

"I envy you your peace. You men of faith have kept something that the rest of us have lost, something that those monks in the Abbey must have had, and the men who sailed in the ships from the Hard. Singleness of mind. Faith in the value of what you are doing. And, as you say, a rule of life that can be used as a touchstone for all your actions. I envy you your faith; I wish I had it; and maybe my envy of you is one step on the road to getting it."

"Though your rule of life may not be the same as mine yet you have one," said Hilary.

"Of course," said David. "Who hasn't? One could not live without some sort of tradition, convention or even superstition that guides one. But my set of principles are not such restful things as yours. I continually doubt them because I evolved them more or less myself. I have to be continually testing them. Yours, you think, were God-given, so you never doubt them. That's why you're so peaceful, Uncle Hilary."

"I did not accept my God-given principles blindly," said Hilary. "I tested them. If I had not they would have been worthless to me."

"Yet you believed in them enough to think them worth the testing."

"Yes," said Hilary. "And it is strange to me that any man who has seriously considered them, you, for instance, should not think so too."

David was silent, for it was strange to him as well. His subconscious mind knew that he did not want to test Hilary's faith, deeply as he longed to possess it, because he was not willing to make the renunciations it would demand of him. But his conscious mind could not accept that; it was too derogatory a piece of self-knowledge to be accepted by a man who prided himself on his willingness for self-sacrifice.

"There is one principle," said Hilary, "that is, I think, common to every faith and every rule of life by which a man can guide his conduct, and which for that reason can surely be accepted without testing and without questioning."

"Yes?" asked David.

"Faithfulness," said Hilary, and suddenly he swung round on David with almost contemptuous anger. "Unless human beings keep their promises we have no sort of hope of anything but chaos for the future, and yet you propose to let Nadine be faithless to her marriage vows and George continue in his desertion of his children—and God knows faithfulness to children is the most elementary principle of conduct under the sun, even the animals understand it. The treatment of their children by many of the men and women of this generation passes my comprehension. Your cruelty to them, for the sake of your own selfish passions, is a thing I cannot understand." He stopped abruptly. He longed to tell David what had happened at the Vicarage two days ago, but he was bound by his promise to Ben. There was so much that he wanted to say to David upon the subject of the children, but the abrupt check had put it out of his mind. He got painfully to his feet, cursing his inarticulacy.

Yet his sudden short outburst had had even more influence on David than Lucilla's hour-long exposition of her views that had so shaken Nadine. Hilary's curt remarks had been like a blow in the face to David. Lucilla's theory of life as a creative art had appealed to his actor's imagination but Hilary had dealt a blow to his man's pride. . . . So that was what men like Hilary, single-minded men whom he admired, thought of him.

"It's all such a damn mess," he said again, as he had said to Nadine in the garden. Didn't Hilary understand on what an uncertain tenure one held one's life these days? Did he not realize one's eagerness to test one's own theories, to express oneself, to work, to love and to possess before it was too late?

But apparently Hilary did understand. "If you think this life is all there is," he said, "then self-sacrifice must seem to you sheer insanity. If you do not think so then it is only common sense. It all depends on your point of view."

"A thing I'm not yet clear about," said David.

Hilary, leading the way towards the Master-Builder's House for tea, made no answer. He had said his say for the time being and was thankful to have it off his chest. Now he could return to the full enjoyment of his day out.

The Master-Builder's House, now a small hotel, was the largest of the remaining houses of the Hard. The Master-Builder had been a person of great importance and his house the center of the busy thriving little town. It had been frequented by the greatest sea captains of the time and on the day of a launching as many as a hundred and fifty people, merchant captains, captains of men-of-war and all the quality of the district had sat down to dine in the banqueting hall. Though the glory had now departed the flavor of

264

splendid festival still hung about the raftered room where Hilary and David sat waiting alone for their tea.

Hilary looked round him and out of the window at the quiet scene. "Perhaps one day Portsmouth will be as derelict as this is," he said. "Given over to the herons and the gulls, with only an old gray donkey to walk about its streets."

David felt actually comforted by the thought. No matter how appalling our wars and the rumors of them, they inevitably pass away.

The room was hung round with beautiful engravings of sailing ships in titanic storms, of white-wigged sea captains and of intricate drawings of the carved poops and forecastles that had been the glory of the Hard. It had been these last that David had wanted to look at again and he jumped up and went to them.

"Until the boys told it to me again the other morning I had forgotten that story of the wrecked grain ship," said Hilary conversationally, lighting his pipe. "Did the boys make it up, I wonder, or was it part of the original legend that the injured captain had himself lashed to the mast so that he should not desert his job? It sounds to me rather like one of Ben's inventions. Ben's ideal of faithfulness to duty is such that as his dominie I find it quite difficult to live up to." And Hilary, quite unaware that he had unwittingly returned to the former subject, drew placidly upon his pipe and admired the view.

But David again felt that he had been dealt a blow. Faithfulness to duty. There seemed no getting away from it. Surrounded by these portraits of sea captains there wasn't a hope. Leaving the engravings of the carvings for a moment he looked along their ranks almost hoping that just one of them would look as though he had cursed his ship and left it. But they none of them looked like that. Far-seeing, vigilant, courageous men they all looked; hardbitten, wily and ruthless, some of them, but none of them could one suspect of lack of faithfulness to duty. His eyes ran over their names. "Roger Slade, Captain of the Victorious, Man-of-war, 38 guns, launched at the Hard in 1804." "John Wyatt, Captain of the Heroic, West-Indiaman, launched at the Hard in 1795." "Benjamin Ellis, Captain of the Wasp, Man-of-war, 74 guns, launched at the Hard in 1810." He moved on down the room. "Christopher Martyn, Captain of the Blue Bird, East-Indiaman, launched at the Hard in 1816." David stopped short and his exclamation made Hilary turn round in his chair.

He was the best man of them all. He too looked vigilant, far-seeing and courageous, but there was no ruthlessness about Christopher Martyn. His face was clear-cut and sensitive; his figure spare, held very upright with the shoulders braced. There was something taut about his whole bearing, like a rope that is stretched too tightly. One felt that no strain would break his courage but that it might snap that difficult balance of mind and nerves that is beyond control. For this man the point beyond which a human creature can suffer and be sane would come sooner than with the majority.... And he looked absurdly young to be a sea captain.

David left him abruptly and went back to the engravings of the carvings and presently his cry of delight moved the placid Hilary not only to move in his chair but to enquire mildly what the matter was. David unhooked a drawing from the dark corner where it hung and sweeping some empty cups and saucers to the floor laid it on the tea table.

"There!" he cried. "Look at that!"

Hilary, observing it, said of it as he had once of Little Village and the harbor, that it was rather pretty. David could have slain him.

"But, Uncle Hilary, don't you see what it is?"

"I should say it was the design for the carved prow of a ship, or the poop, or something of that kind," said Hilary, pleased with his perspicacity.

"But don't you recognize it?" demanded David.

"No," said Hilary. "I don't come here often, you know, and hung over there in that dark corner I can't say I've ever noticed it."

"All we Eliots are a lot of damn fools," said David hotly, forgetful of his language in his worked-up condition. "We've lived at Damerosehay for donkey's years, amiably wondering how that carving in the drawing room got there, and never even thinking of comparing it with these drawings at the Hard."

"Why should we?" asked Hilary, placidly reading out the lettering beneath the engraving. " 'Detail of the carving about the prow of the East-Indiaman Blue Bird. Designed by Captain Christopher Martyn, executed by Jonathon Cleeves, Master-carver at the Hard.' I don't see," he continued, puffing clouds of gentle smoke, "what it has to do with the carving at Damerosehay."

"But, Uncle Hilary!" shouted David. "It's it!" and his

excited finger traced the lovely leaping spirals of the wood that swirled upwards like waves tossed by the wind.

"It is a little like," agreed Hilary thoughtfully. "But not the same, surely?"

"Of course it's not the same!" said the exasperated David. "What we have at Damerosehay is not the whole prow, it's just bits of it pieced together. But, my God, how marvelously done! I bet you he did it himself."

"Who?" asked the bewildered Hilary.

David fetched the picture of Captain Martyn from the wall, removed a sugar basin and a vase of flowers from the table to the floor with the cups and saucers, and laid it beside the other. Hilary compared the two inscriptions beneath the two engravings and intelligence dawned. He even went so far as to be deeply interested. "Could this Christopher Martyn have lived at Damerosehay?" he wondered. "Martyn. The same name as old Jeremy. Was he Jeremy's father? But Aramante? Where does she come in?"

"That's what I'd give a twelve-months' income to know," said David. He paused while an indignant waitress came in, restored the engravings to their proper place and the crockery from the floor to the table, gave them the tepid tea which was all they deserved, and departed. "Obadiah says she was Jeremy Martyn's mother; yet she does not seem to have been Captain Martyn's wife. . . . You would say that was rough luck on poor Jeremy."

He allowed this to sink into Hilary's slow mind with a rather wicked pleasure. It looked to him as though Christopher and Aramante had been guilty of a love affair rather after the style of his and Nadine's. It was not only in this generation, as Hilary had implied, that the welfare of the children was disregarded for the sake of love.

But Hilary was not disconcerted. He looked across the room at the portrait of Captain Martyn, lit by the westering sun, and said, "No. That man would not have done such a thing." Then he stirred his tea thoughtfully. "Is it possible that the story of the wrecked grain ship is not a legend after all, but true, and that it was Captain Martyn's ship?"

"But of course," said David.

"Why of course?" asked Hilary.

"The blue bird. The ship's mascot. Don't you remember that according to Obadiah's grandfather it was carried ashore singing lustily?"

"That might have been sheer coincidence," said Hilary.

But David shook his head. He knew it wasn't. And he knew, too, why the character of the drawings in Captain Martyn's book had changed. His mind as well as his body had been injured by that appalling storm. A little hesitantly, as though it were a friend's confidence that he did not like to betray, he told Hilary about those drawings.

Hilary was very interested and very pitiful. There had been a time in his own life when he had wondered how much longer his mind would stand the strain of physical pain. He had never forgotten the horror of that time. He too, as well as David, felt that Christopher Martyn was his friend. "I wonder," he said, "if the old Vicar's diaries would throw any light on the story?"

"The old Vicar's diaries?" echoed David.

"Yes. My old predecessor. He was at Fairhaven for

years, you know. He must have known Jeremy Martyn well. I found a lot of his old diaries in a cupboard. They'd been overlooked when his things were cleared out of the house after his death."

"Didn't you read them?" asked the astonished David. Really, old Hilary's lack of curiosity was beyond all words.

"Only here and there," confessed Hilary. "They seemed to be mostly jottings about his garden and what he had to eat. But I kept them. I thought I would go through them thoroughly one day when I had nothing better to do.... But the state in which the old boy left his parish has given me something better to do for the last twenty years."

"I'll go through them," said David. "I'll pick them up on my way home tonight."

Tea finished, David asked the present owner of the Master-Builder's House if he might buy the engraving of Captain Martyn for any price he liked to mention. The offer was refused. These sea captains belonged to the Hard and at the Hard they must stay. David understood the refusal. He would have said the same himself.

They walked on up the hill to the chapel that formed the ground floor of one of the rose-red cottages. Once there must have been a church at the Hard. On Sundays, when the noise of the busy yards was stilled, its bell would have rung out across the quiet river, above the crying of the gulls and the lapping of the water; and masters and workmen with their wives and children, sea captains visiting the Master-Builder, of whom no doubt Christopher Martyn was often one, and seamen waiting for the launching of their ship, would have gathered there to sing their psalms, pray for the safety of those at sea and listen to an hour-long sermon from the chaplain of the Hard. That church had disappeared now but a present-day lover of the Hard had made one of the loveliest chapels in the country, the chapel of Saint Mary, to perpetuate its memory. Outside the door that led to it, on the cottage wall, hung a bell, and fastened to the door was a crucifix. These were the only outward signs of the chapel's existence.

They lifted the latch and went in and Hilary, happily and unselfconsciously, knelt at once to his prayers. David, his arms outstretched along the back of a seat, sat at the back of the chapel and looked about him at the well-remembered details that yet always touched him afresh with their beauty. He liked the dark paneling, the faint smell of incense, the lamp burning before the altar, and the beautiful old altar frontal embroidered with roses and carnations. Above all he liked the statue of the Madonna carved out of very dark wood. She was an unusual Madonna for she had the broad plump comfortable face of a country woman, just the sort of face that must have been seen years ago at the Hard, the face of a buxom wife and mother going about her business in the busy town or kneeling Sunday by Sunday, her children clinging to her skirts, saying her prayers in the shipwrights' church. Her homeliness contrasted oddly but delightfully with her crown, with the lily in her hand and the cherubs at her feet. She did not look of English workmanship, but David knew nothing of her history. He would have liked to think that some English sea captain had brought her home from abroad in one of the ships built at the Hard; but that would have been too much to hope for.

Anyway, wherever she had come from, the crown upon her homeliness seemed to glorify common labor just as the stillness and peace of the Hard glorified the busy days that once had been and now were over.

What in the world, thought David, could Hilary be praying about or for? He hoped it wasn't for him. He disliked being prayed for. He didn't think it was fair. For all you knew, under the compulsion of it, you might find yourself doing something heroic that you didn't in the least want or intend to do.

He got up and went outside and wandered up and down the grass verge of the steep little road between the cottages. The wind had risen a good deal and the sky was packed with hurrying gray clouds. The smoke from the cottage chimneys was tossed and torn as soon as it emerged and the donkey's fur was blown up edgeways. David noticed that the sun, seen now and again between the hurrying clouds, had a halo or wheel round it. At Little Village they had a saying:

"The bigger the wheal
The stronger the geal."

There's a gale coming, thought David. Curse it. The end of our fine weather. A blight fell upon him and he shivered. He felt horribly alone.

Hilary, by contrast, emerged in an irritatingly cheerful mood. David looked at him suspiciously as they got into the car.

"I have every right to pray for whom I like," said Hilary placidly, answering the look.

"I suppose you have," said David gloomily, and started the car for home. On the top of the moor a drenching shower of rain caught them, and they had to put up the hood. After that he drove as fast as he dared, the gray car traveling so quickly that it might have been one of the storm clouds racing before the wind. Yet however fast you travel, thought David, braking violently at the Vicarage gate, you cannot outdistance your own thoughts.

He went with Hilary into the study and was given half-a-dozen small shabby calf-bound volumes. "There you are," said Hilary. "If you can find anything of interest in that welter of green peas and early strawberries, and the consequent indigestion, you'll be lucky. The old man was very much taken up with his own affairs. Good night, David. Thanks for the drive. I enjoyed it. One can't go to the Hard too often."

The lane from Big Village to Little Village rose a little before it dropped down to the Harbor, and from its crest one got that sudden view of the Island and the sea that David and Lucilla had seen on the day they found Damerosehay. As David topped the rise the sunset burst upon him and once more he violently braked the car. The wind, that had been raging up out of the southwest for an hour past, had torn the clouds apart and then suddenly dropped at the turn of the tide. The great mass of banked cumulous clouds behind the Island was a glory of gold and orange, violet storm clouds passing slowly across it. Overhead the rent gray sky showed patches of cold blue and green. As David watched there was a slow wonderful intensification of color. The white cliffs of the Island flushed apricot, the

Island itself seemed all built of gold. The water reflected the colors of land and sky and the painted hulls of the boats glowed as though at any moment they would burst into flame. Even the old Castle, crouched like an animal upon the water, took on a strange soft bloom of violet color that melted its grimness into momentary beauty. Then there was as gradual a fading. The cumulous clouds slowly changed to mother-o'-pearl against a sky of pale lavender, while the Island, the Castle and the ships slipped away into rose-colored mists. Then it was all gray as a dove's wing, and only the Island lights, shining out across the darkening Estuary, told of the glory that had been. David started the car again, aware that he had been watching for a very long time, for what he had seen had been not so much a sunset as a writing on sky and sea whose meaning was beyond the power of mortality to grasp. "If one had not seen it one would not have believed it," he said to himself. "If that could be true anything could be true." He still felt very desolate, but mixed with his desolation was a queer feeling of excitement and expectation. Beyond the confines of this earth there was surely something to be known that could not be known now but one day would be as clear as daylight.

Nadine met him at the hall door. "What a sky!" she said. "Did you see it? Obadiah's gone home muttering. He says there'll be the devil of a storm before long."

In the darkness of the hall they clung to each other, and Nadine, for the first time since David had known her, was crying. They clung as desperately as though they were being dragged apart; yet there was no one with them in the hall but the shadows.

After he had taken Lucilla to her room and said good night to Nadine and Margaret, David went back to the deserted drawing room with the old parson's diaries. He put them on the table beside Lucilla's chair and went to the window, opening it wide. It was pitch dark outside, without a glimmer of moonlight or starshine, and ominously still. The quiet oppressed him. It was no settled peace but only the stillness before storm. He went back to the fireplace, kicked the logs into a blaze and turned up the lamp. The light flickered up over the dark woodwork above him. Just so, thought David, had the flung spray once rippled over its surface. Then he settled himself in his chair and turned his attention to the diaries. Pooh-Bah had long since gone off to his comfortable bed, but the Bastard, with whom it was a matter of principle to offer companionship to any member of the family who looked a little lonely, settled down too and propped his hairy chin on David's shoe. . . . David was sitting in Lucilla's chair, the chair of the head of the family. The Bastard liked to have some one in that chair. It gave him a feeling of stability. Pinioning David's foot to the floor with his chin and rhythmically thudding his tail on the parquet he signified that, please, he would like David always to be here when Lucilla was absent.

As Hilary had said, the diaries were mostly taken up with the old parson's garden and interior, what he had put in them both and his subsequent sufferings, but there was a certain amount of parish gossip, notes about the weather and the habits of birds. The old parson had apparently been very interested in birds, as indeed dwellers between sea marshes and inland woods can hardly fail to be. "Saw a Black Throated Diver today," said one entry, "and walked up to Damerosehay to ask Jeremy Martyn if he had also seen it. He had. Never can I see a rare bird but Jeremy Martyn sees it first. He tells me that on Wednesday last he certainly saw an Arctic Skua out on the marshes. I do not believe it. Nor do I believe that he sees Storm Petrels and Sabine's Gulls so often as he says he does." A little later came a much more exciting entry. "Jeremy Martyn declares he saw a Golden Oriol in his garden today. I have never seen one in mine. I am inclined to think that old Jeremy romances about his birds. Take, for instance, the ridiculous story about the Blue Bird, not a Kingfisher, which he declares he sees at rare intervals in his garden. It seems that Captain Christopher Martyn, his father, who died years before I came to Fairhaven, became possessed of an American Blue Bird during his travels. This he carried always with him as his mascot and the first—and last—ship which he commanded was named after it. In the wreck of this same ship at Fairhaven in the early years of the century, in the worst storm ever known in these parts, the bird was saved, but in the subsequent confusion, both Captain Martyn and the unfortunate lady who shared his fortunes being smitten with illness, it escaped into the Damerosehay garden and was never seen again until the day of the Captain's death twenty years later. From that date onwards Jeremy Martyn vows he has occasionally seen it. Was there ever so nonsensical a tale? Jeremy is a charming old man, and his amazing generosity to the poor most praiseworthy, but un-

276

doubtedly he is a little touched. Not for a moment do I believe that he saw that Golden Oriol. I have never seen one."

Then Jeremy and his birds momentarily disappeared from the diaries owing to a distressing rheumatic attack which seized the old parson to the exclusion of all other thoughts from his mind. It was in another volume altogether, apparently overlooked by Hilary, that he noted that he felt better with the appearance of warm and settled weather, and had walked up to Damerosehay to tell Jeremy that he had seen a Ring Ouzel. So had Jeremy. Much annoyed the old parson had refused an invitation to dinner but had thought better of it upon hearing that Jeremy had just fetched up from the cellar the very last bottle of his famous port, laid down in 1799 by Mr. Richard Martyn, the Captain's uncle, who had built the house of Damerosehay.

"Whilst discussing our port, which I am told is bad for rheumatism but don't believe it," wrote the old parson, "Jeremy once more mentioned that he had seen his Blue Bird. I hope my smile was not too incredulous, for I am sincerely attached to the generous old gentleman and consider his foibles to be entirely harmless, but apparently it was slightly so, for he said to me, 'Old friend, you don't believe that tale. Never mind. But I'll tell you a tale that *is* true, and if you don't believe it then may God forgive you, for unbelief will show in you a most un-Christian frame of mind.' At this I gave him my best attention and accepted a second glass of port, for I am convinced that port, if it be truly excellent, is possessed of most medicinal qualities. His tale was the story of his father and mother and whether it be true or no I cannot say. I merely set it down here exactly as he told it.

" 'Human nature,' he said to me, 'is the most foolish and dastardly thing ever created by an otherwise intelligent creator. Give me birds,' he said, 'give me birds every time.' At this I endeavored to pull him up slightly, for his remark seemed to me to have about it a flavor of the blasphemous, but he refilled my slightly depleted glass and continued with his narration. 'Human nature must always think the worst,' he said. 'My neighbors here have from the very day of my birth insisted upon thinking that I was the illegitimate son of Captain Christopher Martyn. In point of fact I am not his son at all, I am the perfectly legitimate child of Louis du Plessis-Pascau. But would my neighbors believe it? No. At last, partly in acquiescence to their insistence, partly because Captain Martyn had named me after my mother as the heir of Damerosehay, but chiefly because I was proud to bear his name, I changed my name to Martyn and referred to him always as my father.'

"I expressed myself as astonished at my old friend's remarks and begged to be told his correct history. The association of Captain Martyn and Aramante du Plessis-Pascau had, I knew, always been considered by the neighborhood to be a most discreditable one and I told him I should be happy to have it proved otherwise. At this he handed me one of the very delicious Damerosehay apricots, and continued with his story.

" 'My mother,' he said, 'was an English girl, an orphan, the niece of a doctor resident at Seacombe on the Estuary, in those days a very flourishing little seaport indeed. Her uncle had brought her up and she was therefore a resident of this district and remarkably devoted to it. At the age of sixteen she married, against her uncle's wishes, Louis du Plessis-Pascau, the descendant of a French gentleman who had fled with his family to Seacombe at the time of the French revolution, and with him she emigrated to Australia. Here she was exceedingly unhappy, for she was of the breed of those who sicken and droop, away from the bit of earth where they have been born and bred. . . . Her soul, she said, was always in Hampshire. When she went away she left it behind her, but when she came back it flew to her breast like a homing bird, and then she was herself again. . . . Moreover her young husband was an improvident scamp, and their poverty was soon very great. After only two years of married life he died, leaving her an expectant mother with hardly a penny in the world.'

"I exclaimed in horror at such a calamity befalling the unfortunate young lady, and he agreed that it had been indeed most deplorable, especially as she had been peculiarly friendless. 'She had a very proud and independent disposition,' he said, 'she did not make friends easily and she would not ask help of the few acquaintances she had. What would have happened to her I do not know had she not met with Captain Martyn, whose Blue Bird sailed into the port of Sydney, where she was then living, just in the nick of time. Poor Captain Martyn was at that time smarting under a terrible indignity. His ship was an East India-man and in his previous voyage, his first as captain, his Blue Bird had been to the East Indies and back in record time. He was a young man and he thought he had deserved well of his company. Yet on returning to England he was commanded to convey, among other commodities, a cargo of donkeys from the Hard to Australia. I have been told that the embarkation of those donkeys caused such a day of riotous merriment as has not been known at the Hard before or since; but Captain Martyn himself was deeply wounded at what he considered an insult to his ship.

" 'And so they met, this young man and woman, both laboring under a sense of injury, and found that they had besides much else in common. Both of them were orphans and both of them belonged to the same beloved patch of country. Aramante was a native of Seacombe and Captain Martyn of Fairhaven, where his uncle Richard Martyn, whose heir he was, had built for himself this fine house of Damerosehay. They made great friends and Aramante confided in Christopher that she had an overwhelming longing: to go home and bear her baby in Hampshire. They made great friends, I say, but with Christopher Martyn it was more than friendship; married man though he was he loved my mother as a man can love only once in a lifetime, that is to say with a devotion that every misfortune under the sun, even death itself, is powerless to quench.'

"Here I thought it my duty to draw Jeremy's attention to the fact that this devotion was most discreditable to Captain Martyn, considering that his affections should have been centred upon the lady with whom he was united in the connubial bond. But Jeremy, merely remarking that Captain Martyn's wife was a faithless young creature incapable of retaining a good man's affection, waved my remark aside as beside the point, noticed at last that my glass was again empty, refilled it and continued his tale.

" 'Captain Martyn,' he said, 'realising my mother's poverty-stricken condition, offered to take her back to England on his ship as his guest. He was returning at once, bound for Seacombe with a cargo of grain and several passengers. He was very honest with her. He told her that he loved her but could not marry her. He told her that though there would be other passengers on board there was no woman among them. He told her exactly what the risks would be; possible risk to her life if her child should be born too soon with only the rough ship's doctor to attend her; certain risk to her reputation. My mother accepted these risks. She was very strong and a good sailor, and she was never one to care what others said of her so long as she herself knew her innocence. My mother was a very brave as well as a very beautiful woman, very confident, self-reliant and determined. She accepted Captain Martyn's offer. She was lodged in his own cabin, all the passengers' cabins being already taken, together with the blue bird in its cage, while he slung a hammock with his first officer.

" 'All went well until they were two days out from home, when they were caught in that famous but terrible storm. You have read about it and heard many a tale of it. Few ships survived it. My mother was a brave woman yet till the end of her life she could never speak of that storm without feeling again the fear and horror of it; the great green sliding hills of sea, the slow climb of the ship up their sides, the shuddering sickening fall into the valleys beyond, the scream of the wind, the gradual splintering and disin-

281

tegration of the ship under the battering of the waves, the terrible fetid atmosphere below decks with every port closed; and my mother near her time and sorely afraid for the safety of her child. Several times, she said, during that terrible two days and a night, Christopher Martyn came down to see her where she lay terrified, in his cabin, his blue bird in its cage swinging from the ceiling, chirruping contentedly as though the wind rocked it in its native forest. The last time he came to her he held her hands for a moment and told her not to be afraid, she and her child were safe in his care and no harm should come to them. Although she knew that one man had little power against the elements, yet, she said, she was comforted and strengthened. She did not see him again until they were wrecked upon the marshes. It was not until afterwards that she heard how as he went up on deck after his visit to her a wave had hurled him against the bulwark, injuring him severely. But he would not go below. He had himself lashed to the broken main mast that he might hold his men together and direct their work upon the ship up till the last moment. He almost did that. It was not until a short half-hour before the end that a falling spar knocked him unconscious. You will say, perhaps, that it was a rather theatrical bit of bravado; yet I think it was typical of the man; he hated to submit to weakness, either moral or physical. Even on the day of his death he was to the best of his ability acting the part of a healthy man.'

"I told my host that I thought the Captain had here got hold of truth. I reminded him that the ancient Greeks in their religious drama acted what they wished to happen, a good harvest, for instance, or protection from storm. The sincere acting of a desired event can sometimes actually create it.

" 'Ah,' said Jeremy. 'If one has sufficient faith. That is mankind's trouble: lack of faith. If we had faith as a grain of mustard seed there would be no limit to our power of creation. We could make of this world an earthly paradise.'

"He became a little absent-minded, thinking over past days, and I had to recall him to himself by saying how curious it was that Captain Martyn should have been wrecked so close to his uncle's house of Damerosehay.

" 'Most providential,' said Jeremy. 'My mother and Captain Martyn and the blue bird in its cage were carried here, and next day I was born, as my mother had wished, in her own beloved county of Hampshire. In this house I first saw the light, here have I lived and here, please God, I will die, and be buried in my garden where my birds will sing over me and the sunshine strike down through the good earth to warm my old bones. This spot of earth is to me as near Paradise as makes no difference.'

"Again I had to recall him to the matter in hand but once I had done so he became very much in earnest, pushing his glass aside, though it was not yet empty, Jeremy being singularly unappreciative of his own good port, and leaning towards me over the table.

" 'When my mother was up and about again,' he said, 'she made a decision which, some would say, ruined her whole life. That's as may be. If life goes on beyond death then her decision must have greatly enriched that part of it which she lives now; if it doesn't then she was of all women the most foolish. Christopher Martyn had been injured not only physically but mentally. The Martyns were a tragic family. The seeds of mental illness were in them. Christopher was a highly-strung man, far too highly-strung for a seaman. The whole stress and strain of the storm, as well as the blow on his head, brought to life in him those seeds which otherwise might have remained dormant. The old man, his uncle, summoned doctors from London and Christopher's wife from Portsmouth. The doctors shook their heads gravely over his condition, and his wife, after an afternoon spent in his company, went back to Portsmouth and most sensibly eloped with a healthy and wealthy young ensign in the Guards. My mother, then, calmly and quietly as was her wont, took a good look at the situation. Here in this house with her and her baby were an old man, frail and feeble, and a young one smitten with what promised to be incurable illness, and both of them devoid of helpful relations. Who was to look after them? Christopher Martyn, you understand, was suffering and melancholic, with a clouded mind, but he was in no sense a madman. There was no need for him to be, in the terrible phrase, 'put away,' if proper care could be given him. A mental asylum, even one provided for the well-to-do, was in those days a terrible place, regarded with shrinking horror by both the sick and the sane. My mother decided that her friend should not go there while the breath of life was in her. She believed that he had saved both herself and her child, and my mother was always very faithful in friendship and very aware of its obligations. She suggested to the old man that she should be nurse and housekeeper to them both, an offer that he

284

gratefully accepted. You will realise the greatness of my mother's sacrifice when you remember that she was a young and beautiful woman and that at this time she did not love Christopher Martyn; she was merely doing what she thought to be her duty.

" 'It was unfortunate for my mother that the old man only lived a year after she made her home at Damerosehay. To a certain extent his presence had protected her from gossip; at his death it broke loose in a venomous flood. She could have lived it down, of course, if she had yielded to the entreaties of her own relatives and left Christopher Martyn after his uncle's death. But this she would not do. While he lived, she said, she would not leave him, and people might think what they would; she cared nothing for what they thought. She was arrogant about it, proud and high-handed. She antagonised the few friends and relatives who still believed in her, and they too left her. What the loneliness of her life must have been, shut up in this house with a sick man and a little child, and she young and high-spirited and beautiful, it is difficult to conceive.

" 'Christopher Martyn lived for twenty years, suffering in mind and body to an extent which one does not like to think of, his life only made endurable by his great love for my mother and for Damerosehay, and by his skill with brush and pencil. He would spend hours over his drawings, and very terrifying I thought most of them were, though full of mystical feeling, yet he got great comfort out of them in his ceaseless childlike grieving over his lost ship and the blue bird that had escaped from its cage in the confusion of the tragic arrival at Damerosehay. He must have been a fine artist and craftsman in his younger days.... That clock which you see there he designed himself when he was staying at the Hard while the Blue Bird was a-building. I am leaving it to my gardener Obadiah, who dotes upon it.... I was very fond of Christopher Martyn. I could not have been fonder had he actually been, as gossip declared him to be, my father. No amount of illness, mental or physical, can ever really obscure a great and gentle spirit. As for my mother, her feeling for him grew with the years from friendship to a love as great as his for her. It was, I think, perpetually nourished by her service to him. When he died then for her the light passed from this world.

" 'Yet she rejoiced in his freedom and she did not weep. We buried him at sea, as he had desired, and on the evening of his burial we saw a bright blue bird winging its way up into the golden sunset sky. It tossed in delight, as a lark does, and sang and sang and sang. Several times since, though you do not believe me, I have seen that bird.

" 'My mother lived for another twenty-five years, and she seldom left Damerosehay. Though she was still a comparatively young woman when Captain Martyn died yet she had spent her strength for him and centred her life upon him for so long that she could not now break away into independent living of her own. She was most truly, to use an old-fashioned word, his relict. Now that she had not got him to wait upon she gave her whole time and attention to his home. The beautifying of Damerosehay was her great absorption. The carving that had been saved from the Blue Bird had been put together as an overmantel for the parlor under the guidance of Captain Martyn himself, but there were many other things that she did to make the house more lovely. Among other additions she made a little chapel which I think she thought of as a monument to Christopher, because it grieved her that his burial at sea had left her with no grave to tend; when she herself came to die she told me to put upon her headstone the texts she would have liked to have put upon his. She took great pleasure in the designing of the windows for the chapel: Saint Christopher carrying the child to safety across the wild waters, as once the Blue Bird had carried me, and that other picture of the glorious freedom from death and suffering which she believed would one day be gained not by men and women only but by the whole natural world as well. "A melodious noise of birds among the branches, a running that could not be seen of skipping beasts." And she planted fruit trees in the garden, and many shrubs and bushes that would increase the joy of the wild birds whose sanctuary it was, and she repaired the crumbling garden walls and set in them those wrought-iron gates that you admire so much. Sometimes, in my comings and goings, I protested at such expenditure for an unknown posterity, for I was unmarried and who would eventually inherit the place I could not conceive. But she said she knew that she and Christopher would have successors at Damerosehay, men and women and children who would love the place as they had done, finding in it the same sanctuary from sorrow and drawing from it the same strength to endure. For them, she said, she laboured. Well, I think she was wrong there. I have been improvident. In my desire to make of Damerosehay a place from which succour flows out to a suffering world I have given away far too much money, and now the place falls to rack and ruin about me. I am an old man, and near my death, with a childless cousin for my nearest relative. Damerosehay, too, is surely near its end.'

"He at last drained his glass and was silent. Outside the uncurtained windows the long June evening was still luminous, for Jeremy dines early. We heard the swans passing overhead and somewhere in the garden there was a blackbird singing. I thanked my old friend for his story. I was, I said, glad to hear the truth of these things, and happy to know them so creditable to all concerned. Then, seeing him disinclined for further company, I bade him good night and went home."

3.

Finding the right entry and deciphering the delicate pointed handwriting had taken a long time. Two o'clock chimed from the clock on the mantelpiece when David at last put down the old parson's diaries. The fire was just a few pale feathers of ashes and the lamp was dim. David lay back in Lucilla's chair, his hands behind his head, and looked up at the darkness of the carved overmantel. The Bastard was still at his feet, still holding him down in his place, his soft snores the only sound in the room.

So now all that he would ever know of his predecessors at Damerosehay was known to him. Christopher Martyn. Aramante du Plessis-Pascau. Jeremy Martyn. His grandmother Lucilla Eliot. They seemed to him closely linked to each other and all four of them so close to him that he could have put out his hand and touched them. There are rela-

tionships of place as well as of blood, and it was Damerosehay that linked those four together. Each owner of it was
in a sense the child of the previous owner because he or
she had lived in and loved this place. And, as Lucilla had
said, children are the children of the mind and soul as well
as of the body. There was a relationship between Lucilla
in her life of service to her children and her grandchildren
that reached back through old Jeremy with his generosity
to Aramante and Christopher in their heroism. Their actions
had bred in them a certain attitude of mind that linked them
together far more closely than any tie of blood could have
done. But what of David Eliot, whom Lucilla had so hoped
would follow her at Damerosehay? He felt himself their
child, their direct descendant; yet his honesty of mind drove
him to ask himself what right he had to claim that relationship. Would he, in their place, have acted as they had done?
Was he capable of their sacrifices? What sacrifices had he
ever made? He knew quite well that in giving up Damerosehay for Nadine, a sacrifice on which he had rather
prided himself, he was not suffering one quarter as much as
he would suffer if he gave up Nadine for Damerosehay. He
suddenly knew, too, now that he had read those diaries,
that Lucilla's conception of truth was a truer one than his
with which he had justified his decision to marry Nadine.
Lucilla's idea of truth as a creative thing had been Christopher Martyn's when with a shattered body lashed to the
mast he had created for the encouragement of his men the
illusion that he still was what he should have been, a captain in competent charge of his ship; it had been Aramante's
when in her service to Christopher she had acted a devotion

she had not at first felt. It would be his and Nadine's if they hid their love for each other from all knowledge but their own and acted in the world's sight the parts of dutiful aunt and nephew. And then, searing him, came Hilary's scorn. What of faithfulness to promises, without which the future must be chaos? And what of the children? Lucilla had kept her promises, she had considered the children; Aramante had considered even children of the future at Damerosehay of whose existence she could have no certain knowledge. Children are the future, and always, it seemed, those whose kinship he desired worked for the future rather than for the passing satisfaction of the present. Evidently they believed in it. They believed it could be worked for and created. They pushed their belief in it on and on even beyond the confines of death and their sacrifices were the obvious result of their belief. They were foolish for this world but wise for the world to come. He envied them their faith. Was it possible that it could be got the other way round, and that faith in immortality could follow upon sacrifices made for it?

He lifted the Bastard's chin gently off his foot and moved quietly about the room, tidying it as Lucilla liked it to be tidied. But he did not feel quiet, for the conflict that had been for so long hidden in his subconscious mind was now in the open. He was fighting it consciously and with desperation.

He put out the light, took the Bastard to his bed and went slowly upstairs. Late though it was there was a line of light showing under Nadine's door. Was she too awake and fighting? As he shut himself into his room there was the first moan in the chimney, the first rush of wind over the roof. The promised gale was on its way. But he hardly noticed it, for the storm in his mind had dragged every sensation down into its own whirlpool.

CHAPTER TEN

I.

By the next morning the wind was high, and still rising, only slackening occasionally when storms of drenching rain swept in from the sea. "White rain," Obadiah called it; a rain so solid that one could hardly see through it. It promised to be the worst gale they had had for years, he said. It was the season of the high tides, too. He paused in his boot-cleaning to rub his stubbly chin and shake his head darkly at Cook, who had only arrived a few days ago and meant to give notice at once now that she had seen the kind of weather they had in these parts. It was her afternoon out and how was she to get along the coast road in all this muck to catch the bus to the cinema, could anyone tell her that? No one could and she went to Margaret to give notice. Jill, too, was depressed, for tomorrow was her afternoon out and Alf had gone away for two days to attend (so he said) his other grandfather's funeral. And Rose the heavy-handed was very low in her mind because her friend the baker's boy had taken up with that red-headed chit at the Eel and Lobster. Altogether the gloom in the kitchen was appalling and throughout the day seeped slowly through the whole house, spreading that awful depression which is characteristic of kitchen gloom only.

David and Nadine, tormented as they both were by a conflict that they could not yet speak of to each other, felt the oppression of the storm. The tumult of it, the rush of wind and water, the rattling of the windows and the screaming in the chimneys, seemed beating upon their nerves. They could not settle to anything. After he had driven the little boys to their lessons, the wind so high even inland that he could hardly hold the car straight upon the road, David tried to go for a walk. It was useless. The wind was too wild and exhausting and he had to go home again.

In the drawing room he found Lucilla serenely teaching Caroline. She was so used to the Damerosehay storms that she alone seemed unaffected by the wind; though she did own that she never remembered one quite as bad as this. Nadine sat near them stitching a little desperately at her embroidery. Her face was paler than usual and her dark eyes violet-shadowed. As David came in she looked up at him and smiled, then dropped her eyes to her work again. David sat down in a far corner with a book, and over the top of it he quietly watched her.

That had been a strange look that she had given him. It had been full of love but full of a desperate pleading. For what was she pleading? That he should not desert her, or that he should not let it break him if she were to desert him? He could not know which it was, for he could not talk to her until his own mind was made up. As the battle in him swayed this way and that he did not forget her, and the suffering which he might cause her if he were to take the part of tradition and leave her for Damerosehay; but it was characteristic of that strain of ruthlessness in him that as he had been willing to sacrifice Lucilla's happiness to one set of principles so he was equally prepared to sacrifice Nadine's to another. One could not help it. It seemed to him that while we are such imperfect creatures there is seldom a clear choice between right and wrong, only between two wrongs. Whatever one does someone must be hurt. The only thing is to choose the wrong that does least hurt to the greatest number. For during the night he had come right round to Lucilla's and Hilary's point of view. It is the community that matters. What he was not sure of yet was whether he was as ready to suffer for his new convictions as he had been for the old. For they asked far more of him. They asked too much. His love for Nadine was like hunger and thirst. Without her it seemed to him that he would have no life at all. Did God, if there was a God, did those fiery spirits whose kinship he wanted, expect one to give up one's very life?

He got up abruptly and went out into the garden to Margaret. Within the high walls there was a certain amount of shelter, and Margaret, in mackintosh and boots, was staking her precious plants against the storm and cutting the loveliest of the flowers before they could be dashed to pieces by the rain. She looked very grim. The glory of her garden was doomed. After this storm it could not be the same again. The summer was over. She had nothing to look forward to now but the chrysanthemums, and then the patient nursing of single blooms in sheltered places. It would be another five months before she could begin to plan again for beds glowing with color and branches heavy with warmth and perfume.... Yet what there still was should be saved.

She straightened herself when she saw David and pushed wisps of untidy hair back from her forehead with the back of a wet hand. "Get some bast from the tool house and come and help me," she commanded.

He obeyed her and soon they were working companionably together. The garden was the one place where David got on well with Margaret and where he could recapture his boyhood's affection for her; for in the garden Margaret shed all her shyness and her gaucherie. Her thick tweeds and her boots, her background of trees and earth and sky, suited her and she knew it. She fitted into them as comfortably as Lucilla into the setting of her drawing room. When she sniffed the scent of the cool wet earth, and felt the worn handle of her trowel fitting into the hollow of her hand, she was as happy as David was when he smelt powder and paint and felt the boards of the theater once more under his feet. As he held a stake ready for Margaret a sudden nostalgia for London and the stage swept over him.

"After all," he said to Margaret, "there's nothing in the world like work."

"Work and one's own home," said Margaret. "It's hard to say which is best. They help each other, and I don't think that one can accomplish much without the other. Be careful what you're doing, David, you're stepping on my violas."

"Are you so devoted to Damerosehay, Aunt Margaret?"

asked David, stepping off the violas and trampling instead upon the mignonette.

"Oh no," said Margaret. "I'm fond of it, of course, but it's not my own home. Mind my mignonette."

What was her own home to a woman, David wondered. To a man it was the place where his forefathers had lived, fathers either of blood or spirit, the place where he had grown up, as he had grown up at Damerosehay. It had gone to the making of him and so to the making of his work. Or else it was the place that he had made out of the proceeds of his work. The two were, as Margaret had said, inseparably connected. But to a woman? Why did Margaret not feel that Damerosehay was home?

"Why, Aunt Margaret?" he asked.

"Because I'm fond of my mignonette. I see no reason why it should be trampled into the earth by your great feet just because its day is over."

"No. I mean I wonder why Damerosehay does not seem home to you?"

Margaret straightened herself and wondered too. "It has not sheltered my children," she said at last. Then she flushed bright red. What a thing to say to a young man like David! It was dreadful the way the garden loosened her tongue.

"But the garden?" insisted David gently. "Isn't the garden home?"

"To a gardener, my dear," said Margaret, "any garden is home. It's home and work together. It's not any one garden, you see, it's the earth and things growing in it that one loves. There are times when I get tired of this particular garden. It's difficult to think of new things to do in it. I'd rather like a fresh one to remake from the beginning."

"Then if you ever had to leave Damerosehay you wouldn't break your heart?" asked David.

"Of course not. If in the course of time you ever live here with your children I shall be just as happy, or happier, living with Hilary. He has asked me to."

"Would Hilary's house seem more like home to you?"

"I think it would," said Margaret. "I could do what I liked in it. Hilary would not mind what I did. He is in so many ways such an utter child that I could do what I liked with him too."

She laughed, thinking of Hilary tenderly and maternally, and David felt a sense of relief, knowing that she would not mind if one day he turned her out of Damerosehay. He looked back at the old house and tried unsuccessfully to picture himself living there with his children. . . . If they were his own children they would be the children of another wife, not Nadine. . . . Just now, loving Nadine so much, it was beyond the power of even his vivid imagination to think of himself as able to love another woman. Yet these things happened. There seemed no wound that in the end time could not heal. He knew that with his mind, though his senses, gripped by pain, could not let him feel it. The senses, capable of dealing only with the moment, make pain seem eternal. The mind, building the future, knows better.

"The bast, dear," said Margaret, patiently, for the third time.

David returned to a sense of his duties, and they worked

on happily together for another hour. The wind swept over them, and now and again the rain drenched them, but neither of them cared. David supposed that he was not a true gardener because he could not agree with Margaret that it was the earth itself that mattered, not a particular walled-in space of it. It was the walled-in space that mattered to him, this particular walled-in space of Damerosehay. In no other garden would he have been content to stand for an hour in puddles of water handing out bast to his aunt.

Margaret, heroically enduring the trampling of her plants, agreed with him that he was no gardener. He seemed never to have the slightest idea of what was beneath his feet.

2.

By lunchtime the rain as well as the wind had so increased that there could be no going out for anybody for the rest of the day; in the afternoon it was therefore all hands to the wheel to keep the children happy and good. It was no easy task, for Ben, who hated noise and turmoil, was jumpy and nervy, Caroline was tearful with fright and Tommy was apparently possessed of a demon of wickedness. By two-thirty he had tied the cats' tails together and dressed up Pooh-Bah in Nadine's best nightgown. By two-forty-five he had given the Bastard Queenie to play with and let out the white mice in the kitchen. By three o'clock there was such a row going on in the dining room, such singing and shouting and beating of drums, that the whole household hastened to the scene of the disturbance to find him, very flushed and bright-eyed and exhilarated, walking round and round the table beating on a silver salver with a poker. A strong smell of alcohol, and a pronounced lurch in his walk, led to the terrible discovery that he had mixed himself a cocktail from the secret store that Ellen kept for the grown-up grandsons and was very drunk indeed. There might have been a very painful revelation of Ellen's and the grandsons' duplicity but for the fine generalship of Nadine, who got her back to the cupboard door and vowed to Lucilla, who entered last upon the distressing scene, that it was only the cooking sherry from the kitchen. As it was it was all most painful, and by three-fifteen Tommy had been very sick. By three-thirty, however, he had recovered, and by three-forty-five David had organized a circus in the drawing room to turn their thoughts.

This was a great success, for David was not the only member of the Eliot family possessed of dramatic talent. Tommy in a scarlet bathing suit jumping through a hoop, Caroline in her party frock playing Red Riding-Hood to Pooh-Bah's Wolf, and Ben's lithe figure turning somersaults were much admired; and Queenie turning color upon each of her colored handkerchiefs in turn was only to be outdone by Bib and Tucker in pink bows riding upon the Bastard's back. It was altogether what David called a commercial as well as an artistic success, for sixpence-halfpenny was taken at the box office for Lucilla's missionary box, and this over and above the expenses of the production, which came to nothing but two eggs which fell out of Red Riding-Hood's basket and were smashed on the parquet floor, and a little cake which Pooh-Bah, not quite certain of his duties as the Wolf, ate by mistake. It was successful, but exhausting, and after a large and filling tea in the nursery they were thankful to settle down round the drawing-room fire and have Lucilla read them "Two Flat Irons for a Farthing." The children loved Lucilla's old-fashioned story books, they liked them far better than their own modern ones. There was something thrilling in the thought that when their father and Aunt Margaret had been children they too had sat on the floor at Lucilla's feet and listened to these very same tales.

But after a little while Mrs. Ewing's beautiful English, Lucilla's gentle voice, and even the lovely leaping flames of the log fire were powerless to hold them. The storm got at them. Now and then the rush of it, and the sheets of rain hurled against the windows, quite drowned Lucilla's voice so that they could not hear what she was reading. The draughts came creeping under the door like live things and the crying in the chimney sounded as though some poor maddened creature was imprisoned there. Now and then, above the wind and rain, they could hear the roar of the angry sea and the poor oak trees in the wood tossing and moaning. Damerosehay storms were always uncanny things but this one was more creepy than usual. The noise of the circus and the clatter of tea had kept it at bay, but now it was right in the room with them. Though none of them spoke of it, yet it captured their thoughts and played upon their nerves so that they were all of them, except Tommy, filled with a strange dreary misery.

Lucilla, while she read steadily on and her face was quiet and composed, was thinking, There is such misery in the world, such torment of mind and body, such fear and storm and conflict. It is all abroad tonight. It is crying in the wind and weeping in the rain. And I have brought all these children and grandchildren into the world. . . . All these children. . . . And soon I shall die and leave them to I know not what. I want them to keep together and to love each other. I want them to stand foursquare to the world. Oh, David, David, please keep them together. Please. What a wind tonight. A horrible wind.

And Margaret thought, Oh, my poor garden. In spite of the stakes there'll not be a thing left standing. I wish I didn't get such rheumatism working in the wet. I wish I wasn't getting old. I wish Cook hadn't given notice. I wish I had a son like David. Oh, my poor garden. I hate these gales.

And Nadine thought, It was Ben, and he saw us. That was why he had asthma. Year after year living with a man you don't love. No one knows what it means. Yes, Grandmother knows. One can't give up a man one loves so desperately. One can't. It's like tearing your heart out. Yet Grandmother did it. She had the courage. I wish I could talk to her. I wish she liked me. Ben had asthma. I have brought these children into the world. It's bad for children to be separated from their father. George is a good father. I can't give up David. I can't. What a vile wind. I hate the noise of it.

And David thought, Was it a storm like this through which he had to guide that ship? All those lives in his charge: the passengers, the crew, Aramante and her child. It is an appalling thing that the lives of others should be so affected by what we do. Especially the lives of the children.

Family life. Community life. National life. Broken promises mean chaos for them all. The more populated the earth the more hampering interdependence becomes. Only the savages have real freedom. I wish I was a savage. Curse this wind! What did he feel like when he realized he had to preserve those lives through that storm?

And Caroline thought, I don't like it. It makes a noise. I wish Mother would have me on her lap.

And Tommy thought, I'll put Queenie in Cook's bed. I wish the house would blow down. It would be fun.

And Ben thought, I don't like it. It's like hammers beating on me. I wish Father was here. I wish I was little again and could ride on his shoulder like the boy in the picture.

And at last none of them, least of all Lucilla herself, listened to a word she was saying. The children seemed glad to go to bed and the grown-ups were glad to have them go. The battering of the storm and their individual worries made them all so restless that the only comfort lay in perpetually doing something different from what they had been doing before. It was a relief to David to write a quite unnecessary letter, a further relief to fight his way to the pillar box with it, a greater one to find it was time to go upstairs and change for dinner.

As he passed the open door of the boys' room he stopped. Tommy was splashing in the bath, and Ben in his blue pajamas was alone in their room, his face pressed against the uncurtained window where outside in the gray twilight the great storm rushed by. To each side of him the colors of the stained glass windows glimmered only very faintly in the strange pallid light that was the stricken day's desperate attempt at a sunset. David tried to picture the room as it had been in Aramante's time. Perhaps she had put a *prie-dieu* in the window where Ben stood now and while she prayed she would have looked across the garden to that break in the oak wood through which one could see the patch of marsh where the *Blue Bird* had been wrecked. In imagination she would have seen it happen all over again, and perhaps autumn by autumn she had watched for the springing of the stunted corn. But of course she had. That was why there was a cornfield in the foreground of the picture of Saint Christopher. "Except a grain of wheat fall into the ground and die..."

Ben gave a little gasp.

"What is it, old man?" David asked, going over to him.

Ben seemed frightened as well as excited, but he did not remove his squashed button of a nose from the glass. "Look!" he said.

"What?" asked David. He could see nothing but the gray whirling twilight, and that bleak stretch of windswept marsh framed in the tossing branches of the oak trees, almost invisible now in the gathering darkness.

"The ship!" said Ben. "It's driving right on to the shingle bank. The sea is coming in over the marshes."

"No, Ben," said David. "How could it? The tide's going down."

"But it is!" cried Ben. "And the ship'll be wrecked!"

"There's no ship there, Ben," said David. "You're dreaming."

"I'm not dreaming, I'm awake," said Ben fiercely. "It is there. It is." And then uncertainty seemed to seize him.

He withdrew his squashed nose from the pane and rubbed his eyes. He sighed and began to tremble. David picked him up, found he was shivering with cold, inserted him firmly into his bed, drew the curtains and lit the candles.

"Never take any notice of what you think you see at twilight," he told Ben. "It's a queer light. Owl's light, the country people call it, because it's uncanny, like owls. Have you got a hot-water bottle?"

"No!" said Ben with scorn. "I don't have a hot-water bottle until November."

David went to the bathroom, burst in upon the dripping Tommy and filled one at the hot tap. . . . Damerosehay might be old-fashioned but its water was always piping hot.

"See me do the porpoise roll," said Tommy.

"No thanks," said David.

But Tommy took no notice of this discouragement. As David went out a realistic side-to-side movement sent the water surging over the top of the bath on to the floor. Hastily closing the door David supposed that Margaret would deal with the mess later, and went back to Ben, who was coughing.

"Now stop that!" he cried in exasperation, and then, more kindly, reproached by Ben's great eyes fixed mournfully upon him, "What is it, old man? What do you want?"

"I'm not coughing to get anything, thank you," said Ben irritably. "I never do. I just cough. I didn't cough to get away from school, like you thought I did. I just coughed a bit more than I was coughing anyhow. I want Father. Mind you, I'm not coughing to get him, I just want him." And he coughed again.

David sat down despairingly upon the bed. All the friendliness that had once existed between himself and Ben had now somehow disappeared. The affection that used to shine in the little boy's eyes when they looked at him had gone. They were dull and without light. Were he again to have a fright, such as he had had over Obadiah's book, it would not now be David to whom he would go for comfort. An unreasonably deep sadness seized David as he realized this. . . . It must have been Ben who had seen them in the wild garden. . . . Such a little thing, such a small maladjustment of what a child considered the right arrangement of things, could apparently upset him disastrously.

It was no good staying any longer with the unresponsive Ben, and he got up. He carefully avoided looking at the window over Ben's bed. He did not want to be told at what cost some men serve the children. "Good night, old man," he said.

"Good night," said Ben sullenly. "It *was* a ship that I saw. I didn't dream it. I don't dream things." And he thrust out his lower lip and glowered at his cousin.

David, seeking after Ben's lost friendship, decided to capitulate. After all, Nadine and he had talked a lot of nonsense about a woman in the wild garden and a man in the drawing room. The whole family was tarred with the same brush.

"Perhaps it was the grain ship that you saw," he said. "Not a ghost ship, there are no such things as ghosts, but a moving picture of what happened once."

"A moving picture?" queried Ben, interested.

"People say," said David, "that everything that once happened in a place leaves its mark upon it, like a photograph on celluloid. Given certain conditions you see it again, just as you see the moving picture when the cinema man puts up his screen and turns a handle."

"What conditions?" asked Ben.

"Sunset seems to be one of them," said David, "and little boys with imaginative minds. And two people thinking of the same thing at the same moment; for you see I was thinking of the grain ship too. And, I think, being unhappy. One's real self gets very sharpened when one is unhappy. It gets able to pierce through and make peepholes in the stuff of everyday life. It's practically the only advantage of being unhappy."

"Oh," said Ben. "Thank you." His tone was a little more cordial and David left him feeling slightly comforted. It is absurd, he thought, how elevated or how dashed one's spirits can be by the approval or disapproval of the children.

3.

The grown-ups' dinner was a depressing meal, for they could hardly hear themselves think above the noise of the storm.

"So early in the autumn for a storm like this," said Lucilla loudly and distinctly above its uproar.

"It's a high tide early tomorrow morning," said Margaret.

"Extra high?" asked Nadine.

"One of the highest tides of the year," said David. "They come in the spring and the autumn."

"I wish," said Lucilla, "that old Obadiah hadn't gone

back to his cottage today. I begged him to stay here, but he wouldn't. Alf is away, you know."

"He'll be all right," said David easily. "It's the safest part of the marsh, with all those dykes."

"I think they told me that one gave way," said Lucilla.

"Sure to be mended again by this time," David assured her.

After dinner the four of them played bridge for the most part in a gloomy silence, for the wind in the drawing room chimney sounded now like guns going off and conversation was even more difficult than in the dining room. Margaret's bridge, also, was a depressing thing; the other three were such expert players that only their affection for her made it possible for them to bear it. Margaret played from instinct rather than from reason, and her instincts were always wrong.

"I thought the king was out," she said.

"Why, Aunt Margaret?" asked David.

"I just felt that it was," said Margaret.

"Well, it just isn't, dear," said Lucilla, who was her partner. "And you've lost us the game.... Not that it matters, darling," she hastily added, fearful of wounding her so easily hurt daughter. "It's only a game."

Only a game, she thought, as she shuffled and dealt. Here she was setting her wits against David's, just as she had done on the night he came home. Only now he had Nadine to help him while she had only Margaret. She wished she could know how the battle was going.

By mutual consent they went to bed early. They had

little hope of sleep, but the bridge was nothing but a farce; it could not take their thoughts.

Lucilla was so weary that she had to ring for Ellen to help her to undress. "What a wind, Ellen," she said. "I'm not nervous, but the noise of it makes one so tired."

"You've more than the wind to make you tired, milady," said Ellen with a world of meaning in her tone.

Lucilla, already enthroned amongst her pillows, raised herself a little and stared at Ellen. But she was too tired to ask questions. "Leave the candles burning," she said. "A little light is consoling with all this noise going on outside. Good night, Ellen."

"Good night, milady," said Ellen, and went out.

Lucilla lay and looked at her lovely room, so softly lit by the two candles. Their light gleamed upon her ebony and ivory crucifix, her miniatures, the silver on the dressing table and the pretty flowered chintz. Now and then the whole house shook under a blast of wind and the noise was unceasing; yet she felt warm and safe in her beloved room, and in that state of exhaustion which is almost peace. I've done all I can, she thought, all I possibly can. She looked at the candle flames that David had said were like hands laid palm to palm in prayer. "Pray," she said to them sleepily. "Pray for the peace of Damerosehay. Let it always be for my children a refuge against the storm." There was a slight cessation in the battering of the rain against the window and she heard the oak trees crying and creaking down in the wood. "Keep us safe," she said, "as you have always done. Fight this storm until it passes." The thought came to her that though she herself had done all she could, yet there was upon her side other strength than her own. The universe was planned as an orderly thing, and those forces that try to wreck its order are always on the losing side. . . . Most unexpectedly she closed her eyes and slept.

Which was more than poor Nadine did, even though her room was at the back of the house, facing the inland fields and woods, and the roar of the storm came to her only distantly. Yet she could feel the shiver of the house when the great blasts struck it, and her own taut nerves quivered in sympathy. She kept the candles alight and resolutely opened her book. It was no good torturing herself any more. She could not give up David and go back to the misery of her life with George. She simply could not do it, and that was that. She was not of the stuff of which martyrs are made. Lucilla had done it, but then she was not Lucilla. A sacrifice like that had been easier for Lucilla than it would be for her. She was different. She felt things more than most people. "That's what everyone thinks," said a voice in her mind. She closed her ears to it and turned a page. She must concentrate on her book or she would go mad. Lucilla had found that if you acted a lie long enough it became reality and happiness was recaptured. What nonsense! And even if it wasn't nonsense for some people it would be for her. She was sure she herself could only capture happiness by the way of her own choice and by no other way. She was very individual. She had more individuality than most women. "That's what every woman thinks," said the voice in her mind. I've a right to be happy, she thought. "What right?" asked the voice in her mind.

"Why you more than your children or George?" Oh, God, thought Nadine, and flung her book on the floor.

It was at this point that Ellen, after a perfunctory knock at the door, entered in a scarlet flannelette dressing gown.

"You'll excuse me, madam," said Ellen, "but I thought you'd like this," and she held out a little pill box in her bony hand.

Nadine opened the box. Inside, carefully wrapped in cotton wool, was a little pearly tooth, decayed at the top.

"What on earth?" she demanded, slightly disgusted.

Ellen, looking quite extraordinarily like a horse, drew up a chair and sat beside the bed. She had not been invited to do so, but that did not worry her.

"You'll excuse me coming to you like this, madam," she said, indicating her dressing gown, "but I'm a lot more comfortable without my corsets. I never seem able to speak my mind in corsets. Can't seem to get enough breath to it."

"But this, Ellen?" asked Nadine, brandishing the pill box. She herself, as she drew a little jacket trimmed with swansdown over her silk nightgown, looked lovelier than the dawn. Her curls were hidden by a lace cap and the absence of lipstick made her face look almost pathetically young. Ellen, however, was by no means softened.

"Most mothers," she said meaningly, "keep all their little dears' first teeth."

"Caroline's tooth!" exclaimed Nadine. "But it's decayed, Ellen."

"Not to notice," said Ellen. "One lady I knew had all the little teeth made into a necklace."

"How perfectly revolting," said Nadine. But she had not

the courage to hand the tooth back. She put it carefully upon her bedside table.

"A very good mother, that lady was," said Ellen, and hitched her chair nearer.

"She must have been," said Nadine, with sarcasm.

And then it began.

"It's only right that. I should tell you, madam," said Ellen, "that I know of your intended marriage to Master David."

"Indeed, Ellen," said Nadine evenly and coldly. But she was a little startled. Ellen's eyes were fixed on her like gimlets and the harsh grating voice rasped upon her nerves. Really, it was too bad of Lucilla to have told their private affairs to her maid.

"No one told me," said Ellen, injured. "Not a word was said to me, though I've been in the family sixty years, but Master David beneath the ilex tree was telling her ladyship the while I was mending a rent in the drawing-room chintz."

"You listened, Ellen," said Nadine.

"No, madam," said Ellen sternly. "It was me duty to mend the·chintz and I'm not a woman to neglect me duty just because, thank God, I retain the use of me hearing." She folded her bony hands and snorted slightly, and her nostrils quivered like those of an old war horse smelling the powder. "And a more disgraceful suggestion than you divorcing poor Master George to marry poor Master David, and separating those poor innocent children from their own loving father, and breaking the heart of her poor ladyship, who's never done you no harm, and she getting old as she

311

is, I never heard in all my born days, madam. You'll excuse me speaking my mind, madam, but I've been in the family sixty years and I'll not lie easy in my grave thinking of the disgrace you've brought upon it. Bigamy, that's what it is, madam: bigamy, adultery and desertion. I know there are laws these days which make such things seem respectable, but what I says is more shame to them in Parliament as passes such laws. They should know better. Making white black and black white. It ain't right; that's what I say. They should read their Bibles, madam, and a little Bible-reading wouldn't do you no harm, madam, if you'll excuse me mentioning it." She paused, took a breath and began again. "As for Master David, madam, well, I won't say what I think of Master David. Spoilt, he was, as a child. I took a slipper to him time and again myself, but her lady-ship, she was always too soft with him. But what I says is, he's young, and old heads can't be expected on young shoulders, and you being many a year older than he is, madam, if you'll forgive my saying so, should know better than to lead him into temptation. And then, madam, it seems to me it ain't hardly right for a young man like that to marry a lady who can't give him children; and you, madam, after the bad time you had with Miss Caroline, may not be able to oblige in that way. Not your fault, madam, but facts is facts, and a crying shame it would be if Master David were to have no children, and he so good with them as he is. And then, madam, Master David is very fond of Damerosehay, and a sad pity it would be if any little dis-agreeableness in the family should part him from it. Well, madam, you'll forgive me speaking my mind, but a more

312

disgraceful suggestion than you divorcing poor Master George and marrying poor Master David and separating those poor innocent children from their loving father—"

And so it went on. Ellen, like all her kind, could repeat herself quite indefinitely, delighted to do so. The cuckoo clock in the nursery had struck eleven just before she came in, and in no time at all was striking half-past, and then it was midnight and still Nadine could not stem the torrent. She tried to do it over and over again but at every effort at interruption Ellen merely raised her voice a little louder and hitched her chair a little nearer. And all the time, as a background to her rasping voice, there was that distant tumult of the storm. A prisoner enduring the Chinese torture of the rhythmically falling drops of water soon goes mad. Repetition can be more exhausting than pain and the continually recurring words and phrases seemed like red-hot nails beaten into Nadine's brain by the strokes of a hammer. "Poor Master George, Poor Master David. Poor Lady Eliot. Poor innocent children. Bigamy. Desertion. Older than he is. Disgrace to the family. You'll excuse me speaking my mind. Poor Master George. Poor innocent children. Poor children. Children."

And then Nadine suddenly discovered that she was alone. Ellen had at last left her and the candles were getting low. She was alone in her darkening room, lying on her face on her bed, with those terrible words and phrases like fire in her brain. She would never get them out now. She knew she would never get them out. Ellen had knocked them in too firmly. Lucilla had put them there, but Ellen had knocked them in. All her life long she had believed that it was right that she should have what she wanted; she had built her life on that assumption. Now Lucilla had shaken her faith and Ellen had destroyed it. Her whole world seemed tumbling in ruins about her.

One o'clock struck. The hour of a new beginning. She turned over and lay on her back staring at the ceiling. In the faint light of the guttering candles she looked old and haggard. It had happened. Once again, as after her first love affair, her world had crumbled. She was not going to marry David. Her youth, together with her desperate striving to prolong it, had vanished. Her self-seeking, born of her youthful longing for joy, had gone too. Stripped of it all she lay looking desperately into the empty void ahead, while the candles guttered and went out. Two o'clock struck.

There seemed nothing in that void ahead. Nothing but a dark emptiness. For an hour she lay, struggling to put George into that emptiness, struggling to force her will to the building up of a new life in the way that Lucilla had done. . . . Acting, acting all the time until one was half dead with weariness, on and on until at last the pretense was reality. . . . Again and again she tried to force her will to this effort and again and again it fell back. It was like a wave beating against some barrier and continually forced back again. The roar of the storm seemed to come right into her and to be part of her own body and soul. The onslaught, the check, the recoil, went on and on until at last from sheer exhaustion she fell asleep.

She woke up to find that it was morning. It was not raining now, and a pale watery light, lit by fitful gleams of sunshine, filled the room. The wind was still blowing but not at gale force. Now and then there were intervals of utter quiet. The outside storm was over.

And so, she realized, was her own. While she slept she must have been still unconsciously fighting and while she slept she had won. She was going back to George. Telling David would be terrible, but she must do it. She was going to build a new life in the way that Lucilla had done and her will was bent to her task. She was more desperately unhappy than she had known a woman could be but she was at peace.

As she dressed she marveled that in the end her will had yielded so easily. It was almost as though something besides her own strength had been fighting for her, while she slept. Quite irrelevantly she thought of that woman in the lilac dress whom Caroline had imagined in the wild garden. Poor little Caroline. Please God in the years to come she would be a better mother than she had been in the past.

4.

David also, on going to bed, resigned himself to hours of reading, but he had a good deal more control over his thoughts than Nadine had and he was able to keep his attention firmly riveted on his book. It was a favorite book, Humbert Wolfe's *Uncelestial City*. In times of storm and tempest, of indecision and desolation, a book already known and loved makes better reading than something new and untried. The meeting with remembered and well-loved passages is like the continual greeting of old friends; nothing is so warming and companionable.

Yet tonight, as so often when the mind is tortured by some undecided question, everything he read seemed to have some bearing upon his problem, all his old friends seemed to have something to say to him and most of the time it was something that he did not in the least want to hear. As the night wore on he came with a leap of the heart to a passage that he usually loved because it made him think again of Van Gogh's picture of the lark above the cornfield.

Shall I not see that to live is to have relinquished
beauty to the sequestration of the dark,
and yet that the spirit of man, benighted, vanquished,
has folded wings, and shall use them as the lark

into the sun beyond the cold clouds flinging
her desperate hope, not reaching where she has striven,
but soaring for ever beyond herself, and singing
high above earth as she is low in heaven?

Shall I not confess that mine own evil humour
and not man's failure forged this black despair,
and, while I wept, high up the golden rumour
of the lark ascending fringed the quiet air?

Yet tonight it made him feel cold with apprehension as he put the book down and thought about it. "To live is to have relinquished beauty to the sequestration of the dark." Was that what life must be, a continual loss of beauty? Youth, love, happiness, health, work, life itself, one left them one by one behind as one went on. "Relinquish." It was a good word. It suggested not the tearing away of treasures but the willing and graceful sacrifice of them.

Beauty to him at this time was all summed up in Nadine's unpossessed loveliness and her adored companionship. Such a relinquishment seemed impossible. He turned away from the thought of it to rejoice in that picture of the soul as a birdlike thing, winged and free even when the evil humors and the despair of a man seemed to himself to keep him earthbound. Men always thought of the spirit of man like that. They even thought of the Spirit of God like that; they pictured him with the wings of a dove. "Fly away and be at rest." At last the mounting lark ascended so high into the light that she was lost in it and was not seen again. If only they would fly back sometimes! If only they would come back to say that they had not disappeared into nothingness but into somewhere. If only they could communicate their peace and tell their wisdom. People said that while one slept one spoke with the dead, though one woke with no memory of it. But that was only conjecture. He turned back some pages and read another passage.

> *You cannot traffick in peace,*
> *. . . . . for Christ*
> *(or whatever name is given*
> *to the secret kingdom of heaven*
> *in which we are and have*
> *this shadow of life, that shadow of the grave)*
> *to those who remain has said,*
> *"Leave the dead to bury the dead!"*
> *Rich though they be, you cannot sell*
> *or buy their miracle,*
> *nor be enriched by it, nor in Jerusalem,*
> *sweet with the bugles blowing over them,*
> *set up your market-place and have increase—not thus*
> *comes peace,*

nor freedom thus. But, slowly
making more holy what is holy
from the guarded pool
of the spirit, swift, cold, and beautiful,
in mists diaphanous his rain
a god draws back again;
and, as the sun builds with the clouds,
                                    of these
he builds his city of peace—
those stoneless streets at whose sweet end
friend meets with friend,
those star-hung towers in which the light of the sun
with the moon's light is one,
and love as visible and exquisite
as the little lamps with which the yew is lit,
so luminously red in the translucent green
of that deep air the lanterns of love are seen—
and the music of meeting and the trumpet at the gate
sounding, "All ye who enter here, abandon hate."
Thus freedom comes, thus peace.

He supposed that if life beyond death existed at all it was created in that way; by a god who took a man's work, thoughts and sacrifices and built with them, stone by stone, his future city of peace. As one lived and worked in this world one made the habitation that was to come. That darkness to which one relinquished one's treasures was not really darkness but the hands of a god. "Relinquish." Whatever way one turned one came back to it again. It was like being caught in a trap.... Oh God, to know that the city of peace was a real city, and not just the creation of desperate longing.... He read on and on and at last, in spite of the noise of the storm, he fell asleep. His last wandering thought, before sleep took him, was that Christopher

318

Martyn had had to relinquish that most precious of all a man's treasures, his sanity.

He woke up with a start. "Yes?" he said, for he was certain that someone had touched and called him. "Yes?" he repeated. "What is it?"

There was no one there, and no sound that could have awakened him except the calling of the plover. The gale was dying away and his room was filled with the gray light of dawn. He felt amazingly peaceful.

But it was not the peace of inaction. Almost in the moment of waking, as though he had been awakened for some particular purpose, he had jumped out of bed and pulled his curtains. His rooms looked east towards that part of the marshes where Obadiah had his cottage. But they could not be seen. Beyond the rushes there was nothing but a sheet of water.

David gasped and looked at his watch. The tide was coming in but it was not yet at its height. Quick staccato thoughts hammered at his brain as he dragged on his clothes. Obadiah! Alf was away. One of the highest tides of the year. The worst storm for years. The dykes had burst. There was no upstairs to Obadiah's cottage. That stream near it had been swollen by the summer rains. And it had poured rain most of yesterday.

He was out of doors and running through the oak wood, one part of his mind vaguely noticing how it had suffered; the moss of the drive was strewn with torn branches and the wounds on the trees showed white in the pallid light. His racing thoughts went on. Those lazy devils could not have mended that broken dyke. God, but he'd make a row

319

about it! Obadiah's life was perhaps in danger. The life of a man who served Damerosehay; a man who served him. He was not going to marry Nadine.... He noticed that the dogs had appeared out of nowhere and were running at his heels.

He was at the harbor and dragging his boat out of the boathouse. He did not waste time arousing Little Village; he did give a shout, but they were all upstairs in bed, asleep and snoring, happily unaware that in another twenty minutes the sea would be entering beneath their front doors. It was perhaps heartless of David not to give them further warning, but it was Obadiah he was bothering about, Obadiah who had no upstairs.

He had got the boat out and was rowing hard. It would have been too risky to get the sail up, for the tide was flowing fast and the depth of the flood water over the different levels of the marsh was incalculable. Mercifully the wind was blowing now directly from the west, and he had its help. "Go home!" he shouted to the dogs, who were swimming after him. Pooh-Bah, who disliked having his royal person assaulted by rudely slapping waves, obeyed, but the Bastard plunged on. "Go home, you old dunderhead!" David yelled at him. But the Bastard, puffing and blowing came on, fighting desperately. He was not as young as he once had been, the tide was strong, and his water-logged mat of hair was heavy about his straining body; but he was aware in his muddled old mind that this was no pleasure trip and he thought it his duty to come too and keep his eye on David. He thrust his black nose skywards and thrashed desperately. "The dear old fool!" groaned

David, and was obliged to endanger the whole expedition by dragging the dripping furry mass in over the gunnel lest it drown. "You old Bastard, you!" The Bastard, his point won, lifted his waterlogged tail with difficulty, rotated it and fawned at David's feet. Then he lay quietly panting and flooding the boat, water streaming from his fur and saliva from his long pink tongue, his eyes shining adoringly through the mat of dripping hair that fell over them.

David struggled on, hard put to it in spite of the favoring wind to negotiate the flow of the tide. Though his attention and all his strength were bent to his task, yet his thoughts, living some queer independent life of their own, as thoughts so often do in times of crisis, still went racing on. And very odd thoughts they were:

I am not going to marry Nadine. I woke up knowing that. How odd. As though I had gone on fighting while I slept and someone or something helped me to make up my mind. Who woke me? I could have sworn that someone woke me to do what I am doing now. Is it true that one meets the dead in sleep? There can't have been a tide as high as this since the storm that wrecked Christopher Martyn. Life will be hell without Nadine. Yet I'll have Damerosehay. I'd rather have had Nadine. It's harder to give up a person than a place. Telling her will be pretty awful. I can't live without Nadine. I've got to. No question about it. My God, the water is right over Obadiah's windowsills!

The bridge had gone, and the stream, after adding its water to the flooding tide, had disappeared too. David rowed straight in over the garden and held on to the stout pole that supported Obadiah's washing line. The ground rose towards the cottage and looking over the gunnel he could see the lost flowers, the marigolds and nasturtiums, bright and beautiful beneath the water. The tallest bushes, the hydrangeas and tamarisks, had their tops not quite submerged and the water was strewn with the little red floating lanterns of the fuchsias.

"Marnin', Master David," said a cheerful voice. " 'Twould a bin just about unkid if ee'd waited till tide was at height, so 'twould. But Oi knowed ee'd come fur Oi. Tarble storm. Tarble wind."

Obadiah, his bedroom window opened, was standing on a chair ankle deep in water. He had dressed himself and sensibly donned his high sea boots, and seemed little the worse for wear. "Can't open door 'gainst this 'ere water," he announced. "Oi'll come through winder."

David got the boat beneath the window and looked in. The water was right up to the mattress of Obadiah's high old-fashioned bed but not yet over it. On the bed the sensible Obadiah had collected his treasures; his best suit, his best boots, his best teapot, a piece of cold ham, his fishing rods, a biscuit tin ornamented with a portrait of Queen Victoria, the grandfather clock that had come from Damerosehay, and many other oddments.

"God knows how we're to get it all in," cried poor David as Obadiah, standing with one foot on the chair and the other on the bed, handed out his treasures one by one. "Oi don't go without me clock," said Obadiah firmly. "Nor me best boots."

Somehow, to the accompaniment of the Bastard's piercing barks, barking being his idea of being helpful, every-thing was got in and stowed away. As Obadiah himself scrambled from the windowsill to the gunnel the sea surged over his bed. The sight of it made David feel suddenly sick. If he had been half-an-hour later, and if last night had been one of those nights when Obadiah refreshed himself so deeply at the Eel and Lobster that there was no waking him the next morning, then he might have been submerged like his marigolds and nasturtiums. Obadiah seemed to feel the same, "It do make Oi feel right gaggly," he told David. "It'll be hard pullin' to Harbor, look see, wi' a down-along wind an' all this 'ere i' the boat."

It was indeed a hard pull home and conversation was impossible. David, straining at one oar while Obadiah pulled on the other, found himself gazing at the grandfather clock propped in the stern; Christopher Martyn's clock that he had designed, and perhaps made, himself. David suddenly grinned. This was another rescue from sea and tempest, but comically different from the other one. That other had been gallant and dramatic, with the great ship rushing to its doom, the captain lashed to the mast, the terrified crew, the beautiful woman in the cabin and the blue bird singing in its cage; but this one, with the boatload of boots and cold ham, crockery, furniture and a wet dog, was simply funny. Yet he hoped it was in the Damerosehay tradition. If Christopher Martyn yet existed anywhere, if he was alive and laughing at him for this ridiculous parody of his own action, it was to be hoped he was yet well contented with the heirs of his home and spirit. . . . David realized that tradition had got him at last. For the family and the place he was sacrificing his personal happiness. The world was well lost for love, they said. They were wrong. Not his world.

"Us came clever," said Obadiah as they reached the harbor.

Little Village had now awakened to the fact that the sea was in the cottages, and agitated but excited heads popped in and out of upper windows.

"Look see," they cried, "Obadiah an' young Mr. Eliot from up the House. Mr. Eliot 'e's fetched Obadiah in from marsh. Deedily done, sir, deedily done. Tarble storm, sir. Reglar white rain, 'twas. Tarble wind. Never seen tide like this 'ere, not anywhen. Tarble storm. Tarble wind."

The Eel and Lobster, like other old inns in those parts, had an outside staircase leading to the upper story. Upon this Mrs. Urry appeared in her dressing gown, her hair most marvelously done up in steel curlers and a scarlet and black rag hearthrug draped over her shoulders. "You come up 'ere, Obadiah," she invited him. "You an' your bits an' pieces. Reg'lar shrammed you look, ol'man, reg'lar shrammed."

David brought the boat up beside the stone stairs, against which the water, now almost at the level of the handle on the Eel and Lobster's front door, was lapping hungrily, and held it there while Obadiah and Urry and Mrs. Urry carted the cold ham, the teapot, the boots, the biscuit tin and the other oddments up the stairs to safety. The male population of Little Village, now in their boats, paddled excitedly about David. "Tide's at height," they said. "Won't rise no 'igher. Wi' this down-along wind, an' the 'igh tide, us is lucky 'tis no worse, look see. Dykes is burst too. Oo's to blame for that? The bloody government." They spat in the water. "Old Obadiah 'e's lucky 'e's not drowned. Mid a bin, but for Mr. Eliot up the House. Tarble storm. Tarble wind."

Their unusual loquacity cheered David and their approval wrapped him round warmly. The cold dull pain that was growing in him at the thought of Nadine was a little eased by it. This was his place. These were his people. Steadying the boat he watched Urry lift the grandfather clock from the stern.

But Obadiah, halfway up the stairs with his best boots, intervened. "Oi'm givin' that thur clock to Master David," he said.

"No, Obadiah!" cried David.

"Oi ain't long for this world, look see," explained Obadiah piously. "It won't be no use to Oi i' churchyard. Seein' it come from House 'tis right should go back thar. . . . Oi knowed ee'd come fur Oi."

David, meeting Obadiah's eyes, saw that he really wanted him to have the clock. Obadiah, though he could not find the words to say so, was very grateful for his rescue and glad it had been the young master who had done it. His clock back again at Damerosehay would be one more link between him and the House. It would stand there forever to show his gratitude.

"Thank you, Obadiah," said David.

Ten minutes later he was in the oak wood, the clock under his arm and the Bastard padding at his heels. It was full morning now and a watery sun shone fitfully through the ravaged branches of the oak trees, laying bars of light across the turf. The sky was pale blue streaked with mother-o'-pearl. The wind, that had been a terrible monster for so long, was now only a thing that sang in the tree tops and tossed the clouds like birds across the sky. It was a very wonderful morning, fresh and clear and bathed in silvery light. A cascade of song poured from the throat of the missel thrush in the wild garden and the blackbird in the ilex tree was caroling softly. The white wings of the gulls were beating everywhere.

Suddenly David noticed that the oak wood was full of living creatures. Brown bright eyes peeped at him from behind the tree trunks and white scuts gleamed as furry bodies popped up and down in the grass. The rabbits in the marsh had fled before the storm and taken refuge at Damerosehay. The wood was alive with them and they were so tame with fright that they did not run away at David's approach.

He swung round and gripped the Bastard's collar, for he would not have them chased or frightened. What with one thing and another he was surely a little light-headed, for he heard himself talking out loud to them. "Sensible little beggars. I'm glad you've come to Damerosehay for refuge. That's what it's for. It's a sanctuary. That's how I shall always keep it."

They continued to pop up and down, their eyes very bright and their ears very pointed, their scuts gleaming as the bars of sunlight fell upon them.

At the front porch David was met by Nadine, Pooh-Bah and the children. "Take the dogs in and shut them up," he said to Ben. "The wood's full of rabbits and I won't have them chased. Get along, all five of you."

He spoke more authoritatively than he had ever been known to do at Damerosehay, and the children hurried the dogs indoors.

"Wherever have you been, David?" cried Nadine. "You're dripping wet."

"Fetching Obadiah in out of the marsh," said David. "Nadine, there's something I want to tell you. I can't marry you."

Nadine looked up at him, her dark eyes enormous and tragic in her white face. "No, David," she said, "you can't. That was something I had to tell you too."

They looked at each other, breathing quickly as though they were tired out. Then she went abruptly in and left him. Explanations would come later. They were both of them stunned by the blow they had dealt each other and neither of them had the strength for them now. David stood staring out across the rushes to the beautiful silvery flood beyond. That hidden dull pain, that had been with him all the morning, had at the sight of Nadine become something that not only hurt inwardly but enveloped him outwardly too. It dragged at his body as well as his mind, pulling him down into misery and at the same time building misery up around him like a wall. The world about him, the bright world of Damerosehay that he loved so much, seemed in some queer way to recede, leaving him alone with his pain. He could have cried out with dismay. Through all the weeks that were to come he was to find out that the sheer loneliness of pain is almost the worst of its terrors.

CHAPTER ELEVEN

I

LUCILLA ONCE more sat in the drawing room waiting for the homecoming of her grandson David. He had gone away on the day after Obadiah's rescue and had been away for six weeks. It had seemed to Lucilla like six years, so great had been her anxiety for him. Her parting injunction of, "For heaven's sake, David, *write*," had been obeyed to the extent of postcards every few days from such places as Bergen, Bruges, Rouen and the Scilly Isles, containing such illuminating remarks as, "Very wet today. Good crossing. Comfortable hotel." "Rotten crossing. Fine days at last. Love to children. Hope you are well." "Nice dogs here but not equal to the Bastard. Love, David."

Beyond that, nothing. The speed with which he seemed to get from Bergen to Bruges had told her how restless he was, the brevity of his remarks how much there was that he could not say. Knowing him she had been able to guess a little at the blackness of his misery but she had not known how he was getting through it. This was his first big trouble and she had hardly known how to bear it; when she had been young she had borne her own troubles, now that she was old she bore her children's and her grandchildren's and found them far worse to put up with than her own had been.

The thing that had most comforted and upheld her had been her growing affection for her daughter-in-law Nadine, who had sailed a fortnight ago for India and George. It is wonderful how one's affection for people grows when they do what you want them to do, and she realized now how unfair she had always been to Nadine. Every evening of that month they had spent together they had sat by the fire and talked and she had come to understand the difficulties of Nadine's motherless youth, the bitter disillusionment of her marriage to George and its hardening effect upon her, the depth of her love for David and the greatness of her courage in putting it from her. Beyond that she had discovered that Hilary was quite right and that Nadine was very fond of her.

"I've always admired you so much, Grandmother," Nadine had said on their last evening together, as the twilight gathered in the garden and the light of the log fire flickered up over the dark wood of the chimneypiece. "I've always thought it was wonderful that you could be so gentle and loving and yet keep your dignity and authority as the head of the family. I don't believe that one of your middle-aged sons would dare to disobey you. The grandchildren all adore you, yet they're a little in awe of you too. You keep the whole family together yet I don't believe I've ever heard you raise your voice, and you have a soft face like a tea rose." She had paused, and then gone on again. "I wish I could be like you, Grandmother. But I can't. I can only dominate if I am hard."

329

Lucilla had pondered. Now that Nadine had mentioned it she had been objectively interested in this question of her own power. "I don't think it's a question of domination, dear," she had said. "I think it's a question of allegiance willingly given to someone whose judgment is trusted. I think my children and my grandchildren do trust me. I don't know why, but they do."

"I do, too," had said Nadine. "It is because of my trust in you that I am going back to George. You say, you have proved, that what I am setting myself to do can be done. If it wasn't for you I shouldn't be doing this. . . . Yet I'm scared, for it really is rather frightening to be so unhappy. I don't know how I'll get through."

"Life is rather an unhappy affair, dear," said Lucilla. "And it's just as well to face the fact. It's essentially sad, woven of gray stuff; yet embroidered with such bright flowers."

"So few and far between," sighed Nadine. "And such long tracts of grayness stretching ahead."

"Don't look ahead, dear," said Lucilla. "Just live one day at a time. However unhappy you are you can still act your part for one more day. And as for trust, well, I think that's what wins it. People like to know that whatever happens they can rely on you to play your part."

Nadine, facing her future, had sighed. "But I'm glad that we're coming back to Damerosehay," she had said. "There's something about Damerosehay that inspires one."

For that was what had been arranged. Nadine was to go out to George, marry him all over again, stay with him for two months in India and then come back with him when the regiment returned to England. Then they would all be at Damerosehay together, Nadine, George and the children, until they found their own home.

The ecstasy of her family over her return to a sense of her duties had almost astonished Nadine. Her rather tentative but most expensive cable to George, asking if she should come back to him and try again, had provoked an almost lyrical reply, even more expensive and mentioning the dates of sailings and undying affection all in the same breath and with no stops at all. The children, when told that Daddy was coming home, had been beside themselves with joy. Tommy had made the house a Hades for noise for days on end, and Ben had put on two pounds in weight in a week; Caroline had said nothing but she had smiled such a lot that she had scarcely been able to suck her thumb at all.

And so, tight-lipped and strained, Nadine had sailed for India surrounded by an aura of family approval and affection that had seemed to give her no comfort whatsoever. But one day, Lucilla hoped, when her enveloping trouble had worn thin enough for the outside world to get through to her again, she would rejoice in its warmth.

Ellen, followed by Tucker the cat, came in with Lucilla's tea. Bib, the kitten, had been given to Obadiah as the solace of his declining years. The dogs, of course, had gone with the children to meet David at the corner by the corn-field.

Ellen, as well as Ben, had most surprisingly put on weight just lately. It was the result of her secret satisfaction at the turn that family affairs had taken. The entire credit, of course, she took to herself. And indeed, thought Lucilla, looking up at the faithful horselike features, perhaps she was right. That midnight interview had not been without its effect on Nadine. Ellen from first to last had been the family salvation.

"Dear Ellen," she said.

"Drink your tea, milady, while it's hot," Ellen commanded, "and don't go feeding Tucker, now. She had her drop of milk in the kitchen before she come in." Then she stood with her bony hands folded on her apron to see that Lucilla did what she was told.

"Sit down, Ellen, for goodness sake," said Lucilla a little irritably.

Ellen snorted slightly and sat down on a hard uncomfortable chair against the wall.

It was Nadine who had told Lucilla of Ellen's alarming visit on the night of the storm; Ellen herself had never mentioned it. She knew that Lucilla knew, and Lucilla knew that Ellen knew that she knew, but they did not say a word about it to each other. This was their code. Lucilla knew that Ellen thought it her duty to become possessed of all the family secrets in order that she might deal with them as she considered they should be dealt with, and that she considered any means which she had to adopt to gain her end perfectly legitimate. Ellen, on the other hand, knew that Lucilla did not approve eavesdropping, unauthorized letter-reading and the like. They could not see eye to eye about these things and so they just were silent.

"Mrs. George must be well on her journey now," said

Lucilla, pouring herself a cup of tea. "She'll soon be with the Major."

"Ah," said Ellen darkly. "And about time too."

How odd it was, thought Lucilla, that out of the whole of their large family only three of them knew, or ever would know, of that love of David and Nadine for each other; herself, Hilary and Ellen.... For George, she and Nadine had decided, was for the sake of his own peace of mind never to be told.... And Damerosehay; somehow she was sure that Damerosehay knew and had mysteriously helped them all to the decision that had been made.

Her eyes went to the clock that Obadiah had given David. It stood now in a corner of the drawing room, its hands standing for ever at one o'clock, the hour of a new beginning, and inside it was Christopher Martyn's book of drawings and the old parson's diaries. David had given them to her with a hurried explanation before he went away. Since then, with Obadiah's help, she had found out the whole story of Christopher, Aramante and Jeremy. She had reveled in it, loving her home the more because of it, and had been surprisingly undepressed by the tragedy of it. The drawings in the book had upset her far less than they had upset Ben and David, and when Obadiah, encouraged by her calmness in face of their horror, had suddenly decided to tell her that Jeremy was buried beneath the ilex tree, she had been rather pleased than otherwise.... She was seventy-eight. The horrors portrayed in Christopher's book she had faced long ago. The nearness of Jeremy's skeleton no more depressed her than the nearness of her own, which on her rheumatic days she was heartily looking forward to getting rid of as he, lucky old fellow, had got rid of his. As for the tragedy of Christopher Martyn, at her age she knew that the miseries of life pass away so quickly while the freedom from them lasts for ever. "He was over-taken, and endured that necessity which cannot be avoided. For gold is tried in the fire, and acceptable men in the furnace of adversity. . . . A melodious noise of birds among the spreading branches, a running that could not be seen of skipping beasts. The whole world shined with clear light, and none were hindered in their labor."

She lifted the teapot to pour herself out another cup of tea.

"You've had two," said Ellen.

"So I have, Ellen," she said, and set the teapot meekly down.

Ellen took the tray away and she was alone again, watch-ing for the first glimpse of the car through the iron gate in the wall. It was late autumn now, verging upon winter. The gales had spent themselves and the earth lay very still beneath a cold clear blue sky. The oak trees were russet in the wood and the wild garden was all overgrown with the feathery splendor of traveler's joy. To Margaret's de-light the frost had spared the chrysanthemums and they made a riot of color in the garden; deep red, tawny, gold and white; the pungent aromatic smell of them mixed with the scent of burning leaves and the salt smell of the sea.

A silver-gray shape slipped past the iron gate in the wall and Lucilla found that her heart was beating suffocatingly. Would he be changed? Would he, perhaps, not love her any more because of what she had done to his life? There was

334

the usual riot in the hall, the usual outburst of shouts and barks and scufflings, and then David was in the room, "Get back, you little demons!" he said, pushing the door against the tumult outside. "Wait!" Then he shut it and came across to her where she stood waiting for him.

He was very changed; older, sterner, and quite unsmiling. Her heart missed a beat and for the first time in her life she dropped her eyes before him. Then she felt him take her face in his hands and lift it. "Are you all right, Grandmother?" he asked, and his voice was gay and just as it used to be.

"Quite all right, David," she answered. "Are you all right?"

"Quite all right," he answered, and looking up she knew that in spite of the change in him he spoke the truth.

2.

But it was not until an hour later, as they sat talking to each other in the drawing room, that she knew how much he was all right. He was very unhappy still, he did not deny that, and doubly so in knowing that Nadine suffered too, but he believed that they had made the right decision. His conviction grew with each day. And there was also growing in him, he told Lucilla, the conviction that because of that decision he was feeling his way towards an entirely new outlook upon things.

"All bereavement, whether fate inflicts it on you or whether the relinquishment is your own, changes you," said Lucilla. "Don't people say that nature abhors a vacuum? Something lost in the present means something new flowing in from the future; often a new or stronger faith. In your loss and gain you are bound to change and to look at things a little differently."

"This life seems now both much more valuable and yet far less worthy of having a fuss made about it than it used to be," said David. "That sounds a complete contradiction, but perhaps you know what I mean."

"It is not now to you the whole tree of life, but the seed," said Lucilla. "Seeds are enormously valuable, the germ of all that is to come is in them, but one can't get as excited about them as one does about the full-grown tree."

"I'm not quite that far yet," said David. "Though that's the logical conclusion that the road I've been traveling lately leads me to. Not much sense in sacrifice if this life is all there is. But I like the simile of a tree, Grandmother. A tree usually has a bird in it."

Then he told her about the gulls at Bergen, wheeling and crying above the flower market beside the fjord, and the dogs in Belgium and the sea birds on the Scilly Isles. Wherever he went, he said, something had reminded him of Damerosehay and he had longed for the moment when he would feel he could go back to it again. As they talked the sky turned from blue to gold and shadows crept out over the garden. The blackbird in the ilex tree started his evening song, and from the wild garden came the voices of the children calling to each other in a last game before bed.

Then suddenly they came tearing helter-skelter through the gate behind the guelder-rose bush, across the lawn and in through the garden door into the drawing room. Ben dashed in first and went straight to David, that shadow that had once been between them entirely forgotten.

"We saw a blue bird in the garden!" he shouted. "We saw a blue bird!"

"We *did!*" yelled Tommy belligerently, though no one had contradicted him. "Not a kingfisher but bright blue like forget-me-nots."

And Caroline, sucking her thumb, nodded vigorously.

David, the children at his heels, went out to investigate, but there was nothing to be seen in the wild garden except the darting leaflike bodies of the tits and the thrush singing in Methuselah; and presently Ellen came out to hale the children off to bed. "A blue bird!" she scoffed. "Moonshine!"

"It was *not!*" said the children indignantly.

"I believe you," David assured them, and they went off comforted.

He lingered in the wild garden. It was incredibly beautiful with that silvery mist of traveler's joy everywhere about him, the purple shadows gathering under the trees and a few golden leaves drifting down silently out of the golden sky. He began to feel almost happy. It was so long since he had felt happy that the strangeness of the sensation was quite startling. "Traveler's joy." That was what he was feeling; the joy of the traveler who returns to his own place. That was what Aramante had felt when she came back to her own spot of earth and her soul flew back to her breast like a homing bird.

And with the happiness there came to him also a new sense of creative power. The fact that he had been able to

337

do what he had done, to love so deeply and yet to relinquish his love, had increased his faith in himself. He looked back with shame to that mood of defeatism at the Hard, when he had thought that the days that are past are better than these days. That was all nonsense. Life was what one made it. As those who had lived before him in this place had built finely, so would he. He remembered a verse in *Ecclesiasticus* that Lucilla had often quoted to him. "And say not thou that former years were better than those of the present time; for that is the talk of a foolish person."

Suddenly from oak tree to lilac bush there was a brilliant flash of blue. Not a kingfisher, as Tommy had said; a paler and more ethereal blue than that. In two strides David was at the lilac bush and had taken in his hands old Mary's blue budgerigar. Incredibly, by some miracle, it had survived rain and storm and the hatred of other birds. Perhaps it had been caught by someone and escaped again. . . . Perhaps, he smiled to himself, it was a fairy bird and could not die. . . . Holding the soft fluttering feathers in his cupped hands David thought that he must return her bird to old Mary; but then he remembered that Hilary had said in a letter that he had given Mary a new budgerigar, a green one, and that she was comforted. He would let the creature go. Undoubtedly it was a fairy bird, or it could not have survived.

He lifted his hands and opened them. The bird spread its wings and flew up and up above the tree tops into the golden sky. David watched as long as he could but suddenly the light dazzled him and he shut his eyes. When he opened them again the bird had gone; earthbound, with eyes that could not stand the glory of light, he had lost sight of it; yet through the little incident the conviction that he had longed for suddenly came to him. "It's true," he thought. "The spirit of man *has* wings."